I0768475

PRETEND YOU'RE MINE THIS CHRISTMAS

A collection

HEATHERLY BELL

Copyright © 2024 by Heatherly Bell

All rights reserved.

No part of this book may be reproduced in any form or by any electronic or mechanical means, including information storage and retrieval systems, without written permission from the author, except for the use of brief quotations in a book review.

Cover by Elizabeth Mackey

Editing by Elaine Caruso

Cowboy, It's Christmas
A MEN OF STONE RIDGE NOVEL

Prologue

Gather up, everyone, because the ladies of SORROW have news! After last year's mess, I had a brilliant idea, if I do say so myself.

You'll remember that last year, Winona James, the country music star, fell in love with one of *our* men, Riggs Henderson (can't say anyone blames her). Well, that means another woman in town, for which we are eternally grateful. Another man of Stone Ridge, settled and happy.

Yet, there are so many more. Even though not all seem ready to settle down (Beau Stephens, I'm looking at you) their *mothers* are anxious for grandchildren, lickety-split! And since we *ladies* do take care of everything that needs doing around here (by the way, some help would be welcome) we've tackled this latest issue, too. The work around here never ends!

But now, with the help of Winona, and all the many connections she has to show-business folk, we have interest from one of them Hollywood studios. The setting of a new reality dating show will be Stone Ridge itself and we will be interviewing women to vie for the heart of "Mr.

Cowboy." I personally have my eye on Wade Cruz, who has recently been permanently sidelined from the rodeo circuit. He's been injured but he'll get over that right quick. His lovely mother raised him to be a proper man of Stone Ridge and helpful in every way. Rose died not long ago, poor lamb, and all of us ladies of SORROW have been delivering casseroles and motherly love to Wade.

Frankly, it's time "Wild Wade" settle down and we want to help him. Yes, we do. He could be our first *Mr. Cowboy*, and with those smoldering rodeo-cowboy good looks, help bring truckloads of women into town.

Because I'll let you in on a little secret: only one woman will win *this* contest, but we have *plenty* of men for them to stick around for.

~ BEULAH HAYES, President of SORROW (Society of Reasonable, Respectable, Orderly Women) and keeper of the *Men of Stone Ridge* bible, tenth edition. ~

Chapter 1

Daisy Carver loved Christmas, but in her opinion, the Christmas décor at the Shady Grind bar and grill had gone a tad overkill this year. The tinsel seemed to be everywhere, bright blinking red and green lights draped across the stage in the back, and bundles of mistletoe hung from the ceiling at approximately every two feet. This had likely been done by a desperate man looking to hook up. There were so many lonely men in their women-scarce town.

And still, no one was even trying to kiss *her*. She'd purposely sat under this mistletoe all night.

The bane of her existence was that Daisy had two older brothers. Two big, brawny cowboys that could take care of themselves in a dark alley. One of them, Jackson, owned this bar and was here tonight. And in case *he* wasn't, there was always her oldest brother, Lincoln. At some point in time, and without her approval, he'd assigned himself as her guardian and protector. Between her brothers and their tattletale wives, Eve and Sadie, it seemed that no man alive would ever dare to approach Daisy unless he was ready to get married to her the next day.

But all she needed was one *brave* man.

She'd dated a little here and there, but every kiss was a dud. Granted, she had a high standard to meet. When she was eighteen, a cowboy had kissed her within an inch of her life. Nothing had ever compared. Though she did get asked out a lot, she was often accused of being too much of a "good girl" and "not fun." That was all going to change. Though marriage, pregnancy, and babies were winding through their town like a virus, Daisy wasn't interested in any of that. Still, when it came to sex, she'd recently decided that she would like to find out what all the fuss was about.

But tonight, she was here simply to forget her troubles and enjoy the show from a seat on the barstool. Her brother Jackson was on the stage playing guitar and singing "It's Christmas, Cowboy," one of his latest country music chart hits. Singing harmony with him was a hugely pregnant Winona James. She'd just had twins seven months ago and must have gotten herself pregnant again the next day. She honestly looked like she'd swallowed a pumpkin. The kind that they sold at the pumpkin patch in nearby Kerrville. This October they'd gone for a personal best with a pumpkin that weighed in at close to two hundred pounds. It won the county contest.

Daisy would never tell her so, but well, Winona looked like she'd swallowed half of that pumpkin. And this time, she wasn't carrying twins. Just one baby. One!

As the song ended and Winona was helped off the stage, Lenny called out, "Hey there, Winona! You think they forgot to take a baby out?"

There was raucous laughter, including from Winona, who shot back, "So I got knocked up again. But I have it on good authority that this one is a *girl*."

A roar of approval at that, because there hadn't been a girl born in Stone Ridge, Texas, for around ten years or so.

"She sings, plays guitar, *and* is having a girl," Jackson said from the stage. "Ladies and gentlemen, let's hear it for Winona James!"

Winona waddled to the bar where her handsome rancher husband, Riggs Henderson, sat on a stool next to Daisy.

"Hey there, Winona," Daisy said.

"Hi, sugar." Winona threw her arms around Daisy. "How are you these days?"

"Oh, you know." Daisy threw a look at the mistletoe hanging above her head. "About the same."

"Ah, I see." Winona caught Riggs's eyes, and waved her hand. "Riggs?"

"Oh, yeah." Riggs leaned forward and bussed Daisy's cheek. "Merry Christmas."

Lord, he smelled good. If he wasn't in his forties *and* married, Daisy would be all over that. Best of all, he didn't scare easily.

Daisy sighed. "Thanks."

"Levi?" Winona called out to the bartender.

"Huh?" When the part-time bartender/horse wrangler turned to Winona, she was pointing to the mistletoe above Daisy's head. He nodded, then leaned across the bar to kiss her cheek. "Merry Christmas, Daisy."

Gee, how exciting. Practically an air kiss. But this would be about as good as it would get for Daisy Carver in Stone Ridge. And it wasn't as if scandalous things didn't happen here, they just happened to other people.

Not *Daisy*.

She was the good girl, as far from her mother's reputation as a girl could get.

It wasn't that she wanted a scandal, but a little excitement would be nice.

Over a year ago, Winona had moved from Nashville to find herself a baby daddy. She'd had a long line of suitors, sure, Daisy heard all about it. But in the end, she'd given up on the idea. Then she wound up accidentally pregnant by Riggs. Some thought Winona would be going back to Nashville eventually, but Daisy didn't see *that* happening. She watched Riggs hold out his hand, and when Winona took it, he smiled and led her out the door.

Jeremy Pine slid into the stool next to Daisy vacated by Riggs.

"Boy, I sure dodged a bullet with that one. Whew." He made a mock swipe of his brow. "Poor Riggs. Got himself saddled with a wife and twins, and another already on the way."

"What do you care about it?" Daisy took a pull of her beer.

"Riggs is a good guy. He should be enjoying his twilight years or some such thing, not bringing up babies."

Daisy snorted. "*Twilight* years? Face it, you're jealous it isn't you. I heard you auditioned for the part as her 'personal assistant.'"

"I wouldn't have taken the job."

"You're too young for her anyway. Winona wanted a *real* man."

Jeremy straightened. "I am a real man, sweetheart. I'm twenty-five now, don't forget."

Jeremy wasn't bad looking and he had a sexy cowboy air about him. Tight Wranglers, tipped Stetson, beard stubble. He was no Wade Cruz, but he had a nice smile and an interesting face.

"So, you want to get out of here or something?"

"Hell, no." He bristled. "Jackson's here. He'll see us leave."

"Coward."

"I'm no coward, just smart as a whip. I don't want to get married yet."

Daisy scowled. "Who said anything about marriage?"

"C'mon, Daisy." He gently put his arm around her shoulder and squeezed lightly, as if giving her sympathy. "It isn't just your brothers. You're a nice girl. And we all know you're a…a…you know…"

"A *what?*"

"A tease," he whispered.

"That's a vicious lie," Daisy lied.

"Why would anyone lie about that?"

"I have no idea! That's my personal business, so how would anyone know whether it's true?"

"I guess it's the way you…act. Plus, your two brothers. No one's turned up dead, so we just assumed—"

"And made an ass of yourself!"

"Well, if it's not true, then." Jeremy removed his arm from her shoulder as Jackson headed toward the bar. "Maybe no one has the guts to find out."

"That's the first thing you've said tonight that makes any sense. There sure are a lot of gutless men in Stone Ridge."

She would correct herself, but she was just too mad. As she'd been taught from the time she was a little girl, the men of Stone Ridge were above reproach. Honest and hardworking ranchers. Traditional. They banded together in times of trouble, helped each other out with broken fences, stuck cattle, emergencies of any kind, and even construction of the new school and clinic.

And they took care of their women. Who were "their" women? Every female from birth to death. As a consequence, a man knew that if he didn't take care of *his* woman, there would be someone else ready and more than willing to take his place. And God help the man who ever raised a hand in anger toward his woman. He'd be run out of town and probably tarred and feathered.

Those were the *good* parts about Stone Ridge and Daisy appreciate them as much as the next woman. The bad parts were unfortunately conjoined with the good ones. All this tradition and protection grated on a young woman who wanted a little adventure. Daisy might have played it safe her whole life, but it was time to broaden her horizons. She was tired of waiting around for something to happen. She would *make* something happen!

A little less protection and a lot more freedom was in order. Though probably neither one would happen tonight.

Jackson joined Daisy and fist-bumped with her. "Hey, Shortie."

"You were good up there tonight," Daisy said. "Are you and Eve comin' over for Sunday dinner this week?"

"I'll have to ask Eve."

"*Please* don't leave me alone with Lincoln and Sadie. The whole night will be about Sammy and how wonderful he is. I hate to tell them, but though I adore Sammy, his ears are too big for his head. So, he's not perfect."

Jackson burst into laughter. "Boy, you sure are easy to rattle these days. We'll be there."

"Thank you!"

"Hey, so how's Wade doing these days?"

"*Wade?*"

Wade Cruz was Daisy's longtime crush and Lincoln's best friend. A rodeo cowboy, he was rarely in town, though he'd made an appearance at his mother's funeral a few months ago only to leave again.

"Lincoln told me that he's back. He got injured and came home. Didn't you hear? Thought you of all people would know."

It felt like the floor had given way beneath Daisy. All the blood rushed to her head.

Wade. Wade Cruz. Injured? When? How? Why?

"Lincoln didn't tell me. No one told me."

"Probably figured you already knew."

"It's not like I keep tabs on him."

Jackson cocked his head and grinned. "*Really?*"

Daisy took one last pull of her beer, set it down, and climbed off the stool. "I'm tired of you teasin' me."

"What? I just got started. Okay, okay." He went palms up. "Shortie, c'mon. Don't go."

She shoved his shoulder, and kept walking, waving him away. When she stepped outside, the sky had darkened to a purplish hue. A chill snapped through the air and she tugged her jacket close. They'd had a strange and early winter, ice storms and snow blanketing areas that rarely saw any. In Hill Country, a foot of snow had fallen not long ago, and temperatures dropped to the thirties.

But some folks knew how to keep warm.

Here and there, couples were kissing in the cabs of their trucks, on the tailgates, and in little quiet corners. Jolette Marie Truehart was in a clinch with some cowboy. Sigh. It had been so long since Daisy had been really and properly kissed. Too long since a certain man had pushed her up against the wall, crashed his lips over hers, sunk his fingers into her hair, and pulled her against him. She remembered well the day and time because it may as well have been written on her heart. She'd been eighteen, and Wade Cruz had kissed her in the bedroom of her family home. Then, as if shocked he'd done it, he ran out of the room so fast he nearly fell on his way out.

Even so, she might not have taken it so personally if he hadn't left town a couple of days later.

She'd called him out on it the next time she'd seen him, weeks later, working as a ranch hand for her father between rodeos.

"I thought *you* of all people weren't afraid of my brothers. You can hold your own."

Wade threw a stack of hay down and wiped his brow. "Who the hell said I'm afraid of 'em?"

"Um, you ran out on me so fast I thought your ass was on fire."

"Listen, Daisy." Wade tipped his hat and gazed at her from under hooded lids. "You need to understand a few things."

She crossed her arms. "And I suppose you're going to tell me these things."

"Now, I can't tell you *everything*. That's something your husband's going to have to do." He slid her a wicked grin and cocked his head. "But the thing is, men and women need to be on an even and equal playing field. It's only right. Both should have the same amount of…experience. Know-how. Catch my drift?"

"I think I do." She suddenly "got" that she was apparently a bad kisser. Humiliation thrummed through her. "But I can learn."

"I'm sure you will, sweetheart. Just not with me." Then he'd walked away and climbed back in the pickup to shove out another bale of hay.

And nearly ten years later, Daisy still hadn't found anyone that came close to that kiss, all thanks to one man.

Wade Cruz.

Chapter 2

Wade's arm hurt like a son of a gun.

This morning, he'd rolled out of bed, and in a hazy fog of sleep he'd forgotten about the compound fracture he'd earned when he'd fallen off a bull in the last qualifying round of the National Rodeo. He'd paid dearly for that memory slip when he put too much weight on his left shoulder. His arm now ached and throbbed, reminding him of the moment the injury had occurred. But no pain had ever been quite like that one. None of his prior concussions, scrapes, cuts, aches and pains. That had been raw, sweltering, bone-grafting, screaming pain.

He'd simply stayed flat on his back where he'd landed while around him everyone ran to help. The sky had been particularly blue that day and he remembered that a bird landed on a stall and a horse nickered. Other than that, Wade couldn't process anything. Not the pain, nor the fact that he'd been so close to another win only to lose it all. And he'd sacrificed far too much to the rodeo already.

But all this knowledge would come later.

Then, he'd noticed the blood, and the bone jutting out

of his skin. Another cowboy passed out at the sight. Wade was simply numb, possibly protected by his body's endorphins. Too bad the relief was temporary. The numbness had worn off soon enough.

Even after surgery, casting, and physical therapy his arm might never be the same.

"This is a career-ending injury," the announcer had said at the time, predicting the future.

Now, Wade staggered to the shower, dressed, and made coffee. He massaged the tightness in his left shoulder caused by the nagging soreness in his arm.

"You won't win," he told his arm.

Last night, when he'd reached for the pain-killing meds the doctor had prescribed, he'd knocked the entire bottle off his nightstand. They'd scattered all over the hardwood floor since he'd not tightened the cap after his last dosage. He wandered back into his bedroom and slowly picked up every last pill and shoved them back in the bottle. Squatting, he swallowed one with his coffee. Sooner or later, he'd wean himself off these, but for now they did the trick of numbing the pain so he could get through his day.

The doorbell rang, and Wade fervently hoped it wasn't someone with another damn casserole for his freezer. A betting man, Wade would stake his life on this being yet another casserole dish.

"Two to one odds," he muttered as he walked to the door.

There, on the other side of his front door was Beulah Hayes herself, carrying another dish.

"Good morning, Wade." Beulah held out the covered plate. "Breakfast."

"You didn't have to do that, Miss Beulah." He took the casserole, using his good arm, and stepped aside. "Come on in. Coffee?"

"Don't mind if I do."

She followed him into the kitchen, no doubt surveying it all. Beulah was president of the ladies of SORROW (Society of Reasonable, Respectable, Orderly Women) and worried far too much about Wade. Unfortunately, she and the ladies thought it was their personal, God-given duty to look out for every man of Stone Ridge. Now that Wade was without a mother, they'd ramped it up.

"I see some progress has been made."

But not enough and she didn't have to say so. Yesterday, Wade had started going through his father's ledgers. Then he'd walked to the north pasture to survey the land. Unfortunately, there was so much to be done, he didn't know where to begin. He mucked the stable belonging to his horse, Dante, and checked in on his old bull, Satan. Before the end of the day, he'd run out of steam. So, he'd watched several hours of film of his last winning season. That was enough to send him to bed early.

Lincoln had been over earlier this week, trying to talk Wade into allowing him to help get the cattle ranch back in business. To do that, he either needed an influx of cash or to use up the last of his savings because his father had left him and his mother with close to nothing.

He scratched his chin. "Ran into a little problem with the barn yesterday. I'll get to it."

"That barn is about to fall in on itself. You need to allow the men to help. That's what we do around here, after all."

"Yum, smells good. What is this?" Wade pulled the tin foil back to peek and change the subject.

"My French toast casserole." She puffed up with pride.

"I had no idea you could make a casserole out of French toast."

"You can make a casserole out of anything."

"I'm beginning to see that." He grabbed a cup from the top cupboard, ignoring the pain in his arm at the stretch.

Beulah had taken a seat at the small white farmer's table in the nook. "I'm worried about you."

"Don't waste your time. I'm fine." He poured and set her coffee down.

"You're not *fine*. Rose hasn't even been gone six months."

"But it was a long time coming." Wade pushed back the memory, ignoring a different kind of ache.

He didn't sit, hoping not to encourage too long of a visit. He leaned a hip against the counter and sipped his coffee.

"I've been thinkin'…" Beulah began.

"Uh-oh."

"I have just the solution to your troubles."

"Really? Have you got a new arm in there for me?" Wade eyed the big brown tote bag she carried.

She narrowed her eyes. "Your arm still aching you much?"

"Nah, it's all healed up," he lied. He was not in the habit of worrying anyone. "Pastor June was by earlier with a casserole. She says the answer to my problems is attending church."

"That never hurts."

"Those wooden pews are hell on a rancher's back."

Beulah shook her head. "You've always been strong as a bull. I do hope you're not as stubborn as one."

"Don't worry, I've quit the rodeo. Or it quit me. Either way."

"That's wise, but it's not entirely what I meant by *stubborn*."

"What did you mean?"

"Wade Cruz, when's the last time you were in a *serious relationship* with a woman?"

"Why, Miss Beulah. I had no idea you cared. And here I thought you were happily married." He winked.

"I'm serious, child. Listen up. Winona has us interest from one of them Hollywood studios. But we have to act fast. Don't you know, we're goin' to have us a reality TV show right here in Stone Ridge, Texas!"

"Did you nominate my house for one of those fixer-upper shows?" He'd been telling everyone who would listen that he would do the work around here himself.

"Why would I do that when we have all the manpower we need, free of charge?"

"But why else would anyone make a reality show here? Does it have to do with a cattle competition?"

Beulah straightened and smiled. "It's a love competition."

"I thought that was against the law."

She squinted. "A *dating* show: *Mr. Cowboy*."

Wade snorted and nearly spit out his coffee. He could just picture it now. A cowboy smiling into the camera, holding a rope instead of a red rose.

He laughed, a full belly laugh, and damn it all, that felt good. "That's…that's pretty funny."

"I don't know what on earth is so *funny*!"

"You're serious?"

"The studio is going to start weeding through the women soon. Interviews, photo shoots, the whole shebang. But it will help pique their interest once we choose a man. They'll pay for a photo shoot of our cowboy, right here in town, no need to go anywhere. Then the studio will select a large group of women and eventually move them to a location right here in town. Probably sometime next summer. They'll stay for weeks while they compete for the heart of a cowboy. A man of Stone Ridge."

"I see, and so you think maybe my house could serve as the location where they'll all stay? It depends on how much time I have." He waved his hand around the kitchen.

He'd quite by accident once watched a preview of one of those dating shows, and the homes provided for the contestants were lavish and large. They'd probably expect a little rustic ambience in Hill Country, but Wade worried he had a little too much rust in *his* mansion.

"No, sugar. I want *you* to be our first Mr. Cowboy."

"See, that's *really* not funny."

"We all just want you to be happy. And a good woman would do that for you. I know we don't have enough of them here, so that's why I've gone out of my way to arrange this for you."

"Well, quickly go out of your way to un-arrange it."

"You don't mean that."

The hell he didn't. He'd lasted thirty-three years without getting hitched, and he didn't see the point anymore. Children would have been the point, according to his mother. But it was too late to make her happy.

Drawing on the manners his sainted mother taught him, Wade forced his voice to be gentle. "I know you mean well, but I'm not interested. And I'm sure there's a lot of men you could approach who would be. Jeremy Pine, for instance. Why not him? He's a looker."

"Jeremy is twenty-five and acts like he's twelve. If we're going to put our best face on this contest, we need a grown man."

"I'm flattered, but still not interested." He uncovered the casserole, found a fork, and took a bite. "Mmm, Miss Beulah, you sure can bake. Come over anytime."

Beulah shook a finger. "Wade Cruz, do not distract me with talk of my superior baking skills!"

At that precise moment, there was another knock on the door. "That's probably Lincoln."

He threw the fork in the sink and opened the door to Daisy Carver.

His heart hopped and started racing as it always did for no apparent reason other than Daisy always had him feeling off balance.

Kind of comical that she would say that, since Daisy was about the only woman in town he'd never dated. It had to do with her age, since she was a good seven years younger. It had to do with her brother, who was Wade's best friend in the world. It also had to do with the fact that Daisy confounded him on every level. He'd never fooled himself into thinking he understood women, but Daisy took his confusion to a stratospheric level.

She was at once Scarlett O'Hara and Daisy Duke. Beauty queen and auto mechanic. Overalls and lipstick. Sweet and ornery. Innocent. Sexy. He could go on, but why bother. She was off-limits. He'd kissed her once in a moment of sheer madness, when he was young and stupid, full of piss and vinegar. The intensity of that kiss had scared him off for good.

And for someone who faced off angry bulls for a career, that said something. It wasn't that he feared Lincoln or Jackson, with whom he could hold his own, thank you very much. But he loved the Carvers, had spent half his life with them, and he couldn't see ruining that by disappointing Daisy as he no doubt would eventually.

He was forever stunned to see her, and forever making efforts to avoid her.

Then she opened her Cupid's bow lips and spoke, shattering the quiet, and reminding him that he was staring. "You're back."

TWO WORDS.

That's all Daisy had to say as she tried to collect her thoughts. As she tried to control the slow roll of her heart and the sense of utter chaos of emotions. She was at once thrilled to see him, while a rope of fear uncoiled inside her telling her to step lively. Guard her heart. Wade was undoubtedly the best-looking man in all of Stone Ridge. Despite that, he was famously single and had been for as long as Daisy could remember. Rumor went he was a bit of a player, but Daisy didn't listen to rumors.

Wade had dark, wavy hair and sensual lips with a smile that always tipped slightly at the corner. And the way he filled out a pair of Wranglers was almost criminal. But Wade didn't *look* injured even if she had it on good authority that he was.

"Hiya, Squirt. Come on in, it's welcome-back-Wade week, apparently." He waved her inside and led her to the kitchen.

Daisy saw Miss Beulah and stopped midwalk. "Hi, Miss Beulah."

"Hello there, young lady," Beulah said. "Will I see you at church tomorrow morning?"

"Of course."

"I'll see you and your grandmother then." Beulah stood and gathered her tote bag. "Now, Wade, just think. You could be happily married in six weeks' time."

Married in six weeks' time?

Oh Lord, he was engaged! Another thing no one had thought to tell her.

I knew this would happen one day. Wade was seven years

older than she was, the same age as Lincoln. She shouldn't be at all surprised he was finally settling down. If the thought made her gut roil, it was her own damn fault. She should have stopped thinking about Wade long ago.

Wade walked Beulah outside. "Thank you for the casserole."

"Think about it. I only want you to be happy."

"Sure." Wade shut the door and turned to Daisy. "What's up? Want some French toast casserole? Say what you will about her, but Miss Beulah can bake."

Daisy just stared at him. She couldn't believe this moment had finally come. Wild Wade Cruz was getting married. Although she didn't understand the rush. Six weeks? Was he madly in love or was the woman pregnant?

He glanced at Daisy and went palms up. "*What?*"

"You look good, all recovered." She took a deep breath, sucked in all her regrets. "Well, I'm very happy for you."

"Um, thanks?"

"No one told me. I didn't know."

"Well, that's because I didn't exactly want it broadcast all over town. I asked Lincoln not to say anything."

"Why not?"

"It happened. Not my proudest moment, Twerp."

Getting engaged was not his proudest moment. At this point, she almost felt sorry for the *woman.*

Daisy swallowed hard. "Just…h-happened?"

"It's to be expected, and though I managed to avoid it for years, it finally happened to me."

"I wish you wouldn't make it sound like a death sentence."

"Sometimes it feels that way. But I've got the ranch, and I'm going to bring it back to what it was before. It's just going to take some work."

Good grief. "Wade, I'm sorry, but I don't think anyone should go into a marriage that makes them feel like they're riding out a death sentence."

Wade narrowed his eyes. "Huh? What are you talkin' about?"

"You're getting married, right? Isn't that what Beulah was doin' here, congratulating you?"

"Wait." He held up a palm. "You thought I was getting married? *That's* why you're happy for me?"

"Why else?"

"I thought you were happy I'm fully recovered from the injury."

"Well, that too, of course." She swept her damp palms across the top of her jeans. "You're *not* getting married, then?"

"No." He chuckled.

"But…you said you'd avoided it for years, and it finally happened to you."

"You thought I meant I was getting married."

"What *did* you mean?"

"The injury. I was lucky, for years, but my luck ran out. No more rodeo for me."

"I'm sorry." But she wasn't sorry that Wade wouldn't be on the road any longer.

"Don't waste your time feeling sorry for me."

"I'm not. I hate that you can't do what you love anymore."

"I'll find something else to love."

"Does that mean that you'll be stayin' in Stone Ridge from now on? No more traveling?"

"That's right."

A moment passed between them. They were both quiet enough for Daisy to hear the sound of her own breathing.

"What did Beulah mean? You could be married in six weeks? I heard her say it."

"I see your confusion now. It's some contest she's dreamed up with Winona. They're going to bring more women into town for our *very* lonesome bachelors." He scooped some of the casserole into a bowl.

"But what does that have to do with you?"

He shrugged. "I'm single. She seems to think I'd be interested in being Mr. Cowboy and having women fight for my attention."

"Why would *you* of all people need any help finding a wife? That's ridiculous! What did you say to her?" Daisy ignored the bowl he set in front of her. "Are you going to do it?"

"Mr. Cowboy? I told her I'd think about it but aw, hell, no."

She accepted the bowl and sat at the table even if she had no intention of eating at a time like this. "Good, because surely one of our Stone Ridge women is good enough to be your wife."

There weren't all that many eligible women in their women-scarce town, but there was Daisy. And Eve's business partner, veterinarian Annabeth. Jolette Marie, and Lucy, a waitress at the Shady Grind. There *were* women available and they'd probably all arm wrestle to get a chance with Wade.

"I'm not *lookin'* for a wife. Beulah and the biddies are just worried about me. They're trying to take up the slack in the nagging department. Doing a good job, too."

Daisy didn't touch the casserole even after he'd handed her a fork. With all the talk of marriage, she'd lost her appetite.

"I'm sorry you were hurt."

"I'm alright."

He seemed to be, at least outwardly, but Daisy didn't believe him for a second. The rodeo had been Wade's life for years. Being sidelined for the rest of his life had to be excruciating.

"You *look* fine."

"Still got all my limbs as you can see. Just a compound fracture." He flexed his left arm and grimaced. "The association took care of the surgery and medical bills, so I stayed in California for a while to recover."

"Linc told me you're going to be working on bringing back the ranch."

"Trying to be a rancher, just like my daddy."

"You're staying…for good?"

She almost couldn't believe this. For half of her life, she'd watched as Wade came back to town and left again. Some said he would sell the ranch after his mother died, and probably never return.

"It's not like I have a choice. This ranch is all I have left in the world."

"Don't make it sound like you're being *punished.*"

"Sorry. You know what I mean. I'm used to a little more excitement than mucking stalls and herding cattle."

"You'll have plenty of excitement now because Beulah will be on you until you agree to be Mr. Cowboy. You know she's never giving up on you. Does she ever give up?"

"You have a point. She'll get the message eventually."

"You're not going to want to hurt her feelings and that's what you're going to have to do to get her to stop."

He winked. "Sweetheart, I have a way with ladies. I can figure out how to say no and not hurt her feelings."

"Yeah, I guess you're pretty good at that, aren't you?"

He ignored her comment. "Do you want coffee?"

"I had coffee before I came over. I need it to open my eyes."

He stopped halfway to the cupboard. "Water? Milk? I think I have milk."

"Wade, I'm not here to eat!" She pushed her bowl away.

"You sure are ornery today, Twerp." He came close and tweaked her nose.

Her anger flashed. "I'm not a kid, Wade."

This is what he did with Daisy. He called her nicknames and tweaked her nose. Tousled her hair.

"Hey, I know that." He patted her head.

"I have an idea. A really good one."

"Uh-oh. Now I'm sinking deep in manure. Two ideas in one morning. I hope at least one of them is good."

"There's only one way Beulah will leave you alone and that's if she thinks you're already serious about a woman."

"Good point." He set his coffee mug down. "But I've been away for a while, so I haven't really dated anyone. I suppose there's always Jolette Marie…"

"No, not *her*. Actually, all you have to do is pretend to date someone."

He crossed his arms and frowned. "Sounds… complicated."

"It doesn't have to be. Like, for instance, I could tell Beulah that we're dating. You…and me."

"No one's going to believe that, least of all Beulah."

"Why wouldn't she?" Daisy stood. "I've dated a lot since you've been gone, and it would just make sense that I'm ready to settle down."

He hooked a thumb to his chest. "And me? Does it make sense that *I'm* ready to settle down?"

"You're going to have to work with me here. At least *try* to follow along. Look, I'm trying to help you. I'm different than all the buckle bunnies you've dated. That means I'm settling-down material. And I'm right here!" She stuck out her arms.

"I see you." He chuckled.

"There's no need to find you a woman from a reality TV show. Those women would be afraid to break a nail and I'm guessing they wouldn't appreciate the natural smell of a cattle ranch. I fix cars for a living and I'm not afraid of a little crap." She straightened. "Or a lot of it."

"You would make any rancher a good wife, true enough."

"So, it's a good idea?"

"Who would know this thing is fake and who would know it's real?"

"We'd have to tell my family the truth, of course."

"Yeah. I could never lie to Lincoln."

"He'd see right through you." She smiled. "But everyone else can believe it. Right? And that will solve your problem."

"Tell you what. I'll think about it."

Chapter 3

Dear Albert,

I'm writing this note with a short update.

Not only did my amazing matchmaking skills bring Lincoln and Sadie together, they also reunited Jackson and Eve. I do hope you're watching from wherever you are in heaven, now that you finally found the light.

Lillian "Mima" Carver assumed that her dearly departed husband had found said light because he'd stopped visiting her. Oh, she wasn't crazy, not according to the doctor anyway. When she'd first started writing these letters to Albert and he'd appear, boots, spurs and all, she'd thought life on the range had finally driven her out of her mind. But the doctor said that as long as she understood Albert wasn't really *there*, and if he brought her comfort, there was no harm done. Although the jury was still out on comfort.

Now in her late seventies, and having raised one son and three grandchildren, Lillian worried she might not have much time left. And she still had one grandchild's happiness to secure.

Her precious Daisy.

She continued writing to Albert:

Not only are Lincoln and Jackson both married and happy, there's a new Carver baby, and another one on the way! Eve is pregnant, too, and although Sadie had a boy, little Sammy, there's still hope for Eve. Of course, I love them anyway, boy or girl. But we could use some girls for the future generation. We don't want this problem happening all over again twenty-five years from now. If you could do something about that and assist me down here, it would be much appreciated. I'm obviously doing all the heavy lifting.

Next up is Daisy, of course, and I will need all the help I can get. She seems bound and determined to fly in the face of everything I've taught her and go after "that Wade." She can't see the rodeo cowboy is a womanizer and a flirt. Still single at thirty-three. His poor sainted mother, God rest her soul. Rose had her own ideas about the two of them. Claimed Daisy and Wade were fated, and she'd seen it in the tea leaves or some such thing. Anyway, he's always been too handsome for his own good, that Wade. Quite a charmer, he is, and not right for my Daisy.

I want someone else for Daisy. Someone closer to her age, like Jeremy Pine, or maybe Maybelle's grandson. There are so many choices for her. Why she insists on this crush she's had on Wade for years is beyond me. Infuriating, really. I blame Hank for foolishly indulging her every whim. I don't blame our son entirely, though, as he'd had a lot to make up for over the years. But perhaps he could have kept his daughter away from the ranch hands better than he managed. Wade worked for Hank when he was off the tour, and now and then I'd catch him flirting and smiling at Daisy.

Lillian set her pen down and stretched. She glanced at her wristwatch and noticed it was nearly time to leave for church. She'd finish this letter to Albert later. It wasn't as if he was waiting for it.

She started down the hall to remind Daisy that it was time to go, when she saw her sitting at the breakfast table.

Fully dressed and drinking the coffee she claimed necessary to life.

"What on earth? I usually have to pull you out of bed to make it on time!"

"You're exaggerating. Don't I always go, every Sunday?"

"We're usually late."

"We won't be today."

Well, wasn't this working out to be a beautiful Sunday morning. Lillian grabbed her coat and off they both went to Trinity Church. Pastor June preached about family and home, two of Lillian's favorite subjects. She sat proudly between Daisy and Eve. Sadie was helping out in the nursery as she couldn't bear to leave Sammy alone yet. Naturally, her grandsons weren't here as they didn't attend often, using the ranch as an excuse. And, she noticed, neither was Wade. No surprise there.

But there sat Jeremy Pine, right next to his mother. Lillian waved. He waved back, the sweet boy. No doubt about it, he and Daisy would make beautiful babies. Her, with the blond hair she'd inherited from her mother. Say what you will about the woman, she was the town's beauty before she hightailed it out of here and left Hank and their three small children.

Yes, *Jeremy*, with matching blondish hair to Daisy's, but a slightly darker shade. Both had green eyes. Lillian could almost see their adorable babies.

The pastor wrapped up the sermon and then mentioned the Nativity play and the need for a few more last-minute volunteers.

Sadie caught up with them as they were all filing out. "Sammy is going to be baby Jesus!"

"He's a little big, isn't he?" Daisy said.

And while Sammy had looked more like a three-month-old at birth, weighing in at a strapping nine pounds, ten ounces, he was still a baby, for crying out loud.

"Do you think they're actually going to use a *newborn*, sugar?" Lillian nudged Daisy. "Sammy is perfect for the part."

"If y'all say so."

Lillian patted Sadie's back. "Best of all, we'll get Lincoln inside the church again. Last time he was here y'all got married."

"Oh, he'll be here." Sadie beamed and cooed at Sammy. "He's so proud. And Sammy just adores Lincoln. Every time he walks in the door, Sammy squeals in delight."

Eve elbowed Sadie. "He's just like his mama."

"Ha, ha." Sadie hip-checked Eve.

Outside, the air was clear and bright with a cold snap coming. Lillian felt it in every one of her arthritic bones. "Let's get on home, Daisy. I have some baking to do."

But they hadn't reached the truck when Beulah accosted them. "Lillian, a word?"

Bless her heart, Beulah meant well with the Mr. Cowboy contest. Lillian was of the mind that she didn't want any of these women being carted in from out of town. She worried they wouldn't be screened carefully enough. They might wind up with some women who didn't mean well, like those simply looking for a so-called sperm donor. Ahem. But now that her men were hitched, she didn't much care if they brought in more women. It might help their future generations, too.

"How can I help you, dear?"

"I just visited Wade yesterday, poor lamb. He's not too keen on the idea of being our first Mr. Cowboy. I'll need your help to convince him." She gave Lillian a conspiratorial smirk. "I know you have a vested interest."

Lillian didn't much want to have this conversation with Daisy present, but Beulah did seem clueless to the predicament. "Can I call on you later? We'll work something out, I'm sure."

"Sorry, Beulah," Daisy piped in. "Wade told me that he isn't going to do it."

"Well, now, I wouldn't jump to that conclusion so fast." Beulah held up a palm. "I don't give up easily. A few more visits from the ladies of SORROW, a few more casseroles, maybe some photos of whom he'd be dating might be of some assistance."

"You have photos of these women?" Daisy asked, sounding a little agitated.

"Not the actual ones, no. I have examples. How can I expect them to sign up without knowing something about the rancher they'll be dating? This is a brand-new reality show, and they'll have no idea who it could be. Only that he'll be a real cowboy."

"That should be enough, for now. Women love their cowboys," Lillian added and met Beulah's gaze, trying to clue her in this conversation should take place out of Daisy's presence. "Daisy, let's go."

"Well, I hate to be the one to give you the bad news, but Wade isn't going to do it because he's already dating someone. She'd be upset."

"Why, he didn't say anything to me yesterday. That little weasel," Beulah said. "Wasting my time like that."

"Maybe it isn't serious," Lillian said, though she hoped it was. She chose to be encouraged that Daisy didn't sound at all upset by the fact.

Lillian didn't much care who Mr. Cowboy would be. Sadie's brother, Beau, would be a fine choice.

"I think it is. Serious enough," Daisy said.

"Who is she?" Beulah leaned in. "Some buckle bunny? Surely not Jolette Marie."

"N-no. It's a nice girl, someone really stable, and ready to settle down. You like her."

"I still don't hear a name." Beulah sniffed.

"It's me." Daisy straightened. "*I'm* his woman."

"MIMA! MIMA, ARE YOU ALRIGHT?" Daisy fanned the church bulletin in front of her grandmother's nose.

She knew that Mima wouldn't like the idea of her and Wade, but she didn't think she'd sway and nearly fall down. Mima acted like Daisy had just announced she'd started dating the devil himself. Daisy and Beulah slowly lowered her to the bench seat right outside the church, and a small crowd gathered around them. Good thing Sadie and Eve had already left, or they'd be having fits.

"Let's give her some air," Winona said.

Delores, Winona's housekeeper and nanny, used the double stroller as a weapon to push people back.

"Get out of my way, child." Beulah elbowed in. "I've got the smelling salts."

"She doesn't need *smelling salts*," Daisy protested. "She's going to be fine."

"Fine? She hardly looks fine. What on earth do you expect when you drop a bomb like that?" Beulah got the smelling salts out of her tote bag.

Mima brushed her away. "Bless your heart. Get that ammonia away from me. I'm fine. I just mistakenly heard Daisy say she was Wade's woman. But I'm old and I've had flights of fancy before."

Daisy chewed on her lower lip and fanned harder while everyone else exchanged worried glances. As soon as she got Mima in the truck, she'd explain the ruse. She should have waited to take Mima into her confidence, but Beulah got so pushy. Suggesting that women would decide whether or not to join the show based on Wade's good looks! Suddenly all Daisy could picture was Victoria's Secret models arriving by the truckload, all for Wade. No, she had to put a stop to this, and the sooner the better. Wade would thank her as soon as he heard. No more casseroles or nagging from the old biddies.

He could remain happily single, as long as he pretended not to be.

"I did *hear* wrong?" Mima pushed the church program out of her face.

"Let's go home where we can talk about this." Daisy offered her hand to help her up.

"That's a good idea," Winona said, now holding one of her twins on her hip. "Go home and take a nap. That's what I'm going to do."

"You and I need to talk, Winona." Beulah waved her hands in the air. "This news puts a monkey wrench in my plans. We need to confer on who will be our Mr. Cowboy. Lots to think about."

"I'll call you." Winona waddled away, Delores following her with the stroller.

On the drive home to the ranch, Daisy tried to explain. "Honestly, Mima, don't you think you'd know it if Wade and I were serious? I'm not *really* dating Wade."

"Well, butter my biscuit, why would you lie to your poor old granny? A shock like that could kill me!" Mima fanned herself using the same now rumpled bulletin.

"I don't know why you hate Wade so much. He's Lincoln's best friend. They grew up together. If you like Lincoln, and I think you do, then you should like Wade just fine."

"Sugar, I don't *hate* anyone. You ought to know better than that. He's just not right for you, that's all."

"Oh yeah? And who is?"

"Someone wonderful. You're beautiful, sugar. Look just like your mama. Everybody says so."

The words sliced through Daisy. She didn't want to be compared to a woman who'd left her husband and three children. For years, she'd tried to be as different from her as possible. Choosing to be a tomboy and picking an untraditional profession to go into. An ugly rumor occasionally drifted through town that Daisy wasn't even Hank's daughter because Maggie Mae had an affair and cheated on her husband. No one believed it anymore, because Daisy was a Carver through and through, but it still burned to think of her mother as an unfaithful woman. Her daddy had never deserved that.

Mima was still talking. "You deserve the best man of all. I think it might just be Jeremy Pine."

It wasn't just the comparison to her mama that spiked hot anger in Daisy, but the suggestion that *Jeremy* was the right one for her. He was a friend, and Daisy liked him, but she wasn't going to marry him. Not in a million years. He didn't even like Daisy.

"What's so great about *him*?"

"Did you see him today at church, sitting right there next to his mama? What a sweet, sweet boy."

Daisy groaned. "I love you, Mima, but you're not going to pick who I date *or* marry. Sorry."

"But why would you lie to Beulah? Did Wade ask you to do this for him?"

"He's too busy recovering from his injury and trying to get a cattle ranch back in business. So, he's not interested in that silly reality show. Beulah came by yesterday, and we could both tell she wasn't going to let it go. He doesn't even know I'm doing this. He's probably going to be upset when I tell him."

Wade wouldn't like it, but they'd probably have to do a few public things to throw others off. He couldn't, for instance, hang out at the Shady Grind and flirt with every other woman, or no one would believe the lie. And they should probably do some of the holiday events in town. It would just be a fun time, for a little while, and in the end, Wade would thank her someday. Probably.

"And what were you doing there *yesterday*, young lady?"

Reminding myself of what a real man looked like? Wondering why Wade still didn't see me as a woman?

In other words, torturing herself.

"I didn't know he'd quit the rodeo and is back home for good. No one told me. I thought he was just home and getting ready to leave again, just as always."

"I didn't tell you because I didn't want you rushing right over there to comfort him. The ladies of SORROW are taking real good care of him."

"He's a friend, and I wanted to see him."

"He should kiss your feet for pretending to date the likes of him. He's a womanizer, that's what. A terrible flirt. Honey, you're too young to know this, but sometimes it's best to settle for a man that isn't *quite* as good-looking. Not as popular with the ladies."

"What about Lincoln and Jackson? The women all think they're gorgeous. Not me, of course, that's disgusting. But you make it sound like they're homely."

"They're *Carver* men, sugar. That's a distinction you must always make. Sadly, not every woman is fortunate enough to marry a Carver man." She shook her head.

Daisy sighed deeply. "You'll need to help me tell the

rest of the family, so no one else has a panic attack. I'll tell Lincoln, and you can tell Jackson and them."

"And your father?"

"I'll tell Daddy, too. But he's always *liked* Wade."

"Hank likes everyone and everything since he got engaged to Brenda. Still, don't take advantage of this new and easy nature of his when you tell him."

Later that day, Daisy wondered if she should go up the hill to the large cabin where her father always stayed and tell him first. Not far from the large family home where Daisy still lived with Mima, his cabin was closer to all the cattle operations. But Brenda Iglesias, who was a constant presence in her father's life these days, would probably be there with him. They'd practically moved in together, and Brenda had quit her job as the live-in maid for the True-harts. She now did Mima's previous job of feeding the cowboys three squares a day.

Daisy liked Brenda, but after all these years, it was plain weird to see Daddy with a woman. Her father had always been such a hard and fierce man. She was painfully aware to be his favorite, and he demanded a lot more from her brothers than he ever did from her. She'd always believed it unfair. Daisy had been allowed to make the decision to go to school to be an auto mechanic, whereas for both of her brothers, they were expected to be ranchers.

She'd never even questioned the fact that she'd been fortunate to be born a girl in Stone Ridge. Over the years, a few men had left town to find a bride, but that still hadn't fixed the men-to-women ratio. Of course, like most women, Daisy saw this as an advantage, and now Beulah and the biddies were trying to change all that.

Well, now she had a timeline. Because even if Wade

didn't get chosen as Mr. Cowboy, if they brought this show to town odds were one or more of the runner-ups would be after him.

And she couldn't let that happen until she finally had a chance for Wade to see *her* as a choice.

Chapter 4

When Sadie got home from church, she realized Sammy had fallen asleep during the car ride. She carefully unstrapped him from the car seat and lugged him inside, hoping he'd stay down for at least an hour. But the minute she crossed the threshold of their cabin, Sammy woke up as if completely rejuvenated from a fifteen-minute snooze.

Predictably, the moment he saw Lincoln, Sammy squealed in delight and kicked his legs.

"Your son just got the part of baby Jesus in the Nativity play!"

The moment Lincoln turned to her, Sadie knew something was horribly wrong. He gave Sammy a half-hearted smile, not his usual, *look out, I'm-about-to-throw-you-up-in-the-air* look.

"Congratulations, Sammy." Lincoln rose and took Sammy from her, then kissed Sadie's temple. "Hiya, bride."

She went into his arms, and he used his free arm to pull her in tight. Her cowboy's arms were so strong and warm that she nuzzled into the deep embrace. She'd loved

Lincoln Carver since she was a girl, and still couldn't believe they were married. Sometimes the happiness was so strong that she could almost feel it in the air around them, sparkling and snapping like a live wire, wrapping around her heart.

All three of them stood in the expansive entryway of their large cabin for a few minutes until Sammy squirmed.

"I'll make lunch." Holding Lincoln's hand, she pulled him into the kitchen.

The cabin Lincoln had built, with help from his daddy and brother, was so new that Sadie could smell the fresh scent of pine wafting all around them. She was still getting accustomed to all the room they now had, too, when for almost a year they'd lived in her cramped cabin on Lupine Lake. Now, they had a two-story "cabin" with a large dining room, kitchen, and three bedrooms upstairs. They were far enough from Jackson and Eve's cabin and the main house down the hill to have their privacy, but still close to family.

Sadie made turkey sandwiches with all the fixings and opened a bag of potato chips as Lincoln played with Sammy. She'd been worried that Lincoln wouldn't be happy about them having a baby this soon, since they were still practically newlyweds. Sammy hadn't been planned, but as Linc promised, they had adjusted their plans, and he didn't seem at all burdened by Sammy. He was the light of Lincoln's life.

She watched out of the corner of her eye as he threw Sammy up in the air a few times, each time easily catching him. The first time he'd done that she'd nearly had a heart attack. But Lincoln would never fail to catch his son. He would, however, sometimes fail to tell Sadie when he was burdened with a problem, because he claimed he didn't want her to worry.

Sadie set Sammy in his high chair and let him pummel a couple of chips with his fist, occasionally taking a bite or two.

Next to her at the large farmhouse table, Lincoln ate his sandwich quietly. The silence between them was thick with worry. She could almost hear his thoughts.

Finally, Sadie was able to take no more of this. She reached for his hand. "What's wrong?"

"Nothing." He squeezed her hand as if to reassure her.

"*Something's* wrong. You need to tell me."

"I don't want you to worry if nothing comes of it."

"I promise I won't worry."

He snorted. "You won't keep that promise."

"Alright, I lied, because I'm already worried. So, it won't make a difference once I know *why* I'm worried."

"Gah! Bee!" Sammy said, having smashed all his chips into dust.

Sadie gave him another chip. "Here you go."

"Is that good, buddy?" Lincoln asked Sammy.

"Cooscoo!" Sammy replied with his drooly smile.

"Stop avoiding the subject. Remember, you said on the day we got married there was nothing we couldn't get through together?"

"And we'll get through this, too. I just don't know if everyone else will."

That sounded ominous and Sadie immediately knew. "Rusty."

Lincoln slowly nodded. "Yeah."

Before she and Lincoln were married, an old rodeo cowboy had started sending Hank emails. They'd thrown her father-in-law into such a funk that Lincoln had taken over, as he so often did. Rusty claimed to have had an affair with Lincoln's mother, Maggie, and that she'd told him Daisy might be his daughter.

Sadie now lost her appetite. Tension coiled through her stomach like a snake. This had to be killing Lincoln. How long had he kept this to himself?

"What's happened?"

"He's very ill, supposedly dying, and would like to see Daisy again just once before he goes. He's leaving everything he has to her."

Sadie swallowed hard. "Even if…even if he's not one hundred percent sure?"

Lincoln met her eyes, his eyes hooded and unreadable. "He must be sure."

"Well, he can't be. Daisy has at least a fifty percent chance of being Hank's daughter."

Daisy was so close to her daddy. She would be devastated to know she wasn't his biological daughter. Devastated to know the ugly rumor she'd refused to believe was true.

"I'm going to have to tell her." Lincoln took her hand and squeezed it. "Soon."

The words lay between them like little bombs.

A while ago, Lincoln had personally met Rusty, even driven him by Daisy's auto shop, so he could take a look at her from a distance. But Rusty had violated that agreement and hopped out of the truck. He'd talked shop with her, without letting her know who he might be. It was the last agreement he'd made with Lincoln and he'd honored it so far.

But Lincoln had wondered if he should have told Daisy the truth instead of shielding her and protecting her.

"She'll forgive you."

"For keeping this from her? I'm not sure that she will. Maybe the right thing to do was to bring it all out in the open, have the DNA tests, be done with it all."

"You were worried of what it would do to Daisy if she

wasn't Hank's daughter. She still had a fifty-fifty chance and no matter what, she *is* Hank's daughter. You meant well and Daisy will understand."

"I don't know." Lincoln ran a palm down his face, and even Sammy couldn't make him smile. "I've got to talk with my father this afternoon."

"Are you going to tell him?"

"Maybe. But we have cattle business to discuss anyway."

Sadie spent the day playing with Sammy, grading papers, and planning the last week of lessons before Christmas break. The kids were so excited about the holidays that she didn't think they'd accomplish much, but she still had to try to keep their attention. But Lincoln wasn't home for dinner, probably off brooding. This protectiveness of his sometimes went too far. She wanted to be his soft place to fall, always, and that involved knowing what was eating at him. Now she knew, at least, but still had no idea how to comfort him if he wanted to brood.

Sadie gave Sammy a bath and put him to bed in his crib. He took few naps, but the one redeeming grace was that he'd slept through the night early on. When she put him to bed at seven o'clock, chances were good he wouldn't wake up until six the next morning. That meant she and Lincoln always had the evenings to themselves, making love and behaving like they did before they'd had Sammy.

"Good night, honey." Sadie shut the light off and left the door ajar.

She'd just washed her face and brushed her teeth when Lincoln got home. She ran down the steps to meet him.

He stood in the foyer, Stetson tipped, eyes weary.

"I told Hank," he said, closing his eyes and pinching the bridge of his nose. "He didn't take it well."

Sadie went into his arms.

"Where were you? I wish you'd come home earlier, maybe to give Sammy a bath."

At least it would distract him if nothing else.

"I'm sorry." He crushed her against him, so tightly that for a moment she couldn't breathe. "I love you. More than you'll ever know."

"And I love you, but I don't like it when you brood." She tweaked his chin.

"Point taken."

Then he kissed her, the way only Lincoln could. Warm, deep, with a passion that always made her knees liquid.

"You're forgiven," she said breathlessly when he broke the kiss.

"Let's go to bed," Lincoln said, tugging her up the steps.

He wore the same wicked smile he did when he wanted to tear all her clothes off. This was *her* Lincoln, the one she'd loved for half her life.

She followed him upstairs, where she took his mind off everything else but her.

ON MONDAY, at work, Daisy decided she'd practice this new dating-Wade thing even if she still hadn't told him it was happening. Because she worked forty-five minutes away in Kerrville, there wasn't much of a chance anyone here would tell him before she did. So, when Bob, the tire specialist, asked her to go on a date for what had to be the hundredth time, she didn't just say no because she didn't date coworkers who were twenty years her senior.

"I'm sorry, but I'm dating someone." She wiped motor oil off her hands. "We're pretty serious."

"Figures." He shook his head in disgust. "Who's the lucky guy?"

"Wade Cruz."

"The rodeo star?"

"That's him."

She let the idea sink in, letting it roll around her mind like melted chocolate.

Daisy and Wade are dating.

Did you hear Daisy and Wade are a thing?

I thought Wade would never settle down, and now along comes Daisy.

They make a cute couple.

She wasn't going to lie. It was a nice feeling.

"Man, that was a heartbreaker of a ride. I watched when he went down. He had a real chance at being the best in the world, and now his career is over. What a tough break."

Daisy never watched the rodeo. Too scary. Lincoln had also done some rodeoing in his day and that's about the time Daisy stopped watching. It was terrifying to watch her big brother put himself in danger, not to mention Wade.

"He's recovering nicely."

This was another lie as she wasn't quite sure that he *was* recovering well. But if he wasn't, he'd certainly put on a good act.

Daisy went about her day, fixing a few sets of brakes and taking out and replacing an old alternator with a new one. Lou was planning on closing down for two weeks during the holidays, which meant that Daisy had to earn all she could in the next several days.

On her lunch break, she crossed the street to her favorite coffee shop and ordered a hot mocha latte and an egg bite. Even Lou was getting into the spirit of the holidays, dragging out the sad, greased-stained artificial tree in his office and setting out garland haphazardly inside the shop. All in all, it was a normal Monday on the job.

Until she recognized the man. Again, he sat in his truck across the street from Lou's Auto Shop. Short, graying hair, goatee. Every time she glanced in his direction, he made it a point to look away. He was obviously casing the shop, though she wondered what he found valuable at Lou's. Lou rarely carried cash in the register, and everyone paid with plastic these days. Sure, tires and alternators could be expensive, but he'd be better off robbing the coffee shop.

"Lou, that man is here again," Daisy said, hooking her thumb.

"What is it with that guy?" Lou scratched his temple, leaving a streak of engine oil. "Last week he told me he was having lunch with his girlfriend. I've never even seen him with a woman."

"He's obviously lying. I think he's hoping to break in, maybe while you're gone."

"Well, there won't be anything left to steal. If he wants this old desk and chair, he's welcome to them. Heck, I'll do fine with the insurance claim. Get everything around here new again. The missus would be happy."

Daisy had hoped Lou would take this more seriously, because the dude bothered her. There was something very suspicious about him. Like he was sitting there collecting everyone's secrets.

"Did you test the alarm system anyway?"

"Sure, sure. Don't worry so much!" Lou waved her away. "Back to work with you."

Daisy did get back to it, working her butt off for the rest of the day. Three more brake jobs. Those always took so long. She put in some overtime and after work resisted the temptation to stop in for a cold beer at the Shady Grind to give Jackson the fake news. But she wasn't sure he'd be there tonight, and she had to stop telling everyone before she actually told *Wade*. There were two of them in this fake relationship, after all. And he had yet to be informed.

It was true that she'd never known Wade to be serious with a woman, though some believed his high school girlfriend cheated and ruined him for all women. Daisy, of course, didn't want to believe that even if all evidence seemed to support it. All she'd ever known of Wade was a good guy who looked after her when her brothers weren't around. He'd been Lincoln's best friend since grade school, and they'd toured the rodeo together for several years. Eventually Lincoln gave up the dangerous bull-riding events to focus on lassoing, but Wade stuck with dangerous bulls for years.

Driving home, she crossed the entrance into Stone Ridge with the weathered sign:

Welcome to Stone Ridge, established 1806 by Titus Ridge Population 5,010
Women eat free every ~~night~~ Tuesday at the Shady Grind

Now that Jackson owned the bar and grill, things weren't quite as loosey-goosey around here. But Daisy nearly drove off the road when she noticed a new, and large, billboard at the entrance to town:
Mr. Cowboy, a new reality dating show
Coming soon to Stone Ridge
It must have gone up after she'd driven to work this morning. Hideous, it blocked some of the skyline. A giant-sized photo of a handsome man Daisy didn't recognize smiled down on all the "little people." He had sparkling white teeth. But sparkling wasn't a strong enough word. How about blinding?

Well, she'd have to speak to someone at the chamber of commerce about this. She would, too, if they had a chamber. Unfortunately, they didn't, so she'd have to take this up with the biddies of SORROW. They'd gone too far this time, and surely Jackson, and Mr. Lloyd from the General Store, not to mention Pastor June from Trinity Church wouldn't like this, either.

When she got home, Daisy found Mima knitting on the couch in front of the fireplace.

"Did you see that billboard? It's taking up half the skyline! It's hideous. What an eyesore! Why hasn't anyone complained yet? I'm going to file a complaint. That's what I'm going to do."

Mima scowled. "What is this mess? I don't know what you're gnawing on about."

After Daisy explained, Mima chuckled and shook her head. "Oh, that Beulah. I heard that would be going up but didn't know it would be this soon. She thought that might encourage a lucky man to step up."

"Lucky man? *Lucky man?* How would you like to be surrounded by beautiful women, all perfectly lovely, and then have to pick just *one?*"

"Well, sugar, that's how it's done. We're not going to encourage a *harem.*"

"These dating shows are ridiculous. No way anyone chooses his life mate with all that pressure. They have a few weeks to get to know each other and make a lifetime commitment. I can't even decide on a dress in a few weeks."

"That's because you don't like dresses. Speaking of which, sugar, maybe if you wore them more often, like Sadie does…"

Daisy blew out a frustrated breath. "Not this again."

She was far more like Eve, comfortable in her jeans,

boots, and a T-shirt most of the time. Sometimes paired with a flannel shirt if it was cold outside. But Mima didn't seem to understand that Daisy would have plenty of men to choose from if only she didn't have big brothers.

"I wish you'd settle down and not just with your fake boyfriend. If you don't like Jeremy, I'll think of someone else."

"You better find a brave one. Did it ever occur to you that I might actually really *have* a boyfriend if only Lincoln and Jackson didn't scare every one of them off?" Daisy went hands on hips.

"I'm sure they don't do that," Mima muttered.

"Speaking of my fake boyfriend, I have to go over there tonight and tell Wade."

"Oh, wonder how he'll take the news?" Mima's voice sounded deceptively mild.

She didn't fool Daisy. Mima hoped this would all blow up in Daisy's face and that Wade wouldn't go along with it. And while Daisy wouldn't be too surprised if that happened, she hoped he'd at least hear her out while she made her case.

She took a shower and dressed in her new jeans and flannel shirt. At the last minute, she decided on a peace offering in case this didn't go as well as she'd hoped. She grabbed one of the apple pies Mima had baked yesterday and was out the door.

"YOU TOO?" Wade said several minutes later when he took the pie from Daisy. "Well, at least it's not a casserole."

She shrugged. "I remembered you like apple pie."

"That's right, Peanut. It's my favorite."

Wow, he hadn't called her Peanut since she was *twelve*. This was going from bad to worse. She followed him into the kitchen, unable to take her eyes off his behind. Wade wore those Wranglers of his extremely well. Tight in all the right places. What would he do right now if she grabbed him and kissed him the way he had planted one on her all those years ago? She was better at kissing now than she'd been back then, the first time she'd ever been kissed. Wade had been her first real kiss and she could still feel the way her ears had buzzed and her brain stopped processing thoughts.

"Um, so, did you do any more thinking about what I suggested?"

He set the pie down and quirked a brow. "You were serious about that."

"Of course. This idea will work."

"I don't think it's such a good plan."

"Why not?"

At the moment, he seemed to be struggling to form words, and she worried he was in pain. Then he grimaced and rubbed his elbow, proving it. "Just…take my word for it, okay?"

"Well, it's too late. I already told Beulah at church, and it worked. Everyone thinks we're dating and they're already looking for someone *else* to be Mr. Cowboy." The words came out in a rush and, boy, did she feel stupid when his eyes grew wide, then narrowed. "So, you're welcome."

"I wish you hadn't."

But she wasn't scared. Instead, she was gall-darned mad. Fury spiked through her and her heart raced as fast as a cornered rabbit's.

"Really, Wade? I'm so awful that you can't even *pretend* that you're mine?"

He flinched, and she realized he couldn't stand the thought of hurting her. She bit her lower lip to keep from crying.

"That's…that's not the problem."

"Then, what is it? If it's my family, I already told you we won't lie to them."

"I wish that were it, but that's not it, either." He rubbed the stubble on his jaw.

"Are you going to *tell* me? Do you already have a girlfriend?"

"No, but I wish I'd thought of that."

"Huh?"

"I'm not fast enough on my feet or I would have thought to tell you that I already have a girlfriend. Another fake girlfriend, so I can't have you be my fake girlfriend as that might offend her. Maybe that would have worked."

She felt dizzy with the lies. "Gosh, you lost me."

"That makes two of us."

He took several steps toward her, so close she could smell the leather of his boots and see the gold specks in his caramel-brown eyes. It didn't escape her fondest memories that he'd only been a little closer than this the time he'd kissed her. He reached to tug on a lock of her hair, further enhancing that memory. Now she could almost smell the peaches that had been ripe that September. If she dared to close her eyes right now, she might also remember the taste of his lips on hers, his warm tongue exploring.

But she didn't dare close her eyes because she didn't want to miss a thing.

"This is playing with fire. If we spend too much time pretending, I'm going to fool myself. And then we're going to wind up in bed. Which wouldn't be a good idea."

This sounded like a fine idea to her. It sounded like an adventure and she was ripe for one of those.

When his thumb lowered to trace her bottom lip, she nearly lost her balance. "Wh-why not?"

He took a step back, breaking the spell. "Because I'm too old for you."

"No, you're not. Maybe when I was eighteen you were, but not now. That age difference has a way of not being quite as important anymore."

"I'm also a broke-down cowboy, in case you hadn't noticed." He held his left arm out.

"I don't care about any of that."

"Maybe I do."

"I don't think that's fair. You should let me decide."

His gaze slid appreciatively down her breasts, to her legs. "Damn, Peanut, you're all grown up, aren't you?"

She was glad she'd worn her new jeans tonight that were a size too small.

"Well, I'm glad you noticed."

"Oh, I noticed." He sent her a slow and easy smile. "Okay, look. If we're going to do this, we'll damn well do it my way."

Chapter 5

Wade was already exhausted. Maybe it was the meds. They made his brain fuzzy while they simultaneously took care of the pain. He would need a full night's sleep to find a way out of this mess.

Pretending to be anything more than friends would be playing with fire.

Daisy Carver was beautiful. To Wade, she always had been. He didn't care that she dressed casually and never made an effort to look particularly feminine. No long and manicured nails on her. No hair extensions or false lashes. Just long, natural blond hair and equally long legs. She usually kept her hair in a high ponytail which gave her a perpetually girlish look. But tonight, the second time he'd seen her in as many days, she'd let her hair down. And he was a goner. He pictured fisting a handful of that hair while he kissed her until she begged him to stop. Or asked him to never stop.

A thick layer of sexual tension had always flickered between them, one that, try as Wade might want to deny, had never gone away. He could tell himself this heap of desire and lust was happening to him now because he hadn't been with a woman in so long. But although accurate, that wasn't the reason he now stared at Daisy like he wanted to take her to bed and keep her there for days.

The point was, he'd like to think he was a better man than that. She of all women deserved better than a dried-up rodeo cowboy with a practically lame arm. If he felt this way at thirty-three, what would he be like at fifty? He didn't want to saddle her with an older man and his orthopedic problems, all due to his lifestyle choices. All due to wanting to be the best in the rodeo and to indulging an addiction to adrenaline rushes.

When he'd had to start over and pick a new career, ranching was his only option. Stone Ridge was home, even if he didn't have quite the same attachment that some of the ranching families had to the land itself. Too many memories of his mother here. She'd held on to this land so tightly Wade wondered if in the end it had killed her. To Wade, land was just dirt, and he didn't know why people were willing to die over it.

Daisy was a rancher's daughter through and through and she loved this town with the same reverence that his mother had. She deserved a man who wouldn't slowly die stuck in this small town.

He was off-limits, too old for her, too experienced. It didn't matter that she made his heart switch like a kitten's tail. They were never going to happen.

But he supposed, if she wanted to pretend for a while, it might help him out.

"Okay, Peanut."

This is what he did with Daisy. He called her nicknames and tweaked her nose. Tousled her hair. Kept it affectionately tender and nonsexual. Safe. But his skills with women were sorely rusty as he hadn't even been with a woman in one long year. He seemed to remember being a whole lot more charming than this.

"But if we're going to do this, I have a few rules of my own."

"Okay." She took a seat on his living room couch, tucking one luscious leg under. "Tell me."

Those jeans she wore were so tight he half wondered if she'd painted them on. He tried hard to focus. Parameters. Boundaries. He needed them before he lost his fool head. Again.

"Light PDA. Hand-holding, kisses on the cheek, that kind of thing."

"Are you *kiddin'* me? No one's going to believe we're for real. Not with your reputation."

He used to be proud of that reputation, had been when he was younger, but now it stung to think even Daisy categorized him there.

"I'll make it look real. Don't you worry about that."

"What about a light kiss on the lips? No tongue."

"Tongue is out of the question."

"In public, sure. I agree."

"Correct me if I'm wrong, but that's all this is. In public fake dating."

"Sure, but we should spend a little time in private practicing all this or it's sure going to look ridiculous."

He squinted. "Ridiculous?"

"Fake."

"Uh-huh. Which it is."

"Wow, I can't believe you're being this thick. Work with me here!"

The problem was he wanted to work her. He wanted to work her so good she'd have trouble walking the next day. Oh, crap. *No.* Those thoughts weren't allowed in his head.

Okay, maybe just in his head where they could do no harm.

He was enjoying the fantasy and didn't realize Daisy was staring at him.

"Does that make sense?" she asked.

While indulging himself, he must have missed something. "Does *what* make sense?"

"The Riverwalk this weekend? Our first out-in-public date. Everyone will be there."

He hadn't planned on the Riverwalk. In fact, he hadn't been out of the house much. Once in a while he dropped by the Shady Grind, but with Lincoln MIA these days, Wade had begun to grow sick of all the rodeo questions.

How many concussions have you had, in total?

How many bones have you broken?

What happened? Did you lose your focus?

Did you hear the bone crack?

How much blood?

He wished he could claim a lack of focus on the day he'd broken his arm. Instead, everything had gone perfectly that day. He'd been enjoying the attentions of a buckle bunny just minutes before, but no one took his focus off the ring. His focus had always been key in his success. The problem was his age, and a body breaking down from all the beating it took over the years. And unlike Lincoln, Wade had failed to quit while ahead. Now he was the focus of commentary on what could go wrong on the way to the top. How close one could come and still lose it all.

Yeah, that was him. A cautionary tale.

"Sure, yeah. The Riverwalk. That sounds okay." He ran a hand through his hair. "You keep everyone away from me that wants to talk about the rodeo. Deal?"

"You don't want to talk about the rodeo?"

"It's all anyone ever asks me about. I'm sick of talking

about the accident. Tired of talking about this arm." He touched it lightly.

"Does it hurt much?"

"Only if I breathe." When she winced, he chuckled. "Just kiddin', Peanut. I'm good."

"Also, stop calling me *Peanut*. I'm not twelve."

He cleared his throat. "Alright. What other pet name is good?"

"It's a pet name?"

"Sure, what else would it be?"

"I think it's that name you call me when you want to put some distance between us." She crossed her arms. "Like Squirt and Twerp."

Okay, he was officially out of his league here. Daisy wasn't just gorgeous, she was smart as a whip, and nobody's fool. For years, he'd had a steady diet of women who wanted only one thing from him. He gave that away easily enough.

He tried a smile. "You might be right about that."

"I know I am." She sent him a conspiratorial wink. "Since I'm helping you with this, maybe you could help me with something, too."

"Yeah, name it, Pe—uh, name it."

"Well, here's the thing. You might have noticed that I haven't had a serious relationship. Like, ever."

"Hadn't noticed."

"Of course you haven't." She untucked her leg and repositioned herself on the couch, knees pointed toward him. "It's not like I have trouble finding men who are interested in me."

"No doubt."

"It's just that most of them aren't as brave as you are."

He scratched his temple. "How's that, now?"

"I have two big brothers who are overly protective."

"And me. You've got me." He thumped his chest.

"Right. But you're not my brother, don't forget."

"I'll still kill anyone who tries to hurt you."

"Anyway, that's why I'm not all that experienced, you know, at being someone's *girlfriend*."

"Okay. I understand."

"You do?" She brightened.

Now he wasn't sure that he *did*, because the fact that he understood seemed to greatly encourage her. He must have missed something. "Um, do I?"

"Geez, do I have to spell it out for you?"

"Apparently."

She covered her face. "Don't make me do that. It's too embarrassing."

"C'mon, you can tell me anything. I've kept all your secrets. I have no clue what—"

And then he stopped talking. Because he suddenly knew exactly what Daisy was referring to and it hit him square in the solar plexus. Nearly knocked all the air out of him, just like that time Satan threw him during practice and nearly impaled him on a post.

And he found himself wishing he was in that situation right now instead of this one.

"You figured it out," she said quietly, lowering her gaze.

"Daisy, are you a virgin? Is that what you're trying to tell me?"

"Yeah, kind of. A little bit. Mostly."

He ran a hand down his face. Poor Daisy. "*Why* are you telling me this?"

"First, I trust you. You won't tattle, even if everybody probably already knows. But it's nobody's business."

"I'll take it to my grave, sweetheart." He made a motion to sweep his finger across his heart.

"Second, because you should know why I might act a

little awkward on our dates together. Why I might not know all the right moves."

"What part of fake don't you understand? Don't worry about any of that."

"And third, and this is the tough one. Because I thought you might help me with my moves."

All the blood rushed out of his head. It was as if someone had hit him with a baseball bat.

"Moves?"

"How to turn a guy on, that kind of thing. I've waited too long for the right man and this is the year I have a little adventure."

"Why do you want to do that? It's nice…being a virgin." He lowered his voice even if they could only be heard by Dante and Satan.

He could not believe they were having *this* conversation.

"Nice? Are you kiddin' me? It makes me…weird. I'm too old to be a virgin."

"Maybe you should get married. That will take care of it."

"Right, because 'nice girls' get married first." She held up air quotes. "Don't give me that eighteenth-century stuff. I'm a modern woman. I have to be sure I don't marry a man who likes to tie his wife up for sexy times."

Oh, now there went an image he'd never be able to wash out of his brain.

He wanted to tear his hair out. "You are driving me nuts. Look, I don't want to be the guy who 'teaches' you." Now *he* held up air quotes.

This could get complicated. Playing with fire wasn't the right term here. They were fooling around with a nuclear bomb.

Maybe he should have hightailed it out of town the day after Daisy appeared on his doorstep. Hell, he could still get out now while the gettin' was good. He'd leave a note, escape the biddies, *Mr. Cowboy*, and the woman who was single-handedly trying to kill him.

Coward.

See? You won't win, he told his arm. *I'm still young. I can have a life and fool around with a beautiful woman.*

No, this was Daisy, for crying out loud. *Peanut.* But his Peanut was all grown up, and when he wasn't looking, she'd turned into a sexpot.

Gulp. He pulled at the neckline of his shirt. Was it hot in here?

"You did the right thing waiting. You should be in love your first time," he said.

"Were you in love your first time?"

Hell no. In fact, someone older had initiated him, which made him wonder if he was playing the double-standard card. He'd been sixteen, and granted, tall for his age. She'd been twenty-five or so, visiting her cousins when she found him in the barn one night. Wade thought she'd been looking for Lincoln, whom she'd flirted with all night, but she shook her head and said "no." She'd straddled him, lifted up her skirt, and that was all she wrote.

He didn't even remember her name.

"Okay. I think it's time for you to go home. My head hurts."

She rose, a look of concern in her eyes that immediately made him sorry he'd said anything. "Not your arm?"

"My arm is fine compared to my brain. It's about to explode."

She blinked. "Are you mad at me?"

"No, I'm not mad. Just very…"

Torn and confused.

Weary. Injured. You name it.

"It's okay. I've given you a lot to think about." She walked toward the front door. "But remember this weekend. The Riverwalk."

Then she turned and sashayed her cute behind out of his home. Slowly, he closed the door. The framed photo of his mother on the fireplace mantel smiled back at him.

And if she could see him now from heaven, she was laughing and saying: "I told you so."

SOMEHOW, Wade made it through the rest of the week without seeing Daisy. Thank the sweet baby Jesus, the casseroles stopped coming every day, and he had few interruptions. No more mention of Mr. Cowboy or how important it was that he settle down with a good woman. Maybe he could actually get some work done around here.

Lincoln came by a few times, to check in, and yell at him to take care of his arm and do his physical therapy. Then he'd offer to do some of Wade's chores and only leave when Wade kicked him out.

Wade's arm hurt every day, but especially after a long day of ranch work. He found himself taking several pain pills a day, hating that he needed them. Someday this would get better. His arm would be fully healed and with any luck no residual pain. But the pain made him feel old, lame, and useless. Still, being permanently sidelined from the rodeo meant he had to find another way to make a living. For the rest of his life.

When he went into the barn for feed or equipment, he glared at the Model T that sat there like a relic of times gone by. An antique, a gift from his father. Mocking him.

On Tuesday and Wednesday, Wade worked on the

fence line. He was so bored that he nearly fell asleep standing up. Safe to say, ranching was nothing like the rodeo. He imagined the only adrenaline shot he might have was if the barn fell down, which at this point looked like three to one odds. He'd take that bet.

Dante and Satan were the only animals left on a formerly large cattle ranch. Once, they'd had thirty head of cattle, two bulls, a stable of horses, pigs, and goats. He might not be much of a rancher, but his father had been, and *his* father before him. Wade might have been a rancher, too, but early on Jorge Cruz saw something special in Wade.

He noticed that his only son was fearless. When Wade was ten, he'd walked across the top of the wood pigpen fence, fallen in, and nearly been lunch. He'd tried to explain to his father that he thought he'd clear it and only missed it by an inch. He'd do better next time.

"There won't be a next time! Boy, don't you got any good sense? If you get hurt, your mother will kill me."

But despite that threat, Wade was always getting hurt. He fell from trees, which he climbed because it would be crazy not to.

But he'd never fallen off a horse. He'd been riding since age five, and they'd never owned anything but well-behaved, docile, and trained quarter horses. Then, when Wade was about twelve, he'd mounted a horse his father was considering purchasing. Something spooked the paint, and he bucked, trying to throw Wade off. The owner yelled. Wade's father cursed. His mother cried, but the horse bucked for several seconds before anyone was able to control him.

It had been the time of Wade's life. He never fell off, no matter how hard that horse had bucked.

And his father saw gold.

From that day on, Wade started training for the rodeo.

"What would you think if you could see me now, Dad?" Wade muttered now as he pounded another nail in the fence.

Things had gone well for several years. His father supported Wade's training, sometimes selling off cattle to pay for expenses. Once Wade started touring and earning money, he put it right back into the ranch. For a while, the cattle operation thrived. His mother was happy, and Wade loved that he had a part. The part he enjoyed. Not the fence repairs, hay bales, pulling cattle out of ditches, tagging, and mucking.

He enjoyed flying on the backs of horses, lassoing steer, the crowds cheering. He sat on bucking bulls. He got to listen as the announcers talked about him. They called him cocky but gifted. Bold. Daring. "Wild Wade" became his nickname early on as he racked up the wins. He hadn't known what an adrenaline junkie was at the age of sixteen, but he did now. And Wade had simply been born that way.

He didn't blame his father for making the most of Wade's talents. He did, however, blame him for ruining what might have been.

A truck came up his driveway, kicking up gravel. The red, long-bed truck was familiar, and Wade immediately recognized his closest neighbor, Riggs Henderson. Their lands abutted each other.

Wade met him, fist-bumping when Riggs climbed out of his truck.

"You know, you could hire some help around here," Riggs said, eyeing Wade's boots. Probably also eyeing the state of Wade's ranch. "Just call me or Sean over anytime. Free of charge."

"You're busy enough with the twins."

"Between Winona and Delores, I'm lucky if I get to hold one of them for longer than a few minutes," he chuckled.

"Don't forget I worked for Hank between tournaments."

"I'm sure it will all come back to you." Riggs nodded. "Again, I'm sorry about your mother."

"It had been coming for some time."

"Still isn't easy."

"No. Guess not."

It was, however, easier when he didn't have to think about it. When he didn't have to live in the same house where she'd died. When he could ride bulls and forget his pain. Now, he was here and every day felt like a struggle, and not just because of his arm.

They walked quietly for a few minutes, their boots kicking up gravel. "There's a cattle auction coming up. Sean and I are going. You got a plan?"

Here was the thing. Everyone seemed to think Wade Cruz should be rolling in the money. All those winnings over the years. Hundreds of thousands of dollars. Compounded interest. He *could* have been well-off had he always been in control. Unfortunately, he'd made the mistake of trusting his father. His own flesh and blood. He hadn't known that Jorge Cruz liked the casinos. When he'd died suddenly, Wade and his mother learned the truth.

Eventually, Wade managed to bring back possibly half of what he should have had in a lifetime of earnings. He'd done that by entering every tournament he could for years. By working for Lincoln's father during off-season. Saving and socking everything away. Then he'd been sucker punched by his mother's cancer and a truckload of medical bills Wade slowly paid off.

What he had left of his savings would have to do because he had no options left. No more competitions, no more so-called "easy" money.

"The plan is to make this a working cattle ranch again."

Chapter 6

Daisy had been waiting for the Riverwalk all week long. After her last week of work at the auto shop before they closed for the holidays, generous Lou gave everyone a bonus. After work, Daisy went to buy a new pair of boots with her bounty.

She'd decided on a pair of low heels with blue inlays, her typical style, when Jolette Marie came up beside her. Since there were no shoe stores in Stone Ridge (or hair and nail salons or much of anything else) everyone came to Kerrville to shop. Either that or they ordered online and waited. And waited.

"Oh, those are *cute*," Jolette Marie said.

"Thanks. I need a new pair for the Riverwalk."

These were practical but also pretty. And the price was right.

"Same reason I'm here." Jolette Marie held up a kickass pair of boots with a killer heel. They were black with red inlays.

Daisy reconsidered. She should get boots with a heel. Much sexier. If she didn't buy a sexy boot, was there any point to this at all? Picking up a similar boot with heels, Daisy gasped at the price. This would be almost her entire bonus.

"What's the matter? Don't have your size?" Jolette Marie, daughter of the wealthiest man in Stone Ridge, didn't have to worry about price tags. "I'll help you look."

For several minutes, Daisy pretended this was the issue. They looked for a size eight, when Daisy was a size seven.

"You know what? I'm going to buy these." She held up the first pair of boots. Damn the torpedoes.

"Suffer for fashion, I always say."

"Smart." Daisy didn't like to suffer, though, for fashion or anything else.

She paid, waving goodbye to half her bonus. It would be worth it if Wade found her feet sexy.

"Are you going with anyone to the Riverwalk?" Daisy asked, making conversation as they walked outside with their packages.

"Several someones." Jolette Marie winked.

She was one of the women who didn't want to settle down with just one guy when there were so many to choose from. It occurred to Daisy that she might find a kindred spirit in Jolette Marie but for a different reason.

"Hey, did you see that billboard they put up?"

"Hilarious."

"I think it's ugly. An eyesore."

"So does my daddy. He claims he's going to sue." Jolette Marie snorted.

Daisy didn't think her kindred spirit would be an old multimillionaire, but so be it. "Good for him."

"Well, Daddy says he's going to do a lot of things that he never does."

"Aren't you worried about all these women they're going to be bringing into town? To take *our* men?"

But then again, why would Jolette Marie be worried? She was beautiful and had the attention of every single man in town. Even Lincoln had dated her for a while before he and Sadie fell in love. The most unfair part of all this to Daisy was that Jolette Marie had older brothers who didn't seem to give a hoot what she did with her life. Or whom she dated. Lucky stiff.

"Don't worry." She waved her hand dismissively. "Those women won't stick around for long."

Daisy hoped not. She thought about it as she drove back into town, once more having to pass by the giant man with the blinding smile. Hopefully she and Wade would be able to pull off this fake-dating thing. From time to time, a news story would come out about the handsome rodeo star who was forced to cut his promising career short. Daisy was no fool. This was precisely the kind of man those reality dating shows wanted. Former football and baseball players. What if the producers came into town and got wind of the fact that a retired rodeo star lived in Stone Ridge, still famously single?

Maybe then even Beulah wouldn't be able to stop them from coming after Wade Cruz.

THE STONE RIDGE RIVERWALK was a pale imitation of the larger San Antonio Christmas Riverwalk to the north. But in a rare show of collaboration, every holiday season Stone Ridge and their sister town, Nothing, put on their own much-smaller version. This had been going on for several decades, since before Daisy was born. Because Nothing, Texas was known for...well, nothing. The Riverwalk had become their claim to fame. Even if it was held along the riverbanks that ran through Stone Ridge.

Stone Ridge had Titus Ridge, and Founder's Day, but Nothing had no clue who had founded them. Or why.

Booths were always set along the banks of the Guadalupe River which curled through Kerrville, Stone Ridge, and down to Nothing. A show of bright-colored blinking lights lit up the night sky, with holiday lights hung between the trees. Every few feet had fresh Christmas trees decorated by the children of both towns. The effect was scenic, but Daisy had never been able to capture or do it justice with a photograph.

"Are you ready, Miss Daisy?" Wade's slow smile was knowing and conspiratorial as he'd held out his good arm.

He'd dropped by to pick her up at the ranch, good manners on display to the point that Mima scowled only once. Dressed in a pair of jeans tight in all the right places, he wore a long-sleeved white button-down and a black Stetson.

She now strolled alongside Wade, holding his warm hand. They'd walked by a few booths, Daisy's feet already hurting.

Wade noticed. "Everything okay?"

"New boots." She should have broken them in first.

His gaze had lowered to check out her, yes, *sexy* feet. "Nice. But they look uncomfortable."

"Come right on over here, Daisy Mae," Lenny called out from his booth. "Take a load off."

Lenny was a retired postal worker who never met a job he didn't like. Since retiring, he'd been a part of Stone Ridge's volunteer fire department. He also played a clown at birthday parties and had recently purchased a broken-down golf cart which he used to drive folks around downtown. Now that they had a medical clinic in town, he'd park himself outside and wait for the pregnant ladies. Of course, he didn't charge for any of these services, as that was not the Stone Ridge way. He simply liked to keep busy.

Today, he'd fashioned a massage table into one like the kind found at malls in bigger cities. The chair was an office-style one on wheels that he'd probably borrowed from Eve's veterinarian office.

"Need a massage?" He wiggled his fingers.

"Um…"

"You seem to be having a little trouble walking," Lenny said, throwing a small towel over his shoulder. "I studied the five-point system for stress relief."

"Lenny," Wade said, voice thick with humor, "I think you're pushing decency boundaries here."

"Son, I firmly doubt that."

"You're not touching my feet," Daisy said, though they hurt like she'd stepped on a nail.

Earlier, Jolette Marie had been walking in her new boots as if on a cloud. Wonder how long it would take Daisy's feet to get numb enough to where she'd stop feeling them.

"Oh good! Lenny, please. My shoulders," came Winona's voice. She waddled to his booth.

Riggs followed her, pushing the double stroller with their twin boys.

"Right this way, Mrs. Henderson." Lenny made a big sweep of his arm.

"This pregnancy has been hell on my back," Winona said, and smiled at both Daisy and Wade. "Hiya, guys. I'm sorry, did I cut ahead of you?"

"No, we're just…trying to decide." Wade cocked his head and fought a smile.

Winona began to moan as Lenny massaged her shoulders. Oh, geez. Daisy flushed a little. Winona must be one of those screamers she'd read about and seen in the kind of movies she wasn't supposed to have watched.

"Should I be jealous?" Riggs asked, parking the stroller next to the booth.

"Oh, baby, it's just that your massages never last long enough," Winona said.

"Try wearing some clothes next time." Wade chuckled, and he and Riggs fist-bumped.

"How do you think we got in this mess?" Winona laughed, patting her belly. "I can't stay away from the man."

All this moaning and talk about making babies and not wearing any clothes was making Daisy a little hot. And with Wade standing right next to her, his warm body and large hand holding hers…she almost forgot she *had* feet.

"I think I'm going to take my girl to get some roasted chestnuts or some hot chocolate," Wade said. He smiled as Beulah and her husband, Lloyd, walked by.

A couple of women wandered over to them as they waited at the hot cocoa booth run by Pastor June. Daisy recognized them as some of the women who barrel raced in local and regional tournaments. She had a lot more in common with these women, who weren't afraid to break a nail or find a split end. They eyed Wade with something close to resembling hero worship.

"Hey, Wade," Belinda said. "I heard you were back."

"In the flesh," Wade said.

"I'm sorry about your arm," Kari Lynn said. "Tough break."

Wade stiffened noticeably. "Part of the gig."

"It shouldn't have happened to you." Kari Lynn reached to touch his arm. Not his bad one, which possibly meant she didn't even know which arm he'd injured.

Wade put an arm around Daisy. "Yeah, well. It did happen."

"Is it getting any better?" Belinda asked, ignoring the arm he'd draped on Daisy.

"June, is that cocoa ready yet?" Wade asked, clearing his throat.

He was the only one who got away with calling Pastor June by her first name, but she and Wade's mother had been the best of friends. Every Sunday, Wade and Rose used to have dinner with Pastor June and her family.

"Hold your horses." Pastor June handed over the cups and everyone chuckled.

"That's hilarious." Wade took his arm off Daisy's shoulder and accepted the cups.

"Do you think you'd ever give lessons?" Belinda asked. "Because I want to take my racing to the next level."

"Me too, and I'd love some tips."

Both women flanked him at which point something strange happened. Wade slid right into flirtatious mode, like a toggle had been switched.

"Why, ladies, I don't think I'd be the best teacher for pretty women like yourselves. I don't know if I could concentrate on the job at hand."

They giggled, and Daisy fumed. It was a sort of unwritten rule in Stone Ridge that women didn't fight over a man. There were too many of them. But of course, some men were different. Special. Men like her brothers and Riggs Henderson. Beau Stephens. *Wade Cruz*.

She stepped back and left Wade to his fan club because not two feet away from her was Beulah. She would be getting a piece of Daisy's mind in about three...two... one...

"Miss Beulah, I saw the billboard y'all put up and it's a

real eyesore." Daisy crossed her arms and tried to look mean.

"Well, hello to you, too, Daisy. And why should our billboard bother you?"

"It's hideous, and I'm a concerned, tax-paying citizen."

Beulah pursed her lips. "It was decided long ago, child. Maybe if you got your nose out of car engines and looked around, you'd notice something. This town is changing."

"Because you're tryin' to change it!"

"Sugar, maybe you haven't considered this, but it's unfair that there aren't enough women for our single men. And I'm attempting to correct that, with the help of Winona."

"What *I've* noticed is that this project is headed by two women who already have their husbands. So, why should y'all care?"

"I thought you and Wade were together. Why do *you* care?"

"Um, yeah. We are together. But I still care."

She tossed her hair back and looked behind but didn't see Wade where she'd left him. At least Beulah wouldn't be a witness to her fake boyfriend flirting with other women. He had a reputation for being a womanizer and a category-five flirt. Daisy had never believed that, but she'd just seen Exhibit A.

She hated that he was proving Mima's theory about him to be correct. Maybe he hadn't changed at all. Maybe Daisy was fooling herself that he ever could.

"Excuse me, Miss Beulah." This was said by an older gentleman Daisy didn't recognize "But the young lady has a point. Do we really need the billboard to be the size of a jumbo jet?"

"It is not the size of a jet!"

"I beg to differ," someone else said. "Yesterday I swear I saw it all the way from Nothing."

"Y'all always thought you were better than us, just because you're closer to Kerrville."

"Stupid idea, you ask me. Just watch Nothing rise from the ashes and clobber your *Mr. Cowboy* contest."

Daisy smiled. Apparently, she'd started a brand-new rivalry between Stone Ridge and Nothing. Maybe they could have the contest in Nothing.

It's not like they had anything else going on.

She left Beulah to fend for herself. As she strolled, she saw no sign of Wade. Regret pulsed through her. She was never going to be able to compete for his attentions the way other women did. This fake-dating thing would never work. In the back of her mind, yes, she'd hoped that maybe this would lead to a little reality of her own. He could teach her how to behave, how to give signals that she wanted a man, and she'd try it all out on him.

Sadie walked up to Daisy, pushing her stroller with Sammy in it, all drooly faced and gurgling.

"Hey, puddin'." Daisy bent and tweaked her nephew's nose.

"Can you come over for dinner tomorrow night?" Sadie asked, and she looked so worried that Daisy wondered if something could be seriously wrong.

"Sure. Why? Are you okay?"

"Why wouldn't I be?" Sadie laughed it off, rolling her shoulders. "We just miss you, that's all."

"We had Sunday dinner together just the other night."

Sadie held up a palm. "But not at *our* house."

Lincoln caught up to Sadie then, tugging her close. "You coming to dinner, Shortie?"

"Sure."

She saw these two all the time. They sounded so excited about dinner. Weird.

"Um, can I bring Wade?"

"*Wade?*" Lincoln narrowed his eyes. "You don't need to pretend with us."

Daisy shrugged. "He needs a home cooked meal, too."

"Of course he can come. We haven't had him over since he got back," Sadie said.

"But this is kind of a family thing," Lincoln said.

"Oh, it is?" Daisy was even more confused now.

"I think it's okay." Sadie threw him the look that turned her big brother into a piece of marshmallow.

He rolled his shoulders. "Sure. It's fine."

"Have y'all seen Wade?" Daisy turned in a slow circle.

"Look for the women," Lincoln said with a snort.

Eve and Jackson were standing under the long branches of a weeping willow not so discreetly making out. Daisy thought it useless to ask them if they'd seen *anyone*.

She walked a few more steps, looking for the single women as Lincoln suggested. No Wade anywhere. Kari Lynn and Belinda were now chatting with some other men. Had he just left her here? How would she explain that to Mima? Daisy was going to have a serious talk with him because she didn't want him to keep filling the stereotype that had been created for him. He was feeding right into it and he was far better than that.

Then she found him, half hidden in the darkness under a willow tree. He stood, his back against the tree trunk. "Hey."

"Wade? What are you doin' there?"

"C'mere." He beckoned her.

She hesitated, then walked slowly toward him, unsure of why this moment seemed markedly different. Maybe it was the darkness of the night or that he cut such a lonely figure. But she was a type of nervous she'd never been around Wade. Heat pulsed through her. Excitement thrummed. Something new and scary.

This is what you've been waiting for. Don't be afraid. Step out of your comfort zone.

She walked under the branches toward him.

"I thought I asked you to keep me away from people who want to talk about the rodeo. How dare you leave me alone with those piranhas?" He slid her a slow smile.

"Kari Lynn? You seemed to be doing just fine."

"I wasn't."

"Could have fooled me."

"I fool a lot of people. Just didn't think you'd ever be one of them."

That simple statement shocked her because he'd never been so open. But it was true that Wade had never been able to fool her. This was the reason she didn't listen to the rumors. She understood him. She knew the one thing he'd feared the most.

And she knew who had hurt him because she'd seen it happen.

"They just admire you for everything you've done. Your accomplishments."

Even if they'd been a little too flirtatious for Daisy's taste, she also saw that they meant to gain some knowledge from an expert.

"All they want to talk about is the rodeo. I'm done with all that."

"Maybe with tournaments, but they made a good point. You could teach others."

He shook his head. "Not doin' any of that. I'm a rancher now. That's what I need to be."

"No one *needs* to be a rancher."

"When all I have left is a broke-down ranch, yeah. I kind of need to be a rancher."

All I have left.

Daisy didn't like to hear those words coming out of "Wild Wade's" lips. Did he really feel like he had nothing else left in his life? His mother was gone, sure, and he'd been close to her. His father had been dead for a few years and Wade never talked about him anymore. But Wade had friends, admirers, and the entire town of Stone Ridge behind him.

Daisy opened her mouth to tell him the ranch was not all he had left, when he put a finger to her lips.

"First lesson, Peanut. When a man you're interested in beckons you, don't hesitate. Hesitating sends the wrong message."

"Right. You just…surprised me, standing over here in the dark."

"Surprises can be a fun part of a relationship."

She nodded. "And…what else should I do? If…if I'm interested."

"You can always lean close, like this."

"Okay." She stepped closer.

He tugged on a lock of her hair. "If you want a man to kiss you, and you're too shy to do it yourself? Stare at his mouth."

She studied his lips, which as it happened, she'd done many times before. Just not when he was *watching*. Now she felt as if time had stopped and they were the only two people in the world. A low breeze kicked up from the river, sending a shiver down her back. The scent of hot cocoa and rain lingered in the air all around them.

"Just like that," he said, and his voice was low, a soft growl. "It's an invitation."

She couldn't tear her eyes away, hypnotized. The anticipation was killing her. He was going to kiss her. Yes. Maybe? Oh, please. Desire rolled through her with a tiny slice of apprehension. This was the moment she'd been waiting for. For years, she'd wanted to compare. She'd wanted to see if the one time had been a fluke. Because she'd been eighteen, half in love with him for most of her life. Now, she'd kissed a few men since that first time with Wade. Not many, to be sure, but enough to know that nothing had ever met that threshold.

She'd told herself it was her imagination, her memory simply enhancing the moment to far more than it had been.

Wade tipped her chin to meet his eyes, and in a slow and luscious move, he lowered his lips to hers. The kiss was slow. Sweet. And delicious. He tasted like a mix of cocoa and mint. It made her think he'd actually prepared for this moment and that more than anything sent tiny tingles of awareness thrumming through her body. She reacted to him, to the heat of his long and lean body. She reached to thread her hands around his neck and draw him closer. His breathing shifted and he deepened the kiss.

Strong hands pulled her close, hip to hip, enough that she could feel his arousal.

They were both breathing heavy when she heard the distinctive voices of Sadie and Lincoln drawing closer, carrying along with the sounds of children laughing and holiday music playing.

"No, baby, he can't have honey," Sadie said. "Not until he's one."

"Sorry, Sammy." Lincoln chuckled. "You don't know what you're missin'."

Daisy broke the kiss, worried they'd be caught. She slid her hands down Wade's arms. "Should we stop now?"

"Only if you want to." Then he took her hand and led her a bit farther into the darkness.

She proved that she did not want to stop, by once again studying his lips. Damn, it was a good mouth. Sensual lips, the top slightly fuller than the bottom.

"You are a quick study, Peanut."

He kissed her again, this time decidedly *not* sweet. There was an urgency in that kiss, one that pushed her heartbeat into a wild race. She drank him in, unable to get enough.

"Okay, now we're stopping." Wade pulled back.

"Why?"

"I need to take a step back before I do something I regret."

"*Regret?* Like what?"

He met her gaze. "You don't want to know. I need to stop now before I lose control. Before I forget the code I live by."

Her breath hitched. Oh Lord. He was losing control. With *her.* "Wade…"

"I mean it, Peanut." He took a step back. "Not now."

"Did I do something wrong?"

He chuckled. "Not at all."

"Because you said we stop only if I want to."

"Yeah, but now I need to."

She stared at the bulge in his jeans, understanding dawning. Momentarily, she was robbed of the power of speech.

"And it would also help if you don't stare," he snorted.

"Oh gosh, I'm sorry!" She clapped a hand over her mouth.

"Don't be."

Daisy was trying to think of something to say when

over Wade's shoulder she spotted the man who'd been hanging around the auto shop for weeks.

Here at the Riverwalk. He seemed determined, his stride filled with purpose and hostility.

Coming straight for her.

Chapter 7

Wade hadn't done this kind of necking since he was a teenager, back in the days when kissing was the main event.

Sure, there was a certain adrenaline rush from kissing a woman he should *not* be kissing. A few feet away from people who might want to kill him for doing so. But that certainly wasn't the reason his heart raced like it did just before the chute opened. He'd just discovered, quite by accident, that he thoroughly enjoyed the way Peanut, uh, *Daisy* kissed.

Then suddenly Daisy looked over his shoulder, her mouth a small circle, her eyes wide as twin circles. The fear in her eyes had a sobering effect on Wade. It had the effect of ice-cold water being dumped over his head.

"It's…it's *him*."

Wade followed the direction of her gaze and saw a man coming toward them. Out of instinct, he stepped in front of Daisy, meeting the man halfway.

"I need Daisy Mae Carver." The man pointed past Wade to Daisy. "That's her right behind you."

"Who wants her?"

The man pulled a rolled-up manila envelope from inside his windbreaker. "I'm Jeff with Wilson Investigations out of San Antonio. You lose 'em, we find 'em."

"You're that man at the auto shop. I've seen you," Daisy said from behind Wade, then stepped beside him. "And I'm not afraid of you."

The man blinked. "You shouldn't be. Actually, I'm trying to help you."

"I'll take that, thanks." Wade held out his hand.

Jeff hesitated but Wade gave him the look he gave a steer he was about to hog-tie and the man handed it over.

Wade accepted the envelope. "How are you trying to help Daisy?"

"She could come into some money."

"Ha! That's a likely story," Daisy said.

"Quiet, Peanut. Let's hear the man out."

"Actually, the man who hired us has known where you are for quite some time. But it was only last week that my firm was dispatched to locate you, make sure we had the right person, and deliver this envelope to you."

"You couldn't use the old-fashioned post-office method?" Wade turned the envelope over in his hands and read the return address. It was from a law firm. He handed it to Daisy.

"I get paid to make sure this gets into *her* hands. Leaving no chance that some well-meaning person will intervene."

"I don't understand." Daisy opened the envelope.

"What the hell is going on here?" came Lincoln's voice as he joined them.

"This man claims he has something for Daisy and that she could come into some money." Wade gestured to the man.

"Oh God," Sadie said, but it wasn't a happy sound. More of a strangled one.

"What's happenin'?" Jackson joined them, and together he and Lincoln flanked Daisy and Wade.

"Nothing good," Lincoln muttered.

Only then did Wade realize that all the color had drained out of his best friend's face. For a former rodeo cowboy often called "lucky" for avoiding any serious injuries, Lincoln had never looked so scared to Wade.

"Is Rusty dead?" Lincoln asked.

"*Rusty?* Who's Rusty?" Daisy said.

Suddenly Jeff didn't look so certain of himself. "No, he's not dead, and I think I should just leave y'all alone. There's a lot to discuss."

"Not so fast." Lincoln grabbed the man's jacket and pulled him back. "If Rusty isn't dead, why are you here?"

"It's a tricky matter. A family matter."

"Since you just dropped a bomb on *my* family and left me to diffuse it, I suggest you start talking and explain." Lincoln's tone and body language suggested the man wasn't going anywhere.

Wade felt the snap and crackle in the air surround him and he welcomed it. He smelled fear.

But not his own. Lincoln's.

Jeff smoothed down his jacket, scowling. "My client is Rusty's brother. He won't contest Rusty's last will and testament. But if Daisy is going to be the beneficiary of Rusty's estate, then she needs to submit to a DNA test to prove she's his biological daughter."

DAISY FROZE. She must have heard wrong. For a moment, she didn't understand. When Wade reached for her hand and squeezed it, she pulled out of her daze. She wished she understood why this "Rusty" thought she was his daughter. She was *Hank's* daughter. Then a thick sense of dread pulsed through her as she tried to think of reasons this idea would even occur to the man. And only one of them came through as painful as a slap.

Her mother.

"The rumor about my mother…it's t-true?"

"I have no idea what you're talking about," Jeff said, throwing his palms up.

"Thank you for your help. We'll take it from here." Lincoln did everything but use his boot on the man's behind.

"Let's go home." Lincoln turned to Daisy. "We have a lot to talk about."

But Daisy was too busy trying to make sense out of legalese. "Wait. Rusty thinks I'm his daughter?"

"He's *wrong*," Lincoln said.

"What the hell," said Jackson. "Why didn't I know about this?"

"Let's go back to our cabin," Sadie echoed Lincoln. "We need some privacy to talk this through."

People were already staring. Riggs, with that worried look of his, wanting to help but reading the room.

"Well, I'm coming," Jackson said. "This is a load of bull hockey."

"Of course you're comin'," Lincoln said. "Everyone is."

"And so am I," Wade said, quirking his brow. His tone brooked no argument. "We're on a date."

As if he needed an excuse. Daisy wanted him there, too. He was practically family.

Lincoln rolled his eyes, then went palms up. "You too, of course."

Not long after, they were all gathered in front of the

fireplace in the great room of Lincoln and Sadie's cabin. The fire roared, easing the chill in the air, both of temperature and mood.

Sadie returned from putting Sammy down for the night and sat on the arm of Lincoln's chair, curling her arm around him. "Sammy's asleep."

Jackson and Eve were seated nearby on the leather couch, holding hands. Eve was biting her lower lip and Jackson had the same scowl on his face that Lincoln did.

And Wade? He was simply holding Daisy's hand and quietly listening.

Lincoln explained how last year Hank had been contacted by a man who claimed he could be Daisy's father. When even the possibility that Daisy might not be his daughter became too much for Hank to deal with, Lincoln took over.

"Remember the old bowlegged man that came into the shop over a year ago to talk engines with you?"

There had been an older man, but that was so long ago, and she talked to a lot of people at the auto shop. She did remember this older man being about her father's age, and seemingly incredibly gratified that she knew her engines. Because of his enthusiasm, it did seem strange that he'd never come back for the tune-up he claimed his truck needed. But she figured he'd found another shop and never thought about it again.

"I think so."

"That was Rusty Jones." Lincoln took off his hat and dragged a hand through his hair. "He talked me into driving him by your work, so he could just catch a glimpse of you. It was part of an agreement I made with him."

"Agreement…you made with him? *What* agreement?"

"Lincoln was trying to protect you," Sadie said.

"It's okay, baby." Lincoln rested his palm on Sadie's leg. "This is for me to explain."

Lincoln went on to tell Daisy that he'd never intended for Rusty to meet her but had simply agreed for him to watch her from a distance. The old man had violated their agreement and climbed out of the truck before Lincoln could stop him.

"I had a feeling then that wasn't the end of it," Lincoln said. "Unfortunately, our mother contacted him just after she left us and told him that you…you might be his daughter. A product of their one-night stand."

Daisy swallowed hard. Her mother, the buckle bunny. The memories of her were almost nonexistent. But there were some random photos here and there, pictures of Daddy with a beautiful blonde, two boys, and a baby in her arms. Daisy imagined they'd been kept simply to prove that someone had given birth to them. A biological connection.

But Maggie was not her family. Her family was in this room, plus Hank, and Mima, who'd been more of a mother to her than anyone else. Even Eve and Sadie had mothered her from time to time. Daisy had never lacked nurturing. And until now, she'd thought numerous times, at least I have my daddy.

"That might be true." Wade squeezed her hand. "But she could also be Hank's daughter."

"Right. There's a fifty-fifty chance anyway, and it's not like Daisy looks like anyone but…" Lincoln didn't finish his sentence.

"Our mother." And how she hated that.

Maggie had been a beauty queen in her hometown of San Antonio, but clearly heartless.

Until now, Daisy believed she hadn't had any intimate relationships with men because of big brothers who were a little too protective. But she'd been ignoring one blatant and obvious fact. The thought occurred that Daisy had distanced herself from Maggie in every way she could.

She couldn't do anything about her blond hair and green eyes. Instinctively, she hadn't wanted Hank to look at her and think of Maggie. To look at Daisy and be reminded of pain and loss. She'd wanted to be as different from Maggie as she could, and she'd succeeded.

Daisy had been a tomboy, having an affinity for and choosing to work in a male-dominated profession. She'd never been overly concerned about her appearance. Mostly, she dressed for practicality and comfort, not fashion. She'd believed it was due to being brought up on a ranch with two older brothers, cattle, and horses. But Eve and Sadie were brought up similarly and yet eased into that part of their lives that involved hairstyles, makeup, and falling in love with the boy next door. Not Daisy.

And at least one of her dates had referred to her as "uptight," a "cold fish," and the worst of them, a tease.

So, here she was, a twenty-six-year-old virgin, and daughter of a buckle bunny. *Please don't let me also be the daughter of a rodeo cowboy.* A living and breathing, walking cliché.

"Daddy knows about this?"

"He does," Lincoln said. "All except for this latest development. See, Rusty is sick, and he's kept in contact. It's true that he wants to leave everything to you. But he doesn't have any other children. For him, a DNA test isn't necessary. He's willing to take that chance and…I guess you won him over that day when you chatted mechanics. Rusty is also a mechanic. Somehow, he's fooled himself into believing that was in your nature. His influence."

"Do I have to do this DNA test?"

"No," Jackson said. "You don't have to do anything you don't want to do."

"That's right," Lincoln said. "Entirely up to you."

"It won't change anything." Sadie reached for Daisy's hand and squeezed.

"I don't see why I should take the test. I don't want or need his money. His brother should have it."

"This is more about whether you want to know," Eve said gently. "In case you want reassurance."

"No need. I already know I'm Hank's daughter."

"Of course you are," Sadie said.

"Damn straight," Lincoln added.

"No question," Jackson said.

Wade had stayed quiet all this time and Daisy wondered what he thought. She would ask him later, privately. If Wade had a differing opinion, she wouldn't want him to be forced to go against her brothers. But she could almost see the wheels spinning. He had opinions. No doubt about it. When she looked at him, he simply gave her a small smile.

She turned to Lincoln. "You *should* have told me this sooner."

Daisy could already see the worry had been eating at her brother. Sadie sucked in a breath, but otherwise the only sound in the room was the snapping of the wood as the fire consumed it.

"I know."

He hung his head, looking like a whipped dog. Her eldest brother, always taking care of everyone and sometimes neglecting himself. Until Sadie came along. It was the first time she'd ever seen him truly happy.

"Listen, Tiny," Daisy said, using an old pet name for her tall big brother. Always broad shouldered enough to take on the family's worries and his own. "You protected me, as you always do. Thank you."

EVEN IF HE didn't have to drive Daisy home, Wade insisted on walking with her down the hill to the family home where she and Mima now lived alone. After dusk, the evening temps had lowered by at least ten degrees. Nearby, she heard a cow lowing and thought of Daddy. She'd have to see him soon and reassure him that she didn't care what this Rusty man had to say. Hank was her father and always would be.

She and Wade walked side by side in the quiet, his easy gait next to her painful hitch.

"You shouldn't have worn those boots." Wade broke the silence.

Yes, that's just what she expected him to contribute after tonight's bombshell. He'd sat right next to her, heard that she might not be a Carver, and he had nothing more to say than her boots were inappropriate footwear.

"Um, yeah. Well, they're pretty."

"I didn't think you cared about that sort of thing."

"Maybe I do."

"This is ridiculous." He stopped on a dime in front of her. "Get on my back."

"What are you *talkin'* about?"

"Your feet are killin' you and that's enough pride on your part. I can't take any more of this."

"I'll be damned if I climb on your back like I can't walk. That's just humiliating."

"More so than having blisters on your feet for days?"

"Look, I'm not some *buckle bunny* that's got to be weak so that her strong cowboy can take care of her."

Oh *man*. Where had that come from? She hadn't meant to sound so defensive.

Wade stared her down. "No, you're a pain in the ass is what you are."

"You take that back!"

"I will if you climb on my back. We have several more yards to go and your grandmother will kill me twice if you walk inside the house limping." He cleared his throat. "I'm afraid she's going to think…other things."

"What other…? Oh. Oh," Daisy said as it slowly dawned on her.

"Yeah, if I'd had sex with you behind that tree, or in my truck, believe me, you would be limping."

Her face must have flushed and darkened to the red color of a stop sign. It was surely hot enough to fry a flapjack on it.

"Fine, then."

He lowered his body enough that she could climb on him, then straightened, tucking his arms under her knees. And it actually wasn't all bad, this piggyback ride. Kind of fun. She remembered how once, just after Eve and Jackson had started dating as teenagers, she saw them fooling around in a similar fashion. Back then she'd thought both of them a couple of idiots but now it made a whole lot more sense. It was simply an excuse to touch.

And she appreciated having a reason to tighten her arms around Wade's shoulders and plaster her body against his. Lowering her head to an inch from the crook of his neck, she inhaled his fresh clean scent. It would be like this if they made love, she imagined. Flesh against flesh, their bodies sliding against each other…

Wade's bad arm seemed to be trembling which yanked her right out of her happy place. This couldn't be good. "Is carrying me hurting your bad arm?"

"No, but thanks for asking."

She was quite familiar with the quiet stoicism of a stubborn cowboy, so she shifted her weight as best she could and repositioned herself. Unfortunately, that made her slide down some, and Wade used his back to pull her up.

"Stay still," he ordered.

Weren't they a pair? Her with her dumb feet and him with an injured arm. He still hadn't mentioned anything about it tonight.

They walked a few more steps before she couldn't take it anymore. "Aren't you going to tell me what you think?"

"About *what*?"

"You know what! The stupid DNA test."

"Yeah? What of it?"

Oh, so he was going to pull this slowpoke cowboy thing on her. "Would *you* do it?"

He was quiet for several seconds. "What I would do doesn't matter. You have to do what's right for you."

She jumped off his back when they were a short distance from the house. "And what if I don't know what's right for me?"

He shoved his hands in his jacket and gazed at her from under hooded lids. "I take it this isn't about the money."

"Of course not." She crossed her arms and shook her head. "I'm afraid."

"You're not afraid of anything except maybe getting kissed. And I think we took care of that tonight." He tweaked her chin. "But me? I'm a risk-taker, so if you're asking what I'd do, then I'd want to do it."

"You'd take the test?"

"Not for the money, of course. The old man can keep it. But I'd want to prove it to myself. Prove that I'm right."

"You'd do something scary because you think you'll get the answer you want?"

"Yeah, guess I'd be betting on myself. That's the only kind of bets I've ever made. But you're talkin' to someone who thrives on a good adrenaline rush. Guess I'd be nervous for a while until I found out. You might call that scared. I would just call it the anticipation of a sweet moment of victory. Every time I got on a bull I didn't know if he'd throw me into next week or if somehow, through skill and good luck, I'd hang on. Maybe I'd be killed, or maybe I'd live."

"You did that every time?"

"That's half the fun of it for me." He snorted. "Was."

In the past few minutes, Daisy's thoughts had run the gamut. On the one hand, she needed to know. She craved reassurance. Safety. That had always been important to her. The other side of her was too afraid to know because if she didn't get the right answer, it could change everything. It would be devastating.

"I don't think I'll ever be able to stop thinking about this if I don't take the damn test."

"Don't let that happen. You could let this go. Forget it."

"But I'm not like you. I don't like the anticipation. Not knowing. Maybe I want it to be over with. I want to prove what I already know."

"You do what you want, and no one will judge you for it." He took her hand and led her to the door. "Good night, fake girlfriend. I had a good time."

"Sure, me too. Until that man showed up, I was enjoying everything about the night."

"Yeah. Me too." He gave her a wicked smile.

Hand on the front door, she turned once more to see him walking back to Lincoln's cabin, where he'd parked his truck.

"Wade," she called out and he turned. A thin sliver of moonlight glinted off his dark Stetson, making it appear almost gray.

He slid her an easy smile and cocked his head. "Yeah?"

"I…I want you to go with me. To take the test."

"You're going to do it."

She nodded.

"If you need me, I'm there."

She cracked the door open, then watched him hike slowly back the way they came before she shut it.

Mima was sitting at the kitchen table, a skein of yarn in a basket, her needles whipping away. "Well, *someone* is finally home."

When she glanced up, she must have read Daisy's mind, because her eyes narrowed, and she threw her knitting down. "What's wrong?"

Everything Daisy had learned tonight and every doubt she'd ever had that the rumors about her mother were true rose like bile in her throat. The ugliness of it all threatened to cut off her air supply.

Her mother wasn't sure *who* her father was. What kind of a woman…

"It's…it's…I'm…not…"

"Oh, baby girl!" Mima threw her arms open wide.

And Daisy went into the arms of the woman who'd raised her and cried her heart out like she hadn't done since she was a little girl.

Chapter 8

Dear Albert,

Well, the worst has happened. I thought I'd dealt with enough pain for two lifetimes or more. Watching my daughter-in-law walk out on her three children was enough to shatter this poor, old heart. My poor lamb Lincoln, the oldest, feeling responsible for everyone. Jackson, his mother's pet, completely lost and wondering what he'd done to chase her away. But the worst of them was my baby girl, Daisy.

The precious child was only three and cried every single night for her mother. Those wails and cries of pain were enough to kill most old ladies. Fortunately, I'm stronger than Texas dirt. Well, you remember all this. You were there. Trying to help, usually going out in the barn or out in the fields to hide. I don't completely blame you for that. Hank did the same and they were his children, after all. But no one knows what to do with grieving children.

I didn't much like Maggie to begin with, but after she left her children, I hated someone for the first time in my life. Hank was of no use, as he had his own demons to handle after Maggie left him.

But now this.

And I thought I'd already had the lowest opinion of Maggie I could possibly have!

Wherever you are, I imagine you already know that Daisy might not be Hank's daughter. I don't believe it, naturally. Of course, she's Hank's daughter! Any other thought is just too terrible to think. Daisy has always been closest to her daddy. He was big enough not to punish her for looking just like her mama. And he would never abandon any of his children, our Hank, but least of all his Daisy.

After all that mess that Maggie left in her wake, Daisy became her daddy's shadow. There was no question in my mind that she wanted to make sure he wouldn't also leave her. And to think all this time I've been worried about "that Wade" taking her away from us. Now I'm worried that circumstance will. If Daisy takes the DNA test, and she isn't Hank's daughter, will she want to do that "I gotta go find myself" thing all the young'uns do? That could take her out of Texas, let alone Stone Ridge!

Worse, will she think there's no hope she won't turn out just like her mother?

She's a Carver through and through. It isn't just that we raised her to be a kind young lady, completely different from her heartless mother. If nothing else, we know for a daggum fact that she's Maggie's daughter. But look how different she is from her! Biology doesn't matter, anyway, only family does. The family that raised you, and I think Daisy must realize this.

"If she doesn't realize it, then you're goin' to have to show her." Out of the blue came Albert's familiar deep drawl.

Lillian jumped. Albert sat on their bed, leaning back on a pillow, legs crossed at the ankles. The old man's ghost hadn't visited her in over a year.

"Albert! This is a fine how-dee-do! Where have you been, old man?"

"Busy. There are a lot of interestin' things to do over there."

Lillian didn't bother asking. He wasn't real. This was just her imagination, after all.

"Sounds like there's another mess goin' on down here. Makes me almost glad I'm dead."

"What do you think I should do?"

"Stay out of it."

"How can I stay out of it when there's a chance my Daisy could fall apart? I can see it in her eyes, she's tempted to take that DNA test!"

"Let her."

Let her. Well, it was a thought. After all, fear itself shouldn't be a reason to hold back from learning the truth. From *confirming* the truth.

"Anything else, old man? You seem to be dripping with advice today."

"You're goin' to need to talk to her about Maggie. We never talked about her. Daisy deserves to know the truth about her mother. It's not all black and white and I can see that now."

Talk to Daisy about Maggie.

Why didn't she think of that? Oh, wait. She just did. "Right. She should know that Maggie wasn't *always* terrible."

"This is what I'm sayin'."

Maggie did have some good qualities, after all, or Hank wouldn't have married her. Yes, Lillian realized, he'd still been reeling over losing Brenda. But for a time, he and Maggie had been happy. It was important that if on the long odds Daisy wasn't Hank's biological daughter, she'd find some connection to the goodness in Maggie, however small.

"What if we're all wrong and Daisy isn't Hank's daughter?"

"We will deal with it when we cross that bridge."

"Yes, thank you, Albert. I've decided. I will neither

encourage nor be against this testing thing. I'll be neutral. Like Switzerland."

"Woman, if you manage that, I'll come back from the dead and eat my daggum hat."

DAISY ROLLED out of bed the next morning, her thoughts a jumble. She'd stayed up too late last night, reading and re-reading the request for a DNA paternity test from Rusty's brother. He wanted it to be done at a reputable center he'd chosen and wanted to be present when it was done. Apparently, the man was seriously worried. Or maybe he simply thought Daisy to be a gold-digger type after some poor old man's fortune.

These DNA tests could be done with kits anyone could order online, though they weren't as accurate. And anyway, how could she get Rusty's DNA? She didn't want to see the man again after he'd talked to her just like she was anyone else he'd meet on the street. *He* could have told her the truth then and saved her poor father and brother from dealing with this secret.

Of course, she could get Daddy's DNA to compare it to hers, but then *he'd* find out.

She didn't want him to know that she was even considering this. It might hurt his feelings to think she had any doubts. And he had enough on his plate with calving season coming up. He was finally happy again, in a relationship with Brenda, whom Daisy had recently learned was his high school sweetheart. She'd never asked many questions about Maggie, and certainly no one ever talked about her. Daisy didn't realize until recently that her mother hadn't been Daddy's first love even if they'd married young.

That was Brenda Iglesias, Eve's mother. Had Maggie

somehow stolen Hank away from Brenda? Another thought too terrible to process. Because no matter who her father was, Daisy couldn't get away from the fact that Maggie was her *mother*. Daisy was even named after her. She made sure never to use her middle name and hated when she'd been called on as "Daisy Mae" in school until she corrected everyone.

"Just *Daisy*," she'd say. "Daisy Carver."

Daisy picked up the landline phone in her bedroom and dialed the number of the establishment listed in the papers.

"I'd like to, um, make an appointment. Please."

"Mornings or afternoon better?"

"Either. The soonest you have."

The receptionist asked a few more questions, and Daisy made the appointment. Just a few days away. Soon, she'd have her answer. And then came that feeling Wade loved. Anticipation. It made Daisy sick with fear. She'd have made the appointment for tomorrow if one had been available. She wanted to stop feeling like she was standing on the edge of a precipice, bracing herself for a fall.

Last night had been a catharsis. Crying until she didn't think there were any tears left took a lot out of her and she'd slept solid all night long. It was also clear that Mima didn't want Daisy to take the test. So, she'd be one more person she wouldn't tell. Eve and Sadie were the worst snitches, and she wouldn't tell them, either. Her brothers were out of the question.

That pretty much left Wade and she found she didn't mind that at all.

Walking into the kitchen, Daisy found Mima already awake. She'd made her usual king-sized breakfast of grits, waffles, bacon, eggs, and hash browns.

"Good mornin', sugar. Feeling better today?"

Nope, I'm feeling like a truck ran over my heart. The prairie dogs are currently feasting on the leftovers.

"So much better! Thanks for listenin' to me bawl last night. I'm sorry about that." Daisy helped herself to a cup of coffee.

"That's a lot to get off your mind."

"Well, I'm not going to worry about it anymore," Daisy lied. "I don't need a test to prove I'm Daisy Carver."

Mima's eyes widened in surprise. "You mean it?"

"You thought you were going to have to worry about me moping around the house for days until we got the results?"

"I think that's for the best. No good can come out of it, and that man will get his brother's inheritance. As it should be. He's family."

"Should I go see Daddy today?"

"He and Brenda are going to get a Christmas tree, I believe."

"I just worry about him."

"You know Hank. Tough as a rock. He has no doubts you're his so I'm sure he's relaxing."

Daisy doubted that. *Lincoln* hadn't been relaxing. "I should talk to him about all this."

"Eventually you will." Mima patted Daisy's hand.

She and Mima ate breakfast in silence. Normally, Daisy didn't mind. But this morning the quiet closed in on her. Not long ago, this house was filled with Jackson and Eve living here, too. Now, both of her brothers had homes they'd built on their land. A few years ago, Daddy had moved up the hill into the smaller house closer to the cattle operations.

It was just Mima and Daisy in this big house now, except for Sunday dinners. Daisy had some freedom with her bedroom on the other side of the house, and she used a separate entryway so that she didn't wake Mima on the rare nights when Daisy came home late. But she sometimes thought it would be nice to rent a cabin on Lupine Lake for a little more privacy.

"What will you do once I move out of this house?"

"Why? You planning on goin' somewhere?"

"No, but maybe…someday. I should get married, I guess." Daisy shrugged.

She did want to get married, naturally. The right man hadn't come along just yet, or maybe that had been her keeping men away. Remaining pure as the driven snow for all the wrong reasons.

"When that time comes, I guess I'll just roam around this big house by myself. Y'all will visit, I'm sure. It's not like you'll be far, anyway. And I guess Albert will show up more then."

"Huh?" Her grandfather had been dead for years.

Mima waved her hand dismissively. "I like writing letters to him. Then I imagine that he's sitting right there with me, listening."

"That's sweet…I think."

"The man was ornery as all get-out, and not my first choice in a husband. But funny how love works out. Your grandpa was the great love of my life."

Daisy nearly spit out her grits. What was it about this family and all the secrets?

"You never told me that before. Why was Grandpa not your *first* choice?"

"Well, of course, he was. But before we dated, there was someone brighter and shinier. I had my head turned. Luckily, Albert waited for me." Mima shoved some more bacon on Daisy's plate. "All this mess has got me to thinkin'. We should really talk some about your mother. Don't you think?"

As much as Daisy did not want to discuss her mother, she had become front and center in their lives. "Was *she* the reason that Daddy and Brenda broke up? They were high school sweethearts, but my mother was the one who got knocked up. Did she take him away from Brenda?"

"Oh, no. Nothing like that. Much as I wish, can't blame that one on your mother. See, Hank wanted to marry Brenda, but her family didn't approve of him."

"*Excuse* me?" Daisy dropped her fork. "Didn't approve of my daddy?"

"We don't talk about the painful past much around here." Mima chuckled. "Hank is a good man now, but he wasn't quite settled as a teenager. Had a little bit of a wild hair about him."

She couldn't see that in her father. Ever since she could remember, he'd seemed sad and defeated. Lonely. Until Brenda.

"Shows you how wrong you can be about someone," Daisy said, hoping Mima caught a hint about Wade.

He wasn't the man Mima thought he was, either. He'd been hiding from those women and Daisy figured his flirting might have been simply force of habit. Almost like putting on a show. Rodeo cowboys were used to that sort of thing and he hadn't gotten it out of his system yet. She'd love to dig deep and find out what made Wade Cruz tick, but she had her own problems now.

"Her family wanted her to marry Ricardo, and Brenda always did as she was told." Mima put her cup down and stared off into the distance. "A good girl and wonderful daughter and mother. And she and Ricardo were happy for a while. Just as your father and mother were."

"I can't believe how Daddy could have ever loved *that woman.*"

"That woman is your mother," Mima said slowly. "And

with all her faults, and there were many, she gave all three of you life. She didn't have to do that."

"Sorry if I'm not feeling grateful for that today but I'm just…not."

"I don't blame you. We should really talk about her more, but maybe another time."

"What's wrong with right now?"

"Did you forget? Today, we're going to the church to help Pastor June set up. It's the tree lighting ceremony tonight. She got a huge tree from Oregon, came in on a long-bed truck, several feet sticking out, I heard. Plenty of complaints as they drove through Nothing. Anyway, the men have to be there early to help get the tree up. And I signed you up to help Sadie entertain the children. Arts and crafts."

It was the last thing Daisy felt like doing today, but she supposed that she and Wade should be at the event together. Otherwise, Beulah would be sniffing around, asking questions. A few days ago, Beau Stephens had reportedly refused to even consider being Mr. Cowboy. He, too, said he was serious about a woman, but now Daisy wondered if he was lying, as well.

Now Beulah was after Sean Henderson, and Daisy was more than certain Sean would say no, too. Eventually, this would all circle back to Wade, the perfect choice for Mr. Cowboy. Surely Daisy and Beulah were not the only ones who could see that.

AN HOUR LATER, Daisy watched with fascination as the fresh pine tree was hauled up using heavy farm equipment. It took ten big men to do it, among them her brothers, as well as Riggs and Wade. Wade wore his black hat and jean jacket and when he caught her eye, he smiled and winked.

"Did you know Wade's arm still hurts?" Daisy asked Beulah. "He's certainly not going to say no to helping."

"He seems fine to me. Why don't you go give him a massage later, like a good girlfriend would?" Beulah gave her the side-eye.

"That's exactly what I plan to do." Daisy coughed and cleared her throat.

"Winona said the producers have asked for a cowboy who was a former sports star, or a rodeo star. Do you know anyone like that?"

"I do, but he's taken." Daisy crossed her arms. "Would they want a multimillionaire instead? What about one of Jolette Marie's brothers?"

"Hmm. Well, they're all mean as the devil but one of them is fairly handsome. I'll suggest it."

Once the tree was straightened and bolted to the church, the men took a break. Daisy noticed that Eve, Sadie, and Winona had joined their men, so she ran over to be with Wade.

"Hi, Wade." She rubbed his arm, then went on tiptoes for a quick kiss on the lips.

"Hey." Under the brim of his hat, his caramel-brown eyes were soft and warm. "Are you okay?"

"Yes, sure," she said, then loudly, "I'll have to give you a massage later, rub out all the kinks."

Wade sent her a slow smile. "Uh-huh."

"We have to make this look good," Daisy hissed. "The producers want a former rodeo star and obviously Lincoln is taken." She put her arm around his waist, encouraging him to do the same, which he did.

"Sure, baby, of course I'll cook dinner for you tonight. Why, your wish is my command," Wade said loudly enough that Beulah turned.

"Don't be silly. I'll cook dinner for you! I just love takin' care of my man."

"Somebody have our volunteer fire department ready," Lincoln joked.

Everyone cackled with laughter over that one. Burn a few meals and suddenly she was toxic in the kitchen.

"Let's get back to work now," Riggs ordered, always the one to keep everyone in line. "This tree isn't going to light itself."

As with every year since they'd started the tree lighting tradition in Stone Ridge, the inside of the church had been decorated as a winter wonderland. Lights were hung from the beams, green garland and fake snow accenting the large room. Booths were meant to entertain children. Arts and crafts were usually ornament making. Lenny had a booth where he created shapes out of balloons. This year, a lot of reindeers with lopsided ears. Sadie had a booth where she read holiday stories to the children.

Eve and Annabeth brought in cats and dogs that were being considered for adoption. But they always made the parents wait until after Christmas to finalize adoptions. Of course, Mima was always at the knitting booth with Delores and most of the ladies of SORROW. They were selling scarves and caps, and the proceeds would be put in a fund for further town projects.

This year, the new medical clinic had a booth, too. Trixie, the midwife, was giving out lollipops to the children. Dr. Grant was walking around with a stethoscope around his neck, clearly not knowing what else to do with himself.

It was always a marathon day of an event, culminating in the tree lighting. People came and went during the day, always returning in the evening for the real action.

"Okay, Jimmy Ray," Daisy said now. "No *more* glitter."

"Just a little bit more," he said, shaking the jar.

He was on Daisy's last nerve. By the third hour, she'd wanted to go home and collapse in her bed. She hoped to last long enough to see the lights go up. The men had been outside working on that for hours.

"Hey, sweetheart. Is this boy bothering you?" came Wade's smooth drawl, a hint of humor in it.

Daisy's heart surged to see him, and when he looked at her as if he was seeing her for the first time, her knees got weak.

Jimmy Ray scrunched up his nose. "*Sweetheart?* Who's your sweetheart?"

"Do you know what a sweetheart is?" Wade tipped his hat.

"That's what my daddy calls my mommy."

"I call my girlfriend sweetheart," Wade said.

"Is Miss Daisy your girlfriend?" This was from Ellie, one of the few grade-school girls.

"Duh," Jimmy Ray said, shaking out enough glitter to cover a small town.

"Miss Sadie used to be Mr. Carver's girlfriend but now she's his wife," Ellie said. "And I helped."

"It was my idea," Jimmy Ray said.

"How did you help, darlin'?" Wade ignored Jimmy Ray and tousled Ellie's hair, earning a smile.

"I helped write the sign."

"There was a sign?"

"Lincoln had all the children write 'Will you marry me' on a big sign and they were all there when he asked her," Daisy explained.

It was the most romantic thing she'd ever heard of, and coming from her lame-about-romance brother, it clinched the deal. Lincoln was in love and he didn't care who knew it.

"Wow." Wade winked at Ellie. "You might be able to call yourself a matchmaker now."

Ellie straightened. "*Really?*"

"Me too!" said Jimmy Ray. "I'm a matchmaker."

Daisy took the jar of glitter from his hand. "Matchmakers don't like glitter."

A choir of voices sounded like angels, and Daisy turned to see Winona near the entrance leading a group of Christmas carolers. Among them were all the ladies of SORROW, including Beulah, right behind Winona. "O Little Town of Bethlehem" brought quiet to the noisy room.

This song, especially, stopped time for Daisy. The ladies, dressed in gowns reminiscent of the Old West, sashayed through the church. Winona occasionally reached out and ruffled a child's hair or tweaked a nose.

It wasn't until they'd circled the room once that Daisy realized Wade was holding her hand. Here was the only *person* she'd ever known who could stop time for her. Her heart hammered away as his warm, big hand held hers.

Something so simple. Not the first time for her, a handsome guy holding her hand.

But somehow, it did feel very much like the first time, and like a private, sacred moment.

Chapter 9

When the lights were plugged in, the town's Christmas tree lit up the entire town square.

Wade had almost forgotten about all the small-town holiday celebrations. For the past few years, he hadn't been home for much of the holiday, usually getting back in time to celebrate the day with his mother and be off again shortly after, chasing the next tournament win. She understood. Her mounting medical bills were overwhelming, and they were all on Wade.

But his mother used to love this kind of thing. She was always right in the thick of it, helping the ladies of SORROW, volunteering her services wherever needed. Even now, he could almost feel her presence. Everywhere.

He and Daisy were sitting on the tailgate of his truck, watching the lights blink in their random patterns. That tree had been hell on wheels to yank up and he was happy not to have had to do it on his own. His arm had lit up like a coal of fire and he promised himself to take it easy for the next few days. He'd stopped restricting himself from the pain pills and taken them as needed. If he didn't do his physical therapy routine on a regular basis, he wouldn't be able to manage all the chores on his ranch. Or give up the ghost by noon.

Earlier today he'd spent the day looking through the old books his father kept on the ranch operations back in the days when it had been, if not profitable, at least sustainable. The possibilities existed, and if he made a few changes from the way his father did business, he might actually do better. Eventually. Of course, he was a long way from there. He had plans to attend the cattle auction with Riggs, which would require the bulk of his savings.

But sitting here next to Daisy had seriously taken his mind off his problems.

"What are you thinking, Peanut? You're so quiet."

She swung her sweet long legs. "I made the appointment."

He nodded, worrying he'd encouraged her to do this when he'd simply shared what he would have done. For someone who didn't like danger or uncertainty, this had to be killing her.

"Name the time and place."

"Rusty's brother will be there, too. The place had all the instructions and knew to contact him. I didn't have to do anything but call."

"He thought of everything."

"I wonder if he hates me."

The thought unnerved Wade. "He has no reason to *hate* you."

"Well, maybe he thinks I want the money and that's why I'm taking the dumb test. He doesn't know I hope to prove that I *can't* take Rusty's money."

"You don't need to care what he thinks. He's got his agenda. You have yours."

She was silent for several more minutes, and the quiet

calm of the evening descended on them. All of the families with young children had left long ago. Only a few stragglers remained.

"Wade, do you remember my mother?"

Wade had a clear recollection of Maggie Carver. In particular, he remembered the days after she'd left Stone Ridge. Rumors ran rampant. Maggie had been kidnapped by her family, who'd never approved of her moving to the Podunk town. Maggie had emptied their checking account and taken off for the Bahamas. Or Maggie had left town with a rodeo cowboy. He figured that in the end no one must have believed she'd been kidnapped because the law was never involved. Which always made Wade think that she must have left a note or said something…to *someone.*

His mother, along with the ladies of SORROW and others, descended on the Carver household with casseroles and offers to babysit little Daisy. Often, Wade was in tow simply to hang out with his best friend, who didn't talk about his missing mother. This was more than okay with Wade. But for a while, Jackson went everywhere with them as a little tagalong because Lincoln wouldn't leave him behind.

"I remember her as a nice lady, believe it or not." He honestly didn't know whether that would help or hurt but he couldn't lie to Daisy.

Daisy's head jerked back. "How so?"

"She was, well, very pretty, of course." He crossed his arms and cleared his throat, feeling odd describing Lincoln's mother this way. Truth be told, he'd had a tiny crush on the younger Mrs. Carver, just as he'd had on his first-grade teacher. "Nice, too. She made cookies for us kids and to my knowledge was never mean to anyone."

"I don't remember her. At all."

"You were little, so I'm not surprised. But you were her

shadow, her mini-me. Always clinging to her leg and never letting her get too far out of your sight."

Daisy snorted. "Imagine that. And still she made a clean getaway *somehow*."

"For what it's worth, I think she loved you all." Wade reached for Daisy's hand, knowing this might be tough to hear but he would want to know this, were it the other way around. "I think everything is a whole lot more complicated than we can know."

"I just wish I knew *why* she left."

"She didn't leave a note?"

"Don't think so." Daisy took in a deep breath. "But I never asked. Since I can't remember her anymore, it's almost like I can't hurt for what I don't remember losing. The pain is all in theory. In the past. And now…it's less pain than anger. I'm the daughter of a woman who abandoned her family. Her *children*."

Wade understood far too well. He remembered the exact day and time he'd discovered how fond his father was of the blackjack tables. And how he'd used Wade to fund his obsession. In some ways, Wade was a gambler, too, but he'd sworn never to fall down the same rabbit hole that his father had. Every now and then, he feared that he was far too much his father's son. The addiction to gambling, he'd heard, gave the gambler a rush of adrenaline.

Wade wanted to believe that he only bet on himself, but sometimes the similarities between father and son were unnerving.

"I'm not excusing what she did, because there's no reason that makes it okay. But I'm guessing that with everything she left behind, she must have thought she had to leave for whatever reason."

"I'm sure she justified it somehow. I never asked

enough questions about her, but now, with all this happening…it's brought her up again."

"That's only natural."

"There's so much I didn't know. When Daddy started dating Brenda, that's when I found out that *she* was his first love. Not my mother."

This was news to Wade. "Seriously?"

"But I asked Mima, and my mother didn't break them up. They imploded on their own. So, there is that."

"She can't have been all bad," Wade continued. "Nobody is."

"No, obviously. She must have loved us at some point."

"There you are," came Lillian Carver's voice. After a quick appraisal of Wade, she nodded. "Well, hello there, *Wade*."

"Mrs. Carver." He hopped off the tailgate and held his hand out for Daisy. "You look very lovely tonight."

"Why, you charmer."

Funny, it didn't sound as if she believed it. Wade wasn't too surprised. He hadn't been the older Mrs. Carver's favorite person for some time now. She'd always been kind and courteous enough, but she blamed Wade for being the influence on Lincoln's rodeo career. He supposed that was easier than believing that Lincoln had a mind of his own when it came to such things. Mrs. Carver was a loyal sort and he appreciated that more than most.

Besides, he was certain that without Lillian Carver, Daisy would have been truly lost. The matriarch had basically raised two generations of Carvers and had the respect of every man of Stone Ridge. Including him.

"Are you ready to go now, sugar?" Mrs. Carver huffed. "Beulah has left, so y'all don't have to carry on this way."

"We were *talking*," Daisy said.

"Can I drive you ladies home? It would be my pleasure." Never let it be said that his manners weren't impeccable.

Are you watching me from heaven, Ma? How am I doing?

"No, I drove," Daisy said. "Thank you, though."

"Yes, thank you, young man. Your mother would be proud," Lillian said.

It sounded a bit more sincere, at least. "Then I'll say good night."

He tipped his hat, then watched as they got in the truck and Daisy drove off. It was only then that he walked to his own truck alone. He managed to narrowly avoid Kari Lynn, who seemed to be angling toward him but couldn't walk fast enough to catch him.

He did *not* want to teach but it was tough to say no to a lady. The last thing he wanted was to watch others compete in the sport he'd loved his entire life. He couldn't go back, and he just wasn't ready to stand by on the sidelines. For now, he needed to be as far away from the rodeo as he could get. That part of his life was over.

The quiet surrounded him when he arrived at the ranch. He shut off the truck and sat in the cab alone, visualizing his home exactly as it used to be. Pens filled with heads of cattle, a stable full of horses. The red barn, not falling down on itself like now, but filled with equipment and a small tractor. A porch that didn't have peeling paint, his mother sitting on the steps. His father at the head of it all, rounding up the cattle, tagging the young ones. Him, racing his first horse, Trigger, across the plains, not a care in the world.

Now, he was alone. Not even any siblings, since, to hear his father tell it, he'd nearly killed his mother on his way into the world. He hadn't missed siblings much growing up because he'd had brothers everywhere in the form of lifelong friends. Lincoln, Jackson, Riggs, and his crew. Daisy, too, even if it had become harder to think of her as only a friend.

But now, well, now he found himself wishing he wasn't the last Cruz standing. A sister would have stayed behind and cared for their mother while he was off trying to make money the only way he'd ever known how. Instead, he'd left his mother to deal with her illness. He'd barely been home in time to say goodbye.

"I know you have to go," she'd say, palming his chin. "Just please, promise me you won't die before I do. Be careful, my love."

"Mom, you're not going to die."

"Yes, I am. It's just a matter of when."

She'd been right, of course. And though that could be said of anyone, they'd both known she'd already had a timer set. After her funeral, Wade wasted no time leaving again. He didn't want all the sympathy and casseroles. He couldn't stand the pitiful looks from everyone in town.

"Poor lamb. He lost his father (good riddance, if you ask me) and now his precious mother. He's all alone in the world."

But out on the rodeo circuit, he was still "Wild Wade" and no one had the slightest amount of pity for him. Just plenty of jealousy from his competition, and attention from the women. They'd line up outside his hotel room if they could find him. He was the cowboy du jour everywhere he went.

In Stone Ridge, he was just one of many eligible bachelors. Good thing he didn't care about settling down.

Figure he'd missed that train.

Sitting in the office with a cold beer, Wade twisted the cap off and took a pull. He opened his laptop and examined once more what he had left from his winnings. By his account, there was just enough to go into debt with several head of cattle and equipment. He'd have to watch, feed, and protect that cattle, hoping one day they'd feed him.

Take your bets, everyone. Odds are two to one. Will "Wild Wade" save the family ranch or die of boredom in the pursuit?

Hell, he wanted in on some of that action.

At this point, it was anyone's guess.

THREE MORNINGS LATER, the cattle he'd purchased at auction arrived and with them, a lot of tedious but back-breaking work. Wade was up at dawn every morning just like the good old days. He finished his coffee and lumbered outside in his work boots. Satan, who was getting old, seemed to observe the goings-on with mild interest and an occasional disgusted snort. Dante, always the friendly sort, was happy for the company.

And even though Wade hadn't asked for any help, later that morning Riggs and his brother Sean arrived and insisted Wade put them to work.

"I know a couple of ranch hands that work on the cheap," Sean said. "If you ever want to hire anyone just temporarily."

"Let me guess. Rodeo cowboys lookin' for the extra work?"

Not long ago, he'd been one of them, putting in the long hours for Hank Carver. Flirting with Daisy when she'd show up, pretending to help, but actually checking out all the cowboys' backsides. Including his own, he was always gratified to discover.

"It's going to be tough work," Riggs said. "But you can get this cattle ranch working again."

"Hell, for you, this should be easy," Sean said.

"When you're ready to breed, you can have some of my bull semen. Free of charge, of course," Riggs said.

"I've got a lot to do before I'm at that point," Wade said. "But thanks, buddy."

For the rest of the morning, they hauled hay and herded cattle. When a shiny clean truck drove up the lane, Riggs walked to meet his wife.

Winona leaned out the window. "Did you forget? It's time for the doctor's appointment."

Riggs cursed. "Is it noon already?"

Noon. Oh hell.

"This ultrasound should confirm that we're having a girl." Winona smiled, tossing her hair, batting her eyelashes. "And then I'll be the belle of the ball."

Riggs hopped in the truck on the passenger side. "See y'all later. Wade, come over anytime."

Wade turned to Sean. "I forgot I've got an appointment, too."

Sean chuckled. "Leave me to it, then. I'll clean up."

"I hate to have you do that, but I am very late."

Daisy was going to kill him. And he wanted to be there for her. Rushing inside, he took a spit shower, changed into better clothes, and covered his hair with his black Stetson. Breaking speed limits, he got to the Double C Ranch as Daisy was getting in her truck.

"I gave up on you," she said.

"Sorry, Peanut. I got caught up with all the new head of cattle that came in." He patted the door of his truck. "Hop in."

She climbed in and buckled up. "I guess I can't blame you for that. I sure know what it's like. Happens all the time around here."

"No doubt. It's new to me, all this cattle business." He took off down the dirt lane leading to the main road, kicking up dust.

"New to you? You grew *up* on a cattle ranch."

"You forget. I was introduced to rodeo early. My daddy had me in the corral practicing staying upright on a bull more often than not. Not that I complained. Anyway, it's been a while since our ranch was a working one, so it's like starting all over."

"I can help," Daisy said.

"No need, I've got it covered."

She grew silent for the rest of the drive to Kerrville and the clinic where they would meet Rusty's brother. Mark Jones, if Wade remembered correctly. He followed the directions Daisy gave him, and a while later they pulled into the parking lot of a plain-looking building. "Valley Health Clinic" the sign read.

"Okay, let's get this show on the road." Usually, Daisy beat him to the punch, always out the passenger door before he could open it for her.

Not this time. Now, she sat, still buckled up, staring off into space.

He opened the passenger side door. "Peanut? What's up?"

"I'm nervous. Maybe this is a mistake."

"You don't have to do this. We can go right now, turn this truck around and head back to town. Stop in at the Shady Grind for a cold beer."

Snapping out of it, she turned to him with narrowed eyes. "Are you trying to talk me out of this?"

"I'm trying to make you realize that *you're* the one calling the shots here. No one can make you do anything you don't want to do." He met her eyes, tipping his hat to get right in her face. "You hear me?"

"You're so right." She unbuckled. "And I'm doing this because *I* want to and for no other reason."

He held out his hand. "That's my girl."

Daisy hopped down and walked—no, strutted—her

way to the clinic. It put a smile on his face just to watch those swinging hips.

DAISY WALKED INSIDE THE CLINIC, Wade holding the door open for her. Inside the otherwise plain office, there was a feeble attempt at holiday cheer with a tabletop tree on the counter and a clear glass jar filled with candy canes. Christmas music piped through speakers, sounding like the stuff they played in elevators.

An older gentleman was the only other one seated in the lobby and he stood.

"You must be Daisy Carver." Mark Jones held out his hand and offered it to Daisy and then Wade. "Thank you for coming. I hope you understand the situation."

"Sure. Of course I do," Daisy said, feeling far less confident than she thought she sounded. "Yes. That's fine."

"I turned over Rusty's DNA sample. Don't worry, it was done in the hospital by professionals."

"He's in the h-hospital?"

"Yes, Daisy." He lowered his gaze. "Unfortunately, he's dying."

"I'm sorry to hear that." That made sense, of course. He was taking care of things ahead of time like any organized and responsible person would do.

Rusty's brother also seemed very organized. He even had a small hanky in the pocket of his suit jacket.

She couldn't possibly be related to these people.

"Why is he dying?" It sounded like a dumb question even to her own ears. Old people died.

"Congestive heart failure."

Daisy filed that away in case she wound up being Rusty's daughter. She'd have to watch out for signs of early heart disease because it was hereditary. Right? On the other hand, her grandfather Carver dropped dead of a heart attack, too, so either way, she could be screwed. As was fifty percent of the nation, if she recalled the statistics. It was either heart disease or cancer that killed a person. Great. She was rambling. Her thoughts were like wild rabbits, hopping away in the fields, trying not to get slaughtered.

"They're waiting for you." His arm made a sweeping motion to the clerk behind the desk.

"Right this way, Miss Carver." The clerk stood and led the way.

Daisy turned back and found Wade right behind her. She felt her shoulders unkink in relief because she hadn't wanted to ask but it was good to have him follow her. Nice to have someone with her who didn't have a horse in the race, so to speak. Wade didn't care whether she was Hank's daughter or Rusty's. In fact, he didn't even seem to mind that she was Maggie's daughter. He'd said Maggie was nice. *Nice.*

"This is a lot quicker than you can imagine," the lab clerk said as she grabbed a box from the medical cabinet. "Just have a seat. It will be over in no time."

But this was the easy part. The tough part would be the wait. Daisy's heart raced and her palms were damp. In a few minutes, she'd have the start of discovering her heritage. Of understanding who she was. Or simply confirming who she'd always been.

"I just need to swab the inside of your mouth to get some cells and then we're done."

"S-sure." Daisy gripped the edge of the molded plastic chair with both hands until Wade pulled one of them off.

Holding her hand, he squatted in front of her. "You remember what I said?"

"I'm…okay." She nodded, tipped her chin, and opened her mouth for the swab.

It was over faster than Daisy would have imagined. One second to possibly change the course for the rest of her life.

Outside, Mr. Jones waited and stood when she walked out.

"You'll both be mailed the results," the lab clerk said. "It should be no more than a week, maybe sooner."

"I don't want mine sent home," Daisy said. "Maybe I'll just pick it up."

"Send it to my house," Wade said and then gave the clerk his address.

"This place is very reputable," Mr. Jones said. "Are there any questions I can answer for you?"

"About?" Daisy asked.

"Rusty, my brother, the man who might be your father. If you want to see him, we can arrange—"

"No." She could not deal with anything else today. Or possibly this year. Also, she did not want to see this man, who'd had an affair with a married woman. With a woman who had small children at home. "I'm sorry but we have plans."

"Okay, some other time maybe. Depending on how this works out, I imagine." He handed Daisy a business card. "Contact me at any time."

The card was that of an autobody shop. Daisy turned it over in her hands. "You're a mechanic?"

He nodded and tipped back on his heels. "Rusty and I both. He worked for me after he retired from the rodeo. That was his first love, but he's a natural-born mechanic. It's in his blood. Had an affinity for it all of his life. I hear you do as well."

A buzzing sound went through Daisy's ears and the room rocked and swayed.

It doesn't mean I'm his daughter. So what? We're both good auto mechanics. And so are a lot of other people in the world. Coincidence, that was all. Chance.

"I'm sorry to put you through this, Daisy, but Rusty doesn't always think things through. If it's true, and you're his daughter, you certainly deserve the gift he wants to leave you."

Still, her stomach pitched because she did *not* want to be Rusty's daughter. Although it made no sense, standing here, and talking even briefly about him, realizing they had something in common…it stretched the possibility in her mind. It took the breath from her body.

She tucked the card in her jeans and ran out of the waiting room without saying goodbye. Outside in the cool December air, she clutched her chest and tried to breathe. But she was breathing out, and not taking breaths in.

Why, why, why did this have to happen now?

This man had been out of her life for decades and he just showed up a year ago? What on earth made him decide that he suddenly wanted to be a father? Face it, he'd been running from the *possibility* of being her father for decades. If by chance Daisy was his, he'd been fine with another man raising his own child.

Which meant that if she was Rusty's daughter, she'd been abandoned twice.

Twice.

"Daisy, breathe. Just breathe."

She heard Wade's voice, sounding calm and clear and warm. And look at that, he'd called her Daisy. Not Peanut or some other childish nickname. He pulled her into his arms, her back to his front, his arms wrapped around her, hands around the fists she held clutched against her chest.

"I'm s-sorry. Sorry." She forced herself to slow her breaths.

"Don't be sorry, sweetheart." He lowered his head to her shoulder, nuzzling her neck. "You don't need to be sorry."

He smelled delicious. Like leather and fresh-mown grass. She leaned against him, using him as a post to hold her up.

This had all been a mistake. She'd lied to her family. A horrible sense of fear took root in her, raw and pulsating. Fear pulled at her shaky soul. Chest tight, she heard blood rushing loudly through her veins.

She turned in Wade's arms, facing him, burying her face in his warm neck as he bent his head.

And they stood there for several minutes, Wade's arm moving up and down her spine in slow and soothing strokes.

Chapter 10

"Hope you don't mind a stop first. I left Sean to clean up, since I was running late." Wade drove down the highway back to Stone Ridge. "I want to check in before I take you home."

And as it so happened, Daisy didn't want to go home right now. Mima, who had a sixth sense about all of her grandchildren, would know something was wrong. Daisy would just walk right in the door and Mima would figure it out. Then, she'd worry right along with Daisy until they received the results. And she did not want her grandmother worrying about the possibly stupid decision Daisy had just made.

"That's fine." Daisy rolled the window down and propped her head on her stretched out arm. "I need to get my act together before I go home. I'm sorry I fell apart on you like that."

"Hey, any excuse to hold you tight." He winked.

Incorrigible flirt. At least now he was also flirting with *her.*

The thought cheered her a little. She wasn't off-limits to him anymore. And there was that hot and amazing kiss behind the tree. No, she hadn't forgotten. That was the night *everything* changed.

"I guess I haven't been much fun lately."

"Fun is overrated."

"Liar."

He chuckled. "Okay, so I've always liked my fun. But I'm all about the ranching now."

"Which is not always a whole lot of fun."

"Tell me it's rewarding, at least."

"Sure. From what I've seen, it can be. Lincoln sure loves it. Eve, too. Jackson not nearly as much but he does his part."

"And you?" He turned briefly to her, a smile tugging at his lips. "I noticed you seemed to have dodged a bullet there."

"Doesn't mean I don't know my way around a ranch, mister." She crossed her arms and turned toward him, pressing her back against the passenger door. "Mima taught me."

"And what did she teach you?"

"Mostly how to make sandwiches and beef burritos, load them up, and deliver them to the cowboys." She smiled, knowing that Mima knew a hell of a lot more than that about running a ranch.

"Food always has its place on a ranch. Especially burritos."

"Tell me about it. But *some* people think burritos are boring. During the summers, when Sadie is home all day, she scours recipes from *The Pioneer Woman* and that's what she feeds Lincoln. Every single day. It's a wonder he doesn't weigh three hundred pounds."

"She works it off him, I'm sure." Passing the Henderson ranch on the right, he then turned down the long lane leading to his ranch. "Every night."

Daisy wished she understood what all the fuss was about. Sex sounded wonderful. But according to Eve and Sadie, who seemed to believe it their civic duty to keep Daisy pure, it was only good with the *right* person. But of course, they happened to know this because they'd been with the *wrong* man at least once. How else would a woman know? Divining rods?

The Cruz ranch sure looked different from the last time she'd been here, asking Wade to give her some experience. She slunk in her seat, not quite believing she'd even suggested that. At this point she didn't want to bring it up again even if being around Wade tended to inspire all manner of randy thoughts. Maybe it was safer to stay wholesome, as far from her mother as she could get. And last she checked, she couldn't have a baby without sex, so she'd be safe from reproducing, too. At least until she could be certain she had some good genes in there. The Carver DNA.

"Impressive," she muttered, getting out of the car when Wade pulled to the side of the barn.

The pens were now filled with cattle and the place looked like a real honest-to-goodness cattle ranch again. Not like a ghost of its former self.

"I'll be right with you, Daisy." Wade hopped out of the driver's side and headed to the cattle pen.

"Take your time."

Daisy wandered over to the red barn looking for an old truck or farm equipment she could help fix. Every holiday season she was out of sorts and usually wandered around the Double C looking for something mechanical to fix. But recently the ranch had enjoyed a nice infusion of cash from Jackson's songwriting royalties. Every piece of old farm equipment had been upgraded which was nice for the cowboys. Not so great for her.

She pulled a blue tarp off, finding an old classic Model T under it. This beauty was probably worth some money. Sliding her hand down the hood of the classic design, she wondered if this was Wade's, or one of his father's vintage cars. She'd never seen one of his father's cars, but heard he collected them for a time but sold them off. Apparently, he'd kept one.

There wasn't anything else of interest until in a dark corner she saw an antique plastic reindeer. Using a broom for protection against evil spiders, she advanced, wielding it like a sword. She brushed the reindeer off and pulled it into the light shining through several slats in the barn's roof.

A memory tugged of a time long ago when she'd run into this very barn at a family picnic. Wade and Lincoln were teenagers at the time, Daisy probably around ten. She'd climbed up the ladder, looking for her brother, and found a couple rolling around in the hay. But the guy wasn't Lincoln. It was Wade and his girlfriend, making out. Daisy had a clear and mostly unobstructed view of Judy Marie's right boob. It was big and pink and…wet.

Daisy gasped and her hand flew over her mouth.

"Hey, you little rat!" Judy Marie squealed and covered herself. "Get on out of here. And you better not tell on me."

"I'm sorry!" Daisy cried.

"She's just a kid. What the hell is wrong with you? Go on, Squirt." Wade winked. "Go find Lincoln."

She'd nearly fallen off the ladder trying to fly back down. A few months later, Judy Marie broke Wade's heart by cheating on him. Maybe with someone who didn't have a best friend's little sister interrupting their make-out sessions in the hayloft. In the intervening years, she hadn't seen Wade suffer much in the girlfriend department even if there had never been anyone serious. Daisy would have known if there had been.

After brushing off the reindeer, Daisy found a treasure trove of other Christmas lawn ornaments. There was a plastic Santa with an extension cord, a plastic snowman, and under another tarp, a full-sized sleigh. It was like a gift. She'd found a winter project. Something to keep her mind off those DNA results for the next few days. This could be scrubbed, polished, and oiled.

One after the other, she brushed the holiday loot with the broom and dragged them outside the barn into the bright sunlight.

"What's all this?" came Wade's voice.

"Look!" She made a wide sweep of her hand over the treasures.

"I am. It's a heap of junk. I've been meaning to go through that barn."

"It's not *junk*!" She went hands on hips. "I can fix this. Look. This one probably used to light up. And this sleigh! It should probably go in a holiday parade."

"That's just…sad." He slowly shook his head.

"The kids will love it."

"I'm afraid the *kids* will think Santa has fallen on hard times."

"If nothing else, we can set these outside and give your ranch some nice Christmas charm."

"Christmas charm, huh?" He tipped his hat.

"What? Aren't you going to get a Christmas tree?"

"Well, I hadn't thought of that. I'm a little busy here." He made a sweeping motion.

She turned to see that he'd separated the cattle into two different pens while she'd been busy in his barn. She'd obviously lost track of time.

"That's fine. I'll get the tree for you. And decorate, too."

"Somethin' tells me you're looking to stay busy for a while. Maybe a few days or so?"

"Sure, yeah. You got me. I'm out of work until after Christmas and there's nothing left to fix at the Double C."

"Such a problem." He grinned. "As you can see, I have no such issue here at Casa La Cruz."

"I told you I can help."

"Yeah, everyone keeps offering. I forgot what that was like."

"This is home. And we help our neighbor."

"In this case, we especially help our neighbor if we're lookin' to avoid thinking other, more complicated thoughts."

"Okay, smart aleck. Where's your toolbox?"

THE SENSE of relief that pulsed through Wade was almost palpable. He appreciated the smile and enthusiasm from Daisy, even if misplaced. This was all junk that his parents had never gotten around to throwing out. But hey, if it gave Daisy a project that made her smile, he was on board. Because seeing the way she'd fallen apart after taking that test was more than this cowboy could take.

"Is that your father's old Ford Model T?" Daisy pointed to the tarp she'd removed. "It's a vintage 1926 coupe hardtop. *Very* cool."

The girl knew her cars. He was not at all surprised. "It's my inheritance from the old man."

The car, and this ranch that he'd nearly driven into the ground with his gambling debts. And the *car*, a gift, came with conditions. He walked over to it, pulled the tarp back on to cover it.

Daisy followed him. "It's a classic. And worth something."

"I'm sure it is. And it would be great if my father hadn't insisted that I keep it and never sell it."

The old man's last joke on Wade. What good would a Model T do on a cattle ranch? He needed a new tractor, that's what he needed.

"Well, sometimes things are worth something more than money to the people who give them."

"That's a nice sentiment, though not to someone who needs the money." He tapped the hood of the car. "What am I going to do with this, even *after* I get it running?"

"It doesn't run?"

He could see the wheels spinning in her head. She'd lit up, a fire in her eyes, an anticipation.

"No, it doesn't. Let me guess. You want to *fix* this."

"Oh, I would love to! Thank you, Wade." She practically jumped into his arms. "Thank you."

He tightened his arms around her and lowered them to her waist. He was enjoying this hug a little too much.

It's probably not wise to spend this much time around Daisy. You might be tempted.

They were in a fake romantic relationship, and though the idea had become more enticing to him than he could have ever imagined, it still wasn't *smart.* He put himself in Lincoln's place, an easy thing to do with a friend who was far more like a brother. Would he want *his* little sister dating someone like him? Someone who didn't know the meaning of commitment? She was too good for him. He had nothing to offer her but his friendship and she already had that. Always would. Best not to mess with that and wind up ruining both of them.

He cleared his throat and gently moved her away from

him. "Sure, Peanut. You go ahead and fix away to your heart's delight. Now, let me find you that toolbox."

A few hours later, the sun setting, Wade was ready for a shower and dinner. He found Daisy working on the lawn ornaments. The reindeer were flanking Santa who, though he looked worn and faded, now glowed. Same with the snowman.

"It was just a short circuit." Daisy had found a power cord and extension cord and plugged them into the nearest outside power outlet. "Working fine again."

"Good job." He removed his hat and shoved a hand through his sweat-dampened hair. "Well, I'm hitting the shower. Then I'll drop you home. I'm probably headed to the Shady Grind for a cold beer and some dinner."

"Okay, but I should probably go with you." She rubbed her hands together and brushed off her jeans.

"You don't have to," he said carefully.

"How will it look if you're off at the Shady Grind without your girlfriend?"

"Maybe like we have separate lives and aren't joined at the hip?"

"I guess I can understand why you might think that. But believe me, I know what real couples do."

"I'm not sure that Lincoln and Sadie are the best example." Wade was happy that his best friend had fallen in love, but Jiminy Cricket, the two of them spent *way* too much time together.

"What about Jackson and Eve?"

"Hmm. Also, probably not the best example."

"And Riggs and Winona?"

"Okay!" He went palms up in an "I give up" gesture. "Are you hungry?"

She shrugged. "I could eat."

"Then it's a date."

Though he didn't feel like company tonight, Wade showered, shaved, and dressed to be a proper companion. But the stupid Model T, like his sore and throbbing arm, refused to relent. Daisy had taken off the tarp and exposed a raw nerve ending.

The car was his father's final slap in the face. Something he didn't need, want, or would be able to use, but given to him anyway. It would have been nice had the old man left them anything else, like a life insurance policy for his mother. But no, the old man hadn't prepared for anything. An antique he couldn't sell was Wade's inheritance.

I should sell it, old man. What would you know, or care, wherever you are now?

But Wade would know, and he'd made a promise.

He was his mother's son, after all. Honorable to a fault. She'd taught him that anything worth doing was worth doing well, worth doing honorably, and that went far beyond the rodeo.

"Ready?"

Wade turned to find that Daisy had also spruced up. Somehow. She'd ditched the high ponytail from earlier and her long hair was loose around her shoulders. She never wore much makeup and didn't need any.

"You look…good," he said, like a teenage boy with zero game.

"So do you. I wish I could have taken a shower, too."

"Next time you want to join me, just say the word." He winked. "Or just walk right in."

"Really?"

Right. Well, *that* happened. He'd slipped that little gem out.

"I'm practicing being your boyfriend, Peanut."

"Oh. Well, I never took a shower with a man before."

Frankly, it was amazing that Daisy had remained untouched this long. Either she was right, and there were a bunch of cowards in Stone Ridge, or she'd been the one to keep them all away. But why? Had she really been waiting for someone special? If so, he wanted that for her. He didn't want her to give up what she'd protected so long to just anyone.

"You don't know what you're missing." With that, he tried his best to lead her out the door and into the safety of his truck.

There will be no more talk of showers with the little sister of your best friend. Little sister. Little. Sister.

Hand low on her back, he gently pushed her forward. This worked, until she stopped inches from the safety of the great outdoors. This time, her backside bumped into him, and he swallowed a groan.

"Oh, sorry." She turned to face him, and he'd swear that a tiny electrical shock passed between them. "I was just going to tell you that I'll intercept any talk of the rodeo if you'd like."

"Thanks."

Normally, he would have thought to ask her to come along and do exactly that. But after that "lesson" under the tree at the Riverwalk, he'd remembered that Daisy was not someone he could fool around with. Even if she'd asked for lessons, it was up to him to restrain himself.

The tension between them was thick with something he couldn't even name. An emotion, cloudy, thick and heavy.

"Let's go," he ordered, ignoring the raw pulse of desire that spiked.

The question was how long he *could* ignore this.

• • •

INSIDE THE SHADY GRIND, Wade found stools at the bar, where they served the full menu. The Dallas Cowboys were on the flat screen, Lenny yelling and shaking his fist.

"Learn how to pass!"

A grand total of about five women in the joint. All were surrounded by about three men or more apiece. There was Jolette Marie in the mix, her admirers holding court. No Lincoln, Jackson, or Riggs in sight. Even Sean and Levi appeared to be MIA. Behind the bar was Lucy, one of the regular waiters/bartenders.

"Man, I missed this place." Wade chuckled, glancing up at the mistletoe hanging from the ceiling every few feet.

"Hey, Daisy, Wade," Lucy said, giving the bar a wipe. "Welcome back, champ."

"Thanks, darlin'." Wade winked and got an elbow in his gut from Daisy.

Her gaze slid to the mistletoe, then him, then back to the mistletoe. Ah. Yeah, he caught the hint. Later, he would explain that elbows were not the best way to get a lover's attention.

"C'mere." Hand on the nape of her neck, he tugged her close.

The kiss, a performance, should have been beautiful, chaste, tender. But...there seemed to be no way to kiss Daisy that way. Not anymore. She clung to him, threading her fingers in his hair, drawing him even closer. Drinking him in.

Suddenly her tongue was in his mouth, she was nearly in his lap, and they were engaging in *precisely* the kind of PDA he'd declared off-limits. When and where and how had she learned to kiss like this? She kissed like her whole body was involved and not just her lips. Her whole heart.

"Oh my Lord, you two, get a room," Lucy said with disgust, setting down two cold beers.

Wade broke the kiss, lowering his hand from her neck to settle on her shoulders. He felt the unnerving sensation that he was way out of his league.

"How was that?" she said.

"Um, yeah. Good."

"I'm a quick study."

"Well, well, well. What have we here?" came Lenny's voice.

Wade cleared his throat and grabbed his beer. "What's up, Lenny?"

"I should ask you what's up." Lenny pulled up a stool and sat next to him. "Now that the game is all but a painful memory, we should chat."

"We're about to order some dinner," Daisy protested.

"I'll deal with you later, young lady," Lenny said, shaking a finger. "What are you, twelve?"

"*Excuse* me," Lucy said, polishing a glass. "We don't serve minors."

"She's older than you realize, Lenny." Wade clapped the older man's shoulder.

Older than I realized.

Yep. Not a young kid anymore. Not *Peanut.*

"I'm beginning to realize that. The little whipper-snapper that always wanted me to make a balloon in the shape of a car."

"That was almost twenty *years* ago," Daisy deadpanned.

"Seems like yesterday." Lenny shook his head. "Where does the time go."

Where does the time go, indeed.

"I'll have a Shady Burger with special sauce," Wade said. "Shoestring fries, and whatever my date's havin."

Lenny cleared his throat as Daisy placed her order.

"My, my, my," Lenny said. "Date, is it?"

"Surely you've heard about us," Wade said. "You have your fingers on the pulse of this town."

"Must have missed somethin'. What a riot. Your mother was right, after all." Lenny slapped his knee. "Son of a biscuit eater."

Wade froze. He'd forgotten that people in this town knew far too much about his private family lore. Including too much knowledge about his well-meaning, at times a little too romantic, eccentric, and don't forget melodramatic, sainted mother.

Daisy took a pull of her beer. "What was Mrs. Cruz right about?"

"How about a game of pool while we wait?" Wade interrupted, climbing off the stool and offering his hand to her. "I'm sure I could beat you with my hands tied behind my back, but I'll use them anyway. I don't want to insult you."

Daisy blinked. He did know how to push her buttons. Maybe she shouldn't be fake dating someone who knew her as well as he did.

"Just try it, buddy."

They waited their turn at the table. Next to them, Jolette Marie talked about barrel racing and horse training. The men hung on her every word. Wade had to admit, she knew her stuff.

"What did Lenny mean?" Daisy asked.

"Who knows? He's upset about the game and probably not thinking straight."

No way would he tell Daisy that his own mother swore that he would someday marry Daisy Mae Carver. She'd seen it in a dream, and no amount of rational talk seemed to dissuade her from this crazy belief.

Not when he'd told her that he only thought of Daisy as a younger sister.

Not when he reminded her that he was seven years older than his best friend's little sister.

She insisted, until her dying day. He wondered if she was watching him now as he struggled between his attraction to Daisy and his duty to behave himself around Lincoln's little sister.

"Hey, champ," Jolette Marie said, walking up to them.

How he wished people would stop calling him that. "Hey, there, Jo."

"Hi, Jo," Daisy said. "You were right about those boots, by the way."

"Oh, good. And hey, I had no idea that you two"—she gestured between them—"were a thing."

"Yes, we are," Daisy spoke up. "We're dating now. It's new."

"Remember when we dated for about two minutes, Wade?" Jolette Marie said.

He'd done his best to wipe away that memory. Two minutes was about right.

"I think all those concussions have done their job. Those high school memories are long gone."

Jolette Marie took no offense, laughing and tossing her hair. "Concussions are good for something, at least. But you stood me up."

"Did not."

"You sure did, but you didn't break my heart."

"I'm sure that's tough to do."

"Hey, Jo!" one of the men she'd been talking to, called out. "Come on back, sweetheart. You owe me a kiss."

"No, she owes me a kiss," the other one said.

The third guy shoved another, and Wade's senses went on high alert. Bar fights over women were not common, but also not unheard of. And he'd expect Jolette Marie to be at the center of most of them.

"Now, no fighting, boys. Excuse me, guys." She smiled and went back to her adoring public.

He'd always found her exhausting to be around. They'd gone to school together and she'd been engaged to one of Wade's friends. The poor man had been one of three she'd left at the altar. In a town known for runaway brides, Jolette Marie held the record.

"Finally," Wade said, both at her leaving and the table being free.

He moved forward, and Daisy wrapped her hand around his bicep. "You'll never forget me."

"That's a given, Peanut."

"Or anything about me."

"I'm sure I won't. If I ever dare to forget a thing, I'm sure you'll elbow me in the gut again." He racked them up, then picked his pool cue, and used the chalk.

Daisy did the same. "Point taken. Elbows in the gut are not attractive."

"They're not a problem, but don't exactly inspire a man."

"You were flirting with Lucy."

"Not flirting. Just being nice."

"Maybe you should take 'keep a girlfriend' lessons from me. That looked like flirting, which is *why* I elbowed you in the gut."

"Keep my attention next time."

"And how am I supposed to do that, Wade?"

"You figure it out." He chuckled. "I can't teach you everything."

Lining up, he winked, and neatly made his shot. Then the next, and the next. "I spent plenty of time in a pool hall blowing off steam."

Daisy stewed, crossed her arms, tapped her foot. "I'm pretty good, too, if you'll give me a shot."

He chuckled and prepared to make his next shot when she gasped. "Oh, no!"

"That won't work on me. I have the focus of a—"

When Wade looked up, he lost all concentration and probably several brain cells.

Daisy's top was undone low enough for him to see the red satin of her push-up bra. He swallowed hard.

"I broke a button."

She'd busted more than one, and he didn't appreciate the wolfish smiles on some of the men as they took notice. He sent them all a glare.

"You want to cover up?" he growled.

Shot ruined, concentration pulverized, he shrugged his jacket off and handed it to her.

"Thanks." She put it on, picked up the pool cue, then proceeded to mop the floor with him.

Score:

Peanut: one.

Wild Wade: zero. Zilch. Nada.

Lord help him, he just might be a little bit in love.

Chapter 11

Dear Albert,

Well, I'm in a pickle again. Things have calmed down some in recent days. It seems Daisy will not take the DNA test and simply leave the matter to rest. That's probably for the best as I'm certain she's Hank's daughter. She certainly doesn't need the money the old man wants to leave her, and it should all be left to his brother. I sincerely hope that's the end of the mess.

But lately, I haven't seen hide nor hair of Daisy. She was with me at the tree lighting, and I later found her and Wade outside "talking." Albert, as I live and breathe, it was the kind of "talking" young lovers do. Sitting close. Sultry looks and glances. Knowing secret smiles. This is a lot more than a pretend romance! Now, as you know, I have someone quite different in mind for our Daisy. Not that Wade. He's too wild and I refuse to allow Rose Cruz to be right. Her, and all her whimsy and far-fetched ideas, which had no place on a cattle ranch.

Albert appeared, arms crossed, chuckling, shaking his head. "You just hate that she was right about them two."

Lillian dropped her pen and turned to him. "She wasn't *right*. Mistakes happen when you walk around with stars in your eyes. You bump into things and hurt yourself. That was Rose for you."

Rose also didn't schedule regular doctor visits and by the time she found out she had cancer it was already too late. Lillian was upset with Rose for a few reasons, but the biggest was her having the nerve to die on them. It wasn't fair. She was a good person, albeit a little too eccentric. Too given to far-fetched notions and dreams. But far too young to die, and here was Lillian, pushing eighty. She sometimes wished the good Lord had taken her in the place of Rose.

"She swore that she saw it in a dream. In the future, Wade and Daisy were in love and married. Don't get me wrong, I didn't believe her, either. Bunch of cockamamie stuff. But I've learned things over here, and well, sometimes things are not always as they seem."

"I know better than most that's true. You're not even really here right now. You're just my imagination. And Rose's imagination worked overtime. She always wanted the best for Wade, as any mother would, and of course she wanted Daisy for him."

"Of course." Albert nodded. "She's a Carver. Can't do any better than that."

"And our girl deserves the best. She's been through enough pain in her short life. What I want for her is a loyal and devoted man who will never leave her. Who will choose her every time over *anyone* and *anything* else."

Albert squinted. "And why can't that be Wade, exactly?"

"You want to play dumb with me? Okay, I'll tell you plain as day. Jorge Cruz ruined that boy. And Rose, well, God rest her soul..." She crossed herself. "She wasn't strong enough to stop it happenin'."

"Uh-huh. So, a rodeo champ who made a name for

himself, and paid for his mother's medical bills when his father left her practically penniless? *That's* not a loyal and devoted man?"

"Oh, I see what's happening here. You're trying to confuse me." Lillian waved her hands dismissively.

"I thought I wasn't even really here," Albert chuckled.

"*Of course*, Wade was loyal and devoted to Rose. How could he not be? He's a man of Stone Ridge, after all, born and bred. But when it comes to a lifelong partner, I don't see it in him. He's far too good-looking for his own good. Terrible flirt. He loves women! All the *women* are after him, even in a town without many of them! No. Daisy deserves better."

"You want her to marry an ugly man that doesn't like women? Am I hearing you right?" Albert canted his head.

Lillian's eyes nearly rolled hard enough to fall out of their sockets. "I didn't *say* that."

"As usual, my advice is to stay out of it. But you'll do whatever you want anyway. You've done well so far with the DNA thing, so why not let this go? Daisy will make her own decisions, and there's nothin' you can do about it."

"You're wrong there, old man. There's something I *can* still do, and it might even help *Wade* in the long run."

And with that, Lillian launched Plan A: get Wade hired as the bachelor for the *Mr. Cowboy* dating show.

Fake should never stand in the way of real.

She picked up the landline and dialed. "Beulah? We need to talk."

DAISY HEARD Mima on the phone the next morning, so she gulped down a cup of coffee, skipped breakfast, and decided it was time to see Hank.

She hadn't ridden for a few weeks, and now she

walked to the stables to get her paint horse, Oreo. If Daisy loved anything more than cars, it was horses. She might not be in love with ranch life and all the back-breaking chores, but she loved a horse as much as the next girl. Always had.

She led Oreo out of the stable, brushed her, cleaned her shoes, and saddled her. Oreo was a calm and docile horse and Daisy had loved her from the moment Daddy brought her home.

"Bought you a horse, Pumpkin!" Daddy had announced. "This one is yours."

"Oh, Daddy!" Daisy had easily launched herself into the arms of the best father on earth.

"Missed me, girl?" She now mounted Oreo and stroked her soft forelock. "I missed you."

Daisy didn't get to ride often enough. Too many little distractions here and there took time away from riding, though she never neglected to check in on Oreo. As a teenager, she'd barrel raced for a while mostly to please Daddy. But though she loved horses, she didn't like racing them for competition. And when she didn't have a passion for it like some girls did, she let the sport go. But contrary to what some believed, she hadn't always had a passion for cars.

But in high school, she'd taken a class simply so she wouldn't have to rely on her brothers or her father to change her oil. There, she'd discovered she had a knack for mechanics.

What must it be like to have known one's passion from the time you were a child? It had been like that for Wade, who'd been on a bucking horse since he was a kid. Wade's father sure loved the rodeo and had been proud of his son, said by everyone to be fearless. But no one was completely without fear despite what risk-takers and adrenaline seekers believed. Everyone had at least one person or thing they were terrified of losing.

For Daisy, that had always been her family.

Funny, she didn't see Wade the way everyone else saw him.

He wasn't cocky, no matter what anyone else said. Everyone else saw a flirty, charming, confident rodeo cowboy with a wild hair. The first time she'd seen Wade afraid, he hadn't even known she was watching. As usual, she and Jackson had both managed to tag along with Lincoln to the Cruz ranch.

Wade would have been fourteen at the time and already in training. He'd been pulled away by his father from whatever game they'd been playing outside.

"Son, if you don't practice every day, you'll never be a pro," Mr. Cruz had said.

By then, Wade was training with miniature bulls. She'd watched from the sidelines as Wade had gone up onto that bull and stayed on for several interminable seconds. Daisy's heart had plunged to her stomach as she watched, terrified Wade would fall and be injured. His father had him wearing a helmet and other protection, but that might not be enough.

"That was five seconds less than the last time," Mr. Cruz yelled. "You gotta beat eight. Do it again."

Wade had removed the helmet, and she'd seen the expression in his eyes and been struck dumb. In a moment she'd never forget, Daisy had seen the truth clear as a bell. Wade wasn't afraid of the bull.

He was afraid of his *father.* The one thing Wade feared was disappointing him.

Now, both of his parents were gone, and she wondered what else he could be afraid of losing. He'd lost his career, too, when he'd identified for so long as a rodeo rider.

Was it possible that Wade had nothing left to *lose*?

Her chest tightened. The thought was a punch to the gut.

"I'm not going to think about that now," Daisy told Oreo.

She rode on and waved to Lincoln and Jackson, with a few other ranch hands in the distance, steering cattle. She didn't see Daddy and thought he might be working inside. He was doing less field work these days.

Hopping off Oreo, Daisy tied her to the fence post and walked up the porch steps to the front door. Normally, she would walk right in, but it was still early. Lord knew what she'd find if she walked right in the door like she'd been able to what seemed like not so long ago. Brenda could be inside, half-naked. Though she really couldn't picture that. Brenda Iglesias was so conservative that Daisy bet she didn't even take her clothes off to have sex.

She face-palmed. Okay, yuck. She did *not* want her mind going there.

Daisy knocked on the door, and Brenda opened it. Fully clothed, thank you, wearing jeans and flannel. Her long, dark hair was peppered with gray and pulled back in a ponytail.

"Daisy!" Brenda grabbed Daisy in a hug. "Come in, querida. Do you want some coffee?"

"Yes, please."

"Almost no one comes to visit us." Brenda walked into the modest kitchen.

The small ranch house was cozy these days, Daisy had to admit. When Daddy had lived here by himself, half the time everything was as dark as his mood. Now the curtains were pulled back to let in sunbeams of light. There were bright splashes of color everywhere. Turquoise blue, orange, jade. Everything neat, clean, and tidy. The house looked like a home where a happy couple lived.

It occurred to Daisy that her father had been miserable for years, and she'd been too stupid to see it.

Brenda handed Daisy a cup of coffee. "Hank is in his office looking over the ledgers."

"Oh, okay. I'll go back there in a minute. I need to talk to him." Daisy looked at the floor, wanting to make casual conversation but not really knowing where to begin. "Um, so how have you been?"

"Wonderful! It's all very exciting. Eve is going in for an ultrasound next week and she might find out if she's having a boy or a girl."

"If she's having a girl, she'll probably be given some kind of an award."

"Well, I was lucky to have a girl, so I hope it's hereditary."

Wouldn't it be nice if everyone could only inherit the good parts from their parents and leave the bad parts out? But more often than that, it didn't happen that way. You got the good right along with the bad. If you were lucky, there was a nice balance.

Brenda went on for several more minutes, talking baby showers, due dates, and how likely they were to be accurate. Then labor, and delivery, until Daisy started to tune her out.

"Pumpkin." Daddy ambled in the kitchen. "I thought I heard your voice."

Daisy set her now empty cup down.

"Daddy." She went into her father's arms, always so warm and open.

Brenda briefly touched Hank's arm as she brushed by him. "I'll be outside."

"You never come up here to see me anymore," her daddy said, pulling back from the hug.

It was true, but that was because she always saw him down at the bigger house where Mima cooked Sunday dinners. Lately he'd been bringing Brenda, too, but Daisy had never been up here to see them living together. Getting ready to be married soon. They weren't planning a big wedding because Brenda didn't like all the attention.

"Lincoln told you?"

"Yes, he did." Daddy lowered his head. "I'm sorry you're havin' to go through this. It's not fair to you."

"Not fair to *me*? Daddy, it's not fair to you, either! I think we know whose fault this is, and it isn't yours."

"Well, I used to think that." He closed his eyes and rubbed his forehead. "But I think there's always enough blame to go around when a marriage doesn't work out."

"That's generous, but she's the one who left us."

"And I'm sorry that we never sat down and talked about this." He walked to the kitchen table and took a seat. "If there's one good thing about this mess, it's a chance to talk about your mother."

"I don't know that there's anything to say. She *cheated* on you, Daddy."

"Well, I never broke my wedding vows, but sometimes I think I cheated on her, too."

"No, you didn't." If she'd had any doubts that her father was an honorable man, and Daisy didn't, *Brenda* would have never broken up a marriage.

"But there are different kinds of affairs. I'm learning that mine was an emotional one. Brenda and I remained close even after we were both married to other people. I tried to tell myself it wasn't true, because I did love your mother, but I think I never really stopped loving Brenda."

Oh my, her father sounded so enlightened. It was as if

someone had switched Sam Elliott for Dr. Phil. What in the world.

"I worried that my mother had broken the two of you up, but Mima said that's not what happened."

"No, what happened is I let my feelings get hurt because Brenda's parents didn't think I was good enough for their daughter. And I didn't fight for us the way I should have."

"I can't *believe* they didn't think you were good enough."

Daddy chuckled and patted her hand. "I wasn't always all that good. Mima can tell you if she ever gets a hankerin' to be honest about her children's many faults. I drank too much, had a hair-trigger temper, and possibly had my head turned by a beautiful woman or two."

A beautiful woman like her mother.

"I'm sorry my mother broke your heart."

"Don't you worry about me now. I got my second chance whether I deserved it or not. While I was angry for many years at your mother, it was mostly on behalf of you kids. She didn't do right by you, even if she believed y'all were better off with me."

"She was right about that, at least. Daddy, you should know that I've decided not to take the DNA test."

While Daisy felt guilty lying about this, even now, this was a gift she could give her father. He wouldn't have to worry or wonder while he was supposed to be enjoying his second chance.

"You do what you want to do and don't worry about me or anyone else. This is your life, and I won't be upset if you have to be sure." He reached out, tucked a lock of her hair behind her ear. "But I'm sure. Besides, no matter what biology has to say about it, you're my daughter. You always will be."

Daisy rarely cried. She figured she'd done enough crying after her mother left to get her through the rest of her life. But when there were tears in her hard-edged father's eyes, it was inevitable.

She hugged him, and blubbered through a wall of tears, assuring him that she was *his* daughter.

And she always would be, no matter what those results had to say.

Chapter 12

Wade had a rough night. Between his aching arm and intrusive thoughts of Daisy, this time with her top *completely* off, he'd rolled around in bed like an alligator. Good thing he didn't have to share his bed with anyone. No one pulling on the covers, complaining he didn't know how to share, and no one kicking him to get more room. Lord knew that would be Daisy, were she in his bed. She'd probably clock him should he dare snore and wake her up.

Okay, that's enough thinking about Daisy in your bed.

Nope. Not going there. Moving on.

She hadn't brought up giving her any more lessons since the night of the Riverwalk, and he was just fine and dandy with that. He wasn't going to be forced to take on that responsibility. Okay, not forced. Wrong word. Um… privileged? Yeah, much better word for that deal. So, he wasn't going to be *privileged* to introduce her into the world of sex. That was good. Yeah. Because with that privilege came a huge responsibility. And he didn't need that piled on top of everything else. So, yeah, great news.

Even if he was certain he could make it good for her.

More than good. How about fantastic? Her first time should be memorable. Spectacular. It should be a high benchmark for any other fools to try and beat. Not that they could if they even tried. Oh, he'd make sure of it.

His mother must be having a field day in heaven, looking in on him now and then, watching him tied up in knots over Daisy. Having a good laugh at what she claimed he'd never be able to fight. Destiny. He'd been against the notion of this supposed "destiny" of his for years because Daisy was young and *sweet.* Too innocent for the likes of him. He'd never be good enough for her, and she'd never be "bad" enough for him.

But his mother firmly believed and insisted to her dying day: he and Daisy were meant for each other. She'd seen it in a dream.

He glanced at his mother's framed photo on the mantel. "You think this is funny, don't you?"

He forced himself to do the physical therapy exercises he loved to avoid. This time before sunrise, so he couldn't talk himself out of them. Afterward, the pain was intense enough for him to count the pills he had left and allow himself two.

Then he had his coffee, showered, dressed, and went out before dawn to start his day.

Since he'd need to move the cattle to another pasture for grazing, he drove the ATV out to a good patch of land and pounded posts into dirt to create the start of a cattle drive lane. That took him several hours after which he realized he was hungry. He hadn't thought ahead to bring a lunch pail with him like his father used to, but then again all he had in the kitchen were casseroles. Time for a run to the General Store at some point and load up on cold cuts. He'd been spending too much time eating out at the Shady Grind and it wouldn't hurt to curb expenses.

He parked the ATV at the bottom of the hill and hiked the short distance to the house. It was then that he heard a rustling in the barn and wondered if he now had the mice taking over, too. Super. Time to get a cat. Also, time to get a new barn for that matter, but that would have to hold for a bit.

As he drew closer, he saw a blonde spitfire under the hood of that classic vintage piece of crap.

After the other night's busted button/lacy-red-bra torture, watching her bend over that engine, her heart-shaped butt sticking out, was *not* helping. Why had he always been attracted to bright and shiny buckle bunnies with tassels on their jeans when *this* kind of a woman existed? She was real, earthy, and dirty in the best kind of way. She had his mind doing cartwheels.

And she's *Lincoln's little sister*. Whoa, cowboy! Whoa. That's one ride you'll never recover from.

He groaned. "Peanut! What are you doin' there?"

"Hey, Wade." She straightened, used a rag to wipe motor oil off her hands. "I didn't see you when I came by earlier, so I got busy."

"This is a waste of your time."

"It will never be a waste of my time to restore something old to new again."

"You can't do that. It's an antique. It won't ever be new again. Give up."

"It will still be just as good, and classier, too. They don't make them like this anymore."

"Suit yourself."

"Also, I got you a little surprise inside. It's an artificial tree and a few ornaments. You really *need* a tree. It will cheer you up, believe me."

"What makes you think I need cheering up?"

"You said you *have* to be a rancher, Wade. I hear you

loud and clear. You don't have a choice. You're stuck here with us."

"I'm not *stuck*."

"Really?"

"Trust me. I'm good with my choices. I'm here, or haven't you noticed?"

"Where else would you be?"

He hadn't been much of a gentleman if he'd let Daisy believe that her fake boyfriend would rather be anywhere else. "Hey. I don't want to be anywhere else. Stone Ridge is my home."

While she didn't appear convinced, at least that shut her up for a moment. She gnawed on her lower lip and wouldn't look at him.

"Um, did the mail come?"

The mail. He mentally face-palmed. Of course she would be here, probably every single day, waiting for the results. He hadn't checked the blue wood mailbox at the end of the lane.

"I haven't checked. But he's always late, so he probably hasn't come by yet."

"You'll let me know the minute my envelope comes, right?"

He pulled off his hat and ran a hand through his hair. "I'll go down there and check after lunch. First, I gotta eat."

"You go ahead, I'll just be out here." She went back to her wrenching.

He should have realized she would use the car as a distraction. She could have been using *him* as a distraction, but that wouldn't be a good idea. He'd already established that.

Just keep telling yourself that, champ.

"Not hungry? You don't want some casserole?"

"Ew, no."

He chuckled and shook his head. "Can't blame you."

Inside, he washed up, mainly because of Daisy. He hadn't even shaved this morning but figured he'd let that go for now. He chose the leftover enchiladas casserole, fuming a little bit. Daisy acted like they'd never even kissed, and really...did she kiss *everyone* the way she'd kissed him?

He'd just pulled the plate out of the microwave when someone knocked on the front door. Frustrated, he stomped over, swung the door open, and found Beulah with someone he didn't recognize. A tall brunette in a black pantsuit gave him an eager smile.

"Wade, let me introduce Savannah Ackerman. And this here is Wild Wade, our rodeo champ, in the flesh!"

He offered the woman his hand, then turned to Beulah. "What's this about?"

Beulah waggled a finger. "This is about discussing you as Mr. Cowboy for our new reality show."

"We already talked about this. I'm—"

"No need to play this game with me. I have it on good authority from Lillian Carver that y'all are just pretending. And she would know better than anyone else. At least hear Miss Ackerman out. She came all this way."

"May we come in, Wade?" Savannah asked in a smooth voice. "I'd just like to talk to you for a few minutes."

"Yeah, sure."

He waved them inside and led them to his great room. Propped in the corner stood the tree with a box of ornaments nearby.

"I'm glad to see you're finally gettin' into the spirit of the holiday," Beulah said, nodding toward the tree.

Miss Ackerman took a seat on the leather couch and pulled a folder out of her briefcase. "As you know, we're in developmental talks about this reality dating show here in Stone Ridge."

"It would be good for the economy," Beulah added.

"Yes," Miss Ackerman continued. "But more importantly, it could be good for you. Do you know how many of our former contestants go on to be TV personalities with successful broadcasting careers?"

Wade crossed his arms and sat on the edge of the couch. "Nah, I don't want to be on TV."

"He's already been on TV." Beulah nudged Miss Ackerman's elbow.

"I don't want to be on TV *again*," Wade added.

"That's fine. There are also plenty of other opportunities behind the scenes. Once you're on our show, opportunities open up everywhere." She splayed a series of eight-by-ten photos of women who looked like fashion models.

"These are just some of the ladies who are interested in becoming Mrs. Cruz."

"Wait. What?" He stood. "What do you mean, *Mrs. Cruz*?"

Miss Ackerman held up a palm as if to silence him. "Not right away. Some *day*. And, of course, it may not work out. We understand, things happen. But we do ask for our single men to walk into this situation with the expectation that they are trying to find true love. Their one and only soul mate."

"Miss Beulah? Are you serious right now?" Wade glared at her and hooked a finger to his chest. "*Me?* Married?"

"What's wrong with that, *Wade*? Surely you don't want to be single the rest of your life. You don't have that many choices, seeing that most women your age are already married. You may have missed the boat, son. I'm trying to help you. Our town needs more women. Look at these gorgeous women, and they'd all move to Stone Ridge." Beulah swept her hand over the glossy photos.

"For six weeks," Miss Ackerman said.

"Well, except for the woman he marries."

Wade crossed his arms, ready to dig in his spurs. No one would talk him into this mess. No way. No how.

"I'm not getting married to someone I've dated for six weeks."

"But that's the premise of the show. Sometimes, you have to take a leap of faith."

"Lady, I'm not leapin' anywhere." He touched his arm. "Maybe you heard. I had a career-ending injury and I'm sure that's not too attractive to these gorgeous women. I'm sort of a broke-down cowboy."

"That's actually *very* attractive. We do love our wounded heroes, don't we?" Savannah smiled.

"I'm sorry I can't help you. It's just not going to happen."

"Would an offer of money help?" Savannah said.

"What's going on here?"

They all turned to the sound of Daisy's voice. Great. She was about to find out their little game was over.

"Daisy Mae Carver! I have a bone to pick with you." Beulah shook her finger. "Pretending to date Wade. What a fine mess you've made. Well, I hope you're proud."

"Your grandmother told Beulah we're a fake couple," Wade explained.

"But—"

Beulah cut her off. "It's time for you to do your duty and help us convince Wade to finally settle down and have himself a wife. I know you hate that gigantic billboard, and the sooner we find our Mr. Cowboy, the sooner it's coming down."

"What about my other suggestion? Jolette Marie's

brother? Sean Henderson? Beau Stephens? *Levi?*" Daisy said, with Levi's name sounding like a squeak.

Savannah piped in. "Hello. Daisy, is it? I'm Savannah Ackerman. I've just offered Mr. Cruz the possibility of some money since he's not interested in a broadcasting or entertainment career after the contest ends."

"M-money?" Daisy turned to him, her voice going from squeaky to shaky.

"I can see the ranch needs work and we could help with all that. Now, I can't make any offers without first consulting with one of my executive producers. But though it's frowned on, there might be a way we can do this," Savannah said. "We really want a rodeo cowboy. Obviously, it would be perfect for our *Mr. Cowboy* show. It's all branding."

"Wait a cotton-pickin' minute. Money? Isn't the offer of marital *bliss* enough?" Beulah held a hand to her neck. "I'm absolutely shocked that this would come down to money. Why isn't love enough?"

Savannah chuckled as if she too understood the unlikeliness of one of these women being Wade's true love.

"That's often not enough for young people. Times are different, Mrs. Hayes."

"Butter my biscuit!" Beulah said. "This proves money is the root of all evil."

"Money is also the way I could get my ranch back in business a hell of a lot sooner." Wade couldn't help but point out.

Not that he would consider it, of course. That is, unless he could get it in writing that he didn't have to marry the woman. That would be important. He'd also have to figure out how much his soul was worth.

Savannah stood. "And on that happy note, I will leave

you to consider the idea. And I'll be in touch when I hear back from the studio executives."

Beulah followed her out, clucking her disapproval the entire way to the door. "I do declare. Never heard of such a thing."

Wade closed the door, chuckling. "That was fun."

Daisy stood in the middle of the room, looking as vulnerable and lost as on the day he took her for the test. "You're thinking about this, aren't you?"

"Not in a serious way." He couldn't lie to Daisy.

"Are you *ready* to get married?"

"No, but hell, Beulah is right. I'm thirty-three, and if I'm going to settle down, I guess I should do it fairly soon. Or at least try."

"With a *stranger?*"

He scratched his temple. "Probably not. I'm definitely not one of those who believe in love at first sight. You may not have heard that part, but Savannah said that they understand sometimes these things don't work out. They want me to at least try, but they understand they can't *force* me to marry one of their women."

"You *are* thinking about it!"

"Just *thinking* about it, Peanut. You can't blame me for that." He stalked back to his forgotten lunch. "And I still haven't eaten lunch."

"How can you eat at a time like this? You're about to sell your soul for a little money."

Damn if that didn't hit him square in the solar plexus and he felt it clean as a punch. "Don't judge me. I'm trying to start over. And I don't have any other way to earn money. A little influx of extra cash wouldn't hurt."

"I know!" She brightened. "You could sell the car. It won't take me much longer to get it running."

"No, I *can't* sell the car."

"I swear, I'll work my magic and—"

"Told you. My old man made me promise never to sell it. The car is my 'inheritance.'" He made air quotes. "A gift I'm supposed to hand down from Cruz to Cruz."

"But he's not going to know."

"*I* would know." With a spoon, he served himself a heap of enchiladas.

"Don't let him keep controlling you when he's already long gone. You didn't even like your father!"

"That's not the issue."

"No, the issue is you're being bullheaded and stubborn, and *such* a man!"

"A man?"

"You saw photos of beautiful women. And you're thinking, my, wouldn't it be nice to be surrounded by women and be the only man in the mix. But that kind of thing can be highly overrated."

"As spoken by a *woman*." He snorted.

"Okay, fine. If you're doing this, I'm not going to fix your car." She crossed her arms. "I refuse."

"I didn't ask you to fix it anyway!" Okay, now he seemed to be yelling.

Calm down, idiot. She means well.

"Fine, you jerk! I'm leaving." She turned and stomped out his front door.

"Good. Great!" He stared at the door after she banged it closed, appetite completely gone.

How in the hell had he gotten himself into this holy mess?

Oh yeah, he remembered. He'd come back to Stone Ridge to see if he could resuscitate the ranch he'd inherited with what little money he had left of his savings. Now he was dealing with Beulah, who wanted him to get married, and Daisy who didn't want him to get married.

She wanted to fix his car. And kill him slowly. She'd asked him to teach her how to attract a man, then forgotten the whole thing. Well, he was going to forget about it, too!

Someday.

At times like these, he was almost glad there weren't many women in Stone Ridge.

DAISY WAS SO furious she slammed the door behind her. It was bad enough that Beulah knew the truth but now Wade was actually considering the contest. Just the idea had created a wall of anger so big she almost couldn't breathe. Her breaths were coming short and brief. She didn't want to believe that Wade was the kind of rodeo cowboy Mima had warned her about. An opportunist and a womanizer.

Like Rusty.

No, not Wade. He was the boy she'd loved for half her life, if she were finally being honest. She didn't have a *crush* on Wade. Crushes didn't last for over a decade. The feelings he inspired in her went far beyond physical attraction. Her heart and soul craved him in a way she did not fully understand.

He was hers. He'd always been hers, but just didn't know it.

Tell him. Stop making stupid excuses to be with him. You swore you were going to take risks. Change your life from boring to adventurous.

She'd just reached her truck when Wade came out the front door. "Daisy! We're not done here."

"Oh yes, we are. We're done when *I* say we're done."

"Look, let's talk about this like adults."

"Is that another crack about my age?" Her hands formed into fists and she gave him her back. "I might be younger than you, Wade, but at least *I* have common sense."

"And I don't?"

"Not when you can't see what's right in front of you."

"Let's not fight. We don't do this. We've been friends for a long time. And I don't want to lose…us."

She turned to face him, some of the hot air fizzling out of her at the sound of his soft tone. Because he was right. They were friends, tied together by community and family. And years of memories. She wanted so much more than that, but she couldn't force him to be ready for her.

"Okay."

"Come back tomorrow. Work on the car, or don't. But I know you need to keep busy until the test results come."

"Yeah. I'll be back." She turned to reach for the handle of the truck.

"Okay, good. See you tomorrow."

In the next moment she and Wade had reached for each other at the same time. She was in his arms, and they were both holding tightly to each other. His arms were around her waist, pulling her closer.

"I'm sorry," he whispered those sweet words into her neck and sent a tingle of pure desire slicing through her. "I shouldn't have yelled at you."

"No, it's my fault. I'm sure I'm not making any sense to you. I can barely understand myself."

"You're waiting for news on something potentially life changing. That's not a small thing. I'm an idiot not to realize you're going to be more sensitive than normal."

She pulled back to face him and placed her hands on his shoulders. "No, but it's…it's a lot more than that."

"Are you sure? What is it, then?" He tugged on a lock of her hair.

"I don't want you to be Mr. Cowboy."

"That much is clear. I don't want to do it, either."

"I do want you to have the money and that's what you want, too."

"It would be nice, sure."

"But there's a bigger problem. At least for me. Maybe not for you, though."

What if he said, you're too young for me? I'm too old for you. You're Lincoln's little sister. We're better off as friends, aren't we? I'm sorry but I think of you as a sister or good friend, not as a lover. Not as a potential wife. But don't take this personally.

He could say some, or all of this. Many of the same things she'd been saying to "men who were not Wade" for a very long time. Now maybe she would get the rejection back tenfold.

But she'd made her decision, no matter how scary. She was tired of playing it safe. She'd suggested to Wade that he pretend to date *her* to rescue him from the contest. To "save" him from dating all these women and possibly marrying one of them. Because if this happened, it would be too late to tell him how she felt. He'd be engaged and Daisy would have to find a way to live with that.

"I-I don't want you to date all these women because I want you for myself."

Wade gazed at her from under hooded eyelids she couldn't read. Then she did what he'd advised and lowered her gaze to study his lips.

He kissed her, a soul-reaping kiss that made both her skin and nipples tighten. Her thoughts were a jumble, if they could even be called thoughts. They were more or less snippets of anticipation. Hope, bright and clear. Single words.

This. Now. Mine. Him.

Finally, finally, finally.

Something good had happened to Daisy. Something

precious and special and wanted. The one man she'd always yearned for. Prayed for.

"About time you got honest with me. I've been waiting. I don't even know how long."

"Oh, Wade. I'm a hot mess right now and I know it. But it won't always be like this."

"You're *not* a mess. You're brave and strong. And you turn me on without even trying."

"How do you know I'm not trying?" She smiled up at him, trying to bat her eyelashes.

"Because if you were really trying, I think you would have killed me by now." He tugged on a lock of her hair. "Are you wearing the red bra tonight?"

"No, this one is black." She started to unbutton her top to demonstrate, but Wade stayed her hand.

"Don't tease me."

"I'm not."

"You don't mean to, but it doesn't take much for me when it comes to you. I got hot and bothered watching you wrench on the car."

"And I always thought being good with cars made me less attractive to men."

Wade cocked his head and smirked. "I admit that I prefer you dressed in your Wranglers than in your auto-shop jumpsuit."

"See? I was right."

"That's just because the uniform hides what I know is underneath." His hand lowered and lingered on her behind.

"You don't *know* what's underneath."

"Oh, but I have a *great* imagination."

She kissed him to shut him up. Pulling back, she pressed a finger to his sensual mouth. "There."

"What was that?" One corner of his mouth tipped in a smile.

"You're talking too much. Less talking, more kissing. And more... *you* know."

"More what, Daisy?" He tugged on her bottom lip. "If you can't talk about it, we can't do it."

"Sex."

"Oh, we are going to have sex, but we're going to take it slow."

"Why?"

"Because you deserve someone who will take his time with you, someone who will—"

"Wade, I can make my own decisions. I'm *ready*. I've been waiting a long, long, *long* time for this."

He chuckled. "And I appreciate the enthusiasm."

"It's the right time. You're the right man." A man she'd never regret loving, no matter what else happened between them.

"We're still taking it slow. I'm afraid you're going to have to trust me." He reached behind her to open the driver's side door. "I'll see you tomorrow."

With that, he helped her into the truck and shut the door.

Daisy drove home, and for the first time in several days, she took a deep breath and let the air fill her lungs.

And she didn't once think about Maggie *or* Rusty.

Chapter 13

Lillian found Daisy humming to herself in the kitchen, happy as a bluebird.

"Well now, good morning," Lillian said, walking as if she might step onto a landmine at any moment.

She figured she'd have hell to pay for letting Beulah know the truth. And up in heaven, Rose would be *quite* unamused, but she didn't know what Lillian was going through down here. Only Albert did. Her Daisy needed a man who would never abandon her, for the rodeo, cattle, or anything else. She needed to be first. She required certainty and security. Safety.

"Hi!" Daisy turned, then gave Lillian a huge hug. "I've been up since dawn, so I started breakfast. The bacon is frying, and the grits are in the pan."

Oh good heavens, the girl was terrible in the kitchen. Lillian would be lucky if the grits were edible.

"Thank you, sugar." Lillian helped herself to a cup of coffee. "I have to admit, I expected you to be a little upset with me."

"Why? For telling Beulah I was fake dating Wade?"

"Let me explain—"

Daisy waved her hand dismissively. "It doesn't matter. I'm fine. I know whatever you did, you did it for my own good. And I appreciate it."

Lillian cupped her ear. "Um, what, now? Speak into my right ear. I think I'm going a tad hard of hearing in the left."

"Ha, ha. You're funny."

"You're not upset that Wade is being courted to be Mr. Cowboy? I heard that they're offering him money and Lord knows the boy needs it. I would like to see him bring that ranch back."

"Whatever Wade decides to do, that decision will be entirely up to him."

"Yes, it certainly will be. And I guess it wouldn't be such a terrible thing to see him settle down, find the right woman. Have a couple of kids."

"And will you feel sorry for this woman? Winding up with Wild Wade?"

Lillian worried this was a trick question. "Well, of course not. Rose raised that boy the right way. He's a true man of Stone Ridge. I think I'll be pleased as punch to see him finally settle down. Rose always wanted the best for him."

Even if she'd mistakenly believed that had been Daisy.

"I'm glad to hear you say that." Daisy turned the bacon over in the skillet. "Because he's a friend of the family and I for one want nothing more than his happiness. Whoever that woman works out to be."

"That's very mature of you. I'm quite proud." Lillian patted her back. "I'm sure the right man will come along for you any day now. There are so many available."

"I'm not going to think about any of that for now."

"Of course. You've had a lot on your mind lately. Let's

get through the holidays and Eve's baby shower. Then we'll find someone just right for you."

"Eve and Sadie invited me Christmas shopping with them, so I'll be taking off for a while today. We're going to dinner. Don't expect me back until late. You might as well go to bed."

"Oh, child. Did you leave all your shopping to the last minute again?"

"I'm afraid so."

"Well, don't spend your hard-earned money on me. I already have everything I could possibly want." Lillian took a sip of her coffee, then sent up a little prayer of thanks and mouthed, "Thank you, Albert."

Things were going according to plan, and best of all, Wade would soon enough be happy and settled down with a lovely woman.

Like Rose used to say, "You just can't fight destiny."

"PLEASE SADIE, NOT ANOTHER TOY STORE," Daisy begged. "I still have to find a few grown-up gifts."

She'd been wracking her brain for a present for Wade, but nothing seemed good enough.

"What did you get for Sammy?" Sadie said.

"I thought I was giving him that little push toy that makes all that popping noise?"

"No, that's what Eve is giving him." Sadie turned her gaze in the direction of Eve, now taking a load off, sitting at a table enjoying a Cinnabon roll.

"Then what am I giving him?"

"*That's* why we're here," Sadie said, walking into yet another toy store. "Follow me. I know just the thing."

Daisy followed dutifully, avoiding parents hauling their kids around as they pointed to what they wanted from Santa. As with every store they'd been inside today, holiday music pumped loudly through speakers and every toy ever created had a Christmas version. A Santa doll with a jiggly belly in the front of the store danced to the tune of "Feliz Navidad." But as much as she was enjoying spending the day with her sisters-in-law, listening to talk of sciatica pain in the last trimester, latching-on problems for nursing babies, and when to start solid foods, she really wanted to get out of this shopping hell.

She'd planned to see Wade later and hadn't intended on spending this much of the day shopping. But the minute they'd arrived, it had been one blessed thing after another. They couldn't find a parking space and they'd circled the lot until someone finally left. Then Eve had to find a restroom every few minutes. Sadie kept texting Lincoln to make sure that Sammy was able to survive for a few hours without her.

News flash: he was.

Finally, thank you Jesus, Sadie handed Daisy a plastic fire truck that could double later as a ride-on toy. Braving the lines, Daisy paid, and they both went to find Eve.

"I still need to find Jackson the perfect present," Eve said.

"What? It wasn't that shirt and the boots you got him *five* stores ago?" Daisy said.

"No, that's an okay present but I know exactly what he wants from me." Eve waddled over to the Victoria's Secret store.

Oh, well. This was more like it. Daisy's eyes didn't know what to take in first. She loved all the silky lingerie. Mostly she bought her lacy undergarments online wondering when she'd be able to finally share them with someone. Well, the time had finally arrived. Wade had loved her red bra. She chose push-up bras and matching thongs until Sadie elbowed her.

"These are for you?"

"No, they're for *you*, Sadie," Daisy snapped. "Why? Why can't they be for me? I like lingerie, too, you know."

"Of course you do. These are just so…sexy."

Daisy not so subtly elbowed Sadie out of her way. "Why don't you go bug Eve? She seems to be buying a dominatrix outfit. Maybe you should stop her."

Sadie burst out laughing. "That's called a teddy. But I don't see how Eve can wear those much longer with her growing belly."

"Let her dream."

"I guess this means there's someone special?" Sadie asked, looking through the push-up bras right along with Daisy.

"Maybe. But there doesn't have to be, you know. This is for *me*."

"Yeah, that's what I used to think. Now, whenever Linc buys me lingerie, I know who it's really for," she chuckled. "Why do you think Eve's buying a teddy? It's so Jackson can enjoy his present."

"Nice to know y'all keep the magic alive." Daisy flipped through the bras, looking for her size in a strapless.

"Well, with your brother, it's easy. He—"

Daisy held up her palm. "You're about to cross the line."

"Got it. Hey, I like this new little system we have."

"And thank *you* for no longer going all the way to 'red alert' before I stop you."

They paid for their purchases, and on the way back to Stone Ridge, they again passed the billboard of the man with blinding white teeth. This time Daisy smiled back at him. From now on, she would view this giant man as a win.

As long as his photo was up, Wade was out.

"We haven't talked about *Mr. Cowboy*," Sadie said. "What do y'all think about this reality show Beulah dreamed up?"

"It's silly," Eve said. "I don't see how anyone can find true and lasting love in six weeks."

"Do you know that they're insisting the man be prepared to propose at the end of the show?" Daisy piped in.

"How do you know that?" Eve asked.

"That's how *all* these shows are, Eve," Sadie said.

"I was there when Beulah came over and the woman from the show offered Wade money to do this. They want him to lie and pretend he'd propose to a woman at the end of the show."

"The women probably wouldn't come out to stay in Stone Ridge if there wasn't an engagement at the end of it," Sadie said.

"Beulah thinks some of these women will stick around, just like Winona did when she found out about all the men," Eve said.

"I disagree," Daisy said, and hoped. "There is only one Winona James-Henderson."

"You can say that again." Sadie snorted.

Even if none of them had liked Winona when she'd first arrived in Stone Ridge, a Nashville star with her hair extensions and false eyelashes, they'd all grown to adore her. Riggs had married her, and she'd been a big part of the only medical clinic in town getting up and running as soon as it had. Now Eve wouldn't have to go to Kerrville to have her baby. The baby could be born right in Stone Ridge.

When they passed the clinic on their right, a large pink bow was strung from one end of the clinic to the other with a sign:

It's a girl!

Both Eve and Sadie squealed. "Winona is having a *girl!*"

"See? This problem will be solved in no time. When do you find out what you're having, Eve?" Daisy asked.

She and Winona were having babies within a couple of months of each other.

"I find out next week." She held up crossed fingers.

"I preferred being surprised," Sadie said.

"I like surprises now," Daisy said quietly, not sure if they could hear her.

She'd had her share of them lately. The fact that Rusty thought he could be her father was not a great one. But there were other surprises, too. To learn that her daddy was truly happy now, reunited with the love of his life in a late-in-life romance.

But possibly the best surprise of her life was to learn that Wild Wade Cruz had been waiting for *her*.

WADE CHECKED the mailbox in the afternoon, half anticipating that Daisy's results would have arrived. But still no envelope for Daisy. A few more bills for him even though he'd switched everything to online banking. And today, a letter from the Rodeo Cowboys Association. Ripping it open, he read that they were trying to start an association of retired rodeo cowboys and would love his support. Imagine that. They planned to elect a board and use their former influence to help ranching communities. Sounded honorable, charitable, and also boring. A chance to be a sad old man recreating some of his younger and more active years. That wasn't ever going to be him. He was still young, though this letter made him feel sixty-five. Did they not realize he'd *retired* young, or was this simply a form letter they sent to every cowboy on their massive list?

Depressing. He considered ripping the letter into shreds, then realized the immature response wasn't him. Instead, he'd bury it somewhere in the office with all the other paperwork he still had to go through.

By the time Daisy rolled up late in the afternoon, he was done with his chores for the day. And ready to collapse.

"Hey, there. I got caught up Christmas shopping with Eve and Sadie. It was *torture.*"

He nodded. "No letter today. Sorry, I already looked."

"That's okay. I don't want to think about any of that."

"No?"

"Just happy thoughts are allowed inside this brain." She gestured to her temple.

"I could use some of those happy thoughts." Wade pulled her into his arms, holding tight.

The rush from being with Daisy had become addictive. She'd essentially taken the place of his former adrenaline kicks. She was everything wrapped up in one package for him. Excitement, thrills, danger, and…oddly enough, the comfort of home. Not a normal combination for him.

The other difference was that he'd become eager to please. Maybe far too eager. It felt strange, like walking around in someone else's too-tight jeans. He'd always been a gentleman, but he'd never actually courted a woman since he'd been a teenager. But today, he'd planned to take Daisy to the farthest point of his property that faced west. So they could watch the sunset.

He told himself this was because she wanted to give him something and he wanted her to know that he didn't take that lightly. This was setting the stage for the rest of her life. She didn't deserve less than everything even if he wasn't certain *he* could give it to her. Not his heart and soul, anyway, both of which felt a little battered these days. And okay, sure, she was taking his mind off his own problems so he didn't have to consider whether or not he could truly be happy for the rest of his life simply being a cattle rancher. Point being, he had to try.

It was enough for some, like Lincoln, and it *should* be enough for him.

He was no stranger to hard work, so that wasn't the problem. And he told himself that the issue wasn't having no one cheering him on as he mucked stalls and hauled hay bales. No one timing him even though, truth be told, he often timed himself.

But fame and adulation were fleeting, he understood, and so what if he was no longer the flavor of the month. Every time Daisy looked at him with all her eagerness, every time she kissed him and sent heat spiraling through, he didn't need anything else.

"We should really decorate your tree." She pointed to it.

"Whatever possessed you to get me a tree, anyway?"

"Your mama would be upset that you didn't have one up. *She* always did."

He ignored the ache that memory sent through him. Maybe it was precisely why he'd avoided getting a tree.

"Haven't you had enough Christmas for today?"

"I guess you're right. The stores were full of it."

"Are you hungry?"

"I managed to get out of dinner with Eve and Sadie."

"Great, I packed something to eat."

She deadpanned. "Not a casserole?"

"Do I look crazy? You've made it clear how you feel about those." He took her hand and led her. "Beef tacos."

"You remembered."

"We're going to go watch the sunset."

"Really?"

He grabbed the cooler and strapped it on the new ATV. Tapping the seat, he indicated for her to hop on. Many ranchers used ATVs to get around a large property. He would always prefer a horse, but frankly, they were far more expensive to own and maintain. Until he started to break even, Wade would not be able to take on any more horses. They were a luxury he couldn't afford.

With Daisy a passenger behind him, he didn't even attempt pushing the ATV to the high speeds he craved. He took it easy, a leisurely drive along the outside perimeter of his property, hoping she'd notice much of the work he'd done. His cattle drive a few days ago had his cows now grazing along the north pasture where they had plenty to eat. One advantage of his situation had been plenty of grass after he'd cleared out all the dead brush. This would save him a lot of money on feed for now.

He pulled over at the fence line of the west pasture, and Daisy spread out the blanket. Together, they laid all the food out.

"This is nice," she said, biting into a taco. "I'm surprised you remember how much I love these."

"I remember everything about you, Peanut." For once, this wasn't a line.

He imagined this happened when you grew up with someone. Always noticing every small thing. Remembering. She liked rocky road ice cream and picked out the marshmallows. She told everyone she enjoyed romantic comedies, but he knew her favorite movie was actually *Tombstone*.

"They're from the taco truck, right?"

"Yup."

It made its way down to Nothing every other week. The actual location was top secret because it always varied, but Wade knew a guy who knew a guy.

"Nothing's claim to fame. The *El Abuelo* taco truck." She faced the skyline and the descending sun. "I wish they'd take the stupid *Mr. Cowboy* show over to Nothing."

"They could use the attention, but don't think that's going to happen. Beulah is on this like white on rice."

She put her taco down. "Wade, if you want to do the show, if you really need the money…maybe you—"

"After all this trouble, you're not goin' to tell me I should do the show?"

"No, I don't want you to. You know why."

"We already established that."

"I just figured you'd do whatever you wanted to anyway."

"And you'd be right about that. That's why I'm here right now. This is where I want to be."

"Yeah?" She smiled at him shyly, and he felt a strange pulling and tightening in his chest.

Heartburn, maybe. Damn. Maybe he *was* getting old. But in the next moment he completely rejected that idea outright, reached for Daisy, and rolled with her on the blanket. She wound up on top, straddling him, and wasn't *this* a beautiful sight? Better than the sunset. Her blond hair fell over her face as she bent her head, then tucked her hair behind her ears and smiled down at him. Her eyes were the most mesmerizing shade of green. They were the color of the warm and lush leaves of an apple tree.

A surreal memory punched through him, one of lying on his back looking up at the bright blue California sky. Thinking that life as he knew it was over.

But this didn't feel like the end. It felt like a beginning.

She threaded the fingers of their hands together. "Tell me something and be honest with me."

Here we go. She was going to ruin this moment by asking him about other women. By asking how many women he'd been with. *Too many.* He wanted to forget about that part of his past and leave behind the reputation he'd earned over the years. Lincoln had been no saint, either, by the way, but he'd been far more discreet. Wade had to give him that.

"I'll be honest. Just don't ask me about something you don't want to hear."

"Okay," she said, cocking her head. "How's your arm?"

"Fine. Great." This was, of course, a lie.

But he didn't feel comfortable telling Daisy that some mornings his arm hurt so much he wanted to scream. Cry. Put a hole in the wall, with his *good* arm. He wouldn't do it, of course. What would be the point?

"You *said* you'd tell me the truth. I could feel it the night you carried me on your back. Your arm was working so hard it was trembling."

"That's nothing for you to worry about."

"But I *do* worry because I care about you."

Whenever he'd told a woman that he *cared* about her, it was the ultimate kiss-off. And they knew it. But Daisy wasn't jaded about love. She was still hopeful and eager, like someone he once remembered…oh yeah, him. Before he'd had his first heartbreak.

And Daisy… well, it occurred to him that Daisy might have never had a broken heart.

"Alright, it hurts. Now you tell me something true. Has anyone ever broken your heart?"

"Why do you ask, so you can go beat him up?"

"No, because I want to know."

"Never mind." She rolled off him. "I can't tell you the truth."

The way she pulled away sent daggers of fear slicing through him. Someone *had* hurt her. How bad? He forced himself to take it down a notch, let the fear go.

"Tell me."

"No."

"Whisper it in my ear."

"No," she snorted.

"Spell it."

"No!"

"Charades?"

She laughed and smacked his shoulder. "Cut it out."

He pulled her back into his arms. "Look."

Together they watched as the sun lowered beyond the horizon, the last rays of the sun darkening against the skyline. The night was clear and cool.

"There's going to be a lot of bright stars tonight," he said.

They were quiet for several moments, just listening to the sounds of sparrows twittering in the tree branches and settling in for the night.

"It was you, okay?" Daisy whispered into the darkness. "*You* broke my heart."

She might as well have shoved a knife in his heart.

"When?" He turned her to face him, palming her chin.

"That time you kissed me and ran away. I felt like I'd done something wrong because I enjoyed it when you kissed me like that."

"Sweetheart, I was the one who'd done something wrong. And I shouldn't have run out on you. When I kissed you, I knew I'd crossed a line, and it scared the crap out of me. Not crossing the line, but the way you made me feel when I did."

"It *was* good, wasn't it?" She took his palm and kissed the inside of it.

"You were young. And yes, it was way *too* good for my comfort."

"I don't think it's a coincidence that it's still good between us. There must be a reason."

"I can't argue."

"For once."

And then she smiled against his mouth and kissed him, a kiss so warm and tender that he knew without a shadow of a doubt he was in deep, deep trouble.

Chapter 14

Daisy had just told Wade a difficult truth, and yet he still wasn't being fully honest with her. She understood why, and it was easy not to hold it against him. But his arm was a problem for him. He kept pushing through, working through the pain, but he had no one to talk to. No one but her. Both parents gone, his mother with whom he'd always been so close.

His father, a man Wade seemed to have both loved and mostly feared. Even Lincoln didn't have as much time for his best friend these days, though she would bet that Wade wouldn't tell him the real truth, either. It was easier to be tough. And it was expected from the men of Stone Ridge. Certainly, from a former rodeo cowboy.

And she understood better than he realized. She behaved far stronger than she felt most days because she didn't want anyone's pity. But he hurt, too, and didn't want her to feel sorry for him. Understandable, but it wouldn't stop her from helping him.

In the middle of their heavy make-out session under the moonlight and stars, she casually massaged his arm.

"What are you doin'?" he said through hooded lids.

"I'm trying to ease some tension."

"Baby, you're already doin' that."

"I just don't want you hurting." She sank her fingers in his thick cocoa hair.

"And I don't want you to hurt, either."

While that could be taken many ways, Daisy fixated on one of them. She didn't know what would happen after they entered into this brand-new territory together. It wouldn't just be Mima having a difficult time accepting them. Lincoln would probably not be thrilled, either, but he'd get over it. Eventually. Sadie would help.

The real problem being, of course, what to do if she and Wade *didn't* work out. They *should* be able to seamlessly go back to being friends again because she'd done that many times in the past. She'd dated everyone from Jeremy to Troy. And when it hadn't lasted, they were still friends even to this day. No hard feelings.

This was different, of course, and her heart knew it. She'd already memorized everything about Wade. It helped that she'd been doing that most of her life. She only wanted to be with one man her whole life, and Wade could be her one and only. Forever. She didn't care if he was her first and last. Maybe that's the way it should be, old-fashioned though it sounded. She was okay with that, given her mother's example. Best to be as far away and different from Maggie as possible.

This night couldn't have gone better if she'd planned it herself. Now that the sun had set, only ambient moonlight remained and a spread of sparkling stars. It gave her a courage she might not have had otherwise to take the lead from a man who probably always led.

Straddling Wade, she slowly unbuttoned her shirt, ready to reveal her new plunging demi bra. Judging by his reaction, which she could feel beneath her more so than see, he approved. Wholeheartedly.

"Wait. I want to see this."

Before she realized, he'd reached for a small pen light and shined it on her boobs.

"Wade!" She rolled off him.

"What?" He laughed, rolling to tuck her under him. "Don't you want me to see?"

"I wanted you to see with the benefit of *mood* lighting. You know, the moon! You're cheating. I don't think anyone looks good with a bright light on them."

"You do. But I want you to feel safe."

He dropped the light, then quite skillfully unsnapped her bra. He slowly kissed and licked from the column of her neck, to her shoulders, lowering the strap of her bra. When his warm mouth covered her breast, Daisy's entire body tightened in response.

Wade stopped. "Am I going too fast? Is this too much?"

"No," she whispered. "It's good. I like it."

The tightening of her skin wasn't out of nerves or anxiety. An intense pleasure she'd never experienced before made her want to buck against him. She did, and he groaned in a way that sent waves of satisfaction rolling through her.

Then Wade went after her jeans and panties, lowering them past her hips.

And Daisy got to experience some of what she'd been missing.

"I'M STILL A VIRGIN," Daisy said once they were back at the ranch.

"Only technically." Wade pulled her into his arms.

"You didn't want your first time to be a few feet away from my grazing cattle, did you? In the dark?"

"I'm not complaining."

Far from complaining, she'd been incredibly responsive. It was a crime to think she'd been denied this experience for so long. She was also eager, to the point of wanting to return the favor, as she'd pulled on his jeans. But he'd denied himself that pleasure because tonight had been all about her. He'd simply stayed her hand and told her that was the advanced course.

She batted her eyelashes. "When are you going to let me into that silly advanced course?"

"You have to be patient. Maybe next time."

"Maybe *next* time?"

"Here's something no other man would ever tell you, so I'm glad you picked me." He tipped her chin to meet his gaze. "The first time might hurt."

"I'm not an idiot. I know that."

"And you already know how I feel about hurting you."

"Yes, and I trust you. I feel safe."

"I will make it good for you, as good as it can be the first time. But baby, it really doesn't get much better than what happened tonight."

"That *was* amazing."

"And the rest will be amazing, too, because I'll make sure of it. It won't hurt as much with me, but it will hurt the first time."

"So why is every woman going on and on about sex like it's better than chocolate?"

"Because it is, after a couple finds their groove." He sent her a wicked smile. "And I know we will."

She believed that, too. "I can't wait."

He kissed her again, holding her close, inhaling her sweet scent. He still tasted her on his tongue, and just that thought sent him into a tailspin. Holding himself back from what he had wanted to take tonight was an excruciating exercise in self-control.

"I'm not going to lie. I can't wait, either."

Lately, it was all he could think about. As if he were a teenager going at it for the first time. Excited and eager. And a little nervous, too, but it happened to be his favorite kind of tension. The anticipation before the chute opened, the thrill in the air all around him.

That was Daisy.

Wade walked her to her truck, opened the door, and waited as she strapped in. She gave him one last kiss, deep and promising, and then drove off.

He would be lucky if he slept at all tonight.

PREDICTABLY, Wade tossed and turned all night long. Memories of what he'd done to Daisy the previous night mixed with the anticipation of what he planned to do to her. As soon as possible.

The next morning, he knew exactly what he had to do.

He hadn't been out to Lincoln and Sadie's cabin since they'd moved into the large home Lincoln had built for them on several acres of Carver land. When he'd been home for his mother's funeral, he'd come to see the frame. Then he and Lincoln sat together, for hours, drinking beer, exchanging memories. Lincoln letting Wade be quiet and stew in his grief. Like best friends do.

And it didn't sit well with Wade that his relationship with Daisy had recently changed, and Lincoln had no clue. Most of this was none of his business, but Wade couldn't get past the fact that he had to say something. After all, in the beginning the whole thing had been a lie. He had to tell Lincoln that he was dating Daisy, and he had to frame it in such a way as to let him know that this relationship wasn't business as usual for him. Because it was true, and also the only way he and Daisy could work.

Daisy was a grown-up now and no one needed to protect her, but least of all from him. He would rather be impaled by an angry bull than hurt her. Even if she wasn't in love with him, for the first time in many years, he was the one open to a serious relationship. But if Lincoln didn't get a clue, if Wade didn't share how his feelings had changed, he might feel betrayed. Wade couldn't have that. He wasn't going to hide a thing.

That's how he found himself knocking on the door of the cabin of his oldest friend.

Lincoln opened the door, holding Sammy. "Oh, hey, bud. Come on in. About time you came by to see the place. The only other time you've been here since it was finished was with Daisy. We had other things on our minds that night."

"Yeah, I'm sorry I've been scarce." He shut the door and stepped inside the marbled foyer. "I actually need to talk to you about something, and I probably should have come sooner."

"Don't tell me you're thinking' about doing that stupid reality show. I heard that both Beulah and Mima are after you. You want my advice? Don't let them pressure you. You're just like me. And you're going to have to know a woman a lot longer than six weeks before you propose." Lincoln snorted. "Probably, like, years."

Years. With someone that I've known for most of my life. Someone who in many ways I've always loved.

Someone who his mother believed was right for him even before Wade did. The strangeness of that never failed to amaze him. How had she known? Was it just a coincidence because she liked the Carver family and had been friendly with Maggie? It had to be.

"That's actually what I need to talk to you about."

"Yeah?" Lincoln set Sammy down on the floor and the kid started to crawl around.

"He can do that already?" Wade pointed. "Isn't that early?"

"Hell if I know. But it's sure made our lives a lot more complicated." Lincoln turned Sammy around when he was headed straight for the fireplace. "Forgot I have to stop cursing around him."

"Well, I—"

"Go ahead, I'm paying attention." Lincoln turned Sammy around again. The kid was quick, he'd give him that.

In the corner, there was a playpen. "Can't you put him in that contraption?"

"I would, but he screams his head off. I'm only thinking of you. The screaming is loud. Boy has a good pair of lungs on him. No, Sammy, you can't have that." Lincoln took a pen that had been on the floor.

Sammy screamed, apparently offended that he couldn't start scribbling at eight months, or however old he was.

"Damn, only Sadie can calm him down when he works himself up like this."

And Sammy's face had gone tomato-sauce red.

"Where is she? Taking a shower?" Wade prayed. This confession time wasn't going too well. He would need Lincoln's undivided attention.

"No, she went to meet with Mima, Beulah, and the ladies of SORROW about some knitting-thing fundraiser. She won't be long," Lincoln yelled over the sounds of Sammy's wails.

"Okay, well, listen. You have to know I didn't see this coming. I swear I didn't."

"What?" Lincoln said, swaying the baby back and forth. "Say that again."

"I should come back another time. You're busy."

"No, seriously, just give me a minute to calm him down. I wanted to talk to you about a fishing trip. It's been a while," Lincoln yelled.

"Your bachelor party weekend," Wade yelled back. "Too long ago. We definitely need to do that again."

This was ridiculous. Two grown men couldn't carry on a conversation with a screaming baby in their midst. Lincoln continued to sway Sammy, hand him various toys, and nothing worked. Nothing. Feeling completely useless, Wade made silly faces. They only made Sammy cry louder.

Then came a squawking sound from the walkie-talkie nearby. Lincoln, like so many, used them as a means of communication on a large ranch.

"Lincoln, we need your help pulling a cow out of the mud," came a man's voice and sounded like Jackson. "Got herself stuck pretty good. I got some help already, but it's going to take a few more men. West pasture, same place she did before. Figured you'd want to get this done now. Is Sadie back?"

"No, damn it. Aw, shit fire. Sorry, Sammy." Lincoln spoke into the handset, then turned to Wade. "Watch Sammy? It will only be a few minutes. I swear."

Wade took a step back and threw his hands up as if he'd been asked to sit on a stick of dynamite. "What? That's *not* a good idea. I don't know much about kids. Let me go help pull the cow out."

"Thanks, buddy, but not with your sore arm. I wouldn't be much of a friend. Besides, I know the location better than you do." Lincoln handed a screaming Sammy to

Wade, who took him with the ease he did holding a woman's purse.

"Just hold him and rock him like I was doing. It does nothing but you feel better trying. Be right back."

But the minute the door shut behind him, Sammy was shocked into silence. He simply stared at Wade with a stiff bottom lip as if he couldn't believe his father had handed him off. Backing up carefully, not wanting to risk dropping the kid, Wade took a seat on the couch.

"My name's Wade." Wade cleared his throat. "Um, do you like horses?"

AN INTERMINABLE TWENTY MINUTES LATER, during which Wade told Sammy his entire life's story, Sadie waltzed in the front door.

"Wade," she said, smiling. "What are you doing here?"

Sammy had fallen asleep during Wade's recounting of the National Rodeo the first year he won the grand prize. He'd been holding him for the past few minutes, and the boy was going to be big like his daddy. Wade's arm ached but he was afraid to move the kid.

"Came by to see Linc, and he had an emergency in the field, so he left Sammy with me."

She drew closer and ran a hand through her boy's soft curls. "Did he cry much?"

"Oh, you know, a little. But I bored him to sleep. He pretty much calmed down when I recounted the first time I was on a bucking horse." He shrugged because it was one of his best stories.

"You two look good there together," she said.

"Well, he's asleep. This part is easy."

"He doesn't usually nap for long. I'll put him down in his crib," Sadie said, easily taking him from Wade. She pressed a kiss to the boy's forehead. "Doesn't he look just like his daddy?"

"He does."

A few minutes later, Sadie was back. "How about some iced tea?"

Wade followed her into the kitchen he hadn't seen since it was little more than a framed room. It was spacious, and this he did remember. Granite countertops were offset by gleaming cherrywood cabinets. In the center, a large kitchen island. The colors were blue and yellow, bright and cheerful.

"We haven't seen much of you lately." Sadie set a pitcher on the bench table set against the kitchen's nook. "How's the arm?"

Why was that all anyone ever asked about? Why not ask him about the ranch and his new cattle and equipment?

"It's fine. I've recovered well."

"Doing your physical therapy exercises?"

"Yes, ma'am." He took a gulp of the sweet tea. "I would drop by more often but there's a lot of work to be done on my ranch."

"Of course, you're busy. So is Lincoln. And you know what we've all been through lately. Poor Daisy. And poor Linc, he's been miserable wondering how she'd take it."

"She's handling it pretty well, I'd say. Linc should have trusted that she would."

"You know how he is, trying to protect everyone he loves from any kind of pain."

"Yeah. I sure know."

"The two of you aren't any different that way."

"He's a lot better at it than I am. I seem to wind up hurting the people that I love one way or another," Wade said, wishing he hadn't said that out loud.

He was thinking of his mother, whom he hadn't seen much in her last months. And really, what had been the point of keeping her alive when he didn't have any time to spend with her? He'd paid her bills and kept her treatments going longer, which had stretched her days, for her friends and family. For him, the times he got home. Maybe that had also been selfish of him. Some days the guilt ate him alive, though he knew she'd understood. At one time, in the exuberance of his youth, he'd actually thought he could save her somehow. That money meant good medical treatment and that would equate life. Didn't quite work out that way.

And time was the one thing he would never get back.

"I'm sure that's not true." Sadie studied him, then pushed a plate of cookies in his direction.

He took one, of course. It would be rude not to. They were holiday sugar cookies in the shape of green trees and yellow stars.

"You're not actually doing that reality show, are you? I heard that Beulah figured out you and Daisy were fake dating."

"No, ma'am. They did offer me money, but at this point, I couldn't in all good conscience participate in that kind of show."

"Oh," Sadie said, her eyes wide. It was as if he'd told her everything.

Everything, in one simple sentence.

This is why he loved women.

"Yeah."

"You and Daisy." Sadie folded the edge of a paper napkin. "When…when did this happen?"

"Recently. I didn't plan it. We really were faking in the beginning."

"Well, *you* were, anyway."

"Yeah, but it took me a while to figure that out. I'm an idiot."

"Another way you're like Lincoln. I don't understand how you missed it. She adores you. Always has."

"I know she did at one time, but I thought she got over that. She was always so much younger than me, that it was unthinkable. And awkward. She had a crush on me, that was all. I never acted on it."

Unless one wanted to count that kiss long ago, but he didn't. He'd done the right thing and rushed out of there before he regretted doing more. The idea that he'd been Daisy's first heartbreak had crushed him, just ripped into a piece of his soul.

But he would make it up to her now.

"I know you didn't. And frankly, Wade, she's old enough to make her own decisions."

"That's what she tells me." He managed to crack a smile.

"Are you worried about how Lincoln will take this?"

"Even my oldest friend can't tell me who to date. But it's out of respect for him that I'm here."

"You haven't told Lincoln yet?"

"I tried, but…there were a few distractions, and then a cow got stuck in the mud."

"Oh, not again?"

Wade chuckled. Some cows got stuck in bad patterns.

"I told him I'd come by some other time and we can talk then." Wade stood, not wanting to impose any longer. "Thanks for the tea and cookies."

Sadie followed him to the door. "Wade? I wonder if you'd let me prepare the way first? I'd like to help. I won't tell him anything, since I know you want to do that. But I could…you know, ease him into the idea."

"Whatever you think is best." He reached for the door handle. "I have no intention of hurting her."

Sadie waved her hand dismissively. "I know that."

Wade drove home, a little unnerved by the fact that Lincoln's wife wanted to "prepare" the way for him. Why? To "soften the blow"?

He'd like to think Lincoln wanted to see his sister happy, especially with everything she'd been through recently, but maybe Wade's reputation had preceded him.

And this time he actually cared what someone thought of him.

Chapter 15

Not surprisingly, Sammy didn't nap for long and was up five minutes after Wade had left. Sadie's little boy was always anxious to get moving the moment he woke up. She put the baby gate up and set him on the kitchen floor with a couple of plastic bowls while she made dinner. Meatloaf, Lincoln's favorite.

In a way she was still celebrating the moment when all the worry had been taken off her cowboy's strong shoulders. When Daisy told her big brother that she wished he would have told her sooner, Sadie had wanted to cry with relief. Late that night, they'd stayed in each other's arms long after making love, talking about everything they'd been through from the moment Hank started receiving emails from Rusty Jones.

"Are you glad she's decided not to take the test?"

"Yes, because that means this is really over. We can put it behind us." His warm and calloused hand skimmed down her naked back. "Why? Do you think she should take it?"

"I don't know. I'm glad for you that she decided not to do it. I like having my husband back."

"You like having all my attention, don't lie. I keep wondering when you'll get sick of having me around."

"I'm never going to get tired of you. Just wait and see."

Sadie wanted this kind of happiness for everyone she loved. And certainly, a former playboy could be reformed when he fell in love. She'd seen it firsthand.

Good thing, because Sadie now knew whom all that sexy underwear Daisy purchased was for. Sadie understood what it was like to pine after a brother's best friend. Her brother, Beau, had accepted that she and Lincoln were together, in fact trusted that no one else could love and protect her better than he could. She had faith that Lincoln would eventually do the same for Daisy.

Lincoln showed up just as she was setting the table, looking like he'd been dragged three miles through mud and grass. Mud caked his jeans, shirt, and face. Still, he had a grin on his face because her man was definitely a rough-and-tumble cowboy.

"Oh, phew, baby!" Sadie fanned a hand in front of her.

"What? You don't want a kiss?" He stood in the doorframe of the kitchen, just on the other side of the baby gate, arms splayed wide.

"No. Kiss me *after* you take a shower."

"What about you, Sammy? Want to give your daddy a big hug?"

Sammy squealed and went back to gumming the Tupperware bowl's lid. It was an expensive toy, and Sadie already washed enough dishes for a five-person household these days. She wished Sammy found his actual toys this intriguing.

"I'll be back," Lincoln said and sprinted upstairs.

"Okay, Sammy. No tantrums tonight. I need Daddy in a good mood."

This latest development was not a big surprise to Sadie. She'd seen Wade and Daisy together and you couldn't fake that kind of thing. While she'd fully expected that from Daisy, the surprise had been watching Wade, a bit gobsmacked with love. She'd never seen him so taken with any woman.

But Wade had always been a full-blown flirt, yes, even with *Sadie* before she and Lincoln got together. Pretty much with every woman in town from birth to death, giving Wade the appearance of always being available to *everyone*.

Twenty minutes later, the table was set, Sammy in his highchair, and Lincoln back down from his shower. Dressed in clean jeans and a pearl-button shirt, his hair still damp, he still made her knees liquid. Her heart sped up simply because he'd entered the room, never mind that she worried what she might find when she put her pulse on his feelings about a Wade-and-Daisy relationship. After what she'd been through lately, Lincoln's dial was set to optimize protective mode with Daisy.

"What's the occasion? Are we still celebrating?" He pressed his hand low on her back before he drew her chair back for her. "You don't even like meatloaf."

"I should eat more of it. Meatloaf is good for me."

Careful, Sadie. Don't lay it on too thick.

He smirked. "Yeah?"

"I got to chat with Wade today."

"I'm sorry I had to leave before we were done talking," Lincoln said, serving her and then himself. "I want to get together and go fishing soon, if you don't mind."

"I think that would be a great idea!"

"Wow, *you're* excited. You hate it when I even have to go away for a cattle auction and that's business."

"Well, I miss you. But you deserve some fun with your oldest friend."

"Thanks, baby. I think I will make plans. I have to check the weather reports. I'll be sure not go until after the holidays."

"You know, I was just thinking. Wade really was *so* great with Daisy at the Riverwalk when that man showed up, don't you think?"

"Yeah, he was. I appreciated him handling things until I got there." Sammy squealed and Lincoln tousled his hair. "Everything worked out and that's all that matters."

"Um, do you know if Wade is actually seeing anyone?"

"Besides Daisy, you mean?" He winked. "You know Wade. He'll never settle down."

"Never say never. Isn't that what people used to say about you?"

"That's true. Then you came along."

"I was always right in front of you."

"What can I say? I'm a slowpoke cowboy." He chuckled and squeezed her hand.

"So, since Wade is sticking around and not in the rodeo anymore, I bet he's going to consider settling down with someone special."

"You think?" Lincoln cocked his head as if the very idea puzzled him. He shook his head. "I can't imagine that."

"Then you need to expand your imagination. He's thirty-three."

"I don't see what age has to do with it. He'll get married when he meets the right woman. *If* he meets the right woman. I expected him to come back home with some buckle bunny and hope to make things work with her on his ranch. He had his choice of women on the circuit, now not so much."

"But he *didn't* come home with a woman. I think Wade is more discriminating than you realize." Sadie handed Sammy a piece of bread to gum on. "It was nice seeing you handle him and Daisy dating, even if it was fake."

"It's not like I'm going to find it weird when Daisy winds up in a relationship. It's bound to happen sooner or later. I wonder what's taking so long. She's old enough."

"This is what I'm thinking, too!"

Lincoln grinned. "What is it? Do you have someone to introduce her to? Want to know if I think she'll like him?"

Sadie playfully pointed her fork. "*You* don't have any *idea* of whom she'd like. But no, I think she can find a guy all by herself."

"You're right about that. Daisy does what she wants and always has."

Really, it was uncanny how little insight her man had into other people's love lives. Probably for the best.

"Have you ever thought about the fact that it might be hard on Daisy, finding and keeping a boyfriend? You and Jackson put together can be pretty intimidating. And that's even before they get to *Hank*."

Lincoln grunted. "The *right* man won't be afraid of us."

You can say that again, cowboy.

"You just remember that, baby. You remember that's what you wanted."

"If I forget, I'm sure you'll remind me."

WADE DROPPED by the General Store on his way back to the ranch. He was determined to have food on hand for the next time Daisy came over.

Unfortunately, he wasn't quick enough to avoid Kari Lynn in the dairy aisle.

"Hiya, Wade."

"Hey there, darlin'. You sure look fine today."

Why had he said that?

Force of habit. It was like he got diarrhea of the mouth around women. Reality check. He didn't *have* to be liked by every woman, did he? No. He didn't.

"You're so sweet." She batted her eyelashes. "I thought maybe I'd come by your ranch sometime. I'd love to see what you've done with it."

"Better not. I wouldn't want your pretty boot to step on a nail or a rut. I've got a lot of work still ahead of me."

"Alright, well, when you're done."

"Sure thing, I'll let you know."

"Well, hello there, *Wade*," came Mrs. Carver's voice out of nowhere. She'd appeared at his elbow like a ninja.

"Mrs. Carver, don't you look lovely today."

Kari Lynn took that moment to strut away in a bit of a huff, he noticed, but rather convenient for him.

"Kari Lynn is so lovely and you're *such* a charmer. Do you ever get tired of laying it on so thick?"

Yes. Try exhausted.

Unfortunately, he'd never learned how to turn off the charm. "I never exaggerate. I do think you look lovely."

"What about me is *lovely*, young man?"

He didn't hesitate because he noticed things about women. All women, young or old. "That's a new coat, isn't it?"

Mrs. Carver blinked. "Why, yes. How did you know?"

"I haven't seen you wearing it before."

"How do you know it hasn't been in the back of my closet?"

"It hasn't."

"You're right." She tugged on the buttons of her coat. "Thank you for noticing."

"Welcome."

He would win Mrs. Carver over yet. She was one of the few women in Stone Ridge who didn't fall under his spell. Wade wasn't sure why other than the fact that Maggie had been friendly with his mother. But Lillian didn't think him good enough for Daisy, no shock there. He didn't have a whole lot to offer her but a broke-down cattle ranch, a falling-in-on-itself barn, a house in need of repairs, and a man with an injured arm.

She could do much better than him. Whether or not she should was the real question. He wasn't the most impartial judge at the moment. Clearly, he had an agenda. He didn't want her to find anyone else.

When he got back to the ranch, he found Daisy in the barn wrenching on the car again.

"You don't give up, do you?"

She wiped her brow, her blond hair held back in a high ponytail. "This is a classic. Trust me on this."

"You sure do ask a lot of me." He headed into the kitchen with his bags. "I'll be right with you."

He quickly put away the milk, bread, eggs, bacon, cereal, soup, and other food he'd bought. An utter feeling of domestication settled on him but this time with an ease he didn't expect. How about that, he seemed to be growing up. Just as his mother said he would someday. Maybe he'd make dinner for Daisy tonight. She couldn't cook, and he wasn't exactly a four-star chef, but he could manage. He'd eaten on the road for years, in diners and bars, but for a while there when he'd been trying to save every penny, he'd learned how to cook an exceptional batch of ramen noodles.

From outside came a sound so loud and jarring that Wade instinctively went for his shotgun. But even as he rushed outside, he should have recognized the sound was unique. Different. Not the sound of an animal threat. Not the sound of cattle hooves. Not the sound of a bull loose and creating havoc.

This was the sound of a building coming down.

Terror was a real and tangible vice that clawed at his throat, cutting off his breath.

Part of the barn had fallen in right where Daisy had been working on the car.

Chapter 16

"Daisy!"

Fear uncoiled in Wade like a poisonous snake. The adrenaline rush hit him with the force of a bull coming straight at him. His pulse raced. The sound of his heartbeat thudded in his ears. He couldn't take in a full breath.

He didn't understand why he thought he'd missed this feeling.

"I'm okay." A piece of the barn's old rotted ceiling lay on her legs, but she was surrounded by dust and wood. She kicked the plank off with her feet. "I think."

He cursed. "You're not *okay*. The ceiling fell on you. I told you not to work on this car. Damn it, Daisy!"

"Hey, be nice! The roof just fell on me!"

"Let's get you out of here before the rest of it falls down."

Without another word, he dusted debris off her shoulders, arms, and legs. He picked Daisy up and kicked the door open, carrying her into the house. Setting her down on the couch, he went for his first-aid kit. It was a required staple when he was growing up and he'd used it just last week when he'd cut his finger mending fences. He found it under the kitchen sink where he'd left it, then grabbed some ice and a dish towel.

"Okay, let's see." Plopping himself next to Daisy, he tried to push up the leg of her pants, but the jeans were too tight. "Pull this up so I can take a look at your legs."

Daisy didn't bother tugging, but simply raised her hips, unzipped, and slid her pants completely off. She wore tiny frilly pink panties with only a small swatch covering her. He made a valiant—he was sure—award-winning effort to ignore this, and inspected her legs. *Her curvy, creamy legs and thighs.* And holy cow, even her *ankles* looked delicious.

Okay, so he wasn't doing such a great job of ignoring.

She had a few bloody wounds and scratches on her shins. He used ointment to clean and bandage her. She could have a concussion. He'd had plenty in his life and knew exactly what to look for.

"Did anything hit your head?"

She gave him an odd look through narrowed eyes. "I don't think so."

"I don't *think* so won't work for me. You have to be sure."

"Okay, maybe a small piece hit my head, but it was so small I barely felt it. My body took most of the punishment. I'll probably just be sore tomorrow."

He handed her the towel with ice. "Put this on your head, just to be safe."

"Ahem. Are you just going to ignore the fact that I'm lying here nearly naked?"

"Daisy, cut me a break. My barn just fell on you. You're injured, and I'm worried and trying not to think about how much I would like to pick you up like a caveman and throw you in my bed right this second."

He rose and went to the medicine cabinet to get some anti-inflammatory meds for her.

This he knew exactly where to find and was gratified to see that he had plenty left. In the beginning, after the injury, he'd counted the pills in the bottle and told his arm he'd get through the day with one pill. One. Some days that worked, others it didn't. He kept careful count, however, and tried to beat his own score.

He grabbed a glass of cold water but when he walked back in the room, he almost had to dunk it over his head.

Daisy had removed her shirt, too, and lay there on his couch, up on her elbows, a slow smile crossing her Cupid's bow lips. She had the sexiest lips he'd ever seen in his life and now that he'd tasted them, he couldn't get them off his mind.

"Can you ignore this?" The pink matching bra pushed up her breasts like an offering.

He swallowed hard and his words were more of a croak. "I'm not *ignoring* anything. This is willpower, girl. Are you trying to kill me?"

"Why are you resisting me?"

"I'm trying to do the right thing here, Daisy. You don't need me to throw you over my shoulder and haul you into my bedroom."

"Hm, maybe I do." She chuckled, took the pill and swallowed it, then licked her lips. "Wade, the thing is, when the ceiling fell on me…it hurt my mouth, too. Right here."

Oh man, she was good. Fine, he would play along.

He gently pulled her up by the waist and pointed to the corner of her lips. "Where? Here?"

"Yes, and you better not even *think* about a Band-Aid."

"No, baby. No more Band-Aids for you. I can see that you're dandy. You may have hit your head but you're obviously firing on all cylinders."

He tugged on her full lower lip, then kissed her. *Not* sweetly.

Not tender. The kiss was long and deep and promised everything he meant to deliver. He was done waiting and done being the honorable good guy. *Done, done, done.* She was getting what she wanted tonight.

But he'd have to slow his roll and not just go for sex the way he wanted. The way his body reacted and the way he craved. Hot, sweaty, raw. No frills. Down to basics. That would come later, were he lucky enough to have more than once with Daisy. Tonight, he'd take his time, even if it killed him.

Wade picked Daisy up in his arms and carried her to the bedroom where, for the second time today, he kicked a door open.

This time, his heart raced for a different reason.

His favorite reason in the world.

DAISY STOOD on her bare feet inside Wade's bedroom, facing him, wearing only her new lingerie.

At last.

Minutes ago, when she'd heard the sounds of the crash before part of the ceiling came down, she swore that her life flashed before her eyes.

She nearly wept it was so boring.

Always the good girl. She'd never taken any chances, never laid her heart on the line. *Or* her body. Finally, it was time to create some memories.

Wade took her in, all of her, as if seeing her for the very first time. His hand slid from her waist to her hips. "You're so beautiful, Daisy."

"I'm glad I have your attention." She stepped forward

and went on tiptoes, her arms reaching for his shoulders. "But *you* have too many clothes on."

She slid his jean jacket off his shoulders with his help, then slowly unbuttoned his shirt. Beautiful tanned, sinewy muscles were revealed, a light smattering of dark chest hair, a taut and flat stomach, and…wait. A tattoo? She traced the edges of the design, a long lasso rope that circled his bicep and lowered, ending at his forearm.

The words read, *Do or Die*.

"We were all drunk one night in Oklahoma," he said.

She kissed the tattoo right where the rope met his bicep. "I like it."

Then she ran her hand down the large red scar on his arm and kissed that, too.

"Had I known, I would have had the tattoo done on the other arm. It could have covered up the scar."

"Maybe then you'd have a broken rope, too. But I happen to love this scar. It says that you have a history and a dangerous past that you *survived*."

He met her eyes, his own hooded and dark with heat. "You're a survivor, too, Daisy."

She'd never considered that, but yes, she *was* a survivor.

She'd survived Maggie Mae leaving and now she'd survive everything else, too. She could have been a different girl than the one she'd turned out to be. She could have gone after the attention of men in an unhealthy way. There had certainly been plenty of them always surrounding her. Instead of asking for attention, she'd been too cautious, but there was some good in that, too. She didn't want to make the same mistakes someone else had made before her.

She would have to make her own.

He toed off his boots, then shucked his Wranglers off. Daisy always thought he had a great body, judging by the way he filled out his clothes, but reality went far beyond anything she'd expected. His body was male perfection. A fine work of art, the hard body of a man who had a life filled with tough physical labor. Mending fences, mucking stalls, corralling cattle, pulling newborn calves out, hauling hay.

"What do you want? Tell me." His fingers traced the curve of her face.

"Everything. I want a memory I won't ever forget. Something real. You."

Gently, he pushed her back on the bed and covered her body with his own. He braced himself above her. "I want to give you all you want."

"Finally."

He slid her panties off, then teased her mercilessly with long, deep kisses, his tongue tasting every inch of her flesh as if he could eat her alive. As if he were a hungry man offered a five-course meal. When he pushed her bra aside with his mouth and suckled at her breasts, she went on fire with heat.

Reaching for him, she tried to pull him to her, tugging on the waistband of his boxer briefs. But it occurred to her that she'd forgotten something important. Protection. If there was one thing she'd learned from women like Jolette Marie, who loved to talk about sex, it was *never* to rely on the man bringing the goods. She'd planned to buy condoms, but she'd never gotten around to it.

"Wade, wait. I meant to…but I don't have any… any—"

"Protection? I've got you. It's my job to protect you in every way."

Oh, whew! She hadn't wanted to rely on him, but how nice to know that she could.

Once, she thought she'd be afraid of this moment.

Worried to be so completely bare and vulnerable. Exposed. But she felt nothing of the sort. Instead, she felt cherished, safe, even…loved.

Okay, let's not go there. Don't get ahead of yourself.

This doesn't have to mean love. It doesn't have to mean forever, just because you want it to.

This was a risk, and she was taking it, right along with him. They were in this together, drawn to each other and giving in to this connection between them. An awareness that had always been there. Something deep and unguarded in her assured her that Wade would never be a mistake. She didn't know where the thought had come from or if it simply sprang from her own wish, but it felt real. Powerful. Like fate.

When she orgasmed once more under Wade's skillful ministrations, it was as if she'd left her own body. It was delicious.

"Oh my, that's so much better than chocolate *or* coffee." She threw back her head and moaned.

Wade snorted. "I would hope so."

"But you don't know how much I love coffee. I can't live without it." She reached for him, pulling him to her. "Please. I'm ready."

"Yes, you are. As ready as you'll ever be."

Within seconds he'd protected them both and then slowly entered her. Daisy gasped which made him stop.

"Too much?" Braced above her, he met her eyes, his own so dark and hooded, she hardly recognized him. "Want me to stop?"

"No, don't stop. It feels good. Really."

She didn't want to say it out loud because it sounded a little silly, but she felt a brand-new realization about herself. It seemed as if she now had an empty space inside her waiting to be filled. And she would stretch to make room for him. In her mind she pictured opening up for him, and when Wade went deeper it stopped hurting. She only felt a delightful friction that grew in intensity as he began to move.

A tide rose inside her that, for the life of her, she couldn't hold back. The sensation was one of losing control while gaining it back. She orgasmed again in a flood of waves of pleasure, releasing a tension she didn't know she'd been holding back. Wade followed, giving her the sweetest knowledge that she could bring him this kind of pleasure.

Her body was more powerful than she'd ever imagined.

Afterwards, he rolled and tucked her under his arm. Pressing a kiss against her temple, he said, "I swear it will be better for you next time."

Better? Better than this? No way. "I'm already addicted. How long before we can do it again?"

"Not long." He chuckled. "Give me a minute."

She caught her breath and kissed the scar on his arm. "Wade, do you ever miss the rodeo?"

"Sometimes I do, but I thought I missed the adrenaline rush. I found out that isn't what I miss at all."

"What is it?"

"It's the community. The way we would come together, and everyone knew their part. Even the animals. We competed against each other, but there's also a grudging respect. It's a sport not just anyone can do and we're proud of that. But the main person I've always competed against is myself."

"What does that mean?"

"I wanted to do better each time than I did the last time. It goes back to those early years, sitting on the minia-ture bull that was my first ride. Trying to beat my own score." He hesitated a beat. "Guess it's the way I was taught."

"I remember. Your father pushed you hard."

"You saw some of that."

"And how badly you wanted to please him."

"When I was a boy. But then the rodeo became all mine. The one thing I had that he could no longer control."

They were both quiet for several seconds, just caressing each other. She pressed her cheek against his chest and listened to the thudding sound of his heartbeat.

"Daisy, do you ever worry what will happen if you *aren't* Hank's biological daughter?"

"No, I don't think about that. It won't happen."

"I just wondered. I've been thinking that biology is only one part of what makes a family. Jorge was my father, but I never understood him. I doubt he ever understood me."

"I feel the same about Maggie, but I always had my father. I know him, or at least I thought I did."

She hadn't realized how truly unhappy he'd been for years. Foolishly, she'd imagined that she and her brothers were all he should need. The thoughts of a self-centered child.

"Maybe we don't ever get to know everything about our parents."

"Sure, I know that. It's just…I can't think of what it would do to my daddy." A sob she hadn't expected caught in her throat. "He's already been through so much. And I don't want to add to his pain."

He squeezed her tightly and kissed her temple. "Are you ever going to tell him you took the test?"

"I'm not sure. If I tell him, it will only be because I want to reassure him. But will that make it seem that I had my doubts I was really his daughter?"

"You know him better than I do, but I doubt that. He will understand that you had to be sure. Just please tell me you didn't do this because it's what I would have done."

"No, of course not." She put a finger to his lips. "This is all me. I made the choice."

"To be honest, I use to wonder if I could actually be my father's son. We were so different."

"But you loved him. I know you did."

"Yeah. I would have done anything to please him when I was young. To make him proud. But we had a difficult relationship. It's made me wonder if I should ever have children. I wouldn't want to ruin them the way my dad ruined me."

"You really feel that way? That he *ruined* you?"

"No, guess not. But for him, the rodeo was a status symbol. He'd brag about his son, the rodeo champ. That's not the way of the circuit. We try to keep it real. One day you're on top, the next you might be in traction. And skill isn't *always* a part of this. Sometimes it's luck which, by God, you never take for granted. But nobody liked my father much, and I had to defend him whenever he came around. Make excuses for him. Ultimately, he thought he created me. Turned me into the cowboy I became. You would think he considered the dangers of the profession. I don't think I'd want my son on a bucking bull. There are a lot of risks, and one of them is death."

She shivered at the thought of Wade dying. "You're talking to someone who rarely took any risks in life so maybe I'll never understand."

"It's not necessarily something to admire."

"For me, it is. The biggest risk I've ever taken is taking that DNA test."

"I'm glad to hear you admit it."

"Okay, you're right. It may not come out the way I want it to, and then I don't know what I'll do."

Wade brought her hand to his lips and kissed it. "You'll be okay because it won't change anything unless you let it. Hank is the father who raised you, who loved you, and never left you. That's a family."

But it would also mean she'd been abandoned twice, both by Rusty and Maggie.

"I didn't mean for this conversation to get so serious," Wade said, rolling her on top of him with a slow smile. "I'm ready to play again."

"Oh, yes, I can tell." She straddled him, threading her fingers through his. "Am I ready for the advanced course yet?"

"Let's say *I'm* not ready to show you the advanced course yet. But let me show you something else. And I think you'll like this."

Two hours later, she could say that she did. Oh, very much.

IT TOOK MUCH LONGER than Wade thought it would to disentangle from Daisy.

First, he didn't want to go anywhere else. Second, he didn't want to do anything else.

Third, whenever he thought to go back outside and see about the barn, she'd change his mind. She'd move a certain way or give him a wicked smile and he was gone. Just toast. For someone who had no experience, she was gifted and talented. Incredibly responsive to him.

Normally, he'd have never let anything he owned sit in complete ruin, but he had Daisy in his bed. Eager and willing and sweet. Addictive. He wasn't going anywhere for a while.

And face it, the barn wasn't something that could be repaired overnight. It would take time, effort, and was he stalling? You bet.

"What was it like, when you got injured?" Her head was resting on his abs, silky hair fanned out.

She wasn't asking him how much it had hurt, but the question might have normally extinguished any flame. Or he'd have thought it would. He didn't speak for a moment, simply collecting his thoughts. Beyond those memories of the moment just after the injury, he hadn't allowed himself to think much about that day.

"If you don't want to talk about it, it's okay." Her hand slid up and down his arm, in soothing strokes.

"I was tired, but otherwise I was having a normal day."

Out in California, the day had been warm and dry. His favorite kind of weather. Not as dusty as Texas, but hot and dusty all the same. A typical rodeo. A disastrous outcome for him.

"What happened?"

"I just… I lost my focus."

He wouldn't mention the woman who'd been vying for his affection at that moment, because he'd determined long ago that hadn't been the problem. No woman had ever distracted him from his job and purpose: winning. He still hadn't put his finger on what had gone wrong. Hadn't zeroed in on why and how one normal day went south in an instant.

Were he still riding, he'd have worked this problem out. Analyzed back and forth until he had the answer, just so he'd never repeat that particular misstep again. But as it worked out, he hadn't been pressed to do that. His career was over. Now, he wasn't sure this would be worth exploring. To what end?

"Do you think you lost your focus because of her?"

He didn't have to ask who she meant. Daisy was talking about his mother. "No."

"We'd lost her so recently, and after the funeral you went right back out."

"I had to."

"I know, but…maybe that's why. It was too much, too soon. You were out there again like nothing had happened."

"No, that's not it. I'm sure. I was doing fine."

That's what she'd wanted. She'd wanted him to move on, live, love, and move forward with no regrets, knowing she was in a better place. And that's exactly what he'd done.

"Because I know I wasn't doing fine. I loved her, too, Wade."

"I know. And she sure loved you."

You have no idea. He threaded his fingers through her soft strands of hair, wanting badly to redirect this conversation.

He hadn't allowed himself to wallow in grief because that was not productive. So, he'd moved on, even if that had become exponentially tougher when coming back to his family home. Her home. Try as he might talk himself into the thought that this hunk of junk, this land, was his, too, this still felt like his mother's place. Eventually, he'd put away all her knickknacks and finally clear out her desk.

For now, he would live the rest of his life to the fullest, ignoring the pain in his arm.

And if he ever wanted to forget, he currently had himself a nice distraction. "Daisy?"

"Hm?" She lifted her head and turned to him with a lazy smile.

He beckoned. "C'mere."

She did, straddling him with a smile, and for the next few hours he did his best to distract them both.

. . .

WADE WOKE before dawn the next morning and slid a hand down Daisy's naked back. "Peanut, we have to go see about the barn. I can't believe I let this go all night."

She rubbed her eyes, her sleep-mussed hair falling every which way. "I had you otherwise occupied."

"I enjoyed that a lot more, true, but I think it's time for me to stop being selfish." He rolled out of bed and walked toward the shower. "Care to join me?"

"Yes." She sat up, sheets falling to reveal her beautiful breasts. "Wade?"

"Yeah?"

"I think you definitely need to stop calling me Peanut now." She winked.

"If you say so, sweetheart. But I do like Peanut."

"You should call me 'honey.' Peanuts are salty."

He quirked a brow. "And your point is…?"

She threw a pillow at him, which he caught midair.

After a pillow fight, and a shower together, they'd had a quick breakfast. Quick, because Daisy burned the grits. And the bacon. Fortunately, he had cereal.

"Don't come in the barn until I'm sure the structure is safe enough out here," he instructed.

Wade *had* secretly hoped the Model T would be toast and he could justify junking it and getting it off his ranch. If he couldn't sell it, he could donate it. He didn't need it around but he'd kept it till this point because it made Daisy happy and distracted her from her problems for a while. But no such luck. Not a dent or scratch to be found on the auto. Shit fire!

Daisy, of course, ignored his request to stay away and followed him into the barn.

"This is amazing. Look at how well it held up." Daisy ran her hand down the hood of the car.

"Careful or you'll get a splinter." He handed her a pair of gloves and she slipped them on.

"I wish you didn't hate this car so much."

"I don't *hate* it. Hating it would take too much energy." He bent to pick up pieces of wood, throwing them outside in a pile.

At least a beam hadn't fallen. A shiver went through him. He didn't want to think about the kind of damage that could have done to Daisy.

Daisy picked up a shingle and threw it in the pile. "If you don't hate it, then what would you call it?"

"A bad reminder."

"Of…?"

"Pride. Excess. Ego. Greed." He stopped to think. "I think that's it."

"Wow, no wonder you hate it!"

"The car reminds me of my father's worst traits. You might not remember, but he collected these. Bought one from my tournament winnings every time he could. Said it was an *investment.* For a rancher, that makes very little sense. We invest in farm equipment, ATVs, feed, cattle, horses. Of course, he wound up using these cars to further feed his gambling habit. When he lost, he sold a car, and went back to the tables."

"But he kept this one for you. There's probably a reason for that."

He thought the reason might be that his father simply ran out of time. One more loss and this one would have been gone, too. There was no real way to know. It was only after his death that Wade learned the enormity of his father's gambling addiction. And it had been a punch to the gut. Had Wade known he was funding his habit, instead of simply supporting the ranch, he would have stopped the rodeo a while ago. Or at the very least, he'd have stopped the bleeding. No pun intended.

Daisy stared up at the ceiling, and at the beam of sunlight, no longer held back by the impediment of a roof. "It's time for a good old-fashioned barn raising."

But he'd have to dig deep into the small amount of cash he had left for the materials even if he got the help from his neighbors with manpower. The plan had been to get this ranch profitable and *then* fix the barn.

"I'll start the phone tree," Daisy said.

Chapter 17

The phone tree.

Wade had almost forgotten about that antiquated benefit of living in Stone Ridge. Any time someone needed help, the phone tree was alerted, and all the available men would head to the destination. Because he traveled so much, he hadn't been around for many of them, though he had participated whenever he was home.

The most recent of those times had been when little Jimmy Ray had wandered off after a town barbecue. A whole squad of men organized a search, and it had been Lincoln who found him. Shortly before that, he'd helped on repairs of the town's first school.

Being on the giving end of their system was one thing, but Wade never expected to be on the receiving end of the phone tree.

"Hang on." Wade followed Daisy into the kitchen where she picked up the landline. "I don't need to bother them. I can probably take care of this on my own. I'll just add it to the list."

The growing list.

"Wade, are you too *proud* to accept help?"

Yes.

He scoffed. "Absolutely not. But the phone tree is for people who are desperate. I can take care of this myself."

"Riggs asked for help when someone put a hole in the fence between your properties and let Satan through it. He had to repair it quickly, so he used the phone tree."

"That's different. There's no danger here, as long as *you* stay out of the barn."

Daisy ignored him, picking up the phone. When he reached to take the handset from her, she put a finger to his lips.

"Hello, Mima? Wade needs some men over here. The barn fell down. Yes, you heard me right. It's an old-fashioned barn raising. Tell Lincoln and Jackson, and then the next man on the list. I'm going to stick around and help the men."

She hung up, and when he held out his arms wide, she folded right into them. "There. It's done."

"And how are you going to help us, exactly?" He kissed her temple, taking in the sweet coconut scent of her hair.

"I'm going to take care of the car."

"Of course."

She wrapped her arms around his waist. "I would decorate the tree, but we need to do that *together*. Later."

"Right. We'll decorate the tree and then we'll decorate each other."

"I can't wait to see a big, red bow on you."

"I'm going to put a lot of tinsel all over you." He slid her a slow smile.

"Tinsel?"

"The silver stuff that takes forever to pull off, you find it in the house year-round, and probably still on the tree next Christmas. I'm going to have a lot of fun taking it off you slowly and all year long."

"Aw."

For once, he'd said the right thing, judging by the sparkle in her eyes.

Yes, Daisy. I want to be with you for a long time, should I be that lucky.

He and Daisy pushed the Model T out of the barn and off to the side. They cleared the area of debris and wood. Then Wade went for his hammer, saw, and tools. Not long after, the men began to arrive in trucks. The Henderson brothers, Sean and Riggs, both upset that Wade hadn't run right over there yesterday after it all happened. He almost told them he'd been otherwise occupied and quite distracted but instead told them he'd been sulking.

"That's what we're here for," Riggs said, grabbing his tools from the truck bed. "Neighbors helping each other."

"But I haven't been around enough to help much."

"Well, that will change." Sean clapped Wade on the back.

It was good to know no one resented him for being gone so much, coming back only occasionally to see his mother or work for Hank between tournaments. Wade didn't think he'd been a good enough neighbor, not for years, but he would do better now.

Lincoln, Jackson, and even Hank arrived shortly thereafter, carrying tools and plenty of wood.

"I'll pay you back for all this wood," Wade protested to Lincoln.

"Yeah, you will. You can pay me back next time any of us is in trouble or in need. I'm sure you'll come through." Lincoln turned to Daisy. "Hiya. You got here quick."

"Yeah, well, I was already—" Daisy began, then

stopped. Clearly, she'd lost her nerve. "Um, I was here to work on the car and saw all the damage."

"Did you *already* find a project while you're on furlough?" Jackson asked.

"She's fascinated by my old man's Model T."

"It withstood the roof falling in on it. Solid steel," Daisy said, flexing a muscle.

The way she loved that car was rather annoying. And also, a little inspiring. She didn't give up on old and broken things. Good to know.

"Did you hear it fall, Wade?" Lincoln said.

"Oh, I heard it. Ran for my shotgun until I realized the building had fallen down."

"Lucky thing that no one got hurt," Jackson said.

"Yeah, lucky." Wade met Daisy's eyes. She smiled at their private joke.

Within the hour, a whole crew of men had arrived. Jeremy, Levi, even old Lenny, who brought cold cuts and beer and set it all up on his tailgate. It was incredible to see the outpouring of support. Wade couldn't remember a time when his father had called for help. There had been plenty of times when he needed it, too, but to Jorge Cruz, asking for help meant admitting failure. He'd drilled that into Wade, too, and that's why he'd never asked for help from anyone in digging his way out of the hole that his father created for him.

This would be one more way he'd take a different path from his father. He would take the help same as he would always willingly give it. It was about community, and he'd fallen out of the rodeo just to find one that had always been here.

Around dinnertime, Winona and Delores drove over in a truck loaded with food. They served up fried chicken, mashed potatoes, onion rings, corn, fried okra, peach and apple pies.

"We've been cookin' all day between wrangling twins," Delores said, one baby on her hip.

Winona carried the other one on her hip as she dished out apple pie. If she'd ever been a stuck-up Nashville celebrity, as the rumor went, it sure didn't show. And Wade hadn't tasted food this delicious since his mother's home cooking. The memory brought about a fresh new wave of pain and he pushed it back down. She'd be proud of what they'd all done here today. And happy that Wade had accepted the assistance.

By the end of the day, the new frame was up, and part of the new roof, surprising even Wade as to how much could be done quickly with serious manpower. But the sun was setting and the temperatures dropping. A cold wind rapidly descended, the air moist and…

"It had better not snow," Wade muttered seconds before the first snow flurry fell.

They fell one after another like little pieces of cotton straight into the new barn. Wonderful. It almost never snowed in this part of Texas.

"Look, Joey!" Winona cried out, bouncing the baby in her arms. "It's snowing! Cal! Check it out!"

"Don't get too excited." Lincoln chuckled. "I'll be lucky to gather up the size of a snow cone to show Sammy."

"Everyone who can, meet back up here tomorrow and let's finish up the roof," Riggs ordered. "For now, let's all get somewhere dry and warm."

He took one of his sons and led his wife back to the truck. Delores followed them, holding the other twin. Knowing his time was limited, Wade ran from one man to the next, thanking him personally. Shaking each hand.

"No problem, son. This is what we do," said Hank.

"I'm happy to help." Derek clapped Wade's shoulder.

Wade thanked twenty men or more. The last men he had to thank were his best friends in the world. Lincoln, Jackson, and Beau Stephens. They accepted his thanks, adding their own disappointment that Wade hadn't called them all sooner.

"I still need to talk to you, Linc," Wade said. "But I've taken enough of your time today. Your wife and son are no doubt waiting for you."

"We'll talk soon. I'll be back tomorrow after morning chores." Lincoln headed to his truck, then called after Daisy, "Need a ride home? The roads will be icy."

"No, I'm fine," Daisy said from behind Wade. "Thank you, though."

"If it gets too icy, I'll drive her home," Wade said. "Don't worry."

"Oh, sure. Yeah." Lincoln climbed in his truck and adjusted his long legs. "Thanks."

He exchanged a quick look with Wade, and in that moment, he was sure that Lincoln understood something had changed. In the old days, they could almost read each other's minds. Then Lincoln shook his head as if he were talking himself out of the thought and drove off with a wave.

Wade pulled Daisy close. "He knows."

"Well, so what?" She burrowed her face in his jacket. "He'll be fine."

"I noticed *you* didn't tell him you were here all night."

"I started to, but…best to ease him into this, don't you think? And not start off by letting him know we're already sleeping together."

"Yeah." He pulled her into his arms, knowing she had

to be cold. She wasn't wearing much of a jacket. "Get your sexy butt inside right now before you freeze."

AS IF LAST night and today wasn't enough, Daisy would also have a white Christmas.

She didn't think she'd ever been happier in her life. Just watching Wade's eyes light up when he saw how much help had come his way. Almost the entire town, save some men who were probably too old or too young to be of any assistance. Even Lenny showed up just to help with food and beverages.

Her heart expanded with joy for Wade. He was finally understanding that he didn't have to do this all alone. He'd mentioned missing the community of the rodeo circuit, and hopefully he'd see that he already had that here in spades.

He belonged. He was finally home for good.

"I'll make a fire," Wade said. "Then I'll drive you home."

She watched him work, squatting in front of the fire, the muscles on his forearms and back bunching. Lust swept through her like a tidal wave. She'd seen good-looking men before, but Wade was different. You couldn't label him handsome or a pretty boy. He was strong and…rugged. His dark hair and olive skin made him stand out in a crowd.

When the flames licked out of the fire, Wade came to sit beside Daisy on the leather couch. He put his arm around her, and she curled into his body.

"If you're trying to get rid of me, this isn't the way to do it."

"I don't want you to go. But you don't live here, Pea— I mean, I need to take you home."

That slip to call her Peanut again was classic, trying to throw up his walls again. Creating a safe distance between them. Because this cowboy had taken risks all his life but clearly never many with his heart.

This time, Daisy wouldn't have it. She was a risk-taker, too, damn it, and she'd proved that.

"What are you doing, Wade? Are you trying to put some distance between us again?"

"No!" he protested just a little *too* quickly.

"It's Lincoln, isn't it? It's bothering you that he suspects."

"I tried to tell him. It didn't work out. Today didn't seem like the right time, either." He studied the fire, his fingers playing almost absentmindedly with her hair.

"Please don't pull away from me. Lincoln is going to be just fine. It's none of his business."

"It's just…more than that. I'm in uncharted territory and while normally the thrill of that would be calling to me this…is different."

"How so?"

"When I saw you lying there, part of the barn on top of you…" He squeezed tighter. "It's different when someone you love is in danger. I don't mind it for me, but I don't ever want to see you like that again."

All Daisy heard out of that sentence was the word *love.* "You love me?"

"You know I do. I've known you all your life. Loved you for at least half of it."

"That's not what I meant."

He chuckled. "I know what you meant. You don't let me get away with much, and I like that. Now I realize it's exactly what I need."

"Because I love you, but I'm also *in love* with you. I'm not sure exactly when this happened, but before you say it, this doesn't have anything to do with last night. It's not that I think I have to wind up with the first man I ever slept with, even if it is you. It's just that…it's *always* been you. You know?"

He slid her a slow smile. "What do you mean last night had nothing to do with it? That wasn't love-inducing sex?"

"You know it was."

He kissed her, a long and deep kiss full of promise.

"You're not in this alone. I doubt that I'll ever be good enough for you, but if you'll have this broke-down cowboy, then…I'm in. Sweetheart, I'm all in."

She smiled against his lips and kissed him back with all the love and emotion in her heart.

Because for the first time in her life, Daisy Carver felt truly and wonderfully…chosen.

Chapter 18

Dear Albert,

Well, I am just beside myself with worry. Daisy spends less and less time at home and more at that Wade's ranch. Claims it's something about a car project. Sometimes, I fear she's far more like her mother than any of us want to believe. She's always favored Maggie, looks-wise, but that's where their similarities ended. Because while Maggie thought of herself as the queen of England, little Daisy has always been a tomboy. Chasing after her big brothers, bringing home frogs and sticks.

Boys were her best friends. She rarely played with girls and dolls but preferred cars. But after she became a young lady, I'd be lying to say that I didn't notice little changes here and there. She wore only a certain type of Wranglers, and a size too small. She occasionally had her hair cut and styled by some fancy schmancy salon in Kerrville, and please let's not talk about the shoes.

Now, she's after a rodeo cowboy just like Maggie Mae. What is this mess? Albert, if she winds up pregnant, what am I to do? Help! I need help from beyond!

"Get ahold of yourself, woman! You're hysterical. If I

wasn't a figment of your imagination, I'd have to slap you." Albert appeared, sitting on the edge of their bed.

Still wearing the same Stetson he'd worn on the day he dropped dead halfway to the barn.

"I've always loved you in that hat."

"Want to know what I think? You worry she's more like *you*. After all, you were the one who raised her. The only mother she's ever known."

"You're talking about Ray, aren't you?"

"The rodeo cowboy that broke your heart. Yeah, that's who I'm talkin' about. Luckiest day of your life when you met me. I was the best thing to ever happen to a heartbroken teenager." He tapped his chest proudly.

Truer words were rarely spoken.

"He turned my head around, Albert. So bright and shiny he blinded me with his devastating good looks and attention. I thought he loved me."

"And where was this man from, again?" Albert cocked his head and narrowed his eyes.

"Stop that! You know very well that he wasn't from Stone Ridge. What does that have to do with it?"

"I think you know."

"You make it sound as if there's something in our water."

He shook his head. "Not the water. There's something about the women."

Albert always did know the right thing to say. She'd give him that.

"The biddies of SORROW always talk on and on about how special the men are. But let's talk about you women now. You *know* you're special, so you don't accept scraps from your men. You want to be first, and so you are. Demand what you deserve, and you'll get it. And our women *are* special."

If this were true, and Albert was right, then maybe Daisy also would demand to be first with Wade. This didn't have to be another "rodeo cowboy breaks young lady's heart romance."

This wasn't Lillian's story, after all.

It was Daisy's.

"Wade was raised by Rose, and he will love and treat our Daisy the way she should be."

"Oh, Rose." And just like that, tears flooded her eyes. "She should be here to see this. If only..."

"Those are the two saddest words in the world, you used to say. *If only.* Why not switch it up to 'but instead'? But instead of getting to see her son be with Daisy while she's alive, she'll have to see it from wherever she is right now."

"Albert, surely she's in heaven."

He winked. "Of course, darlin'. Don't you doubt it."

Lillian heard rattling around in the kitchen.

"She's home."

Lillian threw on a housecoat over her nightgown and rushed to the kitchen. Lately, she hadn't been getting up early enough to cook breakfast. She didn't see the point anymore. Now that Brenda took care of the ranch hands and cowboys, Lillian only had herself and Daisy. More often than not, Daisy ate a light breakfast on her way to work. All she seemed to care about was a steady diet of caffeine.

"Good morning, sugar."

Daisy spun around, a big smile splitting her face. "Morning."

Oh, my girl, it is good to see you this happy.

Every once in a while, the memory of those tear-streaked cheeks on three-year-old Daisy stole Lillian's peace. The rest of her life had been spent happily wiping away that pain. Daisy deserved true and lasting love. Happiness and security. A man who adored her. Everything.

"I haven't seen much of you around here lately."

"I'm sorry. I've been getting in so late every night, but I'll start having breakfast with you every morning." Daisy set a mug of coffee down in front of Lillian.

"There's no need. I just wonder who is taking up so much of your time."

Daisy froze in the middle of pouring her coffee and Lillian had her answer. "I've been meaning to talk to you about this."

"What is it, baby girl?" Lillian patted the seat next to hers, indicating Daisy should sit.

She did, but Lillian sensed a thread of reluctance. Fear struck her heart and for the millionth time she wished Albert were here if only to simply hold her hand.

"I have something to tell you and I…hope you're not angry with me."

Lillian steeled herself for the news. It couldn't be horrible news because Daisy seemed happy. Could she already be *pregnant*? But no, Wade hadn't even been home long enough. Maybe they'd run off somewhere to get married? No. She discounted that immediately. That wasn't Daisy's way. She'd want her family there. Perhaps…

"I took the DNA test."

Lillian set her mug down with a thud, and coffee sloshed around inside.

"Please don't be mad."

"I'm not mad, child. Just…surprised. I assume the results show you're Hank's child?" For what other reason could Daisy be so happy?

"I don't know yet. The results will come any day now."

Daisy took a swallow of her coffee. "You're the first person I've told."

"You've been keeping this to yourself all this time? You must be in knots."

What a burden for her poor Daisy.

"No, I told Wade. He was the only one who knew what I was doing. And he's been there for me every step. He went with me to get the test when I asked him to take me. He held my hand. He…he…" Daisy's voice grew thick with emotion and her breath hitched. "We've grown so close because of all this. I just don't think I would have made it through this without him."

"You're scared, aren't you?"

"There are no guarantees. No matter what, I'll always be a Carver. I'll just find out if I'm one by blood, too. But there are all kinds of families and you'll always be mine. The only mother I ever had."

Lillian pushed back the emotion clogging her throat, because if she didn't, she wouldn't be able to talk. She wouldn't be able to reason with Daisy. "It isn't like you to take a risk like this."

"I know. I've played it safe all my life. I dropped my middle name. And I've tried my best not to look like her." Daisy took a breath. "But, Mima, if I'm not Daddy's daughter, we don't *have* to tell him. It might break his heart and I don't want that. I just had to know."

"Why did *you* have to know?"

"Because I don't like not knowing. All my life, this was supposed to be an ugly rumor. What if it's true? I can't be afraid of the truth. No more secrets, not for me."

Lillian nodded slowly. "You will tell *me* the results, won't you?"

"If you'd like."

"Now, of course, I *have* to know."

But Lillian didn't think this was a wise thing to have done since the outcome mattered so much to all of them. Even Daisy, whether or not she wanted to admit it.

"Did Wade talk you into this?"

"No! Why would you say that?"

"The boy has taken a lot of risks in his life. This would be just one more to him. But maybe some things should be better left alone."

"I disagree or I wouldn't have done this. And it was entirely up to me. He had nothing to do with my decision. I think secrets that are kept buried can only hurt people more in the long run."

"What will you do with the money if you're Rusty's daughter? Will you take it?"

"I don't want any of his inheritance, so I'll just let his brother take it all."

"And if he *is* your father, you don't want to know him?"

"I don't see why. He abandoned me just as much as my mother did. It took him years to be curious whether or not he actually had a daughter. Years spent as a rodeo cowboy, having a good ol' time. I don't want to know him now, even if he is my flesh and blood."

Dear Lord, Lillian hadn't *considered* that. If this were true, and this Mr. Rusty was her father, her girl had been abandoned twice. And the one man who had never left her side might not even be her real father. No. *No*, it wasn't possible. Hank was Daisy's father. There could be no other way.

"I'm sorry, I shouldn't have told you any of this. I hadn't meant to, but…you could tell there was something on my mind."

"Thank you for telling me. I'll take this with me to my grave."

"*What?*" Daisy blinked and reached for Lillian's hand. "Why? Is something wrong? Are you sick?"

"Don't worry none, sugar. But I'm old and won't be around forever." Especially the way this heart of hers ached at the moment. *That* couldn't be good.

"Whew, you had me worried." Daisy went back to her coffee.

"You and Wade seem to be spending a lot of time together," Lillian said carefully.

"At first, he was the only one I could talk to about all this. It wouldn't affect him one way or another and so it was easier to talk to him. Then, there was my car project over there. The Model T was taking my mind off my troubles."

"And…that's it?"

She hesitated. "I know you don't like Wade for me."

"Well, I may have overreacted."

"You think? Having a fainting spell when you heard we were dating?"

"*Fake* dating, you mean, or so you said."

"I wasn't lying!"

"But it turned into something real, didn't it?"

Daisy lowered her eyes and nodded.

"And does he feel the same way?"

"Yes."

Lillian could have warned the girl not to play with fire, but then again, she didn't know that Wade's own mother had predicted their love years ago. And if she was right, and it appeared that she had been, a long and happy marriage with many children had been assured.

At least, Lillian hoped, if Rose was right about the two of them then she was right about all of it.

"You know, Rose loved you very much," Lillian said, patting Daisy's hand. "She was quite friendly with your mother. You used to spend a lot of time over there, you and Maggie Mae. Wade used to entertain you, according to Rose. Only he could get you to stop whining."

"I don't remember that."

"No, you were far too young. I probably should have allowed you to spend more time over there after Maggie left us, but you wanted to stay close to home."

Facts were, Lillian did resent Rose for a time after Maggie Mae left. Surely Rose knew *something* about where she'd gone, and why? They'd been close, after all. But Rose claimed not to know.

"I asked Wade about Maggie Mae. He said she was always nice to him."

"Your mother *was* nice, sugar. She made a terrible mistake but until that day, she'd been a good mother to all of you and always done the best she could."

Daisy nodded. "I suppose she had her own issues, whatever they were. Now that I'm older, I can almost forgive her. Maybe she felt second best to Brenda. Maybe she didn't feel loved by Daddy."

"Hank could have done better."

"But maybe sometimes you just can't help who you love."

"Yes, Rose would have said it's written in the stars." Fanciful talk for a rancher's wife, but that was Rose. "Wade is shiny and bright, and he'll take any woman's breath away, but is he solid? Is he someone you can count on? Be sure that he will love you till the day he dies, just like my Albert did. Because I want nothing less than that for you, my sweet girl."

WADE WOKE the next morning before dawn, feeling well rested for the first time in weeks. His arm hurt, as usual, but even that was at an acceptable and bearable level of pain. No pill required. He couldn't give full credit to great sex, though that certainly hadn't hurt anything. But sex had never given him this kind of peace before. It had never given him this kind of…certainty and purpose. Clarity.

He wondered exactly when he'd fallen in love with Daisy Carver. Because, damn, he sure didn't see *that* coming.

Had he fallen for her the night she beat him at pool or the night she cautiously met him behind the tree at the Riverwalk? Maybe it was the day he'd taken her for the DNA test, and she'd shown him a kind of courage he hadn't seen in the toughest and craziest rodeo cowboy.

Realistically, it could have well been the day he kissed her for the first time when she was only eighteen. And something wild and untamed had unfurled inside of him. Something that scared the spit out of him and had him running from her ever since that moment.

But there was no doubt now. When she slid those green eyes in his direction, when she tossed that blond hair, or shook her finger at him, he was a goner. Certified, one hundred percent *lost*. Taken. She gave him back everything he thought he'd lost. All that adulation and approval from the masses was replaced by one little spitfire that gave as good as she got.

And if he lived to be one hundred, he now believed she was all he'd ever need.

Wade was drinking the last dregs of his coffee when Lincoln showed up. Earlier than everyone else, which was no surprise to Wade.

He walked outside to meet him, just as the first rays of the sun were rising. "Hey."

Lincoln shut the door to his truck. "I'm early, so we can talk."

"Walk with me."

The morning air still carried a chill, but as predicted, the patches of snow were nearly gone. Wade walked next to his oldest friend, who might someday be family. He hoped.

"I like what you've done here," Lincoln remarked, nudging his chin toward the pastures.

"There's more work to be done."

"Plenty and always. That will never change."

"Maybe, but someday I'll no longer be in the red and trying to catch up. The ranch will be self-sustaining."

They walked to the edge of the field where in the distance the cattle could be seen, some grazing, some lying down.

"This is about Daisy, isn't it?" Lincoln said. "That's why you wanted to talk to me."

Wade simply nodded.

"Uh-huh. My bride and I talked long into the night. She saw something that I didn't without you even telling her. But I didn't catch on." Lincoln shoved his hands in the pockets of his leather jacket. "How long has this been going on between you two?"

"Not long at all. It really was fake in the beginning. I wouldn't have lied to you. I never have."

"I know." Lincoln nodded. "I'm hardly in a position to judge you. I fell for Beau's little sister, after all. He was okay with it."

"Sadie has loved you half of her life. And Beau knew it."

Lincoln kicked a rock with his boot. "And if I'm being honest, I know Daisy has loved you for half her life, but I had hoped it was a crush. I just didn't see anything ever coming of it. You weren't ever going to settle down. You weren't going to leave the rodeo."

"I never thought I'd say this but I'm damn glad about the injury. Happy to be a broke-down cowboy. If I hadn't been stopped, I would have missed out on the best thing that ever happened to me."

"Daisy?"

"Don't sound so surprised." Wade chuckled. "Swear to God, Linc, I'm in love with her."

Lincoln grinned. "Hot damn. How about that?"

"Buddy, no one's more shocked than I am. Just didn't see this coming. Had I seen it, maybe I would have stepped aside."

"Why?"

"We both know that she can do better than me."

"Nah, I don't know a better man."

"I thought I couldn't fall in love. Thought it had been beaten right outta me. But she surprised me."

"Well, that's our Daisy. She never gave up on you." Lincoln clapped Wade's back.

"She doesn't give up on people. Anyone she loves."

"You're damn lucky to be one of them."

"And don't I know it."

They stood quietly for a few minutes, two old friends watching the sunrise.

BY MIDDAY, Wade had himself a brand-new barn. And it was far better than the first.

After the crew had left, he was just about to rustle up some lunch when he remembered checking the mailbox for Daisy. And the envelope had finally arrived, a plain and white letter-sized envelope from the laboratory. Simple enough. Able to change many people's lives. This little piece of paper might destroy everything, or simply cement it into place. He walked back with the envelope, turning it over in his hands, wishing he had X-ray vision.

Because one thing had become clear to him since the moment he realized he'd fallen in love with Daisy. This suddenly felt like a huge risk to him as well, like one that had the power to upend his world. But only if it didn't contain the right answer. Surely it would. The odds were fifty-fifty anyway, and on some days, he'd call that good odds. He'd been a glass-half-full type of guy for most of his life.

If Daisy wasn't Hank's daughter, it would make no difference to Wade. That hadn't changed. But what had changed was that he understood, whether she wanted to admit it or not, the wrong outcome was going to destroy Daisy. And suddenly the risk felt a lot closer to home for him. He wished maybe he'd tried to talk her out of this, but if he had, maybe they wouldn't have become this close. He might not have fallen in love with her but still be ambling around this big ranch trying to deal with feeling so alone even with an entire town behind him.

He'd felt undeserving of anyone's help, but Daisy had changed all that for him. Because if she loved him, there must be something fundamentally good and worthy in him. And it was likely the same trait his mother saw. He was going to go out on a limb and call that good and worthy thing in him his heart. The one part of him that had never been battered, bruised, and broken on the circuit. He'd protected that organ fairly well, all things considered.

After lunch, someone was at his door again. He opened it to find the lady from the dating show, along with Beulah.

"Hello there, Wade," said Beulah.

"Come on in, ladies." Wade held the door open, making a sweeping motion with his arm. "Would anyone like some lunch? It's a casserole."

"How sweet of you to ask, but no. This should be quick." Beulah looked expectantly at the woman next to her.

Was her name Georgia? Oh no, Savannah.

"Great news, Mr. Cowboy!" Savannah said. "I was able to negotiate a cash offer for you to do the show. The producers are on board. All I need to do is have them watch some film of you in action, roping those cows and riding those bulls. You're exactly what we need. What size tux do you wear?"

"Now there's something you don't hear every day. I have no idea what size I wear, Miss Ackerman, seeing as I don't believe I've ever worn a penguin suit."

"No problem, we'll take your measurements."

Wade held up his palms. "Hold up. I *never* agreed to this."

"Why, Wade Cruz, are you saying no to this generous offer?" Beulah nudged Savannah. "Show him the money. That's all these young people seem to care about."

"Of course." Savannah whipped out what appeared to be a several-inches-thick contract and flipped to a page. She handed it to Wade. "*This* is what we're talking about."

Wade was sure his eyes bugged out of his head. This figure was equivalent to winning a tournament, one of the biggest. This money could secure his future on the ranch. And realistically, when could he ever earn this kind of money again?

All for dating a bunch of women?

And promising to marry one, Einstein.

A lot of money, and he couldn't take a penny of it. No question. He handed the contract back.

"Very generous."

Beulah clapped her hands. "Wonderful!"

"And I can't take it." Wade removed his hat and ran a hand through his hair.

"Why can't you? Don't *tell* me it's not enough money for you." Beulah clutched her chest as if the very thought would bring on full cardiac arrest.

"It's plenty, and I would do it, but the thing is…I'm taken."

"Since when?" Beulah went hands on hips. "I want a *name*, and I want it now. Don't you care about your town, young man? This is your community. You're just lyin' to an old woman just like you did before."

"Not like before. It really is Daisy. At first, we *were* pretending. But I promise you that I'm not pretending anymore. I'm in love with her."

"Butter my biscuit! You mean Rose was right? You and *Daisy?*"

Wade nodded, smiling a little because he didn't seem able to help it.

"What's happening?" Savannah said. "Is he refusing the money? I don't understand."

"Yes, he is," Beulah said, holding up her index finger, pontificating. "Proving, as I firmly believed, that love has *nothing* to do with money."

"Well, of all the nerve," Savannah said. "Do you know how many heads I had to go over to get this money for you? How many hours of *rodeo* I had to watch? And now you refuse it?"

"Don't worry, we'll find someone else."

"Well, I don't know if we will," Savannah said, stalking off. "I don't understand you people."

"Our young ladies in town get first dibs on our men." Beulah followed her. "I thought you understood this. But we have plenty more where Wade came from. Why, I've already spoken to Sean…he's a rancher, and his brother is married to Winona…"

Her voice drifted as she followed Savannah out the front door.

Wade watched all that money walk away, wishing he could have taken it if nothing else for Daisy's sake. If only it wasn't a stupid dating show. He could promise her the future she deserved. Unfortunately, the strings attached to that mess would lose him what he really wanted. Kind of a catch-22.

Besides, he'd just determined the cost of his soul. Priceless.

Which didn't make this any easier.

Chapter 19

The night of the Nativity play arrived, and Daisy expected Wade to meet her at Trinity Church. She'd had to come with Mima, Jackson, Eve, Lincoln, and Sadie because Sammy was starring in the play. It was a family affair. Even Daddy and Brenda came, eager to see Sammy nail the part. The kid was so cute Daisy didn't see how anyone couldn't love him. Perfect casting. Ha!

The manger scene was set up outside the steps of the church, complete with a cow from the Henderson farm, and a couple of lambs from a farmer from Nothing. Some of the kids from Sadie's classroom were playing Mary, Joseph, and the Angel Gabriel. Pastor June was herding them all like tiny cattle.

"Do you think it's too cold outside?" Sadie said, clutching Sammy to her breast. "I don't want him to get sick."

"Now, sugar, don't worry," Mima said. "Our Sammy is made of tough stuff."

"Just like his daddy," Eve said.

"He is the savior to the world, Sadie," Jackson quipped. "You *have* to share him."

"Jackson!" Eve scolded, but she had a smile on her face.

"You're hilarious." Daisy elbowed Jackson.

"Thank you for noticing, Shortie."

"Has anyone seen Wade?" Daisy asked. "He should be here by now."

And then she saw him ambling toward them, wearing his black Stetson and a slow smile. Her heart tugged with an almost painful tenderness. She loved this man so much she almost couldn't breathe when he walked into a room. His gaze landed on her, as usual taking her in like he'd never seen her before, even though they'd practically grown up together. This had always made her feel…new.

"Go kiss your boyfriend like a proper girlfriend does," Lincoln said.

Daisy whipped her head around to see if her big brother was teasing. The expression on his face told her everything she needed to know.

"He told me just this morning."

"Told you what?" Jackson said. "What am I missing here?"

"Keep up, son," Mima said.

"I'll tell you later," Lincoln said, then turned to Daisy. "Or maybe Daisy will."

Taking her cue, Daisy walked straight toward Wade's open arms in front of the entire family. And she shouldn't have been surprised at the chorus of *Aws*. Mostly coming from the women, sure, but she would take it. She heard their voices carrying behind her.

"What a shock," Jackson chuckled. "Like I didn't see this coming."

"It's so sweet and took way too long." Eve sniffed. "I'm so happy I might cry."

"Me too," Brenda said. "Here, I brought some tissues."

"Rose was right all along," Mima said.

"I really don't understand how anyone could have missed this," Sadie said.

"Baba, bibi," said Sammy.

"That's right, Son," Hank said. "About time."

"Hey," Wade chuckled, folding her into his arms. "Guessing everyone knows about us now."

Daisy pressed her face into the warmth of his chest. "And they're okay with it."

"Even your grandmother?"

"As long as I'm happy."

As the play began, Pastor June reading from the Bible, everyone drew closer and assembled. Daisy stood, Wade behind her, his arms wrapped around her waist. The cow began to moo in the middle of the most important scene. One lamb wandered off, and Sammy had a fit when Sadie dared to put him in the makeshift crib and walk a few inches away from him. So, she carried baby Jesus, and the rest of the play had to go on like that.

It was funny, and cute, and just what one expected from a play starring a cow, lambs, children, and a baby.

Later, after the play had ended, and everyone got treated to Christmas cookies and hot cocoa, Wade drove Daisy home to his place.

And even though it was a little chilly outside, Daisy rolled the window down and stuck her head out. She let the Texas wind blow through her hair as she smelled the welcome scent of fresh-cut grass, the humidity in the air a gift at this time of the year.

It just didn't get any better than this. She had everything she'd ever wanted.

When Wade pulled in and parked, Daisy climbed out of the truck and ran into the moonlit field.

"Catch me if you can," she called out, spinning her arms like the lady in *The Sound of Music*.

Like some kind of a loon. That was her. She was a loon now.

Crazy in love and stupid happy.

"I can." Wade easily caught her from behind and pulled her to him. "How old do you think I am?"

"You're not old at all," she said, leaning her back into him.

"Older than you, but young enough to keep up." He spun her around to face him. "Hey. I need to tell you something."

"Tell me something." She curled her hands around his neck.

"Your results came today."

That took the steam right out of her. "Oh."

"You don't *have* to open that envelope." He lowered his arms around her waist, settling his hands at the small of her back. "Not if you don't want to. No one will ever know but you and I."

"But...I took the test. Why wouldn't I open it?"

"It scares you and I can see that now. You don't have to do this."

"You already told me that."

"Maybe I should have talked you out of it."

"Why would you?"

"Because I don't want you to get hurt, and it feels like a bigger chance to take now."

"I love you, too, Wade." She smiled. "Are you scared for me? Because I'm not."

"I love you, and I'm...yeah, a little bit scared."

To know her fearless rodeo cowboy was scared for her was the most tender thing she'd ever seen.

"And just like I was okay when the barn fell down, I'll be okay this time, too. No matter what."

"Swear that to me."

"I pinky swear." She held out her finger.

He took it, wrapped it around his own and brought both to his lips to brush a kiss. "Okay."

In that moment, with Wade's love and quiet, unrelenting support, Daisy considered that she might *not* open the envelope. Why bother when she had everything she'd ever need? She didn't need to know, when her heart was already so certain.

Later that night, she lay tangled in Wade's arms, her cheek resting on his chest. He had a powerful heart, thudding with steady, even beats. It reassured her more than she would have believed. He'd live a long life and she'd never have to lose him.

Not to the rodeo. Not to a reality dating show. Not to someone else.

Here was someone who loved and would never leave her.

"Do you know what we forgot to do again? We forgot the poor tree. It's two days before Christmas."

"We got it late. There's nothing sayin' that it can't go up on Christmas Eve."

"That's what we'll do. Make a night of it."

"Sounds good."

"Hey? Did you ever hear back from the show about the money?"

"Yeah. They came by earlier today. The offer was... generous."

Daisy sat up. "Are you kidding me? I didn't think they

actually would. They never offer money. They must have really wanted you."

"It doesn't matter. I refused their kind offer because I'm taken."

Daisy's heart was a quivering mess of ribbons and curls. "I can't believe you did that for me."

"And I'd do it again."

"What did Beulah say?"

"She didn't believe me at first, and we sure didn't help the situation by lying. But in the end, I convinced her."

"Was she too upset?"

"Not at all. She explained to the lady that the women in Stone Ridge have first dibs." He tugged on a lock of her hair.

"Thank goodness I saw you first." She gave him a long, deep kiss. "But I hate that you didn't get that money."

"It's money I didn't have before so no big loss."

"I'll make it up to you. I'm going to be the best girl-friend you've ever had."

He cocked his head and smiled. "Sweetheart, that's a *very* low bar."

"We can't have that. But I do have an idea."

"What's that?"

She slid one finger slowly down his abs, and lower… watching his expression darken with heat. "I've been read-ing, and I think I'm ready for the advanced course."

"Oh, yeah." He grinned, splaying his hands behind his neck.

And then she proceeded to rock his world.

During the night, Daisy woke to rays of ambient moonlight spilling through the blinds. Wade was asleep next to her, soundly, one arm thrown over her waist. She shifted, not wanting to wake him, but desperately needing a drink of water. Those darn holiday cookies always made her parched.

Sammy was so cute tonight, his dimpled smile so reminiscent of her big brother. He was sort of Lincoln's mini-me. Just like that she pictured Wade's son, a little carbon copy of him. Running around climbing and jumping off everything. She would watch him like a hawk.

Finding a cold water bottle in the fridge, she uncapped it, then walked over to the framed photo of Rose smiling back at her. She picked up the photo and kissed Rose's sweet face.

"I miss you, Rose, and I promise to take care of him. Forever."

The photo was one of those understated professional photos taken for Trinity's congregation directory a few years ago. Pastor June had hired a photographer and asked families to come and have their pictures taken. Daisy remembered the day well, feeling badly for Rose. She took her photo alone. Her husband had died, and Wade was away touring at the time.

She was such a sweetheart that, even though not technically or by blood, in every sense of the word she was a part of everyone's family. Daisy had loved her, too, like a mother or a special aunt.

No one ever thought Wade would be back to stay after Rose died, but somehow both Daisy and Rose knew that he would.

A sense of connection pulsed through her, a deeply rooted knowledge about the past and the future. If Daisy ever had a daughter with Wade, she'd be Rose's granddaughter by blood. And a finer bloodline could not be had. Her children would not just be *Maggie's* grandchildren, but Rose's grandchildren. And Daisy would make sure they'd always know about her.

On the way back to the bedroom, Daisy spied the envelope lying on the counter where Wade had apparently left it. How could something so thin contain such important information? Well, she was no longer afraid of this letter. Nothing here could hurt her when she had everything she needed.

Using a fingernail, she ripped open the envelope, took out the paper, and read. There was some verbiage about the testing process, their accuracy rating, their procedure. Three columns, the one for mother blank. There was a column for alleged father, one for child, and at the top of each "Alleles Called."

Skimming, Daisy went to the part she wanted and for the second time, her life flashed before her eyes.

The lines on the paper were squiggly and hazy.

She had to read it twice. Three times.

The alleged father cannot be excluded as the biological father of the tested child. This conclusion is based on the matching alleles…

WADE WOKE with a start to the guttural cries of a wounded animal. He sprang out of bed. Daisy wasn't next to him but he wasn't processing all coherent thoughts at the moment. Just ones involving the urgency of that horrible sound. Pulling on pants, he ran for his shotgun, and found Daisy lying on the floor in the middle of the kitchen. *She* was the source of the caterwauling.

Curled in a fetal position, sobbing, the damn letter crumpled to her chest.

His heart must have certainly stopped. Just seized in his chest, stunned. Fatally wounded.

No, no, no.

"Daisy?" He squatted next to her, turning her face to him. "Sweetheart, look at me."

She handed him the letter though he didn't really need to read the results. He already knew, of course.

Daisy was not Hank Carver's biological daughter.

Because he didn't know what else to do, he lay on the floor, too, and curled her into his arms. He caressed her hair, her face, her arms, her back. He didn't bother talking but held her close until the guttural wails began to slow. Until her breathing was reduced to the painful sound of halting skips between uneven breaths.

"It's okay, baby. You're still you. Hank *is* your father. And no one else has to know about any of this. It's just between you and me."

"I d-don't care anymore wh-who knows. I'm a joke. The biggest cliché in the world. I'm Daisy Mae, d-daughter of a buckle bunny and a rodeo cowboy who had a one-night stand."

"You know it's not that simple."

"How is it not simple? My mother was a terrible wife, a cheater, and my father was the man who *cheated* with married women! Does it get any worse than this?"

Yes. It gets worse if I lose you. It gets worse if you blame me for taking you to get the test. For inadvertently encouraging you.

It gets worse if you can't bounce back from this.

But she would. Had to. This was Daisy Carver, and she didn't take shit from anybody.

"No, *your* father is Hank Carver, and he does not cheat with married women. He never abandoned you and he never would. That man is your father."

"I wanted him to be more than anything. I was so sure. I wanted to be *his* flesh and blood. And I'm not. I'm just so *angry* with everyone."

"Yeah, I get it."

"These two *people* played with other people's lives and

hearts for a few minutes of pleasure. For sex. No *wonder* I was a virgin for so long."

She gazed at him from under lowered lids, almost seeing straight through him, and in that moment, he wondered if she was seeing a piece of Rusty in Wade. If she was judging him, too, for every woman he'd ever casually slept with. Some of whom, Lord help him, might have been married for all he knew. He'd always asked, always wanted to be sure, but people were known to lie.

The fear that spiked through him was new and fresh and real. He thought for sure he was a dead man walking. This was judgment from someone he loved. Maybe it had all been too good to be true, this love and devotion from someone so pure and good.

He stood and reached for her. "Let's go back to bed. We'll think about this more in the morning. Things will look better, you'll see."

"I don't see how," she said, allowing him to pull her up to her feet. "Should I take the test again? Do you think the test could be wrong?"

He shrugged. Probably not, but why not leave that possibility open for now. But no, it *wasn't* wrong. He felt it. Knew it. And so did she.

"Either way, we both need some sleep. And I swear to you, I will find some way to make this better. To fix this for you." He brought her hand up to his lips and brushed a kiss across her knuckles.

Hand low on her back, he steered her to the bed and pulled back the covers. She crawled in, and in a moment that renewed his hope, she opened her arms.

She didn't have to ask him twice. He curled her into his body, holding her tightly against his chest. "You'll get through this."

She didn't reply, just buried her face in his neck and fell back asleep within minutes.

He dreamed of their children. Someday. One little blonde girl with green eyes like her mother's. She'd be interested in cars, too. And hopefully, with any luck, horses as well. He'd get a lamb and goat or two for the kids. A whole petting zoo.

Their children would grow up never having any doubt of who their parents were, or that they loved each other and were loved beyond measure. Wade would never abandon his family, and he'd never sacrifice Daisy for anything or anyone else. Not even rodeo, Lord help him, and he never thought *that* would ever happen.

He slept soundly all night long.

The next morning, he woke up, annoyed because Daisy wasn't in his arms. But she could be making the coffee or attempting for the second time to fix him an edible breakfast. He told her she didn't need to cook, that he would, but typically the girl wasn't giving up easily.

"Daisy?" he called out. "I'm going to hit the shower, but first, coffee. You've got me addicted, too."

He walked into the kitchen, finding no Daisy. And no *coffee.* Not even the rich, dark smell of it lingering in the air. More than anything, this hit him as ominous. Pulling the front curtains back, he peered outside to find his truck gone. *She'd taken his truck.*

"Damn it, Daisy. Where the hell did you go?"

It was early morning, the day before Christmas, and he knew for a fact not a blessed establishment would be open in Stone Ridge. Everything closed up tight as a drum, even the General Store. The church would be the only place open and he wondered if Daisy could have gone there to yell at God. It was possible, but his first order of business was to check closer to home. The crumpled letter sat on the counter, deceptively innocent. Taunting him. He quickly showered, dressed, and pocketed the letter. Then he went for his only option: the ATV.

He thought he'd calmed her down the night before. But either she'd faked it well, or she'd had her second wind of fury in the morning. While he wanted to believe there was some other, lighthearted reason she'd disappeared from his bed without saying goodbye, he had nothing. Zilch.

She clearly wanted to get away from him before he'd talk her out of whatever fool thing she was about to do. It would help if he could imagine what that fool thing *was* and get there fast enough to stop it. She already mentioned that she didn't care anymore who knew the truth, so maybe she was headed to the Double C.

On the way, he thought of everything he'd done wrong because the way she'd handled this *had* to be his fault. First, he could have more strongly discouraged Daisy from taking the test. He thought he'd been supportive, but at the time he hadn't fallen in love with her. A man protected those he loved from even the possibility of pain.

He should have stopped this test. Daisy wasn't like him, fearless, with possibly a bit of a death wish on his back. Well, that wish was gone now. He wanted to live a long and healthy life with Daisy even if the boredom of life on a ranch killed him. No matter. He'd die a slow death in her arms and would enjoy every single minute.

ATVs weren't meant for highways, even two-lane ones. Wade stuck to the dirt gutters as he pushed the sucker for all its horsepower. He slowed when a pickup came up next to him, and a window rolled down.

"Lose a cow?" Lenny called out.

Wade waved him away.

Lost my woman.

"I'll help you find the cow," Lenny said. "Not doing much else. Just got back from selling the last tree on my lot."

"You sell *trees*, too?"

"Idle hands, devil's work, and all that."

"I'm fine, Lenny! Move it along."

"Okay, champ! But you look a might ridiculous, you don't mind my sayin'." With that, he waved and finally drove off.

Wade could only *imagine* the picture he made driving down the main highway in an all-terrain vehicle. From the cheering stands of a rodeo exhibition to an ATV that was having trouble pushing sixty.

You've come a long way, cowboy.

He'd come home, defeated, to a ranch he almost didn't remember. A man with a bum arm. A beaten man he barely recognized. Now, he was head over heels in love with a woman whose entire life had just blown up.

Fortunately, he was familiar with that type of scenario. And he wasn't going to just sit by and watch *this* destruction happen.

He had to fix this.

Finally, he got close enough to the Double C Ranch to turn down a dirt road that led to Lincoln and Sadie's cabin. Knowing ranchers' hours, they'd be awake. In fact, he'd probably find Lincoln in the fields. But Daisy wouldn't be out there with him. If anything, she'd be inside with Sadie. Crying. Commiserating. She'd have to tell someone in her family, and Sadie was possibly the person least likely to be invested in the outcome.

When he drove by the main house where Daisy lived with Lillian, he didn't see his truck. And he didn't spy it anywhere on their land. Still, he had to take a chance.

He knocked on the door and Sadie opened it, holding Sammy on her hip. "Hey, Wade."

"Is Daisy here?"

Her eyes widened. "No, why would she be *here*? Did you guys have a fight?"

"No, it's nothing like that. But…something happened."

"What?"

"She's upset, you're right about that. Took my truck and left early this morning."

"Did you check Lillian's yet?"

"I drove by and didn't see my truck. Thought maybe you'd seen her earlier."

"I'll call Lillian," Sadie said, and Wade followed her to the landline in the kitchen. "Hi, Mima. Is…um, Daisy awake yet?"

Wade winced. She hadn't spent the night at her home, but with him. What kind of a man didn't know where he'd put his girlfriend?

"No, I just couldn't remember if we were supposed to go to the church tonight at seven or at eight. Oh yes, you're right, I should have asked you first. Seven? Oh, okay. I'll talk to you later." She hung up. "She hasn't seen her since last night."

He palmed his face, trying to think.

"Wade, what happened?"

"I need to find her. I'm worried she…" He pulled his hat off and ran a hand through his hair. "She…"

"Tell me."

Rather than tell her, Wade pulled the folded piece of paper from his pocket and handed it over.

He watched as Sadie's face crumpled.

"Oh, no. I…I suspected this. Did you know she was having the DNA test done?"

"I went with her. That night after she talked to everyone, she considered it. Then she just went for it."

She asked me what I would do, and I told her I'd take the damn test. Should have kept my damn mouth shut.

But he was a risk-taker at heart even if some risks, he'd now learned, shouldn't be taken.

"She asked me to not tell anyone and I didn't."

Sadie reached to pat his arm. "No, I totally understand."

Maybe sensing his mother's distress, Sammy started fussing.

"I...I need to tell Linc." She headed to the walkie-talkies they kept nearby.

Wade stopped her. "Maybe you don't need to do that yet. I'm going to find her, and then we'll come back and discuss this. It isn't the end of the world, and I told her that."

"It must feel like it to her." Sadie held Sammy close, kissed his forehead. "The day before Christmas. Poor Daisy."

"Some gift," Wade muttered, and then his brain woke up.

Gift.

Wade knew exactly where he might find Daisy, and he would need a vehicle.

Chapter 20

Daisy strode through the pasty-white hallways of the hospital. This morning, she'd been awake before dawn and known exactly what she wanted to do. Still, she'd stayed in bed listening to the sound of Wade's quiet and even breaths. Trying to decide if she should tell him about her plan. But if she told him, he'd talk her out of this. Or he'd want to come with her.

This was one thing she had to do alone. Face the man who'd wrecked her family. The man who'd wrecked her life. Were Maggie anywhere to be found, Daisy would do the same with her.

Now, the sounds of her boot heels thudded against the linoleum floor.

She approached the nurse on the second floor of the cardiology wing. "I would like to see Rusty Jones, please."

"Visiting hours are after five o'clock," the snooty nurse said. "Come back then."

"No," Daisy said. "I'm his daughter, and I need to see him now."

"His daughter? Which one?" The nurse flipped through some forms on the desk.

Aw, hell no.

"He has more than one?"

"Two, I think? No one knows each other, apparently. But it's the first time I've seen *you* around." She studied Daisy with narrowed eyes.

"Yes, I've been out of town. Daisy *Mae* Carver. He'll recognize the name."

"Have a seat." The nurse indicated a row of empty chairs. "I'll check with his doctor and see if he's up for visitors today."

Well, if he wasn't up for visitors, Daisy supposed she would stick around until he was. She'd driven all this way, after all, not even taking the time to leave Wade a note. Regret pulsed through her because he'd likely wake up and be worried to find her gone. With *his* truck.

She'd seen the regret in his eyes last night. His girlfriend was the daughter of two horrible people who obviously didn't know the meaning of loyalty. Of faithfulness. Would Wade view her the same way? Had her stupid DNA determined that she'd wind up like her mother? No man would want a wife like Maggie.

Daisy had two strikes against her. She didn't have Hank's DNA, but that of a no-good, cheating, rodeo cowboy. With *three* daughters? Seriously? Were they all illegitimate, or was she the only one? Daisy burned with anger. If Rusty wasn't dead yet, maybe she'd help facilitate that.

A couple of long hours later, the nurse gestured to the room. "You can go in and see him. Make it a short visit."

"Oh, don't worry." Daisy stomped toward the room. "This won't take long."

But when she crossed the threshold of the doorway, all the hot air whooshed out of her. She barely recognized the man she'd supposedly met at her auto shop a year or so ago. That man had been lively and wily. Funny, with his Southwest idioms. Now, his face was pale against his shock of white hair. His arms were attached to various leads, the skin purple and blotchy in places.

He didn't look like he'd ever been on a bucking horse.

"Daisy Mae," he said in a gravelly voice.

"I go by *Daisy*. Just Daisy."

"You look just like your mama. Man, she was beautiful." He beckoned her closer. "I heard the news. And I'm sorry."

Sorry. That's something she hadn't expected to hear out of the man.

"It's too late to be sorry."

"You're right about that, young lady. But I can't go back and change things, so all I have for you is the sorry."

It was hard to argue with that. "I don't want to be your daughter."

"I know."

"I… I'm just here to tell you that I already have a father. His name is Hank Carver and he never abandoned me. He was always by my side, practically my best friend when I was growing up. You and my mother both left me. So, whether or not my DNA matches yours, that doesn't matter to me." She took a breath. "I just wanted to tell you that I already have a family."

"Well said, darlin'. Well said. Hank is a much better man than I ever was. I guess what happened is an accident of biology. And I'm sorry you had to find out. I never wanted the stupid DNA test. I was going to leave you my money either way. It was my fool brother who insisted.

Maybe we'd all have been better off not ever knowin' for sure."

"I thought so, too, but I'm glad I know. Secrets shouldn't be kept in a family. I plan on telling mine the truth and they'll accept me anyway. That's who they are. Good people, like me."

"I'm glad to hear it."

She cleared her throat. "Do I have *sisters*?"

"'Fraid so. They came out of nowhere when word got out I was dyin'. Funny how that is. I had a little money set aside from all my years in the rodeo. You're the only one I thought might actually be mine. The timing and all."

"Or because my mother was kind enough to tell you?"

"Now, I know you must hate her, and I can't blame ya. But ya know, darlin', your mother was a very sad woman. She told me that she'd fallen in love with a man who still loved someone else. After a while it didn't work anymore. She felt that she deserved better."

"You?" Daisy snorted.

"Heck no, not me. I think I was pretty much nothing to her but a diversion. Contrary to what you might think, hookin' up with rodeo cowboys was not something she did all the time. She wasn't what we like to call a buckle bunny. Got the feelin' this was a one-time deal for her. She said she was going back to try to work things out with her fella."

"Did you know that she was married?"

"No, I didn't. Can't recall if I asked."

"You *should* have asked."

"Maybe, darlin', but I wasn't the married one."

"Are all you rodeo cowboys like this?" She waved her hands. "Spreadin' your seed around, makin' the world a better place?"

Daisy had spent her life trying to be different than Maggie. How on earth had she wound up in the same place? Here she was, in love with another rodeo cowboy. Who knew how far and wide he'd spread his seed? The thought choked off her airway.

"We're not all 'seed spreaders,' as you like to say." He held up air quotes. "Some cowboys are family men who travel with their wives. Sometimes the children, too. Others are loners and dead serious about winning. No time for hanky-panky. Only some of us are like me, or how I used to be."

She didn't know that she believed this man, but it didn't matter.

"There's no point in talkin'. I just thought I'd come in person to tell you that I don't want your money."

"Take the money," a man said from behind her. Daisy whipped around to find the other Mr. Jones in the doorway, Rusty's brother. "Hello, Daisy."

"I'm only here for a minute."

He held up a palm. "I understand. Don't let me interrupt, but it's my opinion that Rusty owes you *this* at the very least."

"I owe her a hell of a lot more than that. But this is the best I can do."

"Think of the money as a gift. No strings attached. Rusty doesn't expect you to visit his grave or be a devoted daughter in death."

"Well, that's good. Because it isn't goin' to happen. What about the other women? My…my sisters?" The word felt foreign coming out of her lips.

To think she'd always wished for a sister. Not like this.

"Only one of them had similar test results. You'll share the inheritance with her."

Sister. She had a sister. Not a *real* sister, of course. Not someone who grew up with her, sharing a room, brushing her hair, reading to her, chasing frogs, and collecting rocks and sticks. Not someone who worried about her enough to invade her privacy and ask who the sexy panties were for. *Sadie.*

At the thought, Daisy was caught between a sound that was somewhere between a snort and a sob. Daisy already had two sisters who were more real to her than someone who had a biological link. The words should mean more. Sister. Father. Mother.

"I don't wish you any harm, Mr. Jones," Daisy said to Rusty. "Thank you, but I don't want your money."

With that she turned and left the room. She wasn't going to forgive him. The forgiveness was not hers to give. Hank should forgive, if he wanted to. He would be the only person owed an apology in this scenario. He'd raised another man's daughter all along believing she was his own. It wasn't fair to do that to a man.

Daisy was halfway to the nurse's desk when she heard the sound of Wade's deep voice.

"I don't care when visiting hours are, ma'am, I need to find Daisy Carver and I need to find her now."

The nurse turned her attention from Wade to Daisy when she stopped a few feet away from the desk. Wade's gaze followed and his eyes met hers. Gaze soft and warm, he slowly walked toward her.

It seemed like a lifetime ago since last night when he'd held her while she cried her heart out.

Her feelings had not changed for Wade, but now she had tiny seeds of doubts. Maybe she'd wanted Wade so much that she'd formed him into who she wanted him to be. Loyal and faithful. Trustworthy. Was he all of those things or were those just words, too?

"I'm sorry I took your truck," she said. "But I didn't want you to talk me out of this."

"Forget that." He pulled her into his arms, holding her tightly against him. "I was worried."

"I know."

"You should know that I went looking for you at the ranch, and I showed Sadie the letter."

"That's okay. There's no way I could keep this from my family. I was a dummy to think that I could."

"Sadie wouldn't tell anyone else. We can still keep this quiet, if you want."

"No, I need to do this. It's the right thing." She nudged her chin toward Rusty's room. "That's what I was doing in there with Mr. Jones. Facing him. Telling him exactly what I thought of him *and* Maggie."

"That's my girl."

She buried her face in his warm neck. "I've had a very long morning. And I just want to go home."

THE MOMENT WADE FOUND DAISY, every thought, every emotion he'd had for the past several hours just loaded, locked, and clicked into place. There was no longer even the slightest doubt in his mind that he loved this woman beyond what he'd believed humanly possible. If it hadn't been proven to him once, when he feared she'd been injured, waking up finding her gone solidified his feelings. He'd do anything for Daisy to give her the life she deserved.

He followed her back to the Double C Ranch, and he figured later, they'd both drive back to his house in his truck. First, she would tell her family, and he'd be there to support her. There was so much he wanted to tell her. His life had become clear the moment he stopped resisting his feelings for her. Without a doubt, nothing in this new life of his would ever again be boring with Daisy at his side.

She challenged him in every way and made him a better man. She was simply…everything. And she had to marry him. She had to say yes to the rest of their lives together.

For the first time in his life, he wanted this security and safety with a woman. All the domesticity he'd previously rejected and found dull and complacent. It no longer felt that way. Not with her.

He parked the truck he'd borrowed from Sadie right behind his own.

Daisy hopped out of his truck and walked over to him. "I need to tell everyone. What a Christmas present, right?"

Right. It was Christmas Eve. Tonight, Daisy and her family would be going to the midnight service, most likely. He'd be there with them, too.

"You can wait, if you want."

"No, it's going to be all over my face that something is wrong. And Sadie knows. She can't keep a thing from Lincoln. I just…better get through this."

"If that's what you want. I'm there with you."

Then she fixed him with those deep-emerald eyes and what he saw in them killed him.

Regret.

"I think I need to do this alone, too. You should just go home and I'll…talk to you in a few days. When everything has calmed down some."

"You don't want to spend Christmas together."

"I think it's best…I…I know we made plans, but everything has changed."

"Nothing has changed for me. I love you, Daisy."

"And I love you. That's what kills me. I spent half my life trying to be different than my mother. And now, look at me. I fell in love with a rodeo cowboy. Just. Like. Her."

"Jesus, Daisy. She didn't love Rusty. It's not the same thing."

"Isn't it? I've loved you for so long that maybe I idealized you. You're not this perfect man."

"Sweetheart, nobody is."

"That's not what I meant. But it's just I didn't let myself think about the life you led before. I'm a pretty blank slate, and you're…you're…"

"*Not* a blank slate."

"There's lots of different kinds of cowboys in the rodeo circuit. Some men bring along their wives, girlfriends, families. Others are loners too intent on the win to be distracted. And others are like Rusty, having a good time with every buckle bunny they could find." She took a breath. "Which one were you?"

"Do you really have to ask? I'm the *loner*."

He'd been the cowboy too intent on winning to be distracted by anyone. Except for that last event. He'd lost his concentration and now he understood why. He'd still been grieving for his mother, and the fact was that rather than face his grief, he'd run from Stone Ridge. Run hard, and fast, and far from reminders of what he'd really lost. Everything that mattered.

He'd lost his focus and paid for it dearly.

"Wade, you had a reputation. I wouldn't listen to the rumors, but maybe I just didn't want to believe them. Those rumors about my mother turned out to be true. Secrets don't work. They come out eventually and destroy lives."

"We don't have any secrets. If you want to know whether I was a monk, then no, I wasn't. But I was no *Rusty Jones*."

"I want to believe that." She gnawed on her lower lip and tears sprung to her eyes.

His heart cracked open like a walnut. "But bottom line, you don't."

"Wade, I'm sorry. I don't know if I can do this—"

"No need." He held up a palm. "Don't be sorry. If you don't trust me, we have nothing. I think we're done here."

With that he turned, and hopped in his truck, salvaging a little slice of his pride.

He drove away without looking back, leaving his sore and bleeding heart on the Double C Ranch.

Chapter 21

Plans with Daisy for an all-night tree trimming on Christmas Eve gone, Wade had nothing to do. He'd been invited to the Henderson ranch for brunch, along with nearly everyone else who didn't have other plans, but that wasn't until tomorrow morning.

Merry Christmas to him.

The stupid, sappy—both literally and figuratively—tree stood in the corner. Naked. Lights and ornaments Daisy had brought over lay in a box under the tree. He could trim the tree by himself, of course, but there was no point to that. He'd avoided this ritual for a damn good reason.

Whenever he got himself home in time for Christmas, he'd decorate the tree for his mother. *Her way.* She'd cook a roast and serve him spiked eggnog while she barked directions. They'd argue, eat, drink, and laugh the entire time. Lights went on the way she wanted, meticulously, on every bough. The ornaments one inch apart. He took care of the tree topper. Even he, over six feet, required a ladder. She'd always wanted to get the tallest tree in all the land. The pine needles brushed the top of their ceiling. Ridiculous.

Lord, he missed her.

Wade grabbed a cold beer from the fridge and eyed a casserole he'd defrosted to have food available. For *Daisy*. And man, he *hated* casseroles. Every single blessed one. He hated everything they represented. Condolences issued by way of comfort food. Food that can be easily frozen and served later. Food for the grieving because apparently everyone forgot how to cook when they lost a loved one. Well, this was the last straw. This was final. No more casseroles in his house!

He viciously pulled the covered enchilada dish out of the fridge and emptied it into the trash can. Cheese, tortillas, chili peppers, corn, and meat mushed together in the trash, smelled like day-old tacos, and made his stomach roil and pitch.

Go talk to your horse. You always feel better afterwards.

Wade made his way to the stables and brushed Dante, then took him for a ride around the property. The day was cold and crisp and clear, helping his mood. The cattle grazing in the pasture cheered him even more, and he decided then and there that he would have more horses as soon as financially feasible. ATVs were great, and far cheaper, but there was joy in the majestic animals. And he wouldn't deprive himself of that connection to his past.

Also, he was going to give lessons. Barrel racing, bull riding, lassoing. Teenagers and young kids. He wouldn't push the younger ones like his father had pushed him. He'd let the love of the sport grow naturally. His focus would be one of safety, since he could serve as a cautionary tale.

Maybe Linc would want to be involved and help get this started. After the holidays, he'd give Kari Lynn a call, see if she still wanted his advice. He loved the rodeo, and just because he couldn't participate anymore didn't mean he couldn't help others. There was joy in the competition, and not only in the winning. It would be another way of giving back to the community that he had loved so much. He had a new sense of community.

Different, but still important. Yeah, he was back to stay. Even without Daisy. This was his land. It was no longer simply dirt, and he understood his mother's connection. It was more than land. This was generational. A strong heritage of hardworking folks. Stone Ridge was his town. His mother's home, and now his. Again.

Yeah, he could keep busy. Plenty to do.

Outside the new barn, he spied the Model T where they'd left it. Daisy had worked hard on that car, had it running at one time for a couple of minutes. The girl had talent. And for more than one thing. Not just cars, but also slipping inside a man's heart when he wasn't looking.

Wade slid his hand down the hood, trying to understand the fascination. Seeing this car through her eyes, instead of his father's, he no longer saw a wasted investment but a link to the past. So many people ran from their pasts, but Daisy had chosen to embrace hers. No more secrets, she'd said. He admired the hell out of that.

Wade had always been less of a car person than he was a horse person, but necessity had forced him to learn a few things. And he had the tools. Polishing the beast that had survived a roof falling on it would give him something to do for the rest of the day. Keep his mind off Daisy. He snorted. *That* was a joke. He'd begun to think of this as *Daisy's* car. As he dusted and polished, he had a brilliant idea.

Yes. This would work.

"I finally outsmarted you, old man."

A few hours later, Wade was nearly done with part one of his master plan when a truck pulled up. *Lincoln.* Well,

Wade should have expected this visit. He wiped the oil off his hands and walked to meet him.

His oldest friend looked pale, and stunned, and Wade's gut clenched with worry. As an only child, Wade couldn't imagine the shock of finding that someone you'd grown up with as a sibling wasn't fully related to you by blood.

"I guess you heard," Wade said.

"Yeah." Lincoln dragged a hand down his face. "And I had to get away. All the crying, the hugging, the kissing. I've had enough. Time for a break."

"How's Hank doing with the news?"

"Better than I thought he would. Maybe he was prepared. Same with Mima and Jackson. It's not like any of us hadn't considered this could be a possibility. We just didn't want to believe it and now we have to accept this." Lincoln hesitated for a beat. "Hey, I wanted to thank you for being there for Daisy. It makes sense that she wanted someone who wasn't as connected to the outcome."

Wade liked to think it had been more than that, but he'd recently been humbled. Not everyone believed Wade Cruz was the best thing since Texas became a state. The woman he loved, for instance. Turned out he was right in the first place. He wasn't good enough for her.

"I was honored to help."

Lincoln clapped Wade's back, and they walked toward the new barn. "What are you up to? Take my mind off my family mess."

"Lots of planning," Wade said. "I wanted to talk to you about starting up a clinic to teach rodeo, right here in town. On my land."

"Yeah?"

"Finally got over myself. It would sure supplement my income while I get the cattle ranch profitable. You know what they say, those who can, do. Those who can't, teach."

"Proving once again that those who teach are often the best at what they do."

Wade chuckled at the underhanded compliment. "While I can no longer participate, I can certainly teach the sport."

"That's a great idea, actually."

"Glad you think so. I'm going to need your help getting this clinic started."

"Count on it, buddy. Whatever you need. I'm there."

For the next hour, they were two old friends again. Former rodeo cowboys, arms spread over the fenced corral. Heads bent, making plans. The possibilities of a new future opened up to Wade and some of the weight of losing Daisy lightened. Not all. No, he expected he would carry that for the rest of his life and love her for just as long. He would not be one of those men who married someone other than the one woman who had his whole heart. Hank had shown him what a disaster that could be. Better to wind up alone.

Lincoln walked to his truck. "Guess we'll see you at the family dinner tomorrow?"

"She didn't tell you?"

"Tell me what?"

"We broke up."

"What? Why didn't you *say* something?"

"It didn't come up."

"It didn't come up! What do you mean it didn't come *up*? Shit fire, what did you *do*, Wade?"

"What did *I* do?"

"You must have done *something* to screw this up! She's loved you for half of her life."

"She wanted some 'distance' and 'time.'" He held up finger quotes. "Doesn't know if she can do this. She has this strange idea that because she fell in love with a rodeo cowboy she's following in your mother's wayward footsteps."

Lincoln narrowed his eyes. "What? That's crazy!"

"I agree, but if that's what she thinks, I have to let her go. She doesn't trust me, bottom line, mostly because of Rusty, I imagine. That man keeps ruining our lives just by existing."

"Damn it, Wade! Did it ever occur to you that someone who's been abandoned by both parents might just want a man who will never let her go?"

No. It hadn't.

He was a certified jackass. He'd let his own foolish pride cloud his judgment.

"Shit fire!" Wade threw his hat to the ground. He'd done that only once before, when he'd lost a tournament because of one bad call. "Why didn't I think of that?"

"I'd call you a dimwit, but this is something I would do. Sometimes, when you're too close to the situation, you just can't see it." Lincoln pointed. "And ego gets in the way. You have to fix this. Just because she's gone off plan and she's a little bit confused, that doesn't mean you give up on her. You love her, right?"

"I want to *marry* her, that's how much I love her."

Lincoln let out a low whistle. "Never thought I'd hear *you* say you want to get hitched."

"Same, buddy. Same. And now look at you. I never wanted to get hitched, because I'd never been with Daisy. She changed everything for me. I love her."

"Give her some time and she'll come around. And for the love of God, don't you ever give up on her."

DEAR ALBERT,

Earlier today, Daisy came by to give me the news. She's not Hank's biological daughter.

Merry Christmas!

Here's the thing. I was foolish enough to believe that nothing would ever hurt as much as this news. I thought everything in our lives would change. I don't know why. Because suddenly I looked at this beautiful girl whom I've raised since she was a toddler, and I knew the truth in an instant. Nothing has really changed. Nothing at all. And it never will, as we belong to each other in a way that DNA can't create. We're a family and that's much harder to accomplish than mixing up a bunch of genes while having yourself a bit of fun. If you catch my drift.

All of us gathered together and Daisy told us the truth. We cried, we hugged, we gave assurance of our love. Daisy, my little spitfire, in the center of all this devotion, understanding that this didn't matter to any of us. She has proven to us, time and again, that she's a Carver through and through, biology be damned!

And with that, I wash my hands of this matchmaking business. I'm an old lady and plum tuckered out. Daisy will love who she loves and choose whomever she chooses. Her heart may be broken a time or two, whether by a bright and shiny rodeo cowboy, or simply a rancher's son. Either way. Shit happens, as the cowboys these days are saying.

As long as my darling girl is happy in the end, I don't care who she winds up marrying. And, of course, I have given her my approval of Wade. You would have been proud. He's Rose's boy, and as you said, she raised him right. It's true that he's bright and shiny and oh-so-handsome but something in the way he looks at Daisy shows me that this is different. I think he loves her, Albert. Really loves her.

And, I've chosen to have faith.

DAISY CRIED ALL DAY. Hank held her in his arms first,

then Brenda. Next, Lincoln, Jackson, Sadie, and Eve. Finally, even Sammy got in there with a sweet baby hug.

This was tough enough to endure without a cracked heart, but Daisy had one of those, too.

She hadn't pictured breaking it off with Wade on Christmas Eve but maybe it had been for the best. Rumors often contained at least a seed of truth, and plenty of women referred to Wade as a commitment-phobe. Not marriage material. She'd disagreed, of course, but simply because she'd refused to believe otherwise. Clearly, the name "Wild Wade" wasn't just about his fearlessness on the circuit. He was a rodeo cowboy and with his looks, it was entirely possible that years from now, a child or two would show up on his doorstep, wanting a DNA test.

The services at Trinity Church that night were a blur for Daisy. Pastor June went on and on about gifts. And about unconditional love. Love was patient. Kind. Not rude or prideful, not easily angered. *Keeps no record of wrongs.*

Daisy slunk lower and lower on the bench pew as she listened to words surely meant for her. Guilt spiked like a painful prick. She'd never judged Wade before. Never painted him with the bold, broad brush that some others had. Because she loved him. Always had. Maybe she always would. But at least she'd spare herself from the heartache of losing him to another woman someday.

She wondered if Linc already knew about her and Wade, as he'd disappeared for a few hours, and gave her strange looks during dinner.

She didn't want to talk about Wade. Her heart ached like someone had pierced her chest with an ice pick. Love wasn't supposed to *hurt* like this. She was so tired of losing the people she loved. And she'd loved Maggie with all her heart. Daisy remembered that much. She remembered how Maggie was once Daisy's entire world. Her sun, her moon, her stars.

Someone else had now taken that place in her heart and it wasn't whom she'd expected.

Wade.

Tonight they were supposed to trim the Christmas tree. It was to have been an all-night thing, probably ending by making love under the tree. She wondered what he was doing tonight instead and whether it was possible that he was hurting as much. He had no family and was trying to rebuild a ranch on his own. Her heart ached remembering the look in his eyes when she'd told him that she had doubts about him. It was not what he'd expected from her. She'd hurt him.

But he'd hurt her, too, by so quickly breaking it off and walking away. She might have liked to see him fight for her, for them. The same way he fought for anything that truly mattered to him.

For his mother. For the rodeo. For his ranch.

He hadn't fought for her.

And still, she loved him.

She'd been sliding down a mountain, with no one there to catch her when she landed. Wade had. He'd been there for her and held her for hours while she'd cried every last tear. Another guy would have cut and run. Not Wade.

It was late on Christmas Eve, but still, Daisy picked up the landline in her bedroom and dialed the number on the business card. "Hello, Mr. Jones? This is Daisy. I've given this a lot of thought. And I do want my part of the inheritance."

"What made you change your mind?"

"Someone very special to me needs the money. A retired and injured rodeo cowboy. You can tell Rusty that he's going to help restore an old cattle ranch."

"That's great, Daisy. It's good to know he'll be helping someone, especially a rodeo cowboy. He's going to love that. And thank you for coming by to see him. It meant a lot."

"I'm sorry I wasn't kinder. What happened wasn't entirely his fault and I understand that."

"That's generous of you. I will tell him you said that. Merry Christmas."

Feeling just a little bit better, Daisy hung up and steered her thoughts away from Wade. Sweet memories of reaching for him. His constant and solid presence like an anchor in her life.

"Daisy?" Mima hollered from the kitchen. "Are you asleep?"

Well, had she been asleep she wouldn't be *now*. But she wasn't in bed and likely wouldn't be till late tonight. She couldn't stop thinking about Wade and what she'd done. She'd allowed him to believe she didn't think him good enough for her. This was so far from the truth it was laughable, but she'd practically spelled it out for him.

Love is patient. Love is kind.

Believes all things.

Endures all things.

"I'm not sleepy." Daisy stood under the archway of the entrance to the kitchen. "Do you need something?"

"This is just like when you were little and couldn't fall asleep waiting for Santa Claus." Holding a plate of cookies, Mima tipped her chin toward the table.

Daisy hated to break it to her, but this wasn't at all like waiting up for Santa filled with the wide-eyed excitement of a young child. This was insomnia because her world had been torpedoed. Then she'd blown up the rest of her life and now didn't quite know how to move past this ache.

"I don't need any more cookies. They make me thirsty." But Daisy took a seat anyway.

"Just indulge me one last time."

Tentacles of fear spread through Daisy's heart. "What do you *mean* one last time?"

She waved a hand dismissively. "I'm not dyin'. But I will, someday. It's inevitable, sugar. How much longer can I possibly live? We're not meant to live forever on earth. I'll be joinin' my Albert in heaven someday."

Daisy didn't want to think about Mima being gone, but it did give some comfort to think of them together again. And Daisy could almost picture her grandfather right now, standing in the kitchen as he so often had, watching Mima cook.

"You smell like gravy, woman," he'd say, sniffing her neck.

Mima would raise her wooden spoon to him. "How dare you!"

"And I love gravy." Pop would then grab Mima, spin her around, and kiss her.

She would giggle, muss his hair, and call him *"old man"* with a deep affection.

"Do you miss him?"

"My goodness, of course I do. He was the love of my life."

"You never missed the bright and shiny rodeo cowboy, did you?"

Mima took a bite of the gingerbread man, then chewed thoughtfully. "Well, no, but maybe that's because it wasn't really love. More like infatuation. Albert was the one for me."

People used to tell Daisy that she was infatuated with Wade. A crush. And the worst of them all: just puppy love. Won't last. Will fade with time. But it hadn't faded. If anything, her feelings for him grew deeper and stronger with every passing year. Every now and again, she'd prayed for her feelings to go away because it was too painful to love someone who was always gone and so far out of her reach.

"How do you know it's really love? True love?" Daisy played with a cookie in the shape of a Christmas tree.

"When you can't stop thinking about them. When life without them is unthinkable. When you can't stand the thought of them being in pain or hurting."

Daisy felt all these things, but also a bone-deep disappointment that he'd given up too easily. Too soon.

"And what if they disappoint you?"

"True love has nothing to do with that. People will forever disappoint you. That's our human nature. What matters is if the one you love can be loyal to you. Committed to you. If he'll stick around when things get rough." She took a breath. "And if you can do the same for him. Also, it doesn't hurt if your heart speeds up when he walks into a room."

Daisy's heart had done that for Wade for as long as she could remember. Whenever she'd see him with Lincoln and he'd grin and say, "Hiya, Peanut" she couldn't help but think he meant more than that. Even those two words had always felt like love. In her heart, every time he said those two words, she'd heard, "Love you."

"That's how you feel about Wade, isn't it?" Mima prompted.

"Yes. But I don't want to."

"Why?"

"I thought he was right for me, but maybe you were right all along."

"This is hard for me to say, but I wasn't right at all. Albert made me realize…um, what I mean is, I suddenly came to my senses about all this. The shiny rodeo cowboy in my past had blinded me again. Daisy, not all rodeo cowboys are the same. You can't picture them all as Rusty."

"Actually, Rusty told me that, too. Some cowboys bring their families along on the circuit. Others are the serious kind that have to win every time. And the rest are a lot like Rusty."

"Yes, and Wade was the serious one intent on winning."

"Why do you say that?"

"Oh, sugar. I'm sorry I didn't tell you this sooner, but it really wasn't my story to tell."

"What does that mean?"

"Well, Wade's father liked to gamble. That *isn't* a rumor."

"Yes, that's how they kept Rose alive and paid for her cancer treatment."

Mima shook her head. "No, Jorge left nothing besides a heavily mortgaged ranch."

"And the classic vintage car Wade couldn't sell," she muttered.

No *wonder* he hated that car. It was everything he needed and nothing he could have. Not Wade. He wouldn't break his promise. Wade was a man of his word. That told her everything she ever needed to know about him.

"Most people think Wade should have a lot of money from all his years in the rodeo. Only a few of us know the truth. We keep quiet about it because Rose asked us to. She didn't want to humiliate her family, or Wade. But his father gambled all the money away. Wade *had* to win. He didn't just have to win for the classic ol' rodeo ego, or for the thrill. He won to save his mother. To save the ranch. So, I have no doubt he was serious and determined to win."

"He *had* to win."

"And there were all those times he worked for Hank during the off-season. Did you think he did that simply to flirt with you?"

"No," she squeaked.

Wade's flirting, the way he couldn't seem to say no to a woman, all those things led one to believe something else entirely about "Wild Wade." That he was *exactly* like Rusty.

But I should have known better. I did know better. This is my fault.

She'd let fear stop her again when she'd promised to be done playing it safe.

"I was right about him all along. Except there at the end, I let fear cloud my vision. I let this thing with Rusty confuse me just because I so desperately didn't want to be like Maggie. I've tried to be the opposite of her all my life."

"No one blames you. This whole paternity thing threw you for a loop. It must have felt like your whole world was imploding."

"Wade was so understanding and supportive. He doesn't judge me for being the love child of a rodeo cowboy and a buckle bunny. I didn't want to be this walking cliché. And I didn't want to be *anything* like her."

"Well, sugar, a lot of good women have fallen for a cowboy." Mima patted Daisy's hand gently. "That's why I wanted to have this talk. Ever since your mother left, I've tried to do nothing but protect you. Maybe I went too far. I thought you should have someone like my Albert. Someone who offered you love, safety, and security. I didn't see Wade as safe or secure. The poor lamb has been through so much and I honestly didn't see him staying. And I know you need someone who won't ever let you go."

And Wade had let her go too easily. Yes, she'd been the one to voice her doubts. To define him by two words: *rodeo cowboy* when he'd been so kind to her. He should have argued with her. Fought. And still…

"I do love him. It seems I always have."

"Rose was right about the two of you."

"Rose?"

"Until the day she died, she believed you and Wade were meant to be. That someday the two of you would be together. It was written in the stars, don't you know."

"What? Why didn't I hear about this?"

"Honestly? None of us believed it. It seemed so unlikely. Wade was gone so much, always taking risks, and you were the girl afraid of your own shadow. We all loved Rose but thought maybe she was a little fanciful. But she was a sweetheart, and Lord, how I miss her. I should have encouraged you and Wade, but I had to think of you first before I encouraged what Rose wanted."

Daisy thought back to the night at the Shady Grind when Lenny had said, "You mean Rose was right?" About that time, Wade had done his best to distract her by challenging her to a pool game. Of course, he probably knew what his mother believed but maybe he'd never taken her seriously, either.

"If you love him, take the risk. I took a risk, too, after having my own heart broken. And I found true love with a rancher. It will be different for you. But I swore to Albert that I'm out of this matchmaking business. So, this is entirely up to you. I didn't think it was fair not to mention it since I've not been Wade's greatest fan. That wasn't fair of me. It's Christmas, for cryin' out loud. And I'm going to choose love over fear. Maybe you could do the same."

DAISY WOKE on Christmas morning with dried tears on her cheeks.

She'd fallen asleep with thoughts of Wade. With memories of him from long ago, when they'd been kids. And of the past two weeks as she'd gotten to know and love him so deeply.

Daisy hadn't fallen for a rodeo cowboy. Years ago, she'd loved a beautiful boy with all her heart. That boy had tried everything to please his father, adored his mother, was her brother's best friend, kind and loving, and the only son of a woman whom Daisy loved.

She couldn't wait until after Christmas Day to fix this.

He was the best thing to ever happen to her and she'd been right about him all along. Only fear had stopped her from moving forward. Unfounded fear.

Daisy woke and careened down the hallway to the kitchen, half dressed. "Mima!"

Her socks had her sliding and nearly falling until she righted herself by pressing her palm against the wall.

"Good Lord, child! Don't scare me like that." Mima held a hand to her neck, her gaze dropping to Daisy's half-dressed state. "What is this mess?"

"I have to miss the gift giving this morning. My presents are all wrapped and under my bed. But I need to find Wade. I have to fix this. The thing is, I broke up with him because I made the mistake of thinking he was a rodeo cowboy."

"Well, he *was*. He retired." Mima cocked her head as if dealing with someone who'd taken a knock to the head and forgotten a few days in there.

"That's not the point! He's the 'serious loner intent on winning.' Why did I ever doubt him?"

Mima slowly shook her head. "I don't know why either of us did, sweetheart. He's Rose's boy."

"He is, and I love him so much. I hurt him, and I have

to make it all up to him. Even if it takes me the rest of my life."

"I'm sure you will but I do hope it won't take *that* long."

"Is it too early to go over there? What am I saying? He's always up early. He works so hard on the ranch, on everything."

She glanced outside to judge the weather when she saw the glistening chrome of the Model T. It was parked just outside their home, by the barn.

And had a big red bow on it.

"What is it? You've been standing there for a whole minute. Did it snow or something?" Mima joined Daisy at the window. "Well, son of a biscuit eater, what in tarnation is that?"

"It's a vintage classic car."

"Well, I can see it's a car, Daisy. I'm not *blind*. What is Wade's car doing on my land?"

"I don't know but I'm going to find out." She threw open the front door.

"Now, young lady, not without proper clothe—"

Daisy didn't hear the end of that sentence. She grabbed her boots by the front door and tugged them on, running outside in her long T-shirt.

The Model T had been polished and gleamed to a shine and there was a note taped to the front shield.

He never said I couldn't give this away.
~ Wade
P.S. Merry Christmas

The keys were in the ignition.

It was, by far, the best Christmas present she'd ever had, from the most honorable man she'd ever known.

Mima had followed her outside, a coat thrown over her

shoulders. By then, Daisy had jumped behind the wheel of the car.

"This is a classic," she said. "They don't make them like this anymore."

"You and your cars."

"His father wouldn't let him sell this car."

"That sounds just like him. Idiot man. Leave your son a ranch in need of a major overhaul and don't give him any help in raising the money."

"This is a gift. You don't sell a gift. If anything, you give it away." She smiled. "It's called regifting."

Like her inheritance, a gift from a man who owed her something. A gift of which she would give every penny to Wade.

"Very generous of Wade to give you this car. I think you better take it for a spin. Go thank him. But try to be back in time for gift giving."

After running back inside to change into her jeans and a warmer outfit, Daisy started up the antique and waved to Mima.

Daisy made it three feet before the car stalled.

She got out, looked under the hood, shook her fist, and begged the car gods for assistance. "Don't prove me wrong. I worked so hard on you!"

"Daisy, sugar, *cars* can't hear you," Mima said patiently. "I've told you that since you were a little girl."

"But I can hear me," Daisy muttered as she tinkered under the hood and found the problem. Within minutes, she had the car humming again. She patted the roof of the car and gave Mima a triumphant smile.

"Let's face it. I have a gift. Machines fear me."

But this Model T didn't fear her enough. Not enough to go over twenty-five miles an hour.

"C'mon!" She hit the steering wheel. "I would like to get there before tomorrow."

Thankfully, traffic would be extra light today, not that it was a freeway thoroughfare at any other time. But today, everyone would be curled under a warm blanket still in bed, or maybe already opening presents with their young children. Or with their lovers.

And she was driving a vintage car down the highway, except she thought the word "driving" might be a little generous. She was more or less limping down the road.

Speaking of limping, there was a golf cart right behind her. Driven by Lenny, who didn't understand two words: day off.

"Hiya, Missy. What's doin'?" Lenny called out as he passed her. "Out for a leisurely drive there?"

Riding next to him was Maybelle, Beulah's sister, who lived alone on the dairy farm not far from here.

"Merry Christmas, Lenny," Daisy said, not wanting to be impolite. She nodded. "Miss Maybelle."

"What kind of car is that?" Lenny said. "It looks like an antique."

"It is. Very special." Daisy kept her eyes on the road, for what she had no idea. She'd have plenty of time to brake were a turtle to cross.

This was torture. She wanted to get to Wade and apologize. Kiss him and ask him to forgive her for jumping to the wrong conclusion. It might be faster to walk there.

"Lenny, don't you ever take a day off?"

"This *is* my day off," Lenny said. "We're goin' to brunch over at the Henderson ranch. Winona invited us."

Were they on a date? *Lenny and Maybelle?*

Hey, why not? Love at any age. And with any luck, she'd get to Wade before *she* was sixty.

"I'm on my way to Wade's so maybe I'll see y'all later.

Go on ahead of me, Lenny. I think your golf cart might be faster."

"No question there. What if I push you?"

"I would like to get there in time to set up my punch," Maybelle said. "You know how Winona loves my punch. I'm sorry, young lady."

"Y'all go on ahead. I'll get there."

Lenny went ahead, Maybelle sending Daisy a wave and blowing a kiss. She mouthed, "Thank you" and winked.

Before long, they were a dot in the distance.

Daisy petted the dashboard. "Don't you worry, you're special. So what if you're not particularly fast? Maybe *fast* is overrated."

Wade had taken pains to clean her up. He might have spent all night doing it. Her heart ached and swelled picturing him slaving over the car he hated. *For her.*

Finally, she arrived at the Cruz ranch. Another twenty or so minutes—when she was tempted to get out and push—and she was down the dirt road to the main house. She didn't see any sign of Wade, but his truck was near the barn.

She parked and looked up to find Wade standing on the porch, eyes narrowed. Was he still angry? The gift implied he wasn't, but his tight jaw said something else.

"You drove the car here?" he said, sounding incredulous.

"Yes, why? Didn't you drive it to me?"

"*Drive* it to you? I thought it didn't run for longer than a couple of minutes!"

"Then how did you..." She turned to the car, waving her arms in a flourish.

"Riggs and I used a trailer to haul it over to you." He walked down the steps, slowly. "You drove it here, Peanut?"

Peanut. The nickname that put distance between them,

that made it clear they were again nothing more than friends. She had hoped that it had become his affectionate pet name for her. Now, the wary look in his eyes made her wonder if he'd ever forgive her for being an idiot.

"Um, machines fear me. But don't get too excited. She doesn't want to go above twenty-five miles an hour." Slowly and deliberately, she walked toward him until she was only inches away. "Thank you for my gift. I particularly liked the note. It's…everything."

Dear Lord, he still hadn't said anything. Just studied her from under those hooded eyes.

"Oh, Wade. Please forgive me. You can't be reduced down to two words. You're not just a 'rodeo cowboy.' You're the boy that I've loved half my life and still love. I've been through so much lately that I got confused. I lied to you. Of *course* I trust you. I know you. You're my whole heart."

He stared at her, unblinking, without saying a word. She was so nervous that she kept talking.

"I want to go inside with you and decorate that tree if you haven't already. I just want to pick up where we left off."

He still hadn't moved from the step where he'd been standing. Well, that was it. Other than throwing herself into his arms—which she briefly considered—she didn't know how else to make this up to him. She'd made a mistake from a knee-jerk reaction. Fear, her nemesis. If he couldn't forgive her, then…

Should she tell him about the money? No, she'd surprise him with that later.

"Okay, well." She gnawed at her lower lip. "I guess I'll be going. Merry Christmas."

"Wait a second." Wade came slowly down the rest of the steps.

"Yes?" She closed the distance between them.

"This is my fault. Lincoln reminded me that if I love you, I'm not allowed to just give up. Believe it or not, I didn't." He reached for her hand and brushed a kiss across her knuckles. "It took me less than a day to get over myself. I was just going to give you a little time before I came after you, guns blazin'. I love you, Daisy. With all my heart."

Oh, yes! Her heart was finally full again.

"I didn't know that your mother always saw us being together. You could have told me that."

Wade cleared his throat. "She saw it in a dream and wouldn't stop talking about it. Said that if I didn't get my head out of my butt, I would someday lose you to some other guy."

"That would never happen." She pulled back to meet his eyes. "Actually, it *didn't* happen, and there were several years in there where it could have."

"Meant to be, I guess. That's what my mother said." He lowered his head and gave her a deep kiss. "Thank you for waiting for me."

"I love you, Wade. And there's no way we're not going to spend Christmas together."

"Christmas or Labor Day, you're never gettin' away from me again."

"Please promise me that. Don't ever let me go. Even though I hope we've been through the worst, you never know."

"I promise I won't let my stupid pride get in the way again if you promise you won't believe every foolish rumor about me."

Daisy made the motion of a cross against her heart.

"I've got a gift of my own coming to you. I accepted Mr. Jones's inheritance, and I want you to have it when the time comes. From one old rodeo cowboy to another, one who's a far better man. I like the serendipity of that. Full circle. You deserve it, Wade. You gave up all that money the show offered you to be with me. And I want you to have the ranch working again, back to what it used to be. And I don't want you to break your back doin' it." She smiled what she hoped was a wicked and knowing smile. "I have plans for that back of yours. I need for it to last several more years."

Wade chuckled, wrapped his arms around her waist, and pulled her tight against him. "It sounds like we both found a way to accept a gift we didn't want, so long as we found a way to give it away to someone we love."

"I think that's perfect."

$$\overline{\qquad\qquad\qquad}$$

Epilogue

$$\overline{\qquad\qquad\qquad}$$

Six months later

Dear Rose,

Well, I write letters to Albert. Why not also to you, my dear friend? I hope you know that I miss you dearly, and your boy is doing just fine. We're taking good care of him, yes, we are. We weren't at all sure he'd be okay, what with the injury, and the grief he couldn't bring himself to acknowledge. Daisy has been so good for him, and he for her. You were right about those two. I don't know why I didn't see it.

Sometimes love can happen between the two most unlikely of people, I guess. Especially when they're bound together by the common threads of family, home, and friendship. I don't know why I never saw it before, dear friend. You're right. They're perfect together.

Oh, and the wedding was beautiful! Rather quick, some thought, but why waste time when you know it's right? All us Carvers were present when Wade went down on bended knee after Sunday night dinner at our home. Sadie, Eve, Brenda, and I were sobbing by the end of his heartfelt proposal. I never would have thought those sweet words would have come straight out of "Wild Wade's" lips. What a fine man you raised, Rose. What a fine man.

Daisy almost didn't allow him to finish before she jumped into his arms and said yes. Loudly! She'd been waiting a long time for that moment. In a way, I know you have, too.

The wedding was at Trinity Church, of course, the place that has unfortunately been the site of far too many of our runaway brides. No one was even slightly worried about my Daisy, of course. She nearly flew to the altar. You would be surprised to see how lovely she looked in a white dress with flowing train and sweetheart collar. The girl who loves her jeans and flannel certainly looked like a young Grace Kelly on that auspicious day.

Then again, Wade filled out a tuxedo like a movie star himself. And to think they almost talked him into the dating reality show. Offered him money and still he turned it all down for true love!

Beulah still hasn't given up on Mr. Cowboy, bless her heart. What am I to do? All of mine are hitched and happy so they can roll in more women if they like. There are plenty of men here in need of a good woman. And we are certainly running out of them.

But don't you worry, Rose, your boy has one of the best of our women. Daisy will never stop loving him. And I'm sure babies are coming along, lickety split! If we are lucky enough to get a girl, I will be campaigning for your namesake, a "little Rose."

Well, I best sign off now. Daisy and Wade have invited us all over to the opening of his new rodeo clinic. That poor man, Rusty, died a few months ago and left some money to his daughters. That helped Wade and Daisy to start the clinic, where Wade will be teaching some of his skills. Lincoln will be lending a hand, teaching roping among other things.

I remain your oldest friend, in death as in life. Keep a light on for me, dear Rose.

Kisses and hugs,

~ Lillian Carver

Crazy for You
CHRISTMAS IN STARLIGHT HILL

Chapter 1

If this was all Los Angeles had to offer in the way of single men, Fallon McQueen might as well give up right now. She'd never find a date to her ex-husband Ted's wedding.

A Christmas overkill of tinsel-covered fake trees and strings of red and green blinking lights hung from one end of the room to the other at Anthony's Bistro. The speed dating events were held every Tuesday and Thursday night, kicking into high gear the closer time marched towards the holiday. For some the holiday decorations and music piping through the speakers served as a powerful motivator. *Find someone here tonight, sucker, or spend one more holiday alone.* For Fallon, no more motivation was required. Even so, she'd put the season into her presentation tonight with a tight red velvet dress and matching red pumps. Miss Santa Claus.

Because she needed a man. A very specific man and it would help if his name happened to be Bud. Probably that would be asking too much, but then again, maybe she could have a Christmas miracle just this once.

"Do you like sushi?" Tagg, as his name tag read, now asked.

Whether or not Fallon liked sushi didn't much matter because at this point she had to be flexible. Could Bud be a nickname for Tagg?

Fallon stalled. "Possibly."

"Don't tell me you haven't had sushi. And you're from San Francisco?"

She hated sushi with the red hot fire of a thousand suns but that was beside the point. "No. *Napa Valley*. Starlight Hill."

"*Where?*"

The timer dinged, indicating that her fifteen minutes of 'get to know you' with Tagg had finally concluded.

"Nice to meet you," Fallon said and moved to the next chair.

"Hello there," Danny-boy (as he'd written on his name tag) said. "You're a mighty *fine* looking woman. The Miss Claus dress rocks. Ho,ho,ho."

This guy wasn't going to work because he was a blonde. The hoe joke was the nail in his coffin. Shame.

"Okay, then. Nice to meet you, but I've really got to run."

Fallon stood, slapped the table once to indicate she was done with this round and exited Anthony's. Two weeks of this had produced a big fat zero. The speed dating had been a bad idea. Maybe her worst yet, and she'd had some doozies in her time. The worst of which had to be lying to her mother about having a serious boyfriend. Six months ago. Now she had to go to this stupid wedding and produce said boyfriend, which was a bit of a problem since he didn't exist.

Outside, she took a deep breath of smog-laced air, coughed, and forced her shoulders to unkink. She decided it was safe enough to walk home alone. Due to it being December, the city was lit up for the holidays, providing even more safety lighting than normal. And it was only a few short blocks to her duplex. Fallon slipped off her pumps and switched them with the flats she carried in her bag. Always prepared. That was the ticket. Of course, even she hadn't been prepared when her boss, Delilah, had fired her on the spot for daring to ask for time off at their busiest season. Now Fallon had no job and no man.

Happy Holidays!

About six months ago Ted had announced he would marry on December twentieth which meant that if Fallon went home for the wedding, she'd get to spend Christmas with her son, David. Even though this year wasn't her turn to have him. As long as she agreed to spend it in Starlight Hill she could stay with David at her mother's house while Ted and his new wife were on their honeymoon. David loved Christmas, and Fallon loved David so she wasn't going to miss this chance. Even if it meant she had to produce a man. But Fallon couldn't just have any date for this wedding. Unfortunately, she'd narrowed it down to tall, dark and handsome when her mother pressed for details on her non-existent boyfriend.

"I said sit still, asswipe!" A man's voice rang into the night, rising above the roaring sounds of the freeway and passing cars.

When Fallon rounded the corner to her duplex she came upon a man known all over the world by two short words: Santa Claus. But this Santa Claus looked like a badass, given that he had a man pinned on the ground, his knee pressed into his back. The man on the ground was squirming and shouting out obscenities.

And this was supposed to be a decent neighborhood. "I-is everything okay?" Fallon asked Santa.

Santa gave a quick glance in her direction. "It's all under control, ma'am. Just move along."

"But I live there." Fallon pointed to the duplex just behind them.

"This joker was trying to break into your place when I stopped him."

"So you say," the pinned man said. "I was just out taking a night stroll."

Dressed in black, with a black knit cap and black gloves. Oh God!

"Sure, sure. You'll get your chance to explain it all once the police come. They're on their way," Santa said.

Fallon stomped her foot near the criminal's head. "You've got your nerve! I don't have anything in there worth taking, sir! All you would have accomplished is make me feel so icky I'd have to burn the place down. Next time pick on someone your own size."

Santa quirked a single eyebrow at her but didn't say a word.

"Betsy!" Fallon ran past the two men toward her neighbor's side of the duplex.

Hopefully her elderly neighbor was safe and sound. She finally answered the door though, it being past ten o'clock at night, she took roughly a millennium to open it.

"What on earth?" she asked, holding her cat in her arms.

"I had to see that you were okay!" Fallon shouted at the hard of hearing woman. "There's a man! And a knit cap! I think he was trying to break in!"

"Oh dear," she said, tugging Hercules closer.

"Don't worry, ma'am," Santa said from his place on top of the criminal's back. "I've got this!"

Oh whew, he had it. But who the hell was he? He was dressed like a mall Santa Claus, complete with red outfit, beard, and big-bowl-full-of-jelly belly. But he behaved more like a super hero the way he had that man pinned and unable to budge.

Fallon stared in Santa's direction. "I don't know who *that* Santa is—"

Betsy shut her door.

Okay, so Fallon was on her own. Familiar territory, that, except this time she had company in the form of the criminal and Santa Claus. A few minutes later, the criminal, Santa, *and* the L.A.P.D. It sounded like the start of a demented version of the "Twelve Days of Christmas."

Maybe Kailey was right. Maybe Fallon *should* take her best friend's advice and move back to Starlight Hill.

The two police officers referred to the Santa as Jack, as if they knew him. So maybe he was an off-duty cop. The cops handcuffed the would-be robber, read him his rights, and then shoved him into the back seat. They asked Fallon some questions and a few minutes later were on their way. Fallon was still standing at the curb trying to remember how to breathe when she noticed Santa Jack near her front door. Specifically, next to the overgrown Oleander.

He crooked a finger in her direction.

She walked over. "Thanks so much. I don't know what to say."

"Say you'll get these bushes trimmed. Makes it too easy for someone to hide while they break in. He was coming in through the window. Or trying to."

She'd never thought about it. The bushes were supposed to give her added privacy. Who knew they would give crooks the secrecy to conduct their crookedness?

She worried a fingernail between her teeth. "Could you…I mean is there any way that you would…I know it's silly, because you caught him, right? But what if his…what do you call those people who hang out with the criminal?"

He squinted. "Accomplices?"

"Accomplice! What if his accomplice got in somehow when you weren't looking and he's in my house right now hiding in the closet like in the movies? The ones where you want to yell at the stupid girl for walking inside all by herself. 'No, no! He's inside, you idiot!'" She took a breath. "Maybe you could just…make sure."

He moved closer to the front door. "I'd be happy to check for you. Ease your mind."

"Thank you," Fallon said and unlocked the front door. "Do you have a gun?"

"Nope. Santa doesn't need a gun." He lowered his fake beard.

Holy Santa Claus! She got a good look at an easy smile and the light scruff of a sexy dark beard. He had deep brown eyes, too. So what if he was a little chunky around the middle? As he went through her duplex, opening closet doors, walking through her bedroom and checking the bathroom, Fallon couldn't help but check him out. Because this off duty Santa, as Santas went, was sort of five-alarm-fire hot. He took off his hat to reveal a full head of chocolate brown wavy hair.

Her ovaries wept.

When he pulled off his red and white coat, he also pulled off his fat belly. "Sorry. This is hot."

Oh boy. Yes, she would have to agree. She'd never in her life, except when she was about seven, been so attracted to Santa Claus. But now that the jacket was off she could see a trim, athletic physique under there. He'd worn a white long sleeved t-shirt under the jacket that seemed a half size too small, given the way his muscles strained at the fabric.

"Cleared," he said and turned back to her. "You're good to go."

Fallon batted her eyelashes. "Thank you so much, offi-cer…officer…"

"Jack Cooper, but just call me Jack. I'm not a cop anymore. As in permanently off-duty. By choice."

"I'm Fallon McQueen."

She might have thought him younger if she went by his lean and agile build, but a long look into his mocha eyes said otherwise. The eyes were edgy with small crinkled lines that led her to believe he'd lived a full and possibly dangerous life.

"So what are you going to do now, Santa Jack? Canvas the neighborhoods to rescue poor women like me?"

"Nah. First, 'rescue' poor women like you? Don't think so. Without me here, pretty sure you would have shamed that burglar to death. Anyway, I'm headed off soon. Blowing this pop stand."

"Where to?"

He shrugged. "Don't know yet. Going to figure it out as I go."

Sounded wonderfully odd to Fallon. She'd spent the past few years working two jobs. When an opportunity had come up to make serious money working in L.A. as a celebrity stylist two years ago, she'd made the move. Even-tually she planned to have her own hair salon on Rodeo Drive, if she could ever find an affordable lease. But as a single mom, she couldn't imagine what it would be like to let it all go. Crazy with a capital K, probably.

"You're kidding, right?"

"Nope."

This got to her. He was so incredibly assertive and confident even while stating the most ridiculous fact. Who started over at their age? She'd pegged him to be like her, around mid-thirties. They were supposed to be elbow deep in their careers, moving up the ladder two or three rungs at a time. Kicking off the fools behind them so there might be more room at the top.

"Starting over," Fallon said. "So you have no immediate plans?"

"That's the idea."

This guy seemed *perfect*. Her Christmas miracle. He was gorgeous, Alpha-protective, strong, obviously loved kids and sounded wide open. He had the dark hair and eyes she'd described to Mom. His name wasn't Bud, either, but she could figure something out later. As an added bonus, when Ted laid eyes on this man, his balls would shrivel up inside him and die. Who cared what he did or didn't do for a living? They could always make something up. All she'd told Mom was that her fake boyfriend had a 'very important job.' Mom would finally stop trying to fix her up with all her friend's bachelor nephews.

This deal had to be done just right, carefully and with the utmost finesse so she wouldn't scare off this super-hot guy before he could agree to go to the destination wedding with her and pretend to be her boyfriend.

"How about some milk and cookies?"

Chapter 2

"Why not?"

The blonde was hot and leggy, two of Jack's favorite qualities in a woman. She was dressed in a tight short red dress with white fur lining the edge…very Christmas of her.

Look who was talking. He was dressed as Santa Claus.

So far, this evening didn't bode well for taking it easy for the next few months as he'd planned to do. He'd known her, a perfect stranger, five minutes if that and was already worried about her, which didn't help his personal situation any. He was supposed to be shedding his white knight syndrome, not rescuing someone. But he'd been walking to Original Joe's for a drink after his Santa duty was over, minding his own damned business, when he spotted the low life. One month out of the force and he still couldn't get away from the criminal element.

He watched now as Fallon moved to the small kitchen, poured two glasses of milk and set them on the table. For the first time, he noticed her composure slip as she walked a little unsteadily on her feet. Despite the bravado she'd showcased outside, she had to be dazed and frightened. Break-ins happened every day all over the city, and the victims always felt violated. Even though he'd stopped it, she'd been a witness to how close the crime had come to happening.

"You okay?"

"Oh, sure. Why wouldn't I be?" She set a package of Oreo cookies on the table and sat.

"It's normal to be rattled." He took a seat at the table.

"I'm fine." But her right hand shook slightly as she raised a glass of milk to her lips.

"Maybe I should come by tomorrow and trim those bushes back for you." He didn't seem able to help himself. It was a sickness.

"No worries. I'll get the landlord to do it."

"Good." He almost sighed in relief, except for the fact that he knew damned well he'd drive by tomorrow to make sure it had been done.

"So is this Santa gig something you do every year?"

He nodded. "We take turns for the police officer's association kid's night we have every year. Tonight I was filling in for my friend Henry."

"You must love Christmas." She said this conversationally, as if she hadn't just stepped over her would-be assailant.

To Jack, this meant she might be good at compartmentalizing. They probably had a lot in common besides the red outfits. "I do love Christmas."

Her green eyes lit up. "My little boy loves Christmas."

"You married?"

"No!" She almost shouted. "Why would you think that? I'm divorced, like half of the population."

"Hey, I'm sorry. Take it easy. I assumed you live alone,

and I was kind of hoping maybe you didn't." He wouldn't worry half as much. "No roommates, either?"

"It's just me."

Craptastic. "So where's your little boy?"

"He lives up in Napa Valley with his father. That's where I'm from."

"Kind of had a feeling you weren't from L.A."

She frowned. "Are you? From L.A.?"

"Born and bred."

"You would appreciate my small town."

"Bet I would. I'm sick of the city. Maybe I'll check that place out when I think about landing somewhere." He took a bite of a cookie. Stale. She didn't like these cookies nearly as much as she enjoyed the Little Debbie cakes, given there were several empty wrappers in her bedroom trash can.

"Jack...I'm really grateful for what you did tonight. I don't even want to think about what would have happened if I had come home and surprised him..." The hand holding a cookie trembled.

The significance of what had just happened appeared to dawn on her. No doubt she'd lose sleep tonight and that pissed him the hell off. When the criminals couldn't take your property, they stole your peace of mind.

He was still working on getting his back.

"Look, here's my phone number. Call me if the landlord doesn't take care of the bushes tomorrow and I'll do it." He reached for his wallet and took out his old business card. *Juan Carlos Cooper, Detective, Homicide Division-L.A.P.D.* "That's my cell number. Still got the same one."

"Thanks." To her credit, Fallon took the card and barely blinked when she glanced at it. "So Jack is a nickname?"

"Everybody calls me Jack, including my family."

She gave him the flirty smile again. That smile had him thinking of her long legs wrapped around his back. Given that he was dressed as Santa, he forced his thoughts to more G-rated ones.

"I appreciate what you did for me tonight, and I think you deserve a break from the city. A change of scenery and some fresh air is what you need. A little vacation in wine country."

"It's an idea."

"So I have a proposition for you."

First an attempted burglary in progress and now a proposition from a sexy woman. This night had taken a turn from worrisome to intriguing. "A proposition."

"Well, don't make it sound slutty."

He leaned forward and hooked his thumb to his chest. "Do I look like someone who has a problem with slutty?"

"I'm trying to do you a favor. You sound like you need some direction in life, and you're a nice guy. You saved my life."

"Let's not get carried away."

"You might have saved my life! And I'm going to help you out."

He managed a grin. That might make two in the last ten minutes. Wasn't this an exceptional night? Check him out with all the grinning. "What *kind* of proposition?"

"I'd like you to be my date."

He cleared his throat. "And how do you know I don't swing the other way?"

"Uh. Sorry." She winced and grabbed the edge of her kitchen table, white-knuckling it. "Do you?"

"No, but that was fun." This time the grin went so wide his cheeks hurt.

Fallon let a breath out. "I have to go to a wedding in Starlight Hill."

"Uh-huh. When is this wedding?"

"Next Saturday, but I'm getting there a few days earlier for the tree lighting and the parade. And here's the thing. It would be nice if you could also pretend that we've known each other a little bit longer than we have."

"Longer than—" He glanced at his watch. "Fifteen minutes?"

"More like six months. You'd be doing me a *huge* favor and this wedding will be a nice diversion for you. Think of it as an all-expense paid vacation in wine country."

"A vacation would be nice." He hadn't thought of wine country up north, more like a beach in Maui, but beggars couldn't be choosers.

"And also if you could, like, pretend that you're in-love with me." Fallon wouldn't look him in the eye. "That would be *such* a help."

"You don't ask for much, do you, Sweetcakes?"

"*Sweetcakes*? Where do you get off calling me Sweetcakes?"

"The Little Debbie cakes."

"You checked my bedroom *garbage can*?"

"What can I say?" He shrugged. "I notice stuff."

She didn't say anything for a long beat but then laughed and smacked his shoulder. "All right, I'll forgive you for nicknaming me after my favorite late-night snack. What do you say? What else have you got going on, pal?"

"Let me see if I understand this. You want me to go with you to a wedding and pretend I'm madly in love with you."

"It's not like you have other plans. You're just leaving and were going to figure it out on the way. All I'm doing is giving you a plan."

"Why? Because you can't stand anyone not having a plan?"

"You have to admit it's a little stupid to be our age without a plan."

He found the whole idea incredibly amusing. It had to be the first time he'd ever been asked out by a woman while wearing his Santa suit. "Do I have to put out?"

Her face flushed pink. "Absolutely not! All you have to do is stay through the wedding on Saturday and then you can just go on your merry way the next day."

"Huh. No putting out."

"No."

They sat quietly for the next few minutes as he drank his milk and she picked at her cookie. Truthfully, she was right in that he could use a break from his surroundings. He'd have probably been headed up to Oregon to see his family for Christmas soon anyway, so he could just make this one big trip.

A road trip.

He finished drinking the last dregs of his milk and leaned back in his seat. "Fine. I'll do it."

"Oh, thank you!"

"It's crazy, yeah, but I'm going to be doing crazy for a while. So this is going to fit right along with my current plan."

"Ah ha! So you admit you have a plan!"

"I do," Jack said meeting her gaze. "I have a plan not to have a plan. That's my plan."

"You are so argumentative, you know that? I'll make you a reservation to fly out next Wednesday."

"Nope."

"Does Wednesday not work? You said—"

"Do you have any idea how expensive that plane ticket is going to be?"

"Yes, but I've got miles I've been saving up. Don't worry about the cost."

He couldn't let her do that when he had a much better idea. "If we're going to do this, it's going to be my way."

"And what way is that?"

"Road trip."

"Are you *kidding* me? You want to drive for hours, fighting over the music, making pit stops and getting on each other's nerves? We just met."

"That's all the more reason to spend more time together if we're supposed to pretend we've known each other for months. Plus, I haven't done a road trip in years. Always wanted to go up the Pacific Coast Highway."

"Highway One? That could take forever!"

Driving up north the scenic route could take a good eight hours depending on traffic, but it could definitely be done in one day. He folded his arms across his chest and let her take it all in. He was dead serious about this. If she wanted him to participate in her con, she would do it his way—which in this case literally was the highway.

"This is ridiculous," Fallon said.

Did she mean his idea or hers? "And we're pretty much smack dab in the middle of ridiculous. It should feel homey to you by now."

She threw her head back and groaned. "Fine. Road trip it is."

He rose to leave, grabbing his red jacket and hat. "Lock up tight. Like Fort Knox tight. I'll see you next week."

The timing was perfect for a road trip. Not to mention the fact that Jack would have company in the form of one captivating woman. She was sexy and funny, even if her idea for him to pose as a man desperately in-love with her when they'd just met at the scene of a potential crime seemed a little…off-kilter to say the least. But a scenic drive up the Pacific coast would set anyone's head straight, and he had a good feeling that he wasn't the only one who needed a break from the city. He should have taken the time for a trip like this before now, and not waited until the job had eaten away at him bit by bit until he was little more than an empty corn husk.

For once in many years, he had the time. He had the company. He had the destination. Now he needed the right vehicle.

"Will it make it up the coast?" Jack ran his hand down the hood of the classic Mustang convertible in Pete's Garage.

Pete had retired from the L.A.P.D. and now rebuilt cars in his spare time. He'd completely rebuilt the engine, added chrome rims, and had been trying to find a buyer for months. Being that his friends and clients were all a bunch of police officers, he hadn't been able to unload it until it had passed smog.

"It will get you there in style."

Jack walked around it, kicking the tires.

"Hey, man. You sure about this?" Pete said.

"That's not the greatest sales pitch I've ever heard."

Pete scowled. "I mean leaving the department, genius. You're the best cop I've ever known."

"Thanks. But I'm done."

"Maybe you just need a break."

He did. He'd pushed too hard for too long. Lost people he cared about and relationships that meant something, and nearly lost himself. But he wasn't here to argue. He was here to buy a car. The new and improved Jack was going to be carefree and loose and let people take care of their own damned problems. This week would be about a wedding in wine country. Fun. Carefree.

"Why the hell did you paint it red?" The car had a black top and tricked out rims, but that red reminded him too much of Santa's sleigh.

"What about it?" He lifted a shoulder. "It's Christmas-y."

"Yeah. All I need now are the reindeer."

"In fact..." Pete walked back to his garage, and came back carrying a wreath which he placed on the grill of the car. "On the house."

Red or not, it would have to do. Jack liked the idea of a convertible. It added to the whole cheery thing he'd be rocking next week.

"Merry Christmas," Jack said, and forked over the cash he'd pulled out of his savings account.

The following week as planned, he left every light on,

set the alarm, and locked up his condo. He picked up his duffel bag, put down the convertible's top, slipped on his baseball cap backwards, and headed to Fallon's place. The powerful engine made a gratifying growl that reminded him he was a man, and he drove to the other end of town taking his sweet time. Enjoying the admiring glances from other drivers. December in Los Angeles, where one could almost always count on driving with the top down. It was one of the perks of living here. When he pulled in front of Fallon's duplex the hedges were trimmed back to leave a clear view of the window. A good omen. He'd managed to restrain himself from driving by her house all week. But look at that, something had already gone right.

So far, so good.

Fallon waited for him by the curb with no less than four suitcases surrounding her. "You're late. And what is *this*?" She pointed to the convertible.

He nodded toward her luggage. "I was going to ask you the same thing."

"It's a wedding. I need choices." She tipped her chin.

"Right."

Damn. This was what he got for being single so long. He'd forgotten a woman's little idiosyncrasies, like bringing an entire wardrobe on a vacation. No worries. He'd make this work. He managed to force two suitcases in the far-from-generous trunk and threw the others in the backseat with his bag.

"One bag?" Fallon studied him, obviously worried he'd planned on wearing jeans to the wedding.

"Don't worry. I've got a suit in there." He opened the passenger side door and waved her in.

She slid him a look. "You realize we'll probably have to put up the top when we go through San Francisco."

"Sure."

He hopped in the driver's seat. Turned to give her an effort at a smile, and handed over the extra baseball cap he'd brought. It was going to get windy and all that long wavy hair would be flying all over the place. She accepted the hat and then slipped it on after a beat. Her lips tipped up in a half-smile, almost like she was reluctant to be too encouraging. He understood she wasn't ecstatic about the road trip and probably not about the baseball cap, either.

Tough.

He hadn't seen her since they'd met last week, and she looked prettier than he'd remembered. Long blonde hair fell past her shoulders. Big green eyes and a sweet smile. World class ass. This was a stupid idea, actually, going to a wedding and pretending to be in-love with a woman he might fall for if he let himself. Good thing he wouldn't let himself. He still wasn't ready to go through that again. One thing he'd decided he especially liked about Fallon? So far she hadn't asked too many personal questions. He assumed she'd checked him out and determined he wasn't a serial killer posing as a cop. God, at least he hoped so.

"Seat belt," he said.

"I hope we're not making too many stops." She clicked the belt in place.

"Some." He made no move to pull out onto the street.

"Sometime today?"

"One more thing."

He leaned over and kissed her full on the lips. It was supposed to be quick, a get acquainted kiss so they'd be somewhat familiar with each other. But when hot lust poured through his veins he was stunned. Her lips were soft and invited him to stay awhile. Probably a bad idea. The next thing he realized, his lips practically jumped off hers like they'd been stung.

Her two warm hands were flush against his chest. "What do you think you're doing?"

Exactly. What the hell am I doing? And also: what the hell was that?

"Breaking the ice," he said. Sounded as good of an excuse as any.

She blinked but didn't say a word.

He cleared his throat. "I'm supposed to be madly in-love with you."

Her lips quivered now, in some kind of righteous indignation or confusion. He couldn't figure out which and wasn't about to try.

"But it's fake," she finally said.

"I know. But if you push me away every time I kiss you we're not going to be too convincing."

One finger brushed against her lower lip. "I won't do that once we get there."

"Nice try, but anyone with half a brain can see if a couple has just met or if they're comfortable around each other. It won't matter what we say, it's more about what we do."

"But—"

He pulled out on to the street. "Hey, it's your lie."

⬜

MAYBE FALLON HAD MADE A MISTAKE, getting into this convertible with a part-time Santa. Too bad about the 'I'm-too-young-for-a-midlife-crisis' cherry red convertible Mustang. She was certain it did beastly gas mileage. Still, it wasn't the anticipated long drive ahead of her that bothered Fallon now, or the wind whipping through the car. Or the orange baseball cap.

It was the amazing kiss.

She'd been thinking about that short but devastating kiss for several minutes simply because, though it was possibly all of two seconds long, she'd been kissed within an inch of her life. He was a solid wall of hot male testosterone and oh boy he smelled so good. She wasn't sure she'd ever in her life been kissed with such…confidence. By a man who had a plan to have no plan. She hated that about him. No one at their age should be so laid-back even if it had helped his availability for this wedding week. But he had a good point, too, and one she hadn't considered. Most people would be able to tell that she and Jack had just met a week ago.

"We should take advantage of this long drive to get to know each other," Fallon said.

"And you need to stop jumping when I touch you."

"You might have started with something besides a *kiss*. Like maybe holding my hand."

"You're right, I could have, but I'm not six."

They snaked up Highway One through Malibu. Sunny blue skies, sandy beaches, and in the distance sailboats out for the day. Beautiful scenery if a person was in no rush which Jack made abundantly clear he was not. He drove at a slow enough speed that several cars passed them. But as long as they arrived in plenty of time, Fallon would grind her teeth into dust if that's what it took. As an added bonus, if she'd thought he looked good in a Santa suit that was nothing to how he filled out a pair of worn Levis, a gray Henley long sleeved shirt, and black biker boots.

A few minutes into the drive, Jack pulled over in a rest stop along Malibu beach.

"What is it?" Fallon asked. "It's too soon to stop."

"Photo-op," he said and grabbed his camera from the back seat. "Get out."

"Get *out?* Me?"

"You see anyone else in this car? I want you to stand next to the car so I can take your photo."

"Why?"

"Do you or do you *not* want to convince everyone I'm madly in love with you?"

"Fine!" Feeling a tad ridiculous, she stepped out and stood beside the car as he snapped one photo after another. Click. Click. People were staring.

"Try to smile."

"I *am* smiling." She gritted her teeth and rested her hand on the hood of the Mustang. "How long have you owned this car?"

"About a week. Bought it for the trip."

She dropped her hand. "Are you *kidding* me?"

"Nope. Got a great deal." He reached for his phone then and took a few photos with that, too.

Finally, she was allowed back in the car. "Was that necessary?"

"Absolutely." Jack handed over his phone. "Now I've got photos of my girlfriend, the woman I'm so madly in love with, in my phone. You haven't thought this one through all the way, have you, Sweetcakes?"

"Listen. I do appreciate everything you're doing to help me out, but if you call me Sweetcakes again you're going to be walking funny."

"I'd almost like to see you try that. You don't like Sweetcakes. What do you want me to call you?"

"Fallon!" She shouted and then realized a term of endearment only lent credence to the whole lovers thing. "Or…babe."

"Ah." He peered at her from lowered shades. "Good choice."

And damn it all, he was right again. She hadn't thought anything about this through. Why would she when she'd come up with the idea on the fly right after being nearly victimized? Usually her best ideas came when brainstorming, but Jack was right in that she often had to smooth them over before she'd present them to anyone else. Straighten out the rough edges.

"Let's get our stories straight," she said as he pulled back on Pacific Highway. "I'll need to know what to tell people. What made you decide you didn't want to be a cop anymore?"

He narrowed eyes at her. "Do we want to tell people I'm a cop?"

Former cop, Fallon almost corrected him. "Why not?"

"People don't like cops. They won't talk to them. And it's not that impressive."

"I think being a homicide detective is quite impressive."

He shook his head. "Here's what we're going to tell them. I'm a high-powered defense attorney. I rake in the big bucks."

"You want to be a *defense* attorney? Not a prosecutor?"

He slid her a look. "Do you want me to work long hours for shit pay, or do you want me to have money to burn? You decide."

"Point taken."

"So I'm a wheeling and dealing defense attorney, and I've never been married before. I've——"

"Is that true?"

"None of it is true. I thought that was the point."

"So you've *been* married before?"

"Do you want to know about the real me or the fake me?"

Both. But he was along for the ride and being a good sport about it, too. She shouldn't ask too much of him and he obviously didn't want to talk about his broken marriage. Coincidentally, neither did she.

"Shouldn't you know something about me, too?"

"It's a little more realistic for a guy not to know every little thing about his girl but yeah. Hit me with the headlines. All the need-to-know stuff."

"I've been married before, and Ted and I have a son, David, who's nine now. That's the wedding we're going to. David's father is getting re-married."

"Wait. We're going to your ex-husband's wedding?"

The wedding of one of my ex-husbands. Might be best not to add that just now. "Did I not mention that?"

"You didn't, no."

"Oh, my bad. I know it sounds weird but we have a son together. Ted is…Ted. I have to put up with him."

"That doesn't mean going to his wedding."

L.A. people often didn't understand the small town mentality. But the residents of Starlight Hill were like one large and dysfunctional family.

"I want to see David. When I found out that Ted's parents weren't going to be available to watch him while Ted honeymooned, my Mom was their second choice."

Jack nodded as if that made sense to him on some level.

"We're stopping."

"We are so not stopping. We're only in Santa Barbara!"

"It's lunch time," Jack said and five minutes later he'd pulled into Johnny Rocket's.

"I could have gone at least another hour without lunch," Fallon complained, putting her hand on the door handle.

"Don't move."

She froze. "What now? Why?"

He took off his baseball cap and propped his sunglasses on his head. "Do you always ask this many questions?"

"Yes."

He hopped out of the car and came to her side of the door to open it. "Now you can move."

"That's really not necessary," Fallon said. "I'm sure you want to get points for being a fantastic boyfriend but no one's watching us now."

Still, it was kind of a nice change to have someone open doors for her. Jack went ahead and opened the door for both her and an elderly couple walking in behind them.

"Lover," Jack said as they were walked to their table by the hostess.

She didn't say a word, only stared at him.

"I want to get points for being a fantastic *lover*. I'm too old to be someone's boyfriend."

The cute hostess with a reindeer antlers headband seated them, taking a thorough appraisal of Jack when she handed him a menu. She might as well have licked her lips. "Your waitress will be right with you."

Jack glanced at the menu. "Tell me about this ex-husband."

Fallon hated to think about Ted, much less talk about him. But she understood it would be necessary. "He's a lawyer."

He put his menu down. "Change of plans. I can't be a lawyer if your ex is a lawyer. I'm not that good. He'll sniff me out in no time. You should have said something."

"It's good we're figuring this out now." She thrummed her fingers on the table.

Jack seemed to be daydreaming. "I think I'd like to be the CEO of my own sports equipment company."

"Why can't you be a homicide detective?"

He narrowed his eyes. "We went over this."

"It's just that I've already asked enough of you. Pretending to be in-love with me is a big enough lie."

He went back to studying the menu without another word.

"Order anything you'd like. On me," Fallon said.

"What'll you have?" The waitress sidled up next to their booth.

"Two of the giant burgers, and two sides of sweet potato fries, with two chocolate milkshakes. Actually, make one a strawberry milkshake and one chocolate." He slapped the menu shut. "And whatever she's having."

Fallon snorted. "Hungry much?"

"Just kidding." He spoke to the waitress. "I ordered for both of us."

The waitress didn't say another word but just took off with their orders.

"Why did you do that? I can order for myself. Just because we're in a nineteen-fifties themed restaurant doesn't mean you get to make my choices."

"Yeah?" His warm gaze did a slow slide from her eyes to her breasts. "You just don't look like you eat in places like these often."

Their gazes locked for a moment and neither of them said a word. Fallon looked away first. Maybe she should focus on light conversation to get away from the sizzle of warmth traveling down her stomach to her thighs.

"Don't you have family to spend Christmas with?"

"My parents moved to Oregon a few years ago when they retired, following my older brother and his family. I'll stop by and see them after your wedding. It's good timing. Right direction."

"You'll drive all the way to Oregon after the wedding?"

"Right."

"You can leave the day after the wedding, and I'll just

tell everyone that you can't spend Christmas with us because of work or something."

A few minutes later they were back on "the one" as Jack kept referring to it, making stops along the way so that he could take even more blasted photos. By the time they got to Pismo Beach, Fallon thought she might have an aneurysm if they stopped once more. Jack took an exit off the highway.

"Again?" She gritted her teeth.

"No worries." He glanced at his phone. "We're making good time."

Fallon was about to let him know that not only were they not making good time, but they were about two hours behind her air tight schedule, when he put the GPS down and took her hand in his. It wasn't so much the action that jarred her this time but his touch. She stared at their hands linked together. Stared at his profile as he drove. The feel of his warm hand holding hers did something strange to her equilibrium. She was only a few hours into this road trip and going home was already messing with her head. She was busy wanting things she shouldn't. Remembering what it was like to even have a lover. *Lover.* He'd just had to use that word with her. The truth was she hadn't wanted or needed anyone in her bed in a very long time.

Too long.

"Why are we stopping here?"

He gave her an easy smile. "Monarch butterflies."

Chapter 4

Jack's first instincts had been dead on. Fallon might need this road trip more than he did, and he would make her enjoy it or die trying. Which he just might, if those 'kill' looks of hers were ever given any real power. He recognized himself in her. Too uptight for too long, focused on the end game and not seeing the beauty of what was right in front of her.

A month ago, it had been the same for him.

But now he was trying, trying like hell to grab life by the balls and squeeze tight. If he still had no idea what he would do with the rest of his life, he would figure it out soon enough. He had options. He could always stay in Oregon and pound nails for his brother.

"Pismo Beach is famous for monarchs. They migrate from late October through February." Jack made the turn off the highway and followed the signs to the Pismo Beach Monarch Butterfly Grove. "This might be good timing."

"It's just another tourist trap," Fallon said as he led her by the small of her back towards the tree line.

She didn't seem as resistant to his touch which made

Jack wonder if he should now back off. But he didn't want to because he liked touching her. She was silky soft and all woman. Still, he hardly wanted the added complication of becoming interested in someone when he had no plan. Women were, of course, *so* attracted to that.

The waves crashed in the background, the sea air fresh, salty and clear. It was a good day to be alive and for the first time in years he didn't regret being a part of this crazy messed up world. There was a small trailer with a drawing of a monarch butterfly printed on its side selling t-shirts. They passed by it, following a small crowd to the viewing area where dozens of butterflies congregated in the tree grove. There were so many of them that they'd formed a unique moving pattern, like a wave at a football game. They migrated south for the warmth, sure, but they also seemed to enjoy being together. Sooner or later, Jack would find that again. The knowledge of being connected to something better…something that made a difference. That mattered. It used to be his work, but now it would have to be…something else.

He caught her staring at them, too, a wistful look on her face. "Pretty cool, huh?"

"It's like a quilt."

That was another way of looking at it.

"We should go," she said after a few more minutes. "Lots of miles ahead."

But he couldn't leave without buying a couple of t-shirts, one for each of them. Then he thought about her little boy and bought another one, guessing at the size. She'd gone ahead of him, of course, not being the type of woman to wait for anyone. He sort of liked and appreciated that about her, while being simultaneously irritated by it. Pretty much standard fare for him. The story of his life had been to be attracted to strong women who didn't appreciate his brand of protectiveness. He was half Hispanic, for the love of God. It was practically his birthright.

When he arrived at the Mustang she was sitting on its hood staring towards the trees in the distance. "I'm sorry. I always feel guilty coming to places like these without David."

"Not quite the same as being here." He threw her a kid-sized t-shirt. "Guessed at the size."

She caught it one-handed. "Thank you. He would really love this place."

For the first time since he'd met Fallon McQueen, Jack felt a tightness in his chest quite different from the one that had taken up residence there a few months ago. This one was mildly pleasant and barely recognizable. She loved that kid, and he could see it written all over her sweet smile.

"Tell me about him." He pulled out of the grove's parking lot and headed back to the highway.

Jack pulled on to the freeway and listened to Fallon talk about David. He was a math whiz, liked baseball, and happened to live in a town where the famous Oakland Sliders retired pitcher Billy Turlock ran a kid's sports camp, which gave him plenty of opportunities to develop his skills. Skills, which if you wanted to believe his mother, were those of a future World Series hitter.

"And just in case it comes up, which it probably won't since it was forever ago, Billy was my boyfriend in high school."

"Interesting. And you two are still friends?"

"Small town. Plus, Billy's a great guy. He hired me when I needed a job, and then his wife hired me at their winery for a while. She wasn't his wife at the time…this is a long story."

"I have time."

"You'll see when we get to Starlight Hill that people there are just…different. We help each other out. It's not like L.A."

"So why did you leave?"

"I wanted to do something with my life, not just work odds jobs forever. I wanted David to be…proud of me."

"I'm sure he is."

She smiled at that but something in the quick blink of her eyes told him that Fallon wasn't quite proud of herself. And he would investigate that further, were it his problem to fix. If he hadn't decided that he would stop being so damn curious about other people and get a life.

Fallon turned up the radio when a Bruno Mars song played, and Jack tried to concentrate on the road. Not on the beautiful woman sitting beside him, who seemed to have good rhythm given by the way she bounced in perfect time. Fallon was unfortunately turning out to be far more complicated than he'd initially thought. She had a body like a centerfold's but had her heart in her eyes when she talked about her son. He had hoped she'd be a woman with little on her mind but getting to a wedding and having a good time. No such luck. She was real and genuine, and he couldn't figure out why that bothered the hell out of him.

Because you're not ready for someone like her, genius. Bad timing.

He pulled his mental focus back to the road. A mid-sized pickup truck switched lanes in front of him, carrying a load of Christmas trees. The trees jostled about in the back and didn't look to be tied down properly. Worried him a little. Again, not his problem. He put a little more distance between him and the truck and just as he did several Christmas trees spilled out on to the road. The truck swerved to the left, and Jack briefly wondered why he seemed destined to attract trouble wherever he went. He swerved to the right just as a large fir rolled on to his dashboard with a loud thunk. He tried to avoid the inevitable.

But he still ran over a Christmas tree.

FALLON HAD BEEN RIGHT in the middle of getting down with her semi-bad self when a plunk drew her attention away from the funk. A Christmas tree landed on the hood of their car, and then several more spilled out on to the road. She froze. Jack reacted quickly and swerved presumably to avoid the attack of the Christmas trees. No such luck as he ran over one. Or two. Instead of the smell of road kill, a lovely pine-scented fragrance surrounded her. And probably plenty of tree sap too.

"Are you okay?" Jack's hand curled around her thigh and squeezed.

"I'm all right." She shook off the daze and stared at the hood of the car. "But your car doesn't look so good."

"Yeah."

Steam rose from underneath the hood of the Mustang, meaning that it probably didn't appreciate being hit by a tree. The truck's driver, a man dressed in a floppy Santa hat and candy-stripe red suspenders, ran around the highway waving his arms around and screaming like a lunatic while he picked up Christmas trees. This had all created a commotion and stopped traffic in the lane behind them while cars slowed to a crawl in the passing lane. Some drivers honked, laughed, and asked where they might find the seventy-five percent off sale.

Jack helped her out of the passenger side door and walked her to the side of the highway, and over the guard rail. "Stay here. I'm going to secure the scene."

The man who wasn't going to be a cop anymore sprang into action while Fallon tried hard not to notice that he was sex personified, even while yelling at people to stop staring and move along, or bending to pick up trees.

She fished her phone out and dialed Kailey. "Running a little late here."

"Where are you? Sounds like you're in a tunnel." One of her little boys yelled in the background and Kailey shushed him. "What's going on?"

"I was hit by a Christmas tree."

Dead silence for a beat. "No really. What happened?"

"Really!" Fallon sighed. "We were following this truck overloaded with trees and then a few of them rolled out on to the highway."

"Are you all right?"

"We're fine, but the car isn't. I've got a bad feeling about this."

She'd lost her job, almost been the victim of a crime, and now she'd had an accident with a Christmas tree. Difficult to believe she wasn't stuck under a dark cloud of bad luck lately.

"I still can't believe you got him to agree to come to the wedding with you and pretend to be your fake boyfriend."

"I suspect the man has a hero complex. All that Latin machismo."

He was now helping the police set up cones on the highway while another cop directed all other vehicles around the truck. She was beginning to think that maybe machismo had received a bad rap for too many years. It wasn't half bad from this angle.

"What's he like? Tell me more."

"My god he's pretty."

"Hmmm," Kailey said. "So you want to date him for real?"

"Uh-uh. Not a good idea."

He was now under the hood of the car and from where she stood, not looking too happy. He scowled and ran a hand down his face.

"Rosie wants me to tell you that she'll beg the landlord not to raise the lease if you'll take over the Curl Up and Dye," Kailey said.

An old-fashioned throwback to the seventies hair salon was not what Fallon had in mind for her storefront. She wanted modern and cutting edge.

"Still not interested. I've got to go and figure out what we're going to do about the car."

Fallon hung up with Kailey and went to meet Jack under the hood. "How bad is it?"

He squinted above a puff of smoke. "Thought I told you to wait over there. It's not safe here."

"Excuse me if I'm not the little woman. I want to know what's up."

"I called a tow truck. We'll know more when we get it to a shop."

"A shop!" It was difficult not to clutch her heart.

"Yeah."

Her experience with auto repair shops involved days waiting to hear how bad the damage would be, followed by a quote that made her want to throw up and give up driving for public transportation, followed by another week of waiting for said work to be complete. Surprising herself, Fallon felt genuine disappointment when she realized this road trip had probably come to an untimely end.

Chapter 5

They had the Mustang towed to an auto shop in Pismo Beach. Fallon stood by Jack and listened as the mechanic rattled off lingo she couldn't quite grasp. But she clearly heard the word 'tomorrow.' It would mean she'd miss the welcome breakfast her mother had planned. Fallon didn't much mind, though she knew Mom would be pissed. She'd use it as one more reason to demonstrate that Fallon was still too flighty and irresponsible. As if it was her fault that she'd nearly been impaled by a tree. Mom would just suggest, and maybe rightfully so, that Fallon shouldn't have been driving up in the first place.

After speaking with the mechanic, Jack pulled her aside. "Look, I'll buy you a plane ticket so you don't have to wait. You fly up and I'll wait for the car. I'll get up there as soon as I can."

"You would do that?"

"I checked. There are a few regional airports not too far. You could go see what's available." He pulled out his wallet and handed her his credit card.

"No, Jack. I said I'd pay for everything." She tried to hand it back to him.

"The road trip was my idea. Take the card."

She stared at it in her hands. "But what are you going to do?"

He took a seat on a red-covered vinyl chair in the waiting area of the shop and stretched his long legs out. "Guess I'll go find a motel room for the night. I'm looking at this as an adventure. Someday, believe me, this will actually be funny."

And today is not that day were his unspoken words. She felt bad for him, but she had to get to Starlight Hill.

"Okay, then. I'll see you tomorrow, or whenever you get there. Call me when you're in town and I'll give you directions. I can always make up some excuse, like you had to work late at your super important job."

He shoved hands in his pockets. "This gives us less time to get our stories straight, but maybe we'll just make it up on the fly."

"More fun anyway."

She tried to smile but the thought worried her. If Jack made up something about their non-existent six-month relationship, she had a feeling it would be pretty wild and outlandish and she'd find herself going along with it to keep up the farce. Later, she'd have to live it down and he'd have moved on to…whatever he was moving on to.

Fallon ordered an Uber and walked outside with Jack to move her luggage.

"I'm sorry your road trip ended like this," she said.

When the Uber driver came, a kid who looked to be twenty-something, Jack loaded the suitcases in the trunk of the sedan without any assistance. "I'll see you tomorrow. Make sure you talk me up real good with all my fake future in-laws."

"Okay, Jack. And thank you for an…interesting time."

Should she hug him? Give him a peck on the cheek? Lips? He inspired far more than a peck, so true, but this wasn't really the time or the place standing right in front of Sam's Auto Repair, under the watchful eyes of a fresh-faced college age kid who was already staring. But Jack made the decision for her, tugging her into a hug that didn't feel at all awkward. She found herself crushed against his hard chest and enveloped in his heat. He smelled like pine and salt air and sand and one hundred percent male. She closed her eyes and wondered why someone like Jack would have no plan. But she had enough of her own problems to work out for now. One of them getting to this wedding.

Jack let her go and opened the back passenger door for her. "Seat belt."

"Of course." She took her seat and gave him one last smile before the door shut.

"Dude! Where you going with all that luggage? Are you moving?" Her Man-Child driver asked.

"No. I'm going to a wedding. Take me to the closest airport."

The driver pulled away from the curb, and she glanced behind her to see Jack walk back into the shop.

"Right on. I love weddings. Free food and drinks. I wish I got invited to more weddings."

"Don't worry, you're still young. The invites are coming."

The thought seemed to cheer him. "Airport, here we come!"

Her young driver chatted about school finals, traffic, and pizza, but Fallon barely heard him. She thought about Jack sitting alone in the auto shop. Thought of him getting a hotel room for the night. Alone. What a damn waste. She thought about a man who would restrain a criminal even while dressed in a Santa suit. Who worried about her overgrown Oleander bushes and offered to trim them. Who would drop whatever he'd been *not* planning to do to help her ridiculous situation just because she'd asked. A man who would buy her son a t-shirt when he'd never even met him. A man who would give her his *credit card* to book a flight home because he'd inconvenienced her by being behind the wrong truck.

"Turn around."

"Did ya forget something?"

"Yes, I did."

So she'd be a day late. No big deal. She wasn't going to have Jack drive the rest of his road trip alone. Not when she was getting used to the big Alpha guy. Back at the auto shop, her driver pissed and moaned about cancelling the ride until she told him to charge her anyway. And then, more happily, he unloaded all her luggage and left her at the curbside with one last cheerful wave.

She left the luggage curbside, and found Jack in front of the vending machine. His hands were shoved in his pockets as he stared at the ground.

"You have to promise me one thing, Jack Cooper," Fallon said from the entrance.

Jack turned and a hint of a smile curved his lips as he squinted. "What happened? Don't tell me you got run over by a reindeer."

"I changed my mind, that's what happened. You're a lot more fun than I thought you would be, and I'm in. I just want this last leg of the road trip to be a little less dangerous and a lot more stimulating. Can you think of a way to do that?"

His easy smile changed the geography of his face from gloomy to downright boyish. He had a killer smile.

"I can think of a few things."

DAMN, she was a sight.

She stood in front of him, hands on her hips, flashing him a gift-wrapped smile. He'd never been quite so pleased or genuinely surprised to see anyone. And he'd had plenty of surprises in his life, although to be fair most of them were not positive ones. He'd already resigned himself to the rest of his road trip on his own, which although would still be worthwhile, wouldn't be quite the same without his sassy companion.

It was good to know she'd felt the same way.

He accepted his credit card when she handed it over. "We should probably get dinner and find a nearby hotel."

"I'll call another car. We might even get the same guy. He can't have gone far."

Sure enough, the same kid was back three minutes later. "Dude, you aren't going to change your mind again?"

"Not this time," Fallon said and she helped get the luggage back in the car.

"Where to?" their driver asked. "Airport?"

Jack glanced at Fallon. "With all your luggage, we'll need to get a hotel room before we have dinner."

"Take us to the closest hotel," Fallon said.

"And for dinner, you gotta try Three Amigos!" While their driver sang the praises of their Godzilla-like steak burrito, Jack kept his eyes on Fallon.

Her left hand rested between them and kept bumping into his thigh. When she noticed him studying her, she smiled and folded her hands into her lap as though caught in the middle of some unscrupulous act. But he wanted her touching him. A year ago, after Alicia had left him, he'd been done with women. It had been one long dry spell while he threw himself into work. He'd never cared for casual sex and nothing had changed in that regard. Other than the fact that he wondered whether one night with his pretend girlfriend would count as casual sex. He wondered that so loudly he half worried she might hear him.

They arrived at the Mission Inn Hotel and he unloaded all their bags. An attendant helped carry their luggage inside and Jack tipped him. Inside, the lobby was decked out for the festivities with garland everywhere. Twinkling lights. The haunting melody of *Frosty the Snowman* piped through speakers. Lit mirrors. Sprigs of holly. Pine boughs.

"How may I help you, sir?" the young female desk clerk asked.

Jack was hyper-aware of Fallon standing beside him. She smelled nice. Like a pine tree. Or was that him? "Two rooms."

"Two rooms? *Really*?" the clerk asked, eyeballing him.

"Yes," Jack said through gritted teeth.

"How many nights?" She tapped into her computer.

"One."

She quirked a brow at the luggage around them, enough for a month's vacation, were they all his bags. "I have one room for one night. Now, if you were staying three nights I could give you two rooms."

"How does that make any sense?"

"It's a package deal." She nodded. "Plus, its Christmas and we have the Santas in town."

"The *Santas*?"

"We call it the Santa Convention around here. If I'm going to give up two rooms that's less room for the Santas, so I need to make it worth our while. They're a bunch of old retired mall Santas who go around town just making everyone happy."

"Good. As long as they spread all the happiness around, who am I to complain?"

"Jack—" Fallon said from next to him. "Let me pay for this."

"No."

"Of course, I can give you both rooms for three nights even if you're not staying." She tapped into her computer.

"So you'll *let* me pay for both rooms for three nights and just stay one?"

"Guess it depends on how badly you need those two rooms." More tapping.

Jack fished his wallet out of his back pocket because a fool was born every minute, and he was about to prove it.

"We'll take one room for one night," Fallon said.

"Now that's more like it. My grandma says you should never go to bed angry." The clerk quickly got them checked in. "I just love a happy ending."

"Are you sure about this?" Jack asked Fallon on their way to the elevators.

She simply nodded and smiled. Neither of them had even thought to request a room with two beds. Most of the time, that's how these rooms came anyway, but every once in a blue moon there was a dream called a King sized bed. As he opened the door to room four hundred and seven, Jack saw two double beds with a nightstand between them.

Damn it. I can't seem to catch a break.

"Perfect," he said instead.

Chapter 6

Tonight Fallon McQueen, former head cheerleader at Starlight Hill High and not horrible looking by most people's standards, would share a bedroom with a man who obviously didn't want to share one with her. He'd been ready to shell out enough cash for three nights rather than share a bedroom with her! She tried to tell herself that he might have been trying to be a gentleman. Knowing Jack and his Latin retro ways, she wouldn't be at all surprised. But her fake boyfriend had already offered to spend enough on her and this crazy scheme. She wanted to pout when the room had the classic two double beds instead of a cozy King sized bed. Had that been the case, she'd have accepted Jack's offer to sleep on the floor while she took the bed. Then after a short time, she'd have whispered in her best sex kitten voice: *this is silly. Come up here and join me on the bed. I don't bite.*

And then maybe something would have happened as they lay next to each other. He'd touch her or she'd touch him and they'd be off to the races. But she didn't know who she was kidding here. All those hot looks she imagined seeing in his dark eyes ever since the moment she'd come back to the auto shop were probably only what she wanted to see. In a way it would be nice if this wasn't make-believe, but a bad idea. Jack was too unstable. She'd been carefree once and couldn't go there ever again. She and her son required stability and security. A plan. She wanted a solid relationship and not one with a man who had no idea where he would be in the next month let alone next year.

Besides that, Fallon hadn't ever had casual sex, and it probably wasn't a good idea to start now. She sure wasn't going to suggest it, even if one night with Jack had genuine appeal. She could argue that it would help make their lie more plausible, and if she were a pathetic person that's exactly the approach she would take.

Jack threw his bag on the bed closest to the door. "You sure you're okay with this."

"Of course. Why waste all that money when we can share a room?"

"Good." He unzipped his bag. "We should go to dinner soon. Might be a good idea to go to bed early too. Mechanic claimed he'd have the car ready first thing. I want to be there when he opens."

"I just have to make a quick call to my mother first."

He grabbed his card key. "I'll give you some privacy and take a walk around outside."

Once he was out the door, Fallon dialed her mother. "I'm not going to be there for the breakfast. I'm sorry."

"What have you done now?"

Fallon scoffed into the phone. "Nothing. Just a little car accident I had. But don't worry, I'm fine."

After Fallon had explained, her mother sighed loudly.

"You always seem to attract trouble, but I'm glad you're all right. Maybe we can reschedule. How's Bud doing?"

"He's taking it in stride." Fallon bit her lower lip.

A couple of weeks ago, her mother had demanded to know the name of her boyfriend. Said if he didn't have a name he clearly didn't exist. Fallon had been drinking a beer at the time and…the rest had just kind of happened.

"Mom?" Fallon had waited to ask this question because she had been worried about the answer. When David had been to L.A. this summer to visit, he didn't talk much about his dad's fiancé. And Fallon certainly hadn't wanted to ruin their time together by bringing it up. "Does David like Sally?"

"Oh, you know, he seems to like her all right. But you're still his mother."

Fallon actually wanted David to like his new stepmother. It was best for all of them to get along. It had taken her years to get to this point, but her love for David didn't mean he couldn't also love and have plenty of room for other people in his life. Still, she understood that Ted getting married would change everything. It might be selfish, but she didn't want Sally to spend more time with David than Fallon did. She hung up with Mom but Jack still wasn't back, so she went through her overnight bag and found her make-up case and toiletries. She set up in the bathroom, leaving a little room for whatever Jack had with him. She wondered if he did anything special to his hair, or if he just rolled out of bed with it that way. The actors who were her clients spent good money to get their hair to look the way Jack's did. But by all appearances, Jack was one of those men who put little to no effort into his looks. His hair looked naturally wind-swept half the time, and she had to continually restrain herself from running her fingers through it the way she wanted.

She, on the other hand, looked frightening in the morning. Her hair usually stuck up in at least two different directions if not three, and her pasty white skin made her look ghostly. Jack had that beautiful tan olive skin that went so well with the dark hair and eyes. Maybe she should go to bed with make-up already on, a trick more than a few of her clients swore by.

You know what? Screw it. She wasn't here to impress Jack. He was her *pretend* boyfriend.

Emphasis on pretend.

WHEN JACK GOT BACK to the room, Fallon had changed. She looked fresh-faced and not at all like she'd been hit by a Christmas tree. She wore a pair of tight jeans and a blue sweater, taut against her shapely breasts. All things he was going to ignore if it killed him.

Jack cleared his throat. "Ready?"

The Mission Inn stood directly across the courtyard from the Mexican restaurant their driver had recommended. Jack took Fallon's hand and they walked across the courtyard strung with more fairy lights.

There was a thirty-minute wait at Three Amigos because of all the Christmas parties. After putting his name down with the hostess, Jack led Fallon into the bar area where he found a table and ordered them a couple of Coronas. A mariachi band made its way around the bar taking requests. He took a long pull of beer and scanned the crowd. All around them, couples were laughing, kissing, and tearing open presents. It was, after all, the season. He tried not to think about the conversations they were bound to have this Christmas around the Cooper family dinner table. His mother would ask once again whether there was any hope that he and Alicia might still reconcile (zero) and give her a grandchild before she was six feet under at the Holy Cross Cemetery. His father would want to know why he'd quit police work. His contractor brother would want to know whether he'd be able to work cheaply.

"You haven't told me much about your family." Fallon fiddled with the edge of a bar napkin.

"Mom and Dad, my older brother Manny and his family. All in Oregon. Already upset that I'm divorced. Wait until they hear I quit my job and have no plan. You liked that, right? How do you think they'll take it?"

She wrinkled her nose. "It's not so much that I didn't like it. It seems pretty odd, that's all. But what do I know? I'm the woman going to a wedding with a fake boyfriend."

"My mother is a Puerto Rican Catholic and she hasn't been happy since I divorced so this is going to be more of the same for her."

"Maybe you should lie too."

He winked at her. "Why? You want to come with me and keep up the charade?"

"I'm going to spend Christmas with David, or you know, I would."

"I'm kidding."

Their name was eventually called and they had a quick dinner in the dining part of the restaurant. While a montage of holiday mariachi music piped through the speakers, they kept the conversation on safer topics, learning each other's favorite movies, songs, and sports teams. Fallon didn't have any sports teams she followed, other than David's Little League team, The Rockets, and the Oakland Sliders. Both rather self-explanatory. She had to take out a pen and paper to list all Jack's favorite sports teams, afraid she'd forget some.

After dinner they headed back to their hotel room, where there was no more avoiding the inevitable.

He would have to get a solid night's sleep with Fallon in the bed next to his.

Chapter 7

Fallon had never stayed in the Pismo Beach area before, only passed through on her way to Disneyland. It seemed as if every building, from the auto repair shop to the restaurant to the hotel, was covered with a Mission style adobe-tiled roof. She wouldn't normally notice such things, but keeping her mind on the architecture of buildings was certainly better than where it wanted to be. Because her dirty mind kept going to *one bedroom.* Who would get undressed first? Did Jack sleep in his underwear or had he brought pajamas? Did he snore or talk in his sleep? Or did he walk in his sleep, and if so could she help him to somehow make his way to her bed?

Once he'd opened the door they both walked past the entryway bathroom and then stood quietly for a moment.

"You go ahead—"

"Why don't you—"

They both spoke at once.

Jack waved his hand toward the bathroom. "Ladies first."

Fallon grabbed her stuff and went into the bathroom

to change. She'd had no seduction plans for this trip, and her clothing told the true story. She'd brought her worn, old, comfy and holey Bruce Springsteen t-shirt to sleep in. Usually when she attempted to seduce a man, she…oh god, she'd forgotten. That's how long it had been. As she brushed her teeth she wondered if she'd ever find a good man who was available. Someone who didn't run from commitment and responsibility like they were both toxic waste. As she rinsed her mouth and spit, she wondered if maybe her standards were too high where it came to that. As she flossed her teeth, she glanced in the mirror to remind herself that she was no longer a twenty-seven-year-old ex-cheerleader/single mother. She had built a life for herself in L.A., along with a solid reputation as a celebrity stylist. She could afford to be picky.

Fallon slowly opened the bathroom door and saw that Jack had turned out the lights. Perfect, since she had planned on running to her side of the bed and hopping under the covers before he could see her choice of sleep-wear. But when she walked by Jack's bed he seemed to be asleep. He lay on his back, hands spread behind his neck, breathing softly. He wore no shirt, and the covers were folded to his waist. No harm could be done from taking a glimpse, so she got a bit closer to get a clear look at the man's sculpted pecs and flat abdomen. A light black line of chest hairs trailed down his abdomen and pointed the way south to the Promised Land. She considered pulling back the covers to glance at what lay underneath, but just then her brain cells kicked in full force. She'd been caught in a cloud of lust-induced stupidity, and it had been a long time since one of those threatened to blur her vision. But this man was a light sleeper. Oh, she'd bet her life on it. No. She would not be a voyeur tonight.

Jack opened one eye. "It's not polite to stare."

"Oh, crap!" Fallon ran to her bed and hopped under the covers. "Don't scare me like that."

He chuckled. "Don't scare you by talking?"

"You were asleep. I-I thought you were asleep." She pulled the covers up to her neck.

"Just resting my eyes."

"Next time warn a girl!"

"Fallon? I'm going to rest my eyes for a bit. And by the way, Springsteen is a good choice. I love the boss."

"Big deal. So I like to be comfortable when I sleep."

"So do I."

"Oh, please tell me you're not naked under there."

He gave her an easy smile. "You could have just gone ahead and pulled the covers back to find out for yourself."

Fallon groaned and put the pillow over her head. "I was *not* going to do that."

Jack hopped out of bed and headed to the bathroom. Fallon tried very hard not to peek, but she did anyway. He wore sexy boxer style briefs and his muscular thighs and butt filled them out as nicely as she'd imagined.

He was back in bed after a few minutes, and propped up on one hand to face her. "We should talk about a few things."

"Like what?"

"Things I should know. How long have you lived in L.A.?"

"Two years. I moved down because I had a chance to work at one of the best celebrity salons on Rodeo Drive. I've lived cheaply and saved everything I could because some day I'm going to have my own salon. The only problem is they keep raising the lease on storefronts. Plus, I hate being away from David. I agreed that he should stay in Starlight Hill with his father, but I didn't think it would be this hard."

"You don't like being away from him."

"I miss him so much. Every day. But honestly? It was kind of nice to start over, in a big city where no one knew anything about me. Like a blank slate. I could be anyone I wanted to be. Sometimes, in a small town like mine, people get stuck in a rut." Her throat constricted. "So now you see why I can't afford to be relaxed about the future like you are. I need a plan because I have a son."

"Understood. In my case, I have no ties."

"I assume you were married before."

"We don't talk. No kids. I don't imagine I could quit my job if I did."

"Listen, I realize that you might not see it this way, but you're still very much a—"

"No," he interrupted. "I'm not a cop anymore."

"Okay," she said, letting Jack sit in his denial.

"How'd you do in school?" Jack asked, rolling over now to stare at the ceiling.

"I was a cheerleader in high school." She sighed.

"Unbelievable," he said.

Fallon couldn't be sure but thought he'd mumbled: *"We're practically made for each other."*

"What did you say?" Fallon crept to the edge of her bed.

"Football player. I dated cheerleaders."

"Of course." She laughed. "God, I was so stupid in high school."

"Makes two of us. I don't know about you but I was headed for the NFL and the Hall of Fame. It was a wonder my head fit through the hallways of the high school. Somewhere along the line that didn't work out for me. Humbling."

"For you and so many others." She rolled back to the

center of her bed, willing herself to stop feeling so close to him.

The dark gave off a misleading air of intimacy that shook her. Conversations like these happened in your lover's arms and not with someone you'd just met.

"Go to sleep. We need to get up early and hit the road." He rolled over, showing her his back.

A good, solid, and strong back. Muscular and tanned, and she was totally not thinking about licking it. "Not until you tell *me* something."

"What do you want to know?" he asked, still turned away from her.

"Why aren't you a cop anymore?"

"That's a story for another day."

Chapter 8

The night went far worse than Jack could have imagined.

He barely got any sleep thinking of her right next to him in that flimsy Springsteen t-shirt that fell just above her curvy thighs. All he wanted to do was climb into bed with her and let his hands roam freely under that t-shirt until he pulled it off. She would have rosy pink nipples and he was certain she'd taste like honey. He happened to like nothing more than a real woman pared down to the essentials. Plain t-shirts and no make-up. Real. Fallon was nothing if not real. He'd wanted to ask about the kid because of his insatiable curiosity, but regretted the question immediately after asking it. She was entitled to her privacy. She'd told him anyway, in a raw voice that made his chest tight again. The whole situation had become a hell of a lot worse when he'd heard the pain in her voice and wanted nothing more than to take her into his arms. Like he'd done earlier today, when he thought he'd be saying goodbye to her company on the rest of his road trip. Never would he have imagined that she'd be so soft in his arms, and smell so much like a woman. Sweet. Like fresh air and scented soap. It hit him right then and there how much he missed touching someone. He'd missed the intimacy of a woman's soft moans. Of the sweet spot between her thighs and the muscles that quivered and tensed when he touched just the right way.

All things he had to stop thinking about.

He'd gone to sleep with wood and woken up with wood. Before this became a problem only she could help him with, he had to start thinking about something else. Now. Fallon rolled over on her stomach and let out a soft sigh. Okay, not helping. Her t-shirt had ridden partly up to her stunning ass and he was treated to a half moon. He wanted to kiss that soft-looking round cheek and then work his way up her body until he reached her sleepy mouth. She wanted him too, if last night's peeping Tom show had been any indication. Or maybe she was just curious about him. He felt the same way but something in his gut told him this wasn't right. Not when he had nothing to offer her.

Cold shower time. He kicked the covers off and headed to the bathroom.

The shower water was the shock that he needed, and he stayed under the stream until his thoughts ran back to the job. Fallon was right in that no matter what he said on the subject, he couldn't help acting and thinking like a cop. Regardless, it wouldn't change facts. He wouldn't go back and that was final. Since he'd been promoted to homicide a few years ago his world had turned dark and sinister. Finished off what little had been left of his marriage. He couldn't shake the work off at the end of the day because the days didn't end. And while he realized that all folks lived in the same world in which people hurt the ones they loved in indescribable ways, not everyone got to see the damage up close and personal. Memory cells were cruel. That last case had done him in. A kid.

He wanted to forget.

Fallon wanted to know why, and he wanted to tell her. He would tell her. He just didn't want to tell her in a way that would bring his dark former world into hers. He wanted this trip to relax her, anyway, not wind her up even tighter. He got that she was a single mother, but it didn't mean she couldn't still enjoy her life. She was beautiful and young and deserved to have some fun. With or without him.

He got out of the shower and toweled off, gratified to find her still asleep. It gave him time to get dressed and find coffee. The hotel had a continental breakfast spread downstairs, and he loaded up on muffins, cereal, and two coffees. He had no idea how Fallon took her coffee, so he shoved creamers and sugars into his pockets.

"Are you and your wife enjoying your stay?" the same delusional attendant said from behind the counter as he walked past on his way to the elevator.

"She's not—yes. We're having a great time."

They certainly would be, were she actually his *wife*. When he let himself back in the room, balancing everything, Fallon sat on the edge of the bed rubbing her eyes.

"Hey, sleepyhead."

"Coffee," she mumbled.

He wasn't sure if that was an observation or a request. Trying not to smile at the bed hair, he handed over a coffee cup and pulled cream and sugar packets out of his pockets. "I wasn't sure how you took your coffee."

"Cream."

One word sentences, and with Fallon's proclivity for words he would have to go out on a limb and guess she was not a morning person. "Here you go. You sleep alright?"

"Uh-huh." She poured cream into her coffee.

At least one of them had. He sat on the edge of his bed

and drank his own black coffee, then took a bite of a muffin. Fallon looked a little scary in the morning, but funny how he still wanted to kiss that sleepy mouth.

He cleared his throat. "We should get going as soon as you're ready."

She didn't say anything, but coffee in hand, staggered toward the bathroom. He heard the shower go on and resigned himself to the fact that he would not be invited to join her in there. That's not what this gig was about. This was fake. Pretend. It wasn't as if he was looking to knock boots with someone, but he could see he'd be the wrong guy for Fallon. At least for the next week, though, he would be the right guy. The right fake guy.

And enjoy the hell out of it.

FALLON HAD GUESSED RIGHT. One glance at Jack in the morning, and he appeared just as breath taking as he did in the middle of the day. Probably a morning person, while she could barely form a coherent thought before her first cup of coffee. He'd brought her coffee and cream, even a muffin. Kind of nice.

Thankfully the car was ready when they arrived, and by nine they were on the road again. They would make good time from Pismo Beach, and should arrive in Starlight Hill well before dark. Which meant she had to tell Jack about the name thing. She hadn't been looking forward to it.

"I think I'll start calling you Bud," she said. "Because you've been a real bud."

She couldn't see what his eyes were doing under his dark sunglasses, but his lips turned up in a half smirk. "Yeah, don't."

"Didn't anyone ever call you by a fun nickname?"

"Not sure about fun, but Jack *is* a nickname."

Confession time. "All right, here's the thing. I may have accidentally told my mother that my boyfriend's name is Bud."

"Why? Because it's such a great name?"

"No. And you should just be grateful I wasn't drinking imported beer at the time."

"Jesus."

"Well, she had me on the ropes. I'd stalled for so long about my fake boyfriend that she wouldn't take no for an answer. I'd already told her you were tall, dark and handsome. Very important job. Vague-city. Finally, one day she told me that I'd probably been under too much stress working with entitled celebrities, and she didn't believe there really was a guy. She wouldn't give up until I gave her a name."

"Why did you lie about having a boyfriend anyway?"

"She wanted to fix me up. Her best friend Trudy has a nephew living in Encino. I didn't want to be rude so I just threw it out there. My mother makes me nervous." *Understatement.*

"You could have just said you broke up before the wedding."

"Sure, and she'd have suggested that I bring her best friend's nephew as my date to the wedding. He's a doctor. A gynecologist."

Jack's chest shook a little, as though he were suspiciously restraining a laugh. "Fine. We'll say Bud is a nickname I hate and now you're no longer calling me that."

"Think she'll fall for it?"

"Oh, I'll make sure of it." He gave her a tight lipped smile.

She'd been pushing boundaries and pushing her luck.

Like the almost-peeking thing. And then the asking-about-the-job thing, when he clearly didn't want to talk about it.

"Did we ever decide on your occupation?" she said.

"You seem convinced I should be a cop."

"It's believable."

"Great. I'm a cop again. That was a quick retirement. But we won't say I'm a detective. People ask too many questions I don't want to answer."

"Gotcha." She paused for a beat and then took her chances. "But why, exactly?"

His only response was to quirk a brow.

"Right, right. We're not talking about it. Yet."

Fallon's phone rang and caller ID read, *Little Man.*

"Hi, honey!"

"Where are you? I thought you were going to be here today."

"I'm on my way. The car broke down, but I'll be there this afternoon."

"Grandma said you shouldn't be driving from L.A. It's dangerous and you're irresponsible." He took a breath. "But Mom, did you know that a regulation baseball has one hundred and eight stitches?"

"No, I didn't know that." Fallon frowned.

Sometimes it was good to have a nine-year-old who flitted from one subject to another, but it still hurt that Fallon's own mother was trash talking her to David. Every time she thought she'd made progress on that front, someone moved the goal line. If it wasn't Ted moving the line, it was often her mother. She told herself that it didn't seem to matter much to David, because he still loved her and was always happy to see her. But how much longer would it be before he stopped having confidence in her abilities, too? She'd guess not much longer, since he was four years away from being a teenager.

A few more minutes of conversation about random baseball facts and what David wanted for Christmas, and Fallon hung up with her son. A familiar tug of longing settled in her heart, followed by the uncomfortable sensation of impending doom. It was always this way when she came home for a visit. Her heart expanded and her throat constricted. She was usually in a hurry to get home right up until the plane landed at San Francisco International Airport. Then she'd have to get Kailey on the phone and have her talk her through the rest of the way with cheery can-do affirmations. The truth was that she only wanted David, but that was never possible. Coming home meant she had to deal with some of the small minded people in town who'd decided her three failed marriages meant she was the town's joke. It meant seeing Ted. A wedding meant she would also see her former in-laws. Truthfully, she sometimes felt safer on the streets of L.A.

"Was that your kid?" Jack asked now.

She tried to smile but it felt tight, much like her narrowing throat. "Yeah, that was David."

"What's wrong?"

"Nothing," she said, lying through her teeth.

"Try again."

"Really, Jack, where *is* your trusty flashlight? Shouldn't you be shining it in my eyes right about now?"

"We don't do that anymore." He scowled. "And it's not an interrogation."

Then he just stopped talking. Not another word. She'd forgotten to put on the baseball cap and even with a ponytail, the wind whipped through her hair, filling all the spaces between them. She grew uncomfortable with the loud and stretching silence.

The man was a genius.

"Okay, I'm suddenly not looking forward to being

home again. Some…people talk about me behind my back. And I haven't always had the best support from my mother. And certainly not from my ex."

"Why not? You're David's mother and you deserve respect for that alone."

"Let's just say that some people don't see it that way."

"Then maybe it's up to me, as your fake lover, to help them see it like that." He grabbed her hand and squeezed it hard.

He probably had no clue what he'd said nearly short-circuited her heart.

Once in a while, Fallon managed to make a good choice despite all odds. The greatest of which had been giving birth to David. Another good decision had been furthering her education in cosmetology by moving down to Los Angeles, then working like a fiend for two years to save every dollar for her own salon.

And agreeing to go on a road trip with Jack Cooper, aka Santa Claus.

Chapter 9

Predictably, the closer they got to San Francisco, the more Fallon needed a pep talk. Jack had been mostly quiet on the trip, appeared simply to enjoy the drive, and had asked her to let him know when and if she wanted to stop. The temperature had lowered with every mile as the skylight darkened to gray and overcast, and when Fallon's teeth began to chatter, Jack pulled over in Palo Alto at a service station. He put the top up and pumped some gas.

"All set," he said as he pulled out of the station.

They were approximately one hour and forty-four minutes from home now, according to her GPS. Nice time for a diversion. "Let's go to Fisherman's Wharf when we get to San Francisco."

"Thought we were in a hurry."

"We've made good time, and I would hate for you to miss San Francisco. Maybe just a quick stop to see the bay. There's nothing like it."

He gave her one of his gorgeous smiles which were starting to affect her far more than she'd wanted. "Now you're talking."

After all, she didn't want to ruin Jack's road trip any more than it already had been. Having wasted one valuable night due to the car and tree fiasco, he'd seemed to understand and accept that he couldn't make any more unscheduled stops. She appreciated that, and she wanted to get home. Delaying the inevitable wasn't going to help, and she desperately wanted to see David. Too bad that didn't stop the churning in her gut.

A couple of hours later she'd walked the length of Pier 39 with Jack and shared a bread bowl of Clam Chowder. Fallon grabbed a couple of stocking stuffers for David at one of the gift shops, and Jack loaded more photos into his phone. When he showed Fallon the photo he'd taken of the two of them cuddled on the pier, she thought it looked pretty damned convincing. Then she flipped through a couple of other photos Jack had taken. One of them had her hair whipping in the wind, as she stood overlooking the bay. Another was of her laughing and pointing at a seagull who'd grabbed someone's bread bowl.

She sent some of the photos to her phone and then handed it back to him. "I didn't notice when you took these other photos of me."

"I think they're pretty good." He glanced at the photo she'd left up and then slipped the phone in his pocket. "Anyway, it's convincing."

It was late afternoon when they rolled into Starlight Hill and straight through Main Street. The town always went all out for the holidays, with white fairy lights on every tree, and signs on almost every corner announcing the Christmas Tree Lighting Ceremony tonight. Of course, she'd be there, along with everyone else she'd ever known. Hopefully people would have forgotten about the last time she'd visited—when Stephan, the self-appointed town gossip, had spread an ugly rumor that she'd left town pregnant with Billy Turlock's baby. That one had hurt her almost as much as it had hurt Billy and Brooke. None of it was true, of course, not that Stephan cared. Billy had barely given her a second look after retiring from baseball and coming back to town several years ago and reconnecting with Brooke. But small town gossip never took a holiday, often fueled by Stephan, who had too much free time on his hands.

"What do you think?" she asked Jack as they drove through town. Since Starlight Hill was on the valley's wine trail, there were storefront tasting rooms on every corner.

"I'm more of a beer guy," he said.

"You're in luck. I heard a microbrewery opened recently. And there's a new tap room, too. Fifty-four different types."

Fallon gave Jack directions to her mother's house, in a middle-class residential area of town. When he pulled up in front of the gray and blue split-level and shut off the car, Fallon froze. This was, by far, the worst idea she'd ever had. Mom would see right through her scheme, her superior German nose for bullshit always in prime form. Then Fallon would have to explain why she didn't want to go out with Trudy's nephew the gynecologist.

She turned to Jack. "Maybe…we should re-think this."

"No way." He took her hand and raised it to his lips, then kissed it. "Having too much fun."

"But—"

"She's looking through the window," he said. "Kiss me."

"W-what?"

But he didn't ask again, just pulled her until she was nearly in his lap and proceeded to kiss the living daylights out of her. It went on for several seconds or minutes or hours, Fallon didn't know which. She'd somehow lost track of time. He was a solid wall of heat and she could have leaned on him for hours. His lips were soft and hard at the same time and his tongue tasted like the salt water taffy he'd bought at the pier.

He ended the kiss and then tucked a hair behind her ear. "You need to act like that happens every day."

"Um…yeah."

While she was still trying to recover from the onslaught of blazing heat and chemistry, Jack had come around to her side of the door. "Thanks for waiting. She's still looking."

"Of course she is." Not a comforting thought. It told her that Mom had suspicions. All the vague information and naming her boyfriend after a beer probably hadn't helped her case.

Jack threaded his fingers through hers and together they walked up to her mother's front door and rang the doorbell. Once. Twice.

"You're *sure* she was looking through the window?" Fallon asked.

"She live alone?"

"Yes."

"Then oh, yeah."

The door finally opened, and Beverly McQueen cried out, "Fallon! Bud!"

Oh God. She should probably go ahead and end this charade now.

"Hi, Mom. Here's the thing, he actually doesn't—"

"What Fallon is trying to say is that not everyone calls me Bud anymore, but of course, you can." He smiled and put out his hand.

"I'm sorry, young man, but I'm a hugger!" Mom pulled Jack into a hug.

Of good looking men she should have added, but Fallon

smiled anyway and officially introduced 'Bud' Cooper. "We've had a long drive. Maybe we can just haul my luggage up into my old bedroom and I can go get Ja—Bud a motel room. Then I'm going to go see David."

"Don't be ridiculous! I can't have Bud staying at a motel room. You'll both stay here in your bedroom." She tapped Jack's shoulder. "My daughter thinks I'm a prude. I might be sixty-seven, but I'm a hip grandma I want you to know. I'm sure that you two sleep together and you're certainly old enough to do it under my roof if you'd like."

Fallon couldn't speak for a moment. This house had three bedrooms, and one of them was always set up for David. Should she call Mom's bluff? She had to be bluffing.

"Wow, thanks. I'm sure we both appreciate that," Fallon said.

"Thank you," Jack said.

"I'm just glad you didn't get hurt in one of Fallon's crazy schemes. Driving up the highway when she had to be here for a wedding? Did you see that in a movie once or read it in a romance novel? What gave you that hair-brained idea?" Mom turned to Fallon.

"Actually, it was my idea." Jack said. "It was kind of a bucket list thing."

"Oh." Mom cleared her throat. "I was sure there had to be a good reason."

Fallon helped Jack with the luggage and together they hauled it up to the second story and her small former bedroom with the single double bed. Mom had changed very little about the room and it still had the same yellow daisies wallpaper she'd grown up with on the walls.

Jack brought the last suitcase in and shut the door with his back. "Hip grandma?"

"She suspects something."

Jack cocked his head. "Don't think so. Maybe she's just trying to make you happy?"

She scoffed. "Not a chance."

"Okay, then she's trying to make me happy." Another easy smile. "But I don't like the way she talks to you."

"Get used to it." She plopped down on the bed.

"Never."

Chapter 10

Even if Jack didn't like the way Mrs. McQueen talked to her daughter, it was hard not to put her on his Christmas list after this latest development. This was one small bed in an equally small room. Of course, he'd offer to take the floor since Fallon's mother would be none the wiser once the bedroom door was shut. But he hoped that Christmas would come early for him and Fallon wouldn't let him take the floor. The shiny hardwood floor looked…hard.

There was a knock on the door. "You are staying for dinner?" Beverly had opened the door with only a short hesitation.

So much for privacy. Hopefully that door had a lock on it. Fallon was correct, and her mother was poking around the two of them with a metaphorical cow prod. And she likely wouldn't be done anytime soon.

"I was hoping to go see David—" Fallon said.

"They're all having dinner with Ted's family tonight. You'll probably see him at the tree lighting later."

"Oh," Fallon said, shoulders sagging. "Sure, that's right."

"I hope you like pot roast, Bud."

"I love pot roast," he smiled through gritted teeth.

Beverly shut the door.

"I hate Bud," Jack said.

Fallon lay down on the bed and covered her face with her arms.

"Hey." He pulled on one arm. "What's wrong? I'm the one being called Bud."

She peeked through splayed fingers. "I'm sorry. I made you go through all this with me and now it's all for nothing."

She looked soft on her pillow, blond hair splayed around her like a halo. "You leave the convincing part to me."

That kiss a few minutes ago had gone on for longer than he'd intended because even though he'd been prepared for the blazing heat and desire, he'd still been a little stunned by it. And while he and Fallon had begun to feel a little too real, he enjoyed it. Her. All of it. So far, other than the car mishap, he was having the best time he'd had in years.

He eased up on the bed next to her, and broached the subject before she did. "I'll take the floor if you're more comfortable that way."

"No! You've done enough already. I'll sleep on the floor."

"The hell you will. I'm not letting you sleep on the floor."

"It's only right. I got us into this mess."

"I don't bite." The way she blinked at him made it difficult not to smile. "Unless...do you *want* me to bite?"

"Jack." She laughed and lightly punched his chest. "You do make me laugh."

Finally. Ever since they'd crossed the town limits sign, Fallon had been increasingly edgy. The jumpiness he could handle, but it was that lost and occasionally gloomy gaze in her eyes that got to him. The part of him that always wanted to fix stuff was having a difficult time staying quiet. But he would. For now. He traced her soft lips and reminded himself he was playing a part. Much like the times he'd interview a suspect and pretend he really believed the garbage spewing out their mouths. Nodded in the places where he'd given them enough rope to hang themselves. All he had to do was shut up and listen because most people generally loved to talk about themselves. Occasionally the truth slipped out while they weren't paying attention.

Now he was playing the part of a dutiful and devoted boyfriend. Considering he was never much of a devoted anything other than a son, brother, and cop, this might be somewhat of a stretch.

"You can kiss me again." Fallon stared at his mouth and wouldn't meet his eyes. "I need to get used to it."

She should get used to it, and so should he. Used to feeling a little out of his mind when he kissed her. Kissing should be comfortable and easy after dating someone for months, not like he was about to burst into flames and do her against the wall or wherever they happened to be standing at the moment. He brushed his lips against hers slowly and then more urgently as he met her eagerness. Her mouth opened under his for more and he went for it like a dying man searching for oxygen. When his hand dove under her sweater to touch silky and smooth skin, she moaned into his mouth and he went instantly hard. Temporarily losing track of, or caring, where he was and whose mother was downstairs serving pot roast, Jack got handsy. His fingers nudged her bra aside to tweak her nipple. Fallon quivered and one leg went over his hip as she pulled him closer.

"Dinner's ready!" A voice screeched from downstairs.

Fallon startled and rolled off him so fast she would have fallen off the bed if he hadn't caught her. "Easy, Grace."

"Ooooof," she said, holding on to his arm. "I better get down there and help her."

He watched her stand and straighten her sweater. "I'm going to need a minute. Or two."

She stared at the tent in his pants. Bit her lower lip as if trying hard not to smile. "Sorry."

"Don't be. I'm my own worst enemy."

"From where I'm standing, you don't look like you'd ever be anyone's enemy. Not with that." She licked her lips, smoothed down her hair, and opened the bedroom door. "See you down there."

In the kitchen, Fallon busied herself with setting the table for her mother and trying to forget about the mini make-out session she'd just had upstairs in her childhood bedroom. The sense of dread she'd had since arriving home spread southward but for a different reason. She was no longer pretending. Jack was very much a man she could fall for, a man who made her nerve endings tingle and her heart squishy. But he was quite possibly the worst man for her to fall in love with. And she would do everything in her power to put the brakes on.

It wasn't supposed to be like this. They were supposed to fly out here, not drive and wind up spending the night in a hotel room. For the next couple of nights, he should be staying in a motel room and not in her small bedroom with her. The wedding day was the main attraction, and all this forced togetherness had not been part of her original plan.

"Smells delicious," Jack said as he walked into the kitchen.

He looked delicious, having changed into black jeans

and a gray sweater that complimented his dark hair and eyes. Yum. She wanted dinner and it wasn't the pot roast.

"Thank you, dear," Fallon's mother said. "Just have a seat."

"Sure I can't help?" he asked, coming up behind Fallon to give her a quick hug.

"Babe, just sit down. We're ready." That was pretty good if she said so herself. *Babe.*

He took a seat at the small table, his intelligent eyes quietly observing and assessing.

"Where did you two meet?" Fallon's mother said as she also took a seat.

Oh no. Had they even discussed that? If they had, she couldn't remember.

"The bar."

"A party."

They both spoke at once.

"It was a party at a bar," Jack explained, taking her hand. "Remember, babe?"

"Uh-huh."

"Goodness," Mom said, putting down her fork. "Are you frequenting dangerous bars to meet men?"

"No, Mom. I—"

"It was a lucky thing for me that she did that night," Jack interrupted. "Her friend had chosen to have her birthday party there. What can you do?"

"What friend?" Mom asked Fallon.

"Kyra. My friend Kyra." Fallon did have a good friend and former co-worker named Kyra in L.A.

"I thought she moved away eight months ago?" Mom narrowed her eyes.

"*Six* months ago," Fallon lied. "It was her going-away party. I mean her birthday party. It was both. Her birthday party and going-away party."

Jack gave her a look that said she should stop talking and perhaps go take a sleeping pill.

Mom threw up her hands. "Oh, my goodness. You young people and all your parties."

"We *don't* have a lot of parties. That's why we put them together in packages, to save on party time."

Jack now glared at her. His eyes said *shut up and let me get a word in. I will fix this. It only requires you stop talking. Now.*

And still, she couldn't help herself. "Jack's favorite baseball team is the San Francisco Giants!"

"True story," Jack said and gave a tight smile.

"Why, you're practically a hometown boy," Mom said. "And what do you do for a living? Fallon neglected to tell me, as though it were a state guarded secret. She would only say it was a very important job."

"I'm a cop." He took a drink from his glass and set it down. "She probably didn't want to say because so many people don't like cops."

"I certainly hope that's not true." Mom frowned.

Jack shrugged.

"Our new chief of police is a young man, ex-Marine. He's started a task force to help at-risk youth in our area," Mom said, passing more pot roast to Jack.

"That's great. I worked on a task force for a while, too." Jack said.

"And I thought Fallon was only trying to impress me while being purposefully vague. You *do* have a very important job."

For the first time in a long while, Fallon felt a bit proud of her mother. She'd acknowledged the importance of service to a community, and not just raking in the big bucks like Ted did. Or like Trudy's nephew the doctor. Maybe there was hope for her yet.

"I wish you'd told me the truth and not behaved as if I couldn't be trusted with it, *Fallon*," Mom said.

Aaand that was the shortest moment of pride in history. At least she was being civil to Jack, and that's all Fallon could hope for.

"Actually, come to think of it." Jack set his fork down. "I think I asked Fallon not to say anything. I'm sorry, Mrs. McQueen, but sometimes what I do is not pleasant conversation."

"Of course, I understand." Mom nodded.

The rest of the dinner passed with only light discussion about plans for the coming week. The tree lighting ceremony tonight, the Santa and Friends Christmas Parade tomorrow evening, followed by the wedding. It was a full week of activities fit into a few days, between the holiday events and wedding. Mom criticized Ted and his fiancé for planning their special day far too close to Christmas, but apparently Sally too didn't care much for tradition. It meant that they would be on their honeymoon in Aruba on Christmas Day.

Fallon helped her mother clean up, and they both refused Jack's help. He was instead sent to the garage to gather up the blankets Mom had set aside for them to take to the ceremony.

"I'll see you kids bright and early in the morning," Mom said at the door.

"You're not coming?" Fallon said.

"Too cold out there." She rubbed her arms and practically shoved Fallon and Jack out the front door. "But you two have fun and give my grandson a hug from me!"

The minute she shut the door, Jack stared at Fallon. "We have our parties together to save on *party* time?"

"Do you see what she does to me? I get so defensive

and turn into a blubbering idiot." She headed towards the end of their street for the short walk downtown.

"Next time let me do the talking and just follow my lead. I've got this." As if to prove it, he one-armed pulled her in, the other holding their blankets. "In case she's watching us walk away."

As they approached, a small crowd had already gathered around Christmas in the Park, though it was nothing compared to the size it would be once everyone arrived. The small street park in the center of town was used to light the town's Christmas tree and start the season's festivities. A huge twenty-something-foot spruce was usually delivered from Oregon. It took several tall men and a mini-crane to string the lights every year. A few were already around the bottom of the tree inspecting. Fallon spied all three of the Turlock brothers: Wallace, Billy and Scott, along with Joe Hannigan, Kailey's husband.

She hadn't seen most of these people for months and even then it had been a short trip. After the last nasty rumor, Fallon had dropped by approximately eight months later to clear up any confusion about her non-existent love child. It had been one of the hottest April months on record, and she'd showed up to a barbeque wearing a bikini to demonstrate her very un-pregnant stomach. Brooke and Billy, of course, had known the truth of it all but privately they'd still thanked her for showing up. Of course, the bikini had started off another slew of nastiness as to whether Fallon perhaps had developed an eating disorder in L.A. (not in this lifetime as she loved cupcakes far too much).

"Small town America," Jack said, spreading the blankets on a couple of empty folded chairs. "Yet another item is crossed off my bucket list. This is pretty cool."

Fallon scanned the crowd, looking for David. He would

be around here somewhere, if not with Ted, then with Ted's parents.

"Mom!"

Out of the corner of her eye, Fallon spied David, a blue streak running toward her. She bent down to accept a hug which nearly knocked her down. Her boy was getting big. "Hi, honey."

"You're here! I was looking for you everywhere." He glanced up and gave Jack a tentative smile.

"This is my friend," Fallon began and then couldn't find it in her heart to lie to her son. "Jack. Jack Cooper."

"Hiya!" David stuck out his hand. "My grandma said your name was Bud, but she said that's not a real name anyway. She said that maybe you weren't even a real person, but you are!"

"Bud is a nickname, for some people." Jack grinned and shook David's hand.

"I like 'Jack' better," David said. "Can I sit with you guys?"

"Sure. Where's your Dad?" Fallon didn't see Ted anywhere in the vicinity.

"He's over there with Sally and they're kissing. It's super disgusting." He pointed and made a face.

How she loved that little scrunched-up face. "I'm sure it's not disgusting."

"Yeah." He nodded. "It totally is."

"Mr. Jack bought you a t-shirt when we stopped at a Monarch Butterfly grove on the way." Fallon ruffled David's hair.

"Cool! Thanks!"

She pulled her big boy into her lap and threw the blanket around both of them. He seemed to grudgingly accept that, seeing as the other seats around them had been taken. He would soon be too old to sit on her lap, and all those times she'd taken for granted would be gone. From time to time she thought about having another kid, but that stage of life was running out for her and there were few men who would take a chance on forever with her.

Her thoughts quickly shifted away from her past because everything was good right now for a change. She sat cuddled under the blanket with the love of her life, the scent of a wood burning fire nearby drifting through, the special smell of pine in the night air. It actually felt homey and familiar, in a good way. Jack reached over and took her hand in his. His big hand was warm and hers a solid block of ice. He grinned and her heart squeezed.

Their current mayor, Ophelia Lyndstrom, came forward to a mike by the large Christmas tree. She welcomed everyone and introduced the choir. The white and red robed choir from the local elementary school were trotted out to sing "Oh Come All Ye Faithful," "Winter Wonderland," and ended with "Silent Night." Santa Claus then came out and invited everyone to the parade tomorrow night.

"That's not the real one," David said to Jack. "He's just his helper."

"Right," Jack said. "He actually has quite a few helpers."

Santa officiated the countdown to the lighting of the tree. There were plenty of ooohs and ahhhs from the crowd as the lights went slowly up the tree and when they reached the top they lit up most of the square block. Applause from everyone, another song from the choir ("Oh, Christmas Tree") and then it was all over for another year. As usual, everyone was invited to free cocoa and knock-you-naked brownies for only a dollar over at Em and Silas' diner. Genevieve Turlock, who owned the Sweet

Southern Buns bakery, would hand out her annual free samples of Christmas cut-out sugar cookies until she ran out. That would be soon, if past years were any indication.

"I'm going to get a cookie!" David kicked off the blanket and ran in the direction of Genevieve and her children, who were helping hand cookies out.

"Nice kid," Jack said, standing. "I stopped sitting on my mom's lap when I was six."

"Thank you. He's the light of my life." She stood and was about to ask Jack if he also wanted a cookie when Ted walked up to them, Sally beside him.

"Fallon," he said with a sharp nod. "Meet Sally. Sally, this is Fallon, David's mother."

Jack, bless him, didn't waste any time in throwing one arm around Fallon and tucking her to his side.

"Nice to meet you," Fallon said to Sally's frozen smile. "And this is—"

"Bud," Ted held out his hand to Jack. "Beverly told me. Good to meet you."

Sally's gaze swept over Jack, practically drooling. "Nice to meet you, Bud."

"I'm Ted Andrews, or husband Number Three," Ted told Jack. "Are you going to be number four?"

"Ted, please—" Fallon and Sally both said at once.

Jack's arm tightened around her, not missing a beat. "I don't care what number I am as long as I'm last."

David ran up to them. "Look! I got a cookie in the shape of Santa! And Sally, I heard Mrs. Turlock tell Ophelia that you should have a cookie too because you look like you never eat."

"Okay, David, alright," Ted said, a stiff smile on his face. "Let's calm down now."

"Sure," David said, taking a bite of his cookie. "Can I go with Mom tonight?"

"No," Ted said. "You know the plan. You're spending Christmas with your Mom and you have to stay with us until the wedding."

"Aw, man!" David kicked the ground. "Weddings are so boring."

"We're going to have so much fun soon enough," Fallon said, hoping to distract him. "Just two more days until the wedding."

"We have to go now." Ted spoke sternly. "Say good-night to your mom."

"Night, Mom," David said and gave her a little wave.

No kiss. He was too big for that. Off they went in another direction. Fallon let out a breath. "Well. That went okay."

"*Okay?*" Jack said, brows up. "It would have gone 'okay' had I been allowed to re-arrange that jerk's face."

"Oh, I'm used to Ted. He's Sally's problem now."

"He shouldn't talk to you like that." Grabbing the blankets, he took her hand and led her away from the crowd.

Fallon wasn't used to anyone coming to her defense. A few years ago Scott Turlock had been her biggest ally in town since he was in lock-down hero mode twenty-four seven. They'd never had a 'thing' despite all the rumors that flew around before he met his wife Diana. But Fallon was a little surprised that Jack hadn't yet mentioned the three marriages. People always made fun of that, too. She should have prepared him a little better. Divorced once and divorced three times didn't carry quite the same connotations.

"Aren't you going to ask? You know you want to ask me."

"I'm not one to judge. If I had a spotless house, I might."

"But you haven't been married three times."

"Maybe that means I have far less faith in the institution than you apparently do." He smiled a little at this and squeezed her hand.

They crossed Main Street holding hands. Someone honked and waved. Fallon blinked into the bright lights. The driver behind the wheel was Joe, and Kailey was in the passenger seat. Fallon hadn't seen them in the crowd tonight.

Fallon waved back. "I got married right after high school and that didn't work out because we were too young of course. Not quite a year. A couple of years later I got married again to one of my good friends. Didn't work out because he'd only married me on the rebound. Nice guy, too, but he broke my heart. That one lasted six months. And then I met Ted, got pregnant quite by accident, and so we were married. But I've been on my own now for about eight years. I guess people tend to forget that."

"So you tried marriage for a while and it wasn't your thing."

"I still believe in marriage, but I just haven't met the right one yet." She paused for a beat. "Next time I get married it will be right. It will be forever."

They didn't speak for a few minutes as they walked back to her mother's house, the sounds of the night all around them. All throughout the residential neighborhood, each track home was decorated to the nines in white, red, green, blue and pink twinkling lights, some with battery lit statues of Santa and his reindeer. Mrs. Martinez's house on the corner had a manger scene. Mom's next door neighbor, Marty, had an inflatable snow globe that played "God Rest Ye Merry Gentlemen."

On the sidewalk in front of Mom's, where only one window was decorated in white fairy lights, Jack stopped abruptly. "What would that look like?"

"Forever?"

"The one."

It didn't take long to tell him, since she'd spent the past few years trying to work it out in her head. "He would be a little bit like me, so he'd understand where I've been. Someone married before too. He has to like kids, of course, or that's a deal breaker. Loyal. Kind. A good kisser." And good at other things too, she chose not to add.

He grinned. "You put kissing last."

She'd suddenly become painfully aware that she'd pretty much described Jack to a T. "I know what's important now."

"You've definitely put a lot of thought into it." He brought her hand up to his lips and kissed it. "Let me ask you something else."

"Ask away."

It didn't matter that she was shivering a little more now that the temperatures had dropped even further outdoors. When they went inside her mother's house, they were going to sleep in the same bed. Not just in the same room. The. Same. Bed.

He took off his jacket and placed it around her shoulders. "We haven't known each other for long even if somehow it feels like we have."

"That's true."

"And tonight we're going to sleep in the same bed through no fault of our own. The only question is how much sleep we'll get. Because I don't know about you, but I'm not tired at all."

—————————

Chapter 12

—————————

Jack palmed the back of Fallon's neck and drew her closer. "Scared?"

"I'm a big girl, Jack. I've been propositioned before."

"This is different."

At least he hoped like hell it was different. Because the truth was that by all rights he should be exhausted. He hadn't slept well the night before and then driven hundreds of miles today. But right now he could stay up all night. He was wide awake and alive because *she* did that to him. Excited him. Made him have thoughts and emotions he hadn't in a long time. Made him feel…something.

She wouldn't meet his eyes. "I know."

"Look at me."

Her green gaze rose to meet his, and there was a spark in them that kick-started his heart into next year. "I'm looking at you."

"And?" He tried not to smile.

"Okay, maybe I'm a little bit terrified."

"Why?"

"Because you're strange if *you're* not scared of me after tonight."

"What I saw tonight was a mother who loves her son, and a son who adores his mother. And I also saw an idiot who doesn't talk to you with the respect you deserve."

"Ted is rude to me, but he's rude to everybody. I know that people talk about me behind my back, too, but maybe I deserve it."

"No one deserves that."

"I've made a lot of mistakes, Jack. *Three* of them. Maybe you should run for the hills."

"I'm not worried." He pressed his forehead against hers. "Tell me to back off, Fallon, and I will. Just say the word."

He listened to the pattern of her breathing as it shifted and the breaths came faster. Shorter. He sensed her heartbeat kick up under his fingertips.

"Don't feel sorry for me. I can't stand that."

"Seriously?" He pulled back to study her face. "I will only feel sorry for myself if you say no. But I'll do what you want. Nothing more and nothing less."

Their eyes locked for a moment and neither of them spoke.

"I want you to kiss me. Then I want you to take me to bed, drive me crazy and hold me all night long. And in the morning, if you're still here, I want you to bring me coffee again."

"News flash: I'm still going to be here." He kissed her neck. Licked it. "Do you want cream too?"

"Mmmm. Yes."

Then he kissed her, a long and deep kiss that got hotter and wilder as their tongues met and he tasted her. She was sweet, warm, willing, and everything he needed. She pressed up against him, and he crushed her to his chest. He couldn't get close enough.

"Inside," he heard himself growl.

She fumbled with the key to her mother's house, and he tried to help her. Once inside he raced up the steps right behind her. He couldn't be more obvious about what he was about to do if he sold tickets, but thankfully Mrs. McQueen had retired for the evening. He shut the bedroom door and made good use of the lock.

Fallon had thrown off his jacket and kicked off her shoes. She stood by the edge of her bed in stocking feet and looked smaller. Vulnerable. "I don't do this. It's been a long time for me."

"Me too." He pulled off his sweater and discarded it on the floor. "I'm not going to tell you how long it's been because I'm a guy and that might make me look bad."

"Just looking at you, it's difficult to believe it's even been fifteen minutes."

"It's been the longest fifteen minutes of my life, then." He put his hands on her hips and tugged her close. "But I haven't forgotten how."

"Lucky me," she said as she pulled off her blue sweater.

Underneath she wore a shiny cherry red bra with a front clasp. In two seconds he'd unclasped it and her smooth breasts spilled out into his hands. *Rosy pink nipples.* He tweaked an already hard nipple with his thumb.

"Jack," she moaned, her voice sounding low and carnal. "You're the sexiest Santa Claus I've ever met."

"It's for the kids. For you I have something else."

He pulled her close by the nape of her neck and angled her the way he wanted to kiss her. Hard and deep. She opened up to him, and damn if it didn't feel like she was equally as desperate to get closer. One touch and she responded, giving back as good as she got. Her soft hands were everywhere on him, down his pants, rubbing his chest and abs, and holding on to his shoulders like an anchor.

He bent low and suckled in her nipple. She tasted as sweet as he'd imagined. When she drew in a sharp breath and bucked against him, he nearly lost what little control he had left. He licked, kissed and slowly savored every part of her soft and bare skin. Tugging an earlobes, nipping at the tender spot on her neck, kissing shoulders, arms, breasts and trailing down her stomach. Sizzling heat consumed him. It took over, and he was like a bottle rocket about to burst. He wanted to slow down and take this easy. Not so simple with her. He needed her more than he could remember ever needing anyone or anything else in his life. Fisting a handful of her silky hair in his hand, he kissed her again and again with a fierceness that matched his longing. Then he backed her up to the bed, and gently pushed her back on to it. She twisted the rest of the way out of her bra, and gazed up at him, beautiful eyes luminous and glazed over with lust.

She did it for him. Upside down, sideways, and every which way a man could move or think or feel. He wriggled her tight jeans off as she twisted to help and tossed them to the side. Underneath she wore shiny red panties a perfect match to the bra, making him wonder who'd had the idea to have sex first. Knowing she'd wanted him just as much turned him on like flipping a switch from warm to raging hot fire. He pulled the flimsy material off and flicked it out of his way, kneeled in front of her, and spread her thighs to kiss her right in the middle of all that heat. Her muscles tensed under his hands. She was already wet. He palmed her ass, lifted her up to him and drank her sweet juices. Unable to get enough and unwilling to let her get away from him, he licked and teased. He stopped only when her body shook in tiny quakes and she said his name over and over.

He stopped not because he wanted to stop, but because he had to get deep inside her before he went crazy out of his mind with lust.

FALLON WILLED herself not to cry, because if Jack hadn't been scared off by now, the crying might be the thing to do it. She didn't understand why she felt such strong emotion welling up, either, unless it was because he'd just given her the most blissful orgasm of her life. Or maybe it was because he'd been so sweet and loving and protective tonight. Fake or not, he'd had her back, and she wasn't used to that. She'd never understood what it would be like to have a strong man like Jack in her life, and had half convinced herself she didn't deserve someone like him anyway. To think that she'd met him only a week ago shocked her to the marrow because it seemed as if she'd known him forever.

Once her body stopped shaking, she tried to tug him up. "Come here."

He rose from his knees and got busy pulling off his pants and underwear. An impressive erection sprang out and she licked her lips in anticipation. She wanted to taste him too and to eat him alive if she could. But instead she watched as he tore off a condom packet with his teeth and then slipped it on.

"Jack, wait, I want to—"

"Later," he growled. "I need inside you."

She gasped when he pushed inside her, deep inside her, the delicious heat of him creating waves of pleasure almost too intense to bear. He drove into her, slowly and methodically creating a rhythm which rocked her to the core. Fallon lifted one leg higher and he went even deeper. He groaned and seemed to lose some control then, his thrusts becoming harder and more urgent. Driving her out of her mind.

And he didn't take his eyes off her. "Look at me, babe."

She did, fixating on his soulful dark eyes. Brooding. Edgy.

"Do you like this?"

"Yes," she gasped.

"Tell me what you want."

She could barely formulate a single thought, much less talk. She wanted *this*. More. Him. "You."

"Like to hear that." He kissed her deeply, and she tasted herself on him.

"I'm so close. Jack."

"Let go, babe. Just let go. Come for me."

And she did a minute later, not because he'd asked but because she couldn't hold back a moment longer as she came apart. Her body shook and trembled fiercely as wave after forceful wave of intense sensations hit her. A moment later with one last powerful deep thrust, he groaned and cursed as he came.

He rolled to lay flat on his back and tucked her under his arm. "What are you doing to me?"

She didn't know that she'd done anything to him. Yet. But somehow, she'd experienced a level of intimacy with him that she'd never had before with any other man. It was embarrassing, actually, how close she felt to him right now. He'd probably had great sex like this many times in his life, while for her it felt like the first time.

"You okay?" he asked when their breaths had become more regular and even.

"Not okay. Pretty awesome, actually."

"Good."

Maybe because she wanted him to feel just as raw and tender as she did at the moment, she asked the question again. "You said you would tell me. Why aren't you a cop anymore?"

He didn't pull back or away as she might have expected. Instead he kissed her forehead. "You really want to know."

"Yes."

"Okay." He let out a ragged breath. "Being in homicide, there are images you can never un-see. I was okay with that for six years. And then I had to investigate the death of a kid at the hands of his own father."

"Oh God."

"Yeah. After that, I was done. Finished. Cooked. My captain told me to take some time off. Come back later, he said. Suggested I put in for a transfer to another department. Most of my friends agreed I just needed a break after that case. It did me in. So I resigned."

"I understand," Fallon said, her fingers playing with the short hairs on his chest. "But you can't stop. I've seen it. It's who you are."

"I'm going to have to figure out how to stop. I might pound nails for a while with my brother. Then I'll see where I land next."

Oregon was so far away, especially from Los Angeles. One more reminder to her, as if she needed it, that what they had was temporary. Fleeting. Some of the best things in life were. And considering their entire relationship was supposed to be fake anyway, he'd already given her far more than she'd ever expected.

"I'm going to always remember this road trip. I didn't think I wanted to drive up the coast with you but we had fun. Didn't we?"

"Yeah, we did, babe. We did." His finger traced the curve of her face. "I thought you needed a break as much as I did. You've been working hard towards your future, and I get that, but sometimes you have to stop and play. I figured that out the hard way."

"You're right. I forgot how for a while. It's because I've always wanted to prove to the people who don't think much of me, to Ted and my mother, and all the others, that I'm a good person too. I made mistakes but it was never because I didn't care."

"Or maybe because you cared too much."

Tears stung her eyes and she pressed her face to his neck. "Why is it that you get me and nobody else does?"

His arms tightened around her. "I'd like to say it's because I'm such a great guy. You're never going to find another one like me. I'm a prince among men. Honestly? Maybe it's because we're so much alike."

"How can you say that? Everyone respects you."

"You need to command respect. I never want to hear Ted talking to you the way he did tonight again. Maybe I should be the one to tell him. It won't be as kind coming from me."

It had always just been easier not to engage Ted in arguments since she usually lost. But Jack was right.

She couldn't have David thinking it was okay to speak disrespectfully to any woman, least of all his mother.

When Fallon woke the next morning, she heard voices downstairs in the kitchen. Jack and her mother. Blinking, she picked up the cellphone from her nightstand. Nine o'clock and already several texts from Kailey:

That Jack Cooper is a looker!

When you wake up, call me.

Are you going to the parade tonight? Could use your help doing hair and make-up for the Nutcracker dancers unless you are too busy with Hot Guy, in which case I totally understand.

But I will want details. All of the details.

Fallon wasn't sure she could give out all those details without blushing so maybe it was best to keep it PG. Right. Like Kailey would let her get away with that. She texted back:

Just woke up. Need coffee. Will text you back when I am fully caffeinated.

She sat up and was about to reach for Jack's shirt off the ground nearby when the door to her bedroom squeaked open. Jack walked in coffee in hand. He looked so handsome and best of all, wide awake. Like he'd already showered, but he hadn't yet shaved. And damn he wore the scruffy look well.

"Morning. Beverly talked my ear off, or I would have been here sooner."

"Thank you." She accepted the hot mug of coffee. "What was she going on about?"

He sat on the edge of the bed and brushed a soft kiss across her lips. "Her back door screen doesn't shut right. Easy fix. And the sink in the downstairs bathroom is clogged. A few other things. I've got a list."

"She gave you a *honey-do* list?"

Would her mother *ever* stop embarrassing her? Not likely in this lifetime! But on the other hand, there was only one explanation for this: Mom believed that they were a couple.

He pulled a piece of paper out of his pants pocket. "Yeah, it's okay. I can handle all this in a day tops."

"Don't do it, Jack. Walk away now while you still can. She's going to suck you dry."

"You're the one who's going to suck me dry." He gave her an easy smile and his hand dove under the covers to caress her breasts.

She shivered, intensely aware of the fact that she was still naked as the day she'd been born. "Y-yes, I will."

"Promises, promises."

There was a knock on her door and Fallon slapped his hand away, shoved her cup of coffee into his hands, and dove under the covers.

"Come in," Jack said, sounding as though he were choking back a laugh.

"No! Don't let her come in," Fallon hissed from under the blanket and sheets. "I'm naked here."

The door creaked opened and Fallon heard her mother's voice. "That reminds me. This door needs to be oiled, Bud."

"Got it," Jack said.

"Good Lord, Fallon, aren't you a little too old to be playing hide and seek?"

"Yes, *Mom*."

"I've got to get my cookies down to the bake sale they're having at the parade tonight, and I could use your help."

"Okay, but I might need to meet Kailey to help with make-up later," she said from under the sheets just before the door shut again. She peeked out to meet Jack's ear-to-ear grin.

"You're never too old to play hide and seek, the adult version."

"Stop smiling. She called you 'Bud' again."

He sighed and handed her coffee back. "Yeah, that's okay too."

"No, it's not." She straightened. "I'm going to tell her the truth. All of it."

"As much as I'd appreciate that, I don't think it's such a good idea." He slid her a look. "You're going to tell her we haven't known each other for six months but more like a week? Yet we slept together in the same bed. I don't know your mother as well as you do, but I'm going to go out on a limb and say that won't help."

"Ha! For all she knows that's all we did. Sleep."

He quirked a single brow. "Do you wonder why she knocked this time and waited to be asked inside?"

"Yeah." Fallon was almost afraid to ask. "Why?"

"I told her I'd appreciate it since I sleep naked. I didn't want either of us to be embarrassed."

She gasped. "You didn't!"

"I did." He rose from the bed and slapped her butt. "C'mon, you hussy, there's work to be done."

Thirty minutes later Fallon had showered and dressed and joined her mother in the kitchen to help with the assembly line of butter, eggs, sugar, flour, mixing and baking. Baking cookies at Christmas time was one of her favorite things to do with David. If she moved back to Starlight Hill, she'd definitely see him more often despite Ted. Especially now that Ted would be married again, and presumably busy with his new wife. She could have David every other weekend again like before, watch his baseball games, and maybe volunteer at his school depending on her work schedule. The question remained whether she could live here again in peace, or if she was going to be the cause of nasty rumors again. The question was whether she could make a life here again, open up her own salon, and support herself without anyone's help.

She'd already done that for a couple of years in L.A., which proved something.

Jack continued to work on the back screen door, making sure to show plenty of demonstrations of affection. If he walked by on the way to the garage because he needed a screw or a nail, he'd stop by and nuzzle Fallon's neck, or come up behind her and wrap his arms around her waist. He was incredibly good at this faking thing and had Fallon believing it too. It felt like she'd actually known him for six months already. It was plain weird.

"My God," Mom said after Jack left the room. She flipped open the oven and took out another tray of Snickerdoodles. "I guess I was wrong about barflies. Didn't think you could meet a decent man in a bar, of all places."

Hold the presses: her mother had just admitted she might be wrong.

"Maybe you're not wrong. Maybe I just got lucky."

That much was one hundred percent true. He'd apprehended a criminal for her, agreed to go to a wedding and pretend he was crazy about her, taken her on the road trip of a lifetime, and last night made her eyes roll to the back of her head.

She swallowed a laugh, wondering what her mother would say if she knew how they'd actually met. *You see, he was dressed as Santa Claus and had a would-be burglar pinned on the ground. He specifically told me he had no plans, so he was wide open and available. It was his crazy idea to drive up the Pacific Coast Highway, which took us two days, but I'll never regret it as long as I live.*

"Done with the screen door," Jack announced as he strode into the kitchen. "The sink is next."

"Thank you! Here's a cookie for your troubles." Mom handed him a fresh baked Snickerdoodle from the tray.

Fallon turned to study him as he took a bite out of it. He eyed her as if he'd like to take a bite out of her too and then winked. "Good."

Jack finished the rest of the cookie in two bites, then stepped toward Fallon and pulled her into his arms. He kissed her, letting her savor him for a split second. The taste of sugar and cinnamon and Jack hit her like a fist to the heart.

"See you ladies in a bit." He walked off in the direction of the downstairs bathroom.

Mom stared at Fallon. "He's crazy about you."

No. He was very good at *faking* being crazy about her. She'd sort of won the lottery there. Fallon opened her mouth to say something and then shut it. Let her mother believe it. It had been the plan all along. Fallon dropped another spoonful of chocolate chip cookie dough on the cookie sheet.

"I owe you an apology," Mom said. "I honestly thought

you'd made him up. You've been acting odd since Ted sent his Save the Date. And when you told me you'd been dating someone special so you couldn't possibly go out with Trudy's nephew, I really thought you'd made the guy up. *Bud?* It's like you thought up a name on the spot. But I'll be darned if he's not as real as this butter, and you are a lucky, lucky woman."

"Thanks, Mom."

Fallon swallowed the golf ball sized lump in her throat. She wanted to *be* that lucky woman, not pretend to be her. Just once in her life she wanted a man that wanted her and her alone. Forever. Two years in L.A. and she hadn't met anyone special until Jack. And in a town as small as Starlight Hill, she was not likely to find 'the one.' No, that ship had sailed. Three times.

Fallon took a deep breath. Now was as good a time as any other. "I've got some bad news. I didn't want to worry you too much, but I lost my job."

"Oh, dear."

"It's okay, though. I've got a lot saved up, and I'll find another one."

"Maybe now's a good time to think about moving back. Rosie retired, after all."

"Maybe."

The Curl up and Dye wasn't at all what Fallon had in mind for her salon, but maybe with a little work she could move the place forward and into the new millennium. New state of the art stools, mirrors and sinks. She could do a lot with the place, especially if the lease was reasonable.

It would be nice to be closer to David again.

And closer to Mom, who wasn't always so bad.

"So cute," Kailey said, sticking a bobby pin in a tiny ballerina's bun. "I want a little girl."

Kailey and Fallon were seated in temporary stations they'd fashioned out of plastic crates inside Miss Angela's Dance Hall. The little Nutcracker ballerinas were getting ready for the parade and their march down Main Street following the Santa float. One by one the girls came up and made their requests. French braid, Princess Bun, ringlet curls, pink color spray.

"Don't you have your hands full as it is?" Fallon covered a little ballerina's eyes and finished her off with some hairspray.

Kailey and Joe had two boys, four and five. Tyler and Kyle were inseparable and about as wild as two boys came.

"Sure, but Joe wants a little girl too."

"Joe wants whatever you want," Fallon said with a smirk, as she waved the next ballerina forward.

"That's true." Kailey smiled with orgasmic glow.

"Where are those boys, anyway? I need to give them both a big fat smooch."

"They're with Joe and Wallace, trying to find the perfect spot to watch. The kids are excited to see Scott Turlock drive the ladder truck this year." Kailey met Fallon's eyes. "I'm so glad you're home. How's Hollywood?"

"Smoggy. But you were right. I got an education."

Kailey had referred Fallon to the intensely stressful world of celebrity styling. And while she'd met enough interesting people to write a few tell-all memoirs, and raked in the money working on Rodeo Drive, she couldn't say she'd lived the dream. She still hadn't found a storefront in L.A. that didn't cost so much she'd have to mortgage her entire future.

"I want a French braid," said Lindsey Turlock from the front of the line. "Please."

The girl was the image of her mother Genevieve, with beautiful naturally red hair flowing down to her shoulders. No matter how much of a color expert Fallon had become, this kind of color couldn't be replicated in a bottle. She had already tried.

"Of course, sweetheart." She missed seeing some of these kids almost as much as she missed David. They were growing up, and it was all happening so fast.

Fallon threaded the strands of hair one over the other. Under. Over. She could do this in her sleep, but she still loved it. Honestly, maybe she'd like a little girl too. Someday.

"Any more thoughts on taking over the lease on Rosie's old salon?"

"I'm going to go take a look at it after the wedding."

Kailey squealed. "Yay!"

"Don't get too excited. I'm just going to check it out."

It couldn't hurt. Sure, it wasn't what she'd had in mind. Her own top-tier celebrity salon on Rodeo Drive. The respect of everyone in the community for being a genuine semi-celebrity. For catering to the 'stars.' But she didn't need the reassurance that she was 'somebody' anymore. All she needed was David, Mom, Kailey, and maybe someday someone special in her life again. This whole road trip with Jack had served to remind her, more than anything, that she'd been alone for too long. She'd let past failures determine her future. No more. It didn't mean she had to get *married* again, but she was *going* to fall in love again.

"So where's Jack right now?" Kailey asked.

"He's around here somewhere," Fallon said. "He drove us over in the Mustang, and Hank from the car shop started to bend his ear. You know, car-guy stuff. Asking about the car's wattage or something."

"And so this is really," Kailey bent closer to whisper, "fake?"

"I met him a week ago. What do you think?"

"You're talking to the girl who fell in love at first sight with Joe Hannigan. A week is plenty of time. I'm not the best person to answer that question."

"Well, don't forget you're talking to a three-time loser." Fallon leaned closer to Kailey, and gently covered Lindsey's little ears. "But yes. Fake."

"And you're sure you want to *keep* it that way? Because when it's right, it's right. It doesn't matter how long you've known each other."

"It's for the best. He's the man with no plan, and I have David. I live by a plan."

"I hope you are at least…enjoying yourself." Kailey winked.

"Oh, yeah." And she would very much like to enjoy herself again tonight. Twice.

"Where's David tonight?" Kailey applied a little more rouge on a ballerina's plump cheeks.

Fallon frowned. "The rehearsal dinner. Tonight, of all nights."

"Poor kid."

"I'll make it up to him."

She'd ordered several presents ahead of time to be delivered to her mother's house, and they'd arrived weeks ago. An electric train set and Star Wars figures. PS2 video games, as he'd asked.

When it was time for the parade to begin, everyone spilled out onto Main Street. The streets were blocked off and the parade would begin there. Then it would work its way down Second and Third Street, before winding back to the beginning. Fallon searched for Jack in the crowd, but didn't see him so she joined Kailey, Joe, their boys, and some of the rowdy Turlock crowd. The parade began with the Santa float and all the children hollered and waved at the man of the hour. Ballerinas followed, twirling and pirouetting as Tchaikovsky's "Dance of the Sugar Plum Fairy" piped through speakers propped up behind the float.

"Aw, they look adorable," Kailey said.

"Good job, baby." Joe swept Kailey up in a fierce kiss.

Fallon pushed aside the envy that coursed through her then, sharp and solid as a stone. She wanted that kind of enduring love.

"Look! It's Uncle Scott!" Wallace and Genevieve's son, Brandon, yelled.

Scott waved from the truck, surrounded on all sides by Starlight Hill's finest. Five of the hunkiest guys she'd ever laid eyes on stood on the runners and waved to the crowd. Funny, but good looks notwithstanding, they did nothing for her. Then a red convertible Mustang with the top down, driven by none other than Jack Cooper, slowly followed the fire truck with a stuck-on placard that read

Starlight Hill PD. Seated next to him was Riley Jacobs, the new chief of police.

"So that's who Jacobs suckered into driving him tonight," Joe said. "Apparently their float didn't work out at the last minute."

"That's Jack Cooper." Kailey pointed. "Fallon's date."

"I thought his name was Bud," Joe said.

Fallon couldn't speak. Jack looked so handsome sitting behind the wheel, a big grin on his face.

For a few minutes, she didn't see anyone else at all.

"HEY, thanks for this, Jack. You really saved my ass," Riley Jacobs said as he waved to the crowd.

Jack had given Riley his real name. Even though it seemed half the town was calling him 'Bud,' he couldn't lie to a fellow cop. In the space of a few minutes, he'd learned Riley was a stand-up guy, an ex-Marine, and though a bit younger than Jack, he felt a connection. He wondered if he'd always feel that bond to other cops or if eventually it would wear off. Fallon waved to him from the crowd, her eyes more than a little wide in amazement. Something in the way she met his eyes then, like she couldn't see anyone else, made his chest tight all over again.

"How long you been a cop?" Riley asked now.

"Still shows?"

"I could freak you out and say yes, but actually, there's a rumor going around town that you're a cop."

He'd been in town two days. Fallon's mother must have risen early this morning to broadcast it from a megaphone location somewhere. He had no words for a beat.

Riley laughed. "Small town. You get used to it."

"*Former* cop," Jack said, turning on Second Street right

behind the ladder truck. "Not sure what I'm doing next. I'm burned out. Had enough. Been a cop since straight out of college."

"I hear you. You might want to try small town police work some time. It's more about service to the community than it is anything else."

"Yeah. I love this kind of thing."

But he couldn't really see himself in a small town, not when he'd been L.A. born and bred. He assumed he'd get stir-crazy after too long. Then again, this was Fallon's town. Beautiful, sexy Fallon. He couldn't help but give it props just for that. Last night, their connection had floored him. He'd had great mind-blowing sex before, sure. But he'd never in his life had this off-the-charts chemistry with any woman. So much so that he had lost track of where fake ended and real began.

As they turned on Third Street and started to head back, Riley waved to a very pregnant woman in the crowd. She stood in front of a storefront that read *Giancarlo's*.

"That's my wife. Sophia."

She seemed younger than Fallon, short with wavy brown hair. Not beautiful like Fallon but very pretty. "Congratulations."

"Thanks," Riley said. "This is our first. Any day now."

"How long you been married?" Jack forced himself to make casual conversation.

"Eight years now."

"You must have been young."

"Knew the first time I laid eyes on her. Proposed four weeks later. I won't say it hasn't been a bumpy ride, but I'll never let go for as long as she'll have me."

The parade finally wound back to Main Street, and he and Riley went in different directions. Riley to find his wife and a cup of hot cocoa. It was a cold winter night in wine country, and Jack knew exactly who he wanted to warm him up. He parked the car, put the top back up, and then walked through the crowd until he found her next to a woman with two-toned colored hair.

"Jack, this is Kailey," Fallon said.

"Nice to meet you!" Kailey gave him a hug. "It's so awesome of you to be in the parade, being a visitor and all. That's sort of above and beyond duty."

"That's his specialty," Fallon said with a smile. "Above and beyond."

He grinned, his thoughts running to last night. "No worries, I love to help out when I can."

Though he'd had a good time tonight, he definitely wanted to get out of here and get Fallon into bed. He'd kept count of the days left, though not in the way he'd expected. He hated to see the days running out, but they'd agreed he'd leave right after the wedding. All part of the plan. She would have Christmas with her son. Plus, Jack didn't want to overstay his welcome and follow her around like a love sick puppy dog. He hadn't done that since he'd been a horny teenager and wasn't even sure he'd done it then. The women were chatting about cute ballerinas and the upcoming wedding, and he was doing his best to appear the dutiful lover hanging on every word. He had his arm around Fallon's waist and had tugged her in tight. He nodded in all the right places. It came pretty natural and he felt comfortable. At ease. Except that his thoughts kept running to how fast he could get Fallon undressed once they got to the house. Her mother would be home and likely still awake, so there might have to be some small talk first. He wanted less talk and more naked.

Eventually the girls ran out of words. They all said goodnight, and Jack took Fallon's hand and led her to the

Mustang parked behind the bank. He opened up the passenger side door and waited for her to get in.

"Thank you, boyfriend of the year." She smiled and got inside.

"Welcome." Once inside he started up the car and waited for the heater to do its job since Fallon was already shivering.

He knew the heater would do its duty, but he still pulled her close.

"You don't have to do that," she said. "I doubt anyone can see us in here."

"You never know," he said and kissed her. One tender kiss, brushed against her soft and willing lips. Then another one, not so tender, while their tongues tangled and explored.

Fallon pulled back a little breathless and sat back in her seat. Snapped her seat belt on. "The wedding is tomorrow."

Seemed like a new cold front had come in. He understood he wasn't the ideal man for Fallon. She hated that he refused to have a plan right now and likely nothing much had changed. But dammit, he couldn't come up with a plan just because she needed him to have one. Which brought him around to a point he needed to make.

"Fallon."

"Yeah?"

"You can't seriously believe I'm this great of an actor."

The moon cast a shadow through the windshield and she just blinked in the semi-darkness but didn't say a word.

"But if you don't want to sleep in the same bed again tonight, that's okay with me."

"I didn't say that."

"We have two more nights together. I think you know what I want. Now tell me what you want to do."

She let out a breath. "I think everybody already thinks we're doing it so I don't see why we should be the ones to suffer."

"That's my girl."

He held her hand as he drove back to her mother's house. Once inside, they both made small talk with Fallon's mother about the evening's festivities. Jack excused himself first and walked casually upstairs. He opened the door to her bedroom and spied Fallon's favorite Springsteen shirt on the bed where she'd left it. Picked it up. It smelled like her. Worn and well loved, the detective in him knew there was a story behind it.

The question was whether Fallon would let her guard down enough to tell him tonight.

Chapter 15

Fallon shut off the Christmas tree lights. The angel at the top of the fresh Douglas Fir tree was the same one from her childhood. Mom bought a small tree every year since David was born. Before that, Christmas hadn't been much of a holiday for either of them since Dad passed. But there was nothing like a child to restore the spirit and magic of Christmas.

Two more nights until Jack would be gone and out of her life. She assumed he'd stay in Oregon until he could figure out what to do with his life. Maybe he'd meet a nice woman there and eventually settle down again possibly years from now. She couldn't exactly wait around for him to make up his mind where he wanted to be and what he wanted out of his life. They barely knew each other, anyway, or at least she kept reminding herself of that fact. He was, unfortunately, exactly the kind of man she would have wanted in her life if this whole thing between them had been real from the beginning. She wanted a man just like him, but one who could handle a ready-made family. Because she and David were a package deal.

And she wouldn't force a relationship. Never again. Her entire romantic life had been based on coercing commitments from boys and men. In high school, she'd been convinced Billy Turlock would ask her to marry him but instead he'd gone off to the minor leagues and never looked back. He hadn't loved her. Neither had any of her three husbands she was now convinced. Ted had only wanted to do the honorable thing by her, and she'd fooled herself into thinking that would be enough. That because of their mutual love for their son they could make their marriage work. But the marriage had been impossible when the going got tough. There had to be true love in any long lasting relationship and it couldn't ever be forced. She'd finally learned that lesson and she didn't want Jack doing anything he wasn't ready and willing to do.

And he wasn't ready for her, that much was clear. Ready for sex? Of course. But there again, she expected this was the norm for him. She knew she should be smart and end the intimacy now before it got any tougher for her. Before she felt any closer to him than she already did. She was older now. Smarter. But apparently still a bonafide sucker for great orgasms because she made her way to the bedroom as if there was a sale on shoes in there.

She shut and locked the door behind her.

Jack leaned back in the chair next to the bed, one long leg stretched out in front of him. Fully clothed.

"Hey." He grinned, and her knees went liquid.

"Hey yourself."

He one-hand tossed what looked like a piece of cloth in her direction. She caught her Springsteen t-shirt mid-air. "Don't tell me you want me to wear this to bed."

He smiled wickedly, leaning further back in the chair, hands folded across his flat stomach. "No, I prefer you wear nothing at all. But I do want to know more about the t-shirt."

"What do you want to know? It's Bruce Springsteen. The Boss." She threw the shirt on the bed and moved towards him.

"At Madison Square Garden, specifically. Did you see him there?"

She didn't like talking about any of this. Ever. And she could play a good game of redirection so she stood in front of him and swiftly removed her top.

"Um, yeah. Many years ago."

He slid her a look full of heat and one finger trailed from cleavage down to her stomach. "I could guess that, given the state of the t-shirt."

She unzipped her jeans and slipped them off, chucking them aside. "I think you know everything now."

He pulled her into his lap. "Try again."

No wonder he'd been a detective. It was in his blood. He noticed far more than most people did. He realized the t-shirt meant something to her. Something that went beyond pure comfort. He just didn't know how or why. And now, because she was *such* a smartass, she sat half-naked in his arms. Not able to blame anyone else because she'd done this to herself. Stripped. For him.

She unbuttoned the top of his jeans. "Jack, you're over-dressed for this occasion."

"I will take care of that soon, don't worry."

She pressed one finger gently to the hollow of his neck and sensed the steady thrum of his heart. "You're not going to drop this, are you?"

He met her gaze as one hand stroked her thigh. "No."

"Fine." She took in a ragged breath. "My father was the real Springsteen fan. He took me to my first concert when I was ten. My dad said the man was a poet and a musician. And that's one of the t-shirts he bought me."

His arms tightened around her. "How old were you when he died?"

She narrowed eyes at him. "How do you know he died? He might have just abandoned us."

Jack just quirked a brow.

"Okay. I was twelve."

"Damn." He kissed her shoulder. "I'm so sorry."

"I named David after him. Anyway, it was a long time ago. I lost or ruined most of the concert t-shirts one way or another except for this one. It was a larger size so I didn't wear it as often. You can see it's barely holding together. But I feel comfortable wearing it…and safe."

"Makes sense." His hand rubbed up and down her back in a soothing pattern.

"Are you glad you asked me? Because I already told you I don't want you feeling sorry for me." She licked his neck and pulled up his sweater to run her hand down his taut abs.

He groaned. "Babe, I feel a lot of things for you but you can be sure sorry is not one of them."

"Good." She stood, and pulled him up with her. "Now take your clothes off."

"Bossy." He kicked off his boots and removed his pants and sweater. "I like it."

Now they had both stripped. So much better this way.

His body was solid and perfect. Hard male angles. Olive skin. His hot gaze swept over her, and everywhere his gaze fell his hand followed. She nearly melted to a fleshy pool on the ground. One big hand palmed her ass and squeezed. He pulled her flat against him, and pressed into her, rigid and firm. She licked his neck again, enjoying his salty taste. She took a lengthy tour of him with her tongue, starting at his neck and working her way to his abs and lower still. Seemed high time for her to learn the geography of his body, and she was only on day two of her lesson plan. When she slid off his boxers his body tensed tight as a steel cable. She licked and tasted him. All of him. He didn't let her linger long before he made an innately male sound and flipped her on to the bed.

"My turn." He slipped her panties off and threw them aside. Her bra came off with one quick flick of his wrist.

"Kiss me," she demanded and he didn't wait another moment.

His mouth covered hers in a wild and heated kiss that set her heart on fire. Taking hold of her wrists, he moved her arms above her head and pinned them.

He studied her face, his eyes hooded with desire. "Still scared?"

"Terrified."

She should be. She wanted him. Needed him. Wanted his hands touching her everywhere, tenderly and with his amazing skill. He covered her with open mouth kisses, moving from her sensitive ear lobes, to her neck, to her breasts, her stomach, and south. Not surprisingly, he took his time with every nibble of her skin, with every flick of his tongue, with every soft bite of tender flesh.

"Trust me," he said.

And she did. She'd trusted him from the moment she laid eyes on him. Realizing maybe, on some level, that they were two of a kind. When he released her arms, he slid down her body and moved to nudge her thighs open. His tongue licked her inner thigh and then flicked her core over and over again until she threaded fingers through his hair and nearly went out of her mind.

"Jack," she moaned. "Please."

She heard the sound of a condom packet ripping open and he slid into her, making them both gasp. He moved inside her with firm and unrelenting thrusts. Sure of what he did to her. How he slayed her with every single touch and every single hot kiss. He would take care of her. He was the type of man who would always take care of his woman. And she had him here. Now. For as long as he was here, he would have her back. He would be all hers. Maybe not forever but for right now. It would have to be enough.

"Fallon," Jack groaned and dropped his forehead to hers. "So good."

She wrapped her legs around him and arched her back, taking him deeper. Good was an understatement. It had never been this erotic for her and never this intense.

And she had no idea how she would ever let him go.

FALLON WOKE to the annoying sound of her phone alarm. Her hand reached out to slap the annoying piece of hardware and missed. Twice. It kept going off like a siren in the room. Cracking one eye open, she grabbed the phone from the nightstand.

Wedding Day: gird your loins.

The reminder she'd set last week. Yes, today was D-day. The awful day she'd have to be in the same room with Ted and his relatives. All of them looking down at her from their very educated, very Patrician noses. She sat up, blinked, and rubbed her eyes. Morning light spilled through cracks in the blinds. A cup of coffee sat on her nightstand and under it a note:

I would have woken you up to have your coffee but you were dead to the world. I've gone to get the oil changed in the Mustang before the long drive. See you this afternoon. ~Jack

Fallon took a sip of the coffee. Cold. She drank it anyway. Now that she wasn't going to be able to roll around in bed with Jack and waste away the morning, she might as well get up. She staggered to the bathroom and took a quick shower, dressed, and headed down to the kitchen. Apparently Mom had left the house early as well. Might be a perfect time to finish her Christmas shopping, so Fallon had a pop tart for breakfast and headed out the door. She didn't have a car so she walked into town.

David was taken care of, but she found sterling silver hoop earrings for Mom from the jewelry and craft shop on Second Street and the silver naval ring Kailey had mentioned. Jack was a bit harder to buy for, as was the case with most men. Still, she wandered into Hank's Cars and Hobbies. She didn't need to buy Jack anything at all, since they wouldn't actually spend the holiday together. But she had so much to thank him for. She planned to wrap the gift and card and have him open it on Christmas day with his family.

"These black leather driving gloves would be perfect for Bud," Hank said.

They would definitely look sexy on Jack but so would a paper bag. She wanted something special. Meaningful.

"How about a hood ornament?" Hank nodded. "Every man needs a hood ornament."

"He *does?*" Fallon didn't think so.

It took her nearly an hour of walking down every aisle of auto supplies and grown-up man toys, but she finally found the perfect gift in the back.

"Oh yeah. This is kind of cool, isn't it? I forgot we even had these."

"It's perfect." By the time she was done it would be a personalized gift.

Fallon paid for it and then walked to Genevieve's Sweet Southern Buns bakery for a treat. God knew she deserved one. She was going to the wedding of her ex-husband today. Not that she cared much anymore, but Ted's family didn't think highly of her and never had. They barely put up with her and did so only because of David. Seeing them again would be by far the worst part of the entire day, and that said something.

"Hey there!" Genevieve said from behind the counter.

"I'll have a cinnamon mini-Bundt cake and some coffee with room."

"Coming right up. Hey, thanks for Lindsey's French braid last night. I try, but I don't do nearly as well as you and Kailey."

"We love doing it. Neither one of us has a little girl."

"So where's Bud? I can't wait to meet him." Genevieve poured coffee into one of the big ceramic mugs she collected.

"He's around." Fallon cleared her throat. "Actually, his name is Jack."

"Okay." Genevieve nodded. "I must have heard wrong."

Sure, because Jack and Bud were such similar sounding names. Fallon smiled at Genevieve's kindness and paid for her cake and coffee. The large ceramic mug was pink and white and read *I bake. What's your super power?* Hair and make-up, and falling for men who were not available. Was there a mug for that?

She found a good quiet spot to be alone with her thoughts. She needed to re-work her entire immediate life plan. No biggie. As it worked out, the timing was perfect to move back home. She didn't have a job in L.A., but she did have plenty of money saved which would go a lot further in Starlight Hill than it ever would in L.A. She pulled out her planner and started to make a few notes. First, she'd check out the salon tomorrow, after the wedding. If she could work out a lease with the current landlord she'd run the numbers to make sure she could afford to fix the salon the way she wanted to. When Ted returned from his honeymoon, she could go back to L.A. and give notice to the landlord. Pack. Say goodbye to Betsy next door. Fond memories of the milk and cookies she'd shared with Santa Jack came back. If she stayed in L.A. a while longer and found another job, there was a chance he'd at least be back to pack up and move to wherever he'd intended to land. Maybe he'd look her up. Or maybe not.

Maybe instead it was high time for her to stop fantasizing about any hopes for a future with Jack. Sweet and sexy that he was, he'd become caught up in something momentary with her. Once back in L.A. reality would return. He was either going back to the L.A.P.D. homicide department, or he would move to another department. Jack would never stop being a cop.

She hoped all the fantastic sex she'd had in the past two days would be enough for a while, because after Jack she couldn't imagine being interested in anyone else for a long time. But she'd gone nearly eight years before this without a man. What was eight more? By then, David would be a grown-up and she wouldn't need to be such a stickler about plans. Maybe she could be carefree again like Jack.

The bakery door dinged, making Fallon look up. Stephan, her nemesis. He glanced in her direction and then quickly looked away. Which made no sense, since she'd never faced him down as she'd always wanted to do.

Like she should have done long ago. She'd had no trouble yelling at a burglar (when he was pinned under a strong man) because two years in L.A. working with celebrities had given her an even tougher skin. And you know what? Now was as good of a time as any to tell Mr. Gossip a few things. She stood up and walked over to the man who thought he had the pulse on their small town.

"Merry Christmas," Fallon said.

He gave her a quick glance. "Oh, hey. Look at you. You look *fantastic*! You in town for long?"

"Until after Christmas. But then I'm moving back permanently."

"You are?" His eyebrows met his forehead. "That's… wow, that's awesome."

"Is it? I'm going to need your help. You and I need to make a deal."

His shifty eyes went into overtime shift. "A deal?"

She tapped his chest. "You stop talking about me and spreading ugly lies and I won't kick you in the balls."

He glanced down at his family jewels. "Fallon, really. You take this all a little too…seriously, I think."

"No one asked you to think. I have a son, Stephan, and he doesn't need to hear any more small town rumors about his mother. So what if I was married three times? It stopped being funny a long time ago. Why don't you blog about food or wine…or just anything else. Stop talking about me. Or Billy and Brooke. Or eating disorders. Or I swear…" She glanced down at his crotch with her best PMS look.

Stephan did everything but cup his gonads and then flew out the bakery's door.

"Sorry about that." Fallon turned to Genevieve with what she hoped was an apologetic smile on her face. Given that she was not sorry at all, Fallon didn't think she could pull it off.

"Don't apologize. It's about time someone told him off. I don't even think Brooke has threatened his balls before."

Next stop? Find a good time and place to tell Mom that she would need to show her, as David's mother, the respect she deserved. The respect she commanded.

Chapter 16

There probably *was* no appropriate dress to wear to the wedding of an ex-husband. But after going through all of her many wardrobe choices over the course of the afternoon, Fallon selected the royal blue peplum dress she'd bought on Rodeo Drive one month ago when it was seventy-five percent off. Dressed only in her full length spandex slip, she set up in the hallway bathroom and proceeded to work on her make-up and hair for the next two hours. Unable to decide between the flat iron and curling iron, she split the difference. She straightened and then curled her hair. Pinned it. Took the pins out. She tried a French braid and didn't like it. A Princess Bun was no better. Up or down?

This day was going to be a disaster.

"You in there?" Jack's voice called out from the other side of the door.

She opened the door and her womb contracted. Jack took a step inside, dressed to the nines in a black double breasted suit, caramel colored button down, and striped tie. The man cleaned up well. He looked great naked, but this was definitely a close second.

"Y-you look fantastic."

"So do you." His gaze slid down her skin tight slip. "You sure I can't talk you into going like that?"

She rolled her eyes. "I don't think everyone else would appreciate it."

"Screw 'em."

He pulled her into a kiss that quickly got a little wild and heated considering they were in a small bathroom. Pushed up against the wall, one of Jack's arms on either side barricading her, she didn't want to go to any dumb wedding. She wanted to go back to bed.

"Fallon!" Another screech from Mom downstairs. "I hope you're almost ready. We have to leave soon. And I'm not going to be late because of you!"

"Maybe we could be late because of me." Jack palmed her ass. "Don't worry, I'll calm her down. If we're late to the jerk's wedding, we're late. Take your time."

He closed the door.

"Okay, down it is," Fallon said to the mirror. "And that's final." In the bedroom, she stepped into her dress and black stilettos, zipped up and then went downstairs to meet Jack and Mom.

Showtime.

A few minutes later, all three of them were in Jack's Mustang finding a parking place at Immanuel Methodist Church. The white clapboard building in the middle of downtown still had its original belfry and was a town landmark. David, as it had turned out, was Ted's honorary best man, and he looked adorable in a white mini-tux and cummerbund. But his blonde hair was parted to the side as if someone had used a ruler to do it. From the front of the church, her little boy waved at Fallon and she waved back. The wedding was short and sweet, with some declarations of love and a hard cough from the bride's side when the pastor asked if anyone cared to object now or forever hold their peace.

As the wedding party filed out, Ted's mother Gladys caught Fallon's eye and pursed her lips in disapproval. But Fallon didn't miss the way her eyes swept over Jack, taking him in, a glint of admiration in her eyes. The rest of the wedding party was far more obvious. Sally's maid of honor blatantly eye-fucked him as she walked out, and one of the bridesmaids licked her lips. Fallon gripped Jack's arm a little tighter. She'd wanted this, after all. Wanted everyone to stare at her in envy. But now all she wanted was for all of them to stop gawking at Jack. It made her a little queasy and a lot jealous. Crazy.

"Ready?" Jack asked.

"Yes, please." She stepped out into the aisle first, followed by Jack and Mom.

"You looked much prettier on *your* wedding day," Mom hissed. "All three of them."

Fallon winced. "Uh, thanks Mom."

When they arrived at Serrano's Vineyard on the outskirts of town (Ted was friends with the idiot man who owned it), the party was in full swing. Ted had sprung for a live band, including a brass and horn section. The reception was open table seating and Jack guided Fallon and Mom to an available table, pulling out a chair for each of them. The wedding party arrived nearly an hour later, and poor David looked miserable. They'd probably taken so many photos that he'd never want to sit or stand still again.

The minute he saw Fallon, he headed over to her table. "Mom! Grandma! The wedding is finally over. Now we can have Christmas!"

"We sure can." Fallon smiled and reached out to fix David's unnatural looking part. Force of habit.

"The photographer said this wedding would ruin anybody's Christmas. But not ours!" David said.

Fallon inwardly cringed, Mom gave David her grandmother 'warning' look, and a moment later David was ushered off to the bridal table by Gladys.

"I love that kid," Jack said. "No filter."

The question remained whether he'd still love it when he happened to be on the other end of all the raw honesty. "This should be an interesting toast by the honorary best man. I hope Ted has thought this one through."

"And I kind of hope he hasn't." Jack dipped his head and took a sip from the water glass.

He'd removed his jacket, but even though he was dressed like a cover model he wore the look with casual ease. Each arm was stretched out on the back of the chairs on either side like he owned this table. He'd loosened his tie slightly, and had one long leg stretched out, leaning back with the carefree comfort of someone at a picnic by the lake. His intelligent eyes never missing a beat. Observing.

"You know we're going to dance," Jack said, his gaze going to the dance floor and back to her.

"Eventually." Fallon wanted a slow song, one where she could have every excuse to hold him close and bury her face in his warm neck.

Wine was served and the bride and groom took to the floor with their first dance. The band played *I Only Want to Be with You*. Sally danced next with her father, Ted with Gladys, and finally the entire wedding party crowded the dance floor. David was in the middle of it all, throwing his hands up in the air and jumping up and down in place to Uptown Funk.

"He's celebrating the end of the Wedding Week of Doom." Jack winked.

"Fallon," Mom said. "Aren't you going to dance? You two lovebirds should dance!"

Jack quirked an eyebrow at Fallon.

The band switched to a Sam Hunt ballad, *Make You Miss Me*. Jack stood and held out his hand. Fallon let him guide her by the small of her back to the dance floor where they joined the rest of the now somewhat subdued crowd. It wasn't long before Jack had pulled her in tight enough for her to feel every one of his hard male edges. She laced her fingers around the back of his neck and swayed in time with him. Last night, Jack had said he wasn't that great of an actor, but she still wondered how much of this was for show and how much for real. It shouldn't matter. This was the entire reason she'd asked him to the wedding, even if it had blown up in her face. She wanted them to be the real thing. She wanted forever again for the first time in a long while but once again forever wasn't going to happen. Not for her.

He tipped her chin. "I can hear you thinking."

Hopefully her love-sick haze wasn't written all over her pitiful face. "Everyone's watching us."

"Isn't that what you wanted?"

What she'd wanted had changed, because she hadn't expected to fall for him. Suddenly this display felt like a huge invasion of privacy.

She sucked in a strangled breath. "I'm moving back to Starlight Hill. When Ted gets back from the honeymoon, I'll go back and pack everything up. For a while I thought maybe I'd see you again in L.A. at some point but that's probably not going to happen now."

"I'm sure it's for the best." His eyes were unreadable,

hooded and shut-down. "I won't worry about you living alone. And David needs you here."

"I'm going to look into leasing the old salon where I used to work part-time. Re-model it with the money I've saved up and turn it into my own place. Fallon's Follicles, or maybe I'll just keep the old name, the Curl Up and Dye. The name isn't as important as the fact that it will be mine. And I'll bring a little bit of Hollywood to Starlight Hill."

"If anyone can do it you can."

She smiled at the amount of confidence he had in her, and ran a hand through his full head of hair. He didn't need a haircut, but she wanted to give him one anyway if only to have an excuse to play with his gorgeous head of chocolate brown hair.

"Still don't have a plan for what happens next?"

"Christmas with my folks. Other than that, taking it one day at a time. But you know, plans change."

She met his eyes. "And you'll be a cop again."

"Maybe."

"It isn't wrong to want to help people. To be the only one in the room who notices the smallest of details. It's a gift."

"And a curse?"

"Whatever you do, I know you'll do it well."

Fallon closed her eyes and buried her face in his neck, thinking that somewhere in the world there was a lucky woman who would meet Jack Cooper at the right time.

Jack twirled a strand of Fallon's hair around his finger. She was the most beautiful woman in the room, in his humble opinion. As far as he was concerned, there was no other woman. Her blue dress clung to her curves in all the right places, and he had a difficult time keeping his hands to himself. But he'd be good for now, the attentive lover with the perfect amount of affection for the circumstances. In other words, no ass-grabbing at the wedding reception. It wasn't easy when he'd caught many a deadbeat checking out his date, Ted the Jackass included. He didn't blame any of them. Her looks had caught his attention first, too, but he'd bet not one of them understood how much more there was to her. She'd taken her father's death harder than anyone seemed to know or appreciate from what he could tell. Made some youthful mistakes chasing love and endured the taunts of mean-spirited people. She adored her son. She'd planned, and saved, and scraped by, and now she would have her own business. He'd also fantasized meeting her again at some point in L.A. But he was proud of her for making a tough decision. It hadn't been easy and yet she was here. Still holding her head high.

Later there was dinner and wine. Then much more wine. Plenty of drunken toasts, as at any wedding, but unfortunately David was not invited to give a speech. Probably a wise move. Instead, Ted's brother gave a rambling toast in which he awkwardly praised Ted's great taste in women as his gaze swept over Fallon, and as somewhat of an after-thought, Sally. Seemed as though the jackassery might run in the family. The cake was finally cut, and while Jack wanted more than anything to get out of here and back to Fallon's bedroom, he also recognized it meant the countdown had begun. It was time to gracefully bow out of Fallon's life. Time for his curtain call.

Ted and his wife finally turned to say goodbye to the crowd of guests. Once the couple was finally out the door, the die-hards took to the dance floor and Fallon grabbed David's hand.

"Are you ready to go home?"

"Yeah, guys! Let's rock and roll!" David grasped Jack's hand too.

The kid spun like a top on the way home, talking baseball stats, football, video games and Christmas. Never a dull moment with David around, that was for sure.

"It's going to be time for bed when we get back to the house and your room is all ready for you," Beverly said. "We have a big day tomorrow."

Once back at the house, Fallon's mother retired immediately claiming a monster sized headache due to Gladys and the entire 'plebian' side of Ted's family. She apologized to Jack profusely for having to endure that 'joke' of a wedding. Fallon then took David upstairs to get him ready for bed.

In the living room, Jack lost the jacket and kicked off

the uncomfortable shoes. He slipped off his tie and helped himself to a glass of milk in the kitchen. Quite likely, he was the most sober person in town tonight. He strolled back to the Christmas tree to make sure his present for Fallon was still where he'd put it earlier today.

What seemed like an hour later, Fallon walked in the room. "He's finally asleep. This is almost as bad as Christmas Eve. He was so wound up. It must have been all the sugar in the wedding cake."

She'd changed into dark sweats and a long sleeve white shirt that read: *I make hair contact before I make eye contact.* Big floppy socks on her feet. Hair pulled into a ponytail with all make-up removed. Gorgeous.

"It was a nice wedding, as weddings of idiots go. I've been to a few, believe me, and this was one of the better ones."

She laughed. "Thank you."

"For?"

"Being so wonderful about…all this. And for making me feel like the only woman in the room."

"You are the only woman in the room." He rocked back on his heels and scanned the living room.

"I meant at the reception."

"That part was easy." Jack pulled her present out. "Merry Christmas."

He handed her a box wrapped in gold paper. He'd had to drive to Napa after the oil change in order to find exactly what he'd been looking for.

"I've got something for you, too." She fished a package from under the tree. "But don't open it till you get to Oregon and spend Christmas with your family."

He knew he'd open it before he got out of town. "I want you to open mine now."

"Really?" Her eyes shone as bright as any kid's on Christmas morning. She took a seat on the couch near the tree, tore open the wrapping paper and lifted the lid of the box. Froze.

"Oh, my God."

"Do you like it?"

"I love it." She draped the new Bruce Springsteen t-shirt on. "It's just perfect."

"Yeah?" He pulled her up by the elbows and the t-shirt hung between them. "I want you to think about only one thing when you wear this shirt. I want you to think about making new memories."

Her eyes were suspiciously wet and shiny. "I already have some beautiful new memories."

"Fallon." He pressed his forehead to hers. "I didn't want you to cry, babe. I want to see you smile. You should be laughing and smiling all the time. That's how I'm going to remember you."

She gave him a trembling smile and kissed him tenderly, just a soft brush across the lips. But he pulled her closer and held on tight, her breath warm on his neck. He would always remember the way she smelled like sunshine and chocolate. The way her hair pointed in three different directions when she rolled out of bed. The way she laid across from him without a stitch of clothes or make-up on, still the most beautiful woman he'd ever seen. He had plenty of photos of her in his phone and they would have to do. He couldn't have her, and he knew that. She needed someone who would stay in this little town and carve out a life with her and David. She didn't need a washed-up cop who didn't have a plan for what would happen next. These feelings he had for her would wear off in time he assumed. It couldn't be love because love didn't happen like this. It had been all of two weeks since they'd met. He didn't fall in love easily so this had to be something else. As the type of man and cop who clung to reality and facts, the facts all said he couldn't be in love. It wasn't logical. This odd tightness in his chest at the thought of leaving her, this ache, might be…heartburn. He pulled back to rub his chest.

"Are you okay?" Fallon said.

"Sure." Hell, no. He was sick. Or something.

"Maybe too much rich food tonight." She walked to the kitchen and came back with a pill and a glass of water. "Here, take this."

He swallowed it, doubtful it would help but at this point willing to try anything. The thought of leaving tomorrow, driving alone, no longer held any appeal. When exactly had he become such a sap? He set the glass of water down on the coffee table and took a seat on the couch, stretching his legs. Fallon smiled down at him and then plopped down in his lap. His arms immediately went around her like it was the most natural thing in the world. Strange. He had friends he'd known for ten years that he didn't feel nearly as comfortable with as he did with her.

"Tell me you're going to be alright. That you're not going to let that jackass disrespect you anymore."

"I won't." Her fingers dug through his hair, playing with it. Fluffed it out to the sides and then smoothed it down. She was the only person other than his barber that he'd let play with his hair. Ever. "You would have been proud of me today."

"Yeah?"

"I stood up to the self-appointed town gossip, who's made my life miserable in the past. I do believe I got his attention."

"Good going."

"I'll be okay so you don't need to worry about me. I

always land on my feet. But it doesn't mean I won't miss you."

"Right back at you, babe." He tightened his arms around her as she lowered her head to his chest.

"This used to be my favorite thing to do as a kid waiting up for Santa Claus. My dad told me Santa wouldn't come until I closed my eyes. I'd watch the Christmas tree lights until I couldn't keep them open."

He stroked Fallon's back. By this time tomorrow he'd be in Oregon with his family. Probably goofing off with his brother's sons and stealing fresh baked *galletas* from his mother's oven. He should be looking forward to all of it, spending time with family and relaxing. Instead he was wide awake trying to figure out why he didn't want to move from this position. Wondering if he'd get a wink of sleep tonight.

Eventually the pattern of Fallon's breathing shifted and became slow and regular. He nudged her slightly. "Fallon."

Nothing.

"Babe."

Still nothing. Funny. She couldn't keep her eyes open while he wasn't sure his would ever shut again. He rose with her in his arms and carried her slowly up the steps. She moved, nuzzling his neck and mumbling his name.

"We're going to bed. To sleep." He wasn't sure if he'd said that out loud for his sake, or hers.

He laid her on the bed and covered her with a blanket. She said his name again.

"Yeah. I'm here." He unbuttoned his shirt and slung it on a hanger nearby. Tossed his pants and slipped under the covers next to her.

She rolled towards him and murmured two words quite clearly: "Hold me."

But he'd already reached for her even before she'd

asked. "All night long. And then in the morning I'll bring you coffee. With cream."

One last time.

Chapter 18

Fallon always woke early when David spent the night. Call it mother's intuition. She usually managed to wake before he did. Even so, when she heard the shower going and noted Jack's absence next to her, she assumed he'd beat her to the shower again. There was no cup of coffee on the nightstand, possibly because it hadn't been made. Good. Call her crazy sentimental, but if Jack brought her a cup of coffee this morning she might burst into tears and embarrass them both. She threw off the covers, remembering all too well that she'd fallen asleep last night listening to the steady beat of Jack's strong heart. Several times during the night her eyes had drifted open to find one arm slung over her. He slept soundly but still held her because he always kept his promises. Too well.

Fallon peeked in on David snuggled in bed. She made her way downstairs to the empty kitchen and started the coffee. When Mom padded into the kitchen a few minutes later, Fallon was searching for the mixing bowl.

"What are you looking for?" Mom asked.

"I want to make pancakes for David."

"Here." Mom reached in a cupboard and set a large bowl on the counter. "Where's Bud? He's always up before you are."

"He's in the shower. I'm sure he'll be down in a few minutes."

"I'll want to say goodbye. He's a wonderful man, that one. I wish he'd stay for Christmas."

"He has to work." Fallon added the flour, milk and cracked an egg.

"Shame." Mom grabbed a mug and poured some coffee. "Christmas is a time for family."

Fallon took a deep breath and stopped stirring. "I want to talk to you before David gets up."

"What about?"

"I know I've made a lot of mistakes in the past, but haven't I been a good mother to David?"

"Of course! What on earth does that have to do—"

Fallon held up her hand. "Whatever you think about my personal life is one thing but please don't say it in front of David. He needs to hear good things about me, especially from you."

There was a long beat of silence as Mom sipped her coffee.

"You're right," Mom said, meeting Fallon's gaze. "After your father died, maybe I was too tough on you. I'll try and do better."

"That's all I can ask."

"But David loves you and there's nothing in the world anyone could say to change that."

David ran into the kitchen two minutes later. "Pancakes? Yay! Dad says whenever I'm with you guys I don't eat right so I have to eat all kinds of disgusting vegetables at his house. I love being here!"

Mom scowled. "Let me tell you something, dear,

pancakes are not exactly junk food. And your mother is a wonderful cook."

Fallon gave her mother a grateful smile. She kissed David's cheek and served him a short stack.

"Can we go Christmas shopping today?" David asked between bites. "I didn't get you or grandma anything."

Fallon and Mom exchanged a look. Fallon had always helped David pick a present for his father. In years past, Ted had done the same. "Your Dad didn't take you shopping for us?"

David shook his head.

Perfect. Exactly what she'd wanted to do four days before Christmas. "Okay, we'll get ready and go after we finish eating."

"I'll take him," Mom said. "That way he can surprise you."

"We'll all go and he can take turns surprising us both," Fallon said. "But I need to stop by the Curl Up and Dye."

"Morning." Jack strode in the kitchen, came up behind Fallon and kissed her neck. He helped himself to a cup of coffee as if he'd lived here all his life and then ruffled David's hair. "Hey, kiddo."

David tipped his head back and smiled, a mouthful of pancakes in his mouth.

"Excuse me. I need to get out of this housecoat." Mom pointed to Jack. "Now don't you leave without saying goodbye."

"No ma'am." He sat across from David. "Is it okay if I have some of your pancakes?"

David shook his head and giggled.

"C'mon. It's Christmas."

David shook his head double-time.

Fallon set a plate in front of Jack. "You can have some of your own."

"Sweet."

For the next few minutes, Fallon endured pure torture. Her womb contracted at the sight of Jack teasing her son and racing to see who could finish first. Worse, she had to pretend this was business as usual when it would all be over forever in a matter of minutes. She didn't know how much more of this her weak heart could take. It seemed so easy for Jack to walk away. He might never see her again and he seemed okay with that. She wasn't but she would learn to be. Whether he had a plan for his life, whether or not he was the right man for her, none of it mattered any longer. She'd managed to fall in love with him. And what good timing on her part to love someone for the first time in her life enough to let him go. The first man she shouldn't let go at all.

Well. No one had ever accused her of good timing. Her timing when it came to romantic love more or less sucked.

Appetite non-existent, Fallon cleaned up the dishes.

"Mom, can I go play video games for a while?"

"Twenty minutes. Then we have to get ready to go shopping."

David dashed off, probably unwilling to waste any one of those precious minutes. Jack brought their plates to the sink.

"You okay?" He looped his arms around her waist from behind and pulled her close.

"Of course. I have so much to do today. I didn't plan on the Christmas shopping." She stiffened her spine and didn't lean in to him as she normally might. Her hands were wet and sudsy, after all.

Not taking the hint, he nuzzled her neck. "You're going to be alright."

"I know." Let him think that. She would be eventually because she was nothing if not a survivor.

"Good." He took a step back, his voice curt. "So how do you want to do this?"

She dried her hands with a dish towel and turned to him. "Do what?"

"Act four." He met her gaze, his eyes unreadable again. "Say goodbye."

Of course. Now they were going to have to figure out how to say goodbye. As if she needed one more thing dumped on her plate today. Saying 'so long' to the love of her life would have to fit between cleaning up the kitchen and last minute Christmas shopping.

"I think we should…keep pretending." Just like she would pretend that her heart wasn't breaking.

"Right." He stuffed hands in his pockets. "Like we're going to see each other again soon. Not a big goodbye."

She wouldn't look at him. "That's the only goodbye I want."

"A fake one."

"Why not? We've been faking all along." She moved past him, heading upstairs to get dressed.

He didn't follow.

━━

JACK HAD BEEN TASKED with locking up. He stood and waved to Beverly, David, and Fallon as all three prepared to drive off in Beverly's sedan. Fallon had her attention riveted to the road and wouldn't look at him again, after the 'fake' goodbye. It had involved a frozen smile from her, a short peck on the lips, and a promise to see him back in L.A.

We've been faking all along.

The words stung. He hadn't been pretending for some time. If he were being honest with himself, he hadn't been from the moment she'd turned around and come back to the auto shop rather than fly home on his dime. Maybe he'd fooled himself into thinking that she felt the way he did. That despite their circumstances and timing being off from the beginning, they had something. Something pretty special. Something rare.

Eventually Jack couldn't avoid it any longer. Because he wasn't the type to leave anything undone, he oiled the door hinges of the bedroom where he'd spent the two most erotic nights of his life. Except he wasn't going to think about that now. He went downstairs to make sure the bathroom sink still drained and the back screen door still shut. For good measure, even though he hadn't been asked, he tried every lock in the house to make sure that it worked. Fallon would likely be living here with her mother until she found a place of her own in town. Safe small town or not, no sense in not having a house protected from all the elements.

Then there was nothing left to do but leave.

He slid two more presents under the tree. One for David (baseball cards) and another for Beverly. He grabbed his bag and the present from Fallon. He'd never promised he wouldn't open it until he got to Oregon, so he sat at the kitchen table alone and tore into the candy cane wrapping paper. He took out a model of a red Mustang convertible. She'd cut out the shape of the two of them from one of the photos he'd taken and taped it behind the driver's wheel of the car. Outside, there was a typed label which read: Road Trip on Pacific Coast Highway, 'The One.' There was a card with the present, too, and Fallon had written him a note.

Thank you for the best Christmas ever. You're a good man, Jack, no matter where you land or what you do for a living. Don't worry about your family. They will understand and support your decision. I know you won't believe this, but it's going to be hard for me to stay here without you. You make this place feel like home again, and I know that makes no sense at all. It's my home. If you're ever in Starlight Hill again, you know where to find me.

Love,

Fallon

Jack took a deep breath and slipped the card back in the envelope. Rubbed his chest, which ached again. He hoped he wasn't getting the flu. Or having a heart attack. This card didn't change anything, of course, as she hadn't expected him to open his present until he was in Oregon. She wanted him to go. He locked the house and put the key under a rock as he'd been instructed to do. That pissed him off, but he did it anyway since they both promised it wasn't a normal occurrence to leave a spare key where anyone could find it. Outside, he opened the car trunk and threw his bag in the back. The present he put in the passenger seat next to him along with the card.

He hung a left on Main Street and headed through town on his way to the freeway. A long drive lay ahead of him if he wanted to make it to Oregon before Christmas Eve. His parents and brother were expecting him. There would be roasted pork on Christmas Day and Spanish rice. Flan for dessert. Fallon was right, and they'd all eventually understand why he'd quit homicide and accept his decision to move on. They loved him, and supported all of his decisions, even the ones he hadn't yet made. He only wished he felt as confident about what lay ahead for Fallon. She hadn't had the support she'd needed, and he could see it had led to some bad decisions on her part in the past. But it couldn't be just him who saw inside to the heart of the woman who loved her family. Her friends.

He'd only driven a few blocks before he pulled over in front of Brooke's Wine Tasting Room to take another look at the Christmas card Fallon had given him. Read it again. Twice.

Love, Fallon.

Did she mean it? Could you love someone after having known them for only two weeks? He would have never thought so before meeting Fallon McQueen. But then again, most people didn't experience as much as the two of them had since first meeting. An attempted crime in progress, a road trip on the Pacific Coast Highway, an accident with several Christmas trees, a small town America tree lighting and parade, two erotic nights that would forever headline his wildest fantasies, and pretending to be in love while…actually falling. Because dammit, that's exactly what he'd done.

He'd fallen for her. Hard.

Someone in a car behind him honked and stopped next to him, the window rolled down. "Hey, Bud! You need any help there? Car okay?" Hank again, who seemed obsessed with the Mustang.

"I'm good," he called out and pulled back on to the street.

The car was good. Him, not so much. He seemed a little bit lost and a whole lot confused. Sort of helpless and weak, his two least favorite words in the English language. *Vulnerable.* There was another word he hated. As a detective he always dealt in facts and there were a few obvious ones he couldn't run away from. He found Fallon beautiful and kind and he didn't care what anyone else thought of her. She smelled like sunshine and tasted so damned sweet. She was loyal to her friends and a good mother to her son. She'd done nothing to deserve the way some treated her despite her past mistakes. And she'd found the courage to come home despite all that. Speaking of difficult pasts, he wasn't exactly a prince, but he had a feeling she saw him that way. Which was only one of the many things he loved about her.

Damn it.

If she was serious about loving him, it meant she'd take him warts and all. No plan or just a basic life plan. He hoped that loving her the way he did would make him the right man for her one way or another. Jack turned the Mustang around and headed back to town.

Someone else he recognized from the parade called out, "Hiya, Bud!"

Sooner or later, if he would stay in this town the way he wanted to, and create a life here with Fallon and David, he'd get people to stop calling him 'Bud.' For now, it was a small price to pay. He pulled in front of the empty salon shop she wanted to lease and renovate. She would need some help with that. He could pound nails for his brother up in Oregon, or he could pound them right here for the woman who turned him inside out and upside down until damned if he wasn't right side up again.

There. He had a plan.

He rapped on the door with a sign that read 'Closed, Please Come Back Later.' Yeah, not a chance. The time was here. Now.

She opened the door. "What's wrong?"

Her eyes were red rimmed which hit him hard.

"Did you mean it?" He held up the card.

"You weren't supposed to open it…" She glanced at the ground and then met his eyes. "Yes. It's crazy, I know, but—"

"But we already established we're doing crazy."

"From the moment we met, wouldn't you say?" Her hands fluttered in front of her. "I'm sorry to put that weight on you. I had to be honest. But I don't want you to…to feel like you need to return my feelings. I didn't plan on this happening. I didn't plan on fake becoming so real."

He pulled her into his arms. "Babe, it's safe to say neither one of us planned this. We only wanted to fool a few people but the joke was on us."

"Don't feel like you have to—"

"Fallon, the point is I haven't really felt *anything* for a long time. Until you." He kissed the palm of her hand. "You were right. I'm a cop and eventually I'll go back to being what I am. I love the helping people part. I don't necessarily enjoy all the other stuff, so maybe being a small town cop is who I am."

Her eyes were watery. "You don't have to stay here because of me. Not just because it's going to be hard for me to be here…without you."

"I don't have to. I want to. Babe, I have a new plan and it's you. You and David. If you'll have me." He tugged her in tighter. "I know this all started out as a lie, but somewhere it became real to me, too. And I'm never letting go."

He kissed her with a fierceness that matched the way she made him feel inside. She loved him even when he didn't have a plan. When he couldn't offer her all the security and safety that he wanted to. Someday. He'd work on that because she was everything he'd ever wanted or needed. The rest would all fall into place. The rest would be easy.

"I love you so much, Jack."

"That's good because I love you, too."

She gave him one of her heart-stopping smiles. "I guess we really are crazy."

"Speak for yourself. The only crazy I am is crazy for you."

"Fair warning, but I told Mom the whole truth. That your name isn't Bud but Jack and that we haven't known each other for six months. I was rather vague on how long I've known you. Baby steps."

"What did she say?"

"There was some eye-rolling involved. She'll be okay. It helps that she really likes you."

"Well. I took care of her Honey-Do list." He nuzzled her neck. "We'll take it slow from here on out."

"We sure can't take it any faster. Can you stay for Christmas?"

"Try and stop me."

"But what's your family going to say?"

"When I tell them I'm not coming because I'm spending Christmas with the beautiful woman that drove up the coast with me? The woman I want to spend the rest of my life with?" He chuckled.

"I bet they say: well, hell, son, it's about freaking time!"

Epilogue

Christmas Eve, one year later

Fallon set a gift wrapped video game for David under the tree. She'd have David over bright and early on Christmas morning, where he'd find that Santa had already arrived.

Jack wheeled a ten speed bicycle into the room and stood it near the tree. "And that's the last one. I think."

"You really shouldn't have. We're spoiling him."

"He needed a new bike. I've patched the tire on his old one three times this year. Besides, he should spend more time outside."

She didn't disagree. The past year had brought along a few surprises, not the least of which was that she and Jack had similar views on everything that mattered. Convenient. They loved the outdoors and thought it was important to spend time there, had similar taste in music, appreciated the same kind of pizza and ice cream sundae toppings, loved to read mysteries and enjoyed making fun of the same reality TV stars. They both wanted another child. A girl. In the year they'd spent getting to know each other there had been one fight, but she still couldn't remember what it had been about. More than likely, it had something to do with the spare key she kept outside under a rock since she constantly locked herself out of their home. Jack maintained it wasn't safe but that was the cop in him. Fallon did remember that the argument had ended in the best make-up sex of her entire life.

Another surprise had been the way Ted had quickly fallen into line when he'd discovered that Fallon and Jack were a 'thing' that wasn't going to be going away anytime soon. She had a feeling Jack and Ted had had a conversation at some point, but she hadn't pressed for details.

"Come here." Jack plopped down on the couch and crooked a finger at her.

She didn't need to be asked twice, going into his arms with the kind of ease she'd felt for a year. Never in her entire life had she been so sure, so certain about anything or anyone. Jack had her heart and soul, her mind, and her body. She imagined that was the way it always worked when it came down to true love. This was one hundred percent real. Always would be.

"I'm about ready to give up." He stroked her back. "Where is it?"

"Nice try. You have to wait until tomorrow morning." She'd already learned her lesson the hard way.

She couldn't hide anything from Jack. He always found his gifts like a bloodhound on the scent of a single bread crumb. He was worse than David, too, when it came to being patient.

"Babe, you ought to know better than to hide anything from me," he teased, then tugged on her earlobe. "We still have a few hours left. I won't give up."

"I know," she said with a deep sigh. "That's why your gifts are not in our house."

He froze. "What?"

"They're at Kailey and Joe's and they're dropping them off in the morning on their way to Genevieve's." She giggled a little at that, having finally outsmarted her in-house detective.

"Cheating. Damn." He threw his head back. "You realize what this means."

"Uh-huh. I won."

"It means I have some free time and nothing to do."

"Oh gee, I wonder what you could do with all this free time." She licked and kissed his neck since he'd just given her such great access.

He moaned. "It's time for your surprise."

"Unless it's making love under the Christmas tree I don't want my surprise yet. I'll wait until morning like a big girl."

"Aw dammit, you guessed. It was the tree thing."

"No." Sue her if she loved the idea even if it meant she might be brushing pine needles out of...interesting places for a while. "Really?"

"Get off."

"Right now? *Me*?"

"Do you see anyone else on my lap?"

No, she actually didn't, and that was kind of the idea. But she rose, walked to the tree and smiled. "I'm ready."

"First close your eyes."

"I kind of like this game."

"This is a different one." He dragged his teeth over his lower lip, studying her.

She eyed him and pretended to be annoyed when she loved the way he kept her guessing. And when he flashed his boyish smile again, she'd do anything he asked.

She always did. "Okay, they're closed."

"Hold out your hand," he said.

She held out her right hand, but he bumped it down and raised her left one instead.

He closed her hand around something suspiciously... small.

"You can open your eyes."

Fallon slowly opened one eye and then the other one to find Jack on his knees in front of her.

"Jack!" She opened her fisted hand to find a beautiful solitaire diamond ring.

"That's your surprise. Though I guess it isn't much of one considering I've probably told you a thousand times how much I love you. How happy you make me every day. It's because of you that I'm a cop again and doing what I love. It's because of you that I believe in second, and yeah, even fourth chances. Would you marry me?"

"Yes! Yes!"

He stood to slip the ring on her finger. "Look at that. It fits."

Everything fit. Jack. Her. This house. Her new salon. His job with the Starlight Hill PD.

"We fit." She reached up to kiss him, big sloppy tears clouding her view. "Forever."

"I like the way you think." He pressed his forehead to hers and his hand dropped to the small of her back. "I love you, Fallon."

"I love you more."

"Hope so, because we're going to have to do this all over again tomorrow when the Cooper clan arrives. Try to look surprised. My mother will probably sink to her knees and clutch her rosary beads but don't let it alarm you."

She laughed. "I could have waited until tomorrow, silly."

"I know. The point is I couldn't." He tugged on a lock of her hair. "Now about the tree thing."

She kicked off her red pumps, and he unzipped the back of her red dress with the white faux fur piping on the hem. The dress she'd worn the night she met the right man under the least likely of circumstances.

Jack pulled off his Santa jacket and off came the fake belly.

"Merry Christmas, Santa."

"Merry Christmas, Mrs. Claus."

The Right Man

A NOVELLA

Chapter 1

Trish

Perhaps it might be better if I actually stepped out of my truck and talked to a real, live person instead of practicing my speech by reciting it to my steering wheel.

"Hi, Jimmy," I said to my steering wheel.

No. That sounded too familiar.

"Jimmy, hello. How are you?"

Nope. Way too formal. I tapped my red tipped fingernail on the outer edge of the column.

"Jimmy, I need a favor."

But I could almost see Jimmy "Bull" Hopkins' quirk an eyebrow at that. *A favor.* Only a guess, but I was no longer on his Christmas list. Sooner rather than later, I would have to climb out of the safety of my dusty old blue pickup and strut across the parking lot into the Silver Saddle saloon. Preferably before any of the patrons walking past me noticed I was having a conversation with myself. It was Ladies Night, the last one before Thanksgiving, so it would be crowded inside. Jimmy would be behind the bar, owner, manager and sometime bartender. Force of nature and consummate heartbreaker. Serving up drinks and charm in equal parts. He'd take one long sideways look at me, and… what? Order me out of the bar? No, that wasn't Jimmy's way. Still, it was quite possible that someone else, *not* Jimmy, would suggest I turn tail and leave by way of the same door I came in. That would be because everyone in the small Bay Area town of Fortune, California loved Jimmy Hopkins.

"I'm doing this."

I wrenched my body out of the driver's side door, climbed out and forced one booted foot in front of the other. Chin up. Just like I'd done for all twenty-nine years of my life. Like I had through boot camp eleven years ago when I worried three times a day that I'd made the biggest mistake of my life by signing up.

I hadn't.

Among the many reasons it had been the best decision of my life, the U.S. Army was where I'd first laid eyes on Ranger Jimmy Hopkins. It was where he'd first slid me a crooked smile and said, "Hiya, Boots."

My heart had slid right out of my chest to fall at his feet and I'd stammered, "H-hi."

Now, my red cowboy boots thudded across the asphalt lot as I gave myself a little pep talk. I wasn't just Trish Jackson, Jimmy's ex-fiancé and former assistant manager of the Silver Saddle. I was also Staff Sergeant Trish Jackson, retired U.S. Army. Currently working at Fortune Ranch and reviewing my many options, including going back to school to finish my engineering degree on the GI bill.

But first things first.

I had the not-so-little matter of Thanksgiving dinner this year at my grandparent's home in Gilroy, just south of Fortune, where I'd grown up. I adored Reina and Jorge

Garcia and would not be disappointing them. Fueled by the courage of that love, I threw open the doors to the Silver Saddle and made my way inside. If I'd been worried that the saloon would burst into flames when I walked inside, at least that did not happen. And in fact, I didn't immediately attract any attention as I made my way through the crowded bar.

Autumn colors were everywhere, from the acorn and gourd displays on opposite ends of the bar counter to the haystacks placed in strategic areas around the dance floor. Red, gold, and burnt orange splashes of colorful silk leaves were scattered on the ground, instead of the usual peanut husks. Bertha, the mechanical bull, stood in her usual corner in the back. Nice job if I said so myself. I'd decorated. God, I had missed this place. Practically my second home since Jimmy had bought the place a few years ago, after having followed me out to the Bay Area. I hadn't wanted him to buy it, and tried to explain to the Alabama native that a country and western themed bar wouldn't do well with the Silicon Valley set. But what did I know? There'd been a resurgence in the popularity of country music, with young hip artists like Sam Hunt dominating the charts, young millennials declared country music cool again, and the Silver Saddle took off. Jimmy hadn't looked back since.

I'd worked here side by side with him until last month. Odds were I'd still be working here, were it up to Jimmy, because he wouldn't have fired me. Instead, I'd quit. Now I was working for our friend Emily Parker, helping to plan *her* wedding and all the other weddings that took place on her family's event ranch. Not that it made me sad every day or anything like that. It was just temporary. A job. And this *arrangement* I would suggest to Jimmy tonight was just that. Temporary. One day out of the rest of his life. Surely he'd see the sense in it. My grandparents deserved one last happy Thanksgiving Day before they found out the unfortunate truth. There would be no Hopkins/Jackson wedding this June.

I reached the end of the bar, where I found a stool, folded my hands, and watched Jimmy at work. He was a site, dressed all in black to match his dark brown hair, filling skeins of beer, and mixing drinks in a shaker like the consummate pro. To look at him, no one would guess the entire trajectory of his life had recently been derailed. All those plans we'd made together. Gone in a heartbeat. Because whether Jimmy Hopkins was riding Bertha the mechanical bull, riding a real bull during his short career post-Army as a bull rider, or simply pouring someone a glass of Pinot, you'd never see the man sweat. Never.

It was like a religion with him.

"Hey, bud. What are you having?" Jimmy said to the customer two down from me.

"Gimme a Corona. And a Chardonnay for my lady."

"Comin' right up."

He served the couple of women next to me, turned to the till, then faced me. The moment he actually caught my eye and *noticed* me, I thought his composure slipped for an instant. One brief moment during which I allowed myself to believe that maybe he regretted issuing me an ultimatum.

"Trish." But his dark and hooded eyes gave away nothing else. Zip. One second. That's what I got.

"H-hi."

His square jaw and chin were covered in dark hair. This was new. He'd grown a beard. I never liked the way his bristle felt against my skin, but holy cow, I liked the way it looked on him now. He was hotter than hell and studying me as if he half wondered whether I was an apparition.

"What'll you have?"

"A coke. Please."

He turned quickly to fill a glass from the fountain.

The piping sounds of Brad Paisley singing *Perfect Storm* rolled through the first rate speakers I'd helped Jimmy pick out, the loud din of chatter and laughter ringing in my ears, but so far no one had noticed me. No one except the man next to me, whom I didn't recognize. He alone seemed to be zeroed in on the knowledge that something out of the ordinary had just passed between Jimmy and me. The man's body shifted in my direction and he cradled his beer bottle.

Jimmy set a coke down. "On the house."

"No." I pulled a wallet out of my purse. "I'll pay."

"I don't want your money." Jimmy raised his palm.

"Well, you're going to get it." I threw down two dollar bills.

"Ladies night." He took one of the bills and continued down the line taking orders.

I leaned forward, ignoring the man next to me, now smiling in my direction. "Jimmy, can I talk to you?"

"Busy here." He poured a couple of drafts, mixed a Mojito, then started back down the line.

"When you have a minute." I took a sip of the coke and prepared to wait all damned night if I had to.

"I'm Dan," the man next to me said, offering his hand.

"Trish." I was in no mood to talk and make friends tonight. But at least this guy didn't know me, so he wouldn't judge.

"You're the first pretty lady he's completely ignored."

"Ouch."

He grinned. "Figure that makes you special."

"If by special you mean he wishes he could kick me out then you're right."

"Uh-oh."

"I'm his ex."

"Don't think so. A man never looks at his *ex* like that."

I was about to ask him what he meant and if he would care to elaborate, but he topped off his beer, set it down, and walked off to greener pastures. I didn't blame him. Tonight I felt about as warm and fuzzy as a Molotov cocktail. And I could do about as much damage with all the bitterness I'd been curling up with every night. Too bad I'd recently decided that it didn't look good on me. I had to move on, and I knew it. And after Thanksgiving, I would.

An hour later, I still sat on the barstool. Waiting. As the hustle wound down, Jimmy finished up with a customer and then re-filled my empty glass.

"You okay?"

I supposed that was Jimmy being Jimmy, asking because he was a nice guy and all. And because I'd like to think I also had a little bit of good left in me, I chose not to tell him the truth. I was most definitely *not* okay and quite frankly the jury was still out on whether I ever would be again.

"I'm good." I smiled. "I just…I need a favor."

"Name it."

"I'd like you to come to Thanksgiving dinner with me at Nonna and Poppi's."

He blinked, obviously not expecting this particular request. "Why?"

I drew in a sharp breath and remembered I was made out of tough stuff. *Go for it.* "Because they don't know about us."

He braced long arms against the edge of the counter and hung his head. "What are you talking about?"

"I didn't… tell them yet. I couldn't. Not right before the holidays."

"It's been a month."

I fingered my cocktail napkin. "I know, and I was getting around to it."

"So you want me to come to dinner and pretend like nothing happened?"

"If you mean pretend that you didn't call the wedding off? Yes, that's what I'm suggesting."

He gave me his patient look. "I didn't call the wedding off. *You* did."

"Well, no. There's two ways of looking at that."

"Not the way I see it. So I go with you to Thanksgiving. Then what?"

"And… I'll tell them. After Black Friday. You know how Nonna is always in such a good mood after she scores her deals and finishes her Christmas shopping in one day."

He winced. "That's when you swoop in and ruin her day by telling her we're not getting married?"

"There really is no good time to do this."

"A month ago."

"It's just one day. Your parents aren't in town and I know you had no plans to go to Alabama."

He didn't speak for a beat. "This isn't a good idea."

"Of course it isn't! You think this is fun for me?" I gulped down the rest of my coke. "I just care a lot about two sweet people who love us both and don't deserve to have their Thanksgiving ruined."

"If you want…I'll tell them."

"No!" I didn't want or need Jimmy slaying my dragons. "I'll do it. It has to come from me. I just need this favor. Please. Just this once. Can't you pretend you still love me for one more day?"

Chapter 2

Jimmy

I saw Thanksgiving Day dissipating before my eyes. I'd had elaborate plans I hated to change now. I was going to curl up in front of my plasma TV and watch college football all day. Alone. In my boxers. With a beer, if I wanted. It was the first time I'd been single at Thanksgiving in years. If I was going to give up all the sex, damn it, I was going to take up the marathon football. But now Trish had once again changed my plans. Just as she had from the moment I'd first laid eyes on her. I'd never found it so difficult to say "no" to anyone.

And it pissed me the hell off.

It also pissed me off the way she'd waltzed in and just about every guy in the place turned his head to gawk. She wore her red boots tonight, the ones she had to know drove me crazy, and a short blue dress showing off her long legs. Long, wavy dark brown hair loose. I hadn't seen her for a month and I'd nearly swallowed my tongue.

And then Dan, the new guy, had tried to move in. Not

that I could blame him. I wasn't sure what Trish had told Dan but it seemed to drive the dude away. Good thing, too. It was one thing to tell Trish I was done with the wedding. It was another to observe the love of my life take up with another man right under my nose. Fortune was a small town, but I had no intention of watching when that happened.

And a woman like Trish wouldn't be alone for long, even if her reputation these days as our small town's "Bridezilla" preceded her. When I'd asked Trish to marry me earlier this year, I could have never anticipated those four little words would turn my woman into someone I barely recognized. I'd already phoned my parents, of course, and given them the bad news. We'd broken up. There would be no wedding. They hadn't been thrilled, either, but both of them understood.

A man could only take so much before he was ready to rip off the head of the next wedding cake baker. Then again, it wasn't their fault that Trish changed her mind about the cake once a month. Or that she'd gone through ten wedding dresses. I had no idea what was wrong with the first, second, or ninth dress because God forbid I should see any of them before the wedding. Something about a "train" was the thing wrong with one of them.

Honestly, I didn't care anymore. When the issue with releasing the doves had come up, and Trish and Emily argued, going back and forth on chickens versus doves, I mentally checked out. A week after that, I'd been watching the game when a commercial had come on featuring island destinations. That's when I'd had my best idea to date.

I suggested to Trish that we elope and get it all over with.

"Get it…over with?" Her beautiful face had turned red and her normally full lips were a thin straight line.

"I just want to be married to you, Boots. I don't give a shit about the wedding."

"You don't give a shit about our *wedding*?"

She hadn't heard the "I want to be married to you" part. All she'd heard was what she wanted to hear. Trish had gone tone deaf about anything other than our wedding day, which had begun to feel a lot more like *her* wedding day. One day out of the rest of our lives. And I was just the sap who was to show up and take my vows like a man.

Finally, I'd had enough.

I'd told Trish in no uncertain terms: elope with me, or forget the whole deal. She'd made it clear how she felt about me when she moved out. Elope might as well be a four letter word to her. But I still loved the stubborn woman, so damn if it wasn't tough to say no to her even now, while making her ridiculous request. "Pretend you love me for one more day."

Jesus. She didn't know me at all. Or maybe I didn't know her. One thing was certain. The curse of the wedding day had robbed me of my best friend, my lover, my everything. I was about to say "no" when Trish's eyes started to leak. These were real tears. I ought to know, since I was the authority on Trish's Tears. The tears when I'd put my foot down on the ten-tier cake (which she'd later decided against, anyway) were fake. The tears when I'd dropped to my knee to ask her to marry me had been real.

"Please," she said now. "I won't ask for anything else from you, ever again."

This was cruel. How could I refuse her trembling lips and watery eyes?

"Damn, Trish. Don't cry."

"I'm not *crying*."

My heart pinched as I remembered the new Army

recruit I'd met all those years ago. Trying hard to be brave, looking scared spitless. The Army had changed her. Toughened her up. Only I got to see the soft edges. Sometimes.

I threw down my bar towel. "We'd already be married if you'd listened to me and this wouldn't be an issue."

"It would be a whole other issue! How do you think they'd feel about not being with me on the most important day of my life?"

I had a feeling her family would be fine and get it over it quickly enough. Not Trish.

"Okay. You got it. I'll go with you to Thanksgiving dinner."

"Thank you!"

"But I have to warn you. Your grandparents are going to see right through this. They may not know the wedding is off, but believe me, they'll sense something is wrong between us. You don't give them enough credit."

"You leave that to me."

Chapter 3

Trish

"Jimmy said yes to Thanksgiving," I said to Emily Parker the very next day.

"I knew he would."

We were both sitting in Emily's small home office in a loft above a detached garage, taking a break from making phone calls. They were currently on a search for a photographer for the Jones wedding to be held at Fortune Family Ranch this June. Everything seemed to come together so seamlessly for the Jones wedding, and I wondered once a day why that couldn't have been the case with my wedding.

Later this morning, when Emily went to the south county airport where she worked as a pilot alongside her fiancé, Stone Mcallister, I would go through an Excel spreadsheet of wedding guests for the Jones wedding and start forming table placement. Then I had an appointment scheduled with a new couple who were still looking for a wedding venue.

I sighed. "I guess the only explanation is that he felt

sorry for me. You know Jimmy. He'd do anything for his friends."

"Not anything. He only does what deep inside he already wants to do anyway. Like most Alpha men."

"He didn't *want* to do anything."

Emily waggled her brows. "Maybe he wants to *do* you."

"Emily!" I laughed. "You have a one-track mind, girl."

"Okay, so I love sex. What can I say? I'm in love!"

"Sure, you and Stone do it like rabbits. Jimmy and I used to also, but that doesn't mean we're going to take up where we left off."

"But it's been a month and he's got to be missing you! Think about it. What were you wearing when you asked him?"

"My red cowboy boots and blue dress."

"You look smoking hot in that outfit."

Reason number one I'd worn it, not that Jimmy had noticed. "Thanks."

"I mean, isn't there still a chance for you two?"

Emily, the eternal optimist and romantic. But just because Stone was head over heels in love with her, and she with him, didn't mean she could sprinkle the magic fairy dust over every couple.

"We've been over this. He gave me an ultimatum and it involved the 'E' word. Plus, the things he said about our wedding. He doesn't seem to care about any of it, so maybe he doesn't care about me, either."

"Maybe you could forgive him. It's not the worst thing he could ever say to you."

So said Emily.

"After how hard you and I worked on the perfect wedding, he wanted to run away and elope. He said, and I quote, 'I don't give a shit about our wedding.' It's like I don't even know who he *is* anymore."

"But you two love each other! You should be able to get over this little bump."

But I didn't think that would be possible. It wasn't a little bump to me. I'd looked forward to my wedding day most of my life, or at least since I'd been seven years old. Thought about it and planned it with my mother, who used to cut out wedding dress pages out of catalogs for me. Mom, who'd never had her special day, instead getting married at the courthouse because she was three months pregnant with me.

The marriage hadn't lasted, of course, and I figured any man who was cheap enough to take his fiancée to the nearest judge to "take care of it" wasn't much of a man at all. My father certainly hadn't been. When Mom became sick with cancer and was dying, he'd sent her a Get Well Soon card. And after Mom had died, I went to live with my grandparents, and not with my father.

To this day, anything regarding weddings brought back fond memories for me. Of lazy Saturday mornings spent with my mother, daydreaming about the perfect wedding to the right man. He'd come along, Mom assured me. He'd be special. The One. We'd fall in love, and have a glorious wedding.

A carriage fit for a princess pulled by white horses. A beautiful clapboard chapel in the woods. A reception with an orchestra that would play, "The Most Beautiful Girl in the World" because that's exactly how my husband would see me. The most perfect wedding day would be followed by a long marriage and many children.

Then the right man had come along. He had beautifully dark eyes and wavy hair, a smile that melted my heart, and he didn't give a *shit* about our wedding.

"I don't know about that, Em…"

I didn't want Emily to get her hopes up, because Jimmy

had said in no uncertain terms he'd personally rip the head off of the next wedding "anything" person. I thought he was being unreasonable. He thought *I* was the unreasonable one. Then I'd refused to elope with him, moved out, and he still hadn't changed his mind. So I'd lost him. Maybe the right man was this elusive creature that didn't really exist. Like a magical woodland unicorn.

Just like the perfect wedding had turned out to be, in the end, unattainable.

After Emily left for the airport, I worked on the Jones wedding until it was time for my appointment. Then I shut my laptop, grabbed Emily's clipboard, and came down the steps from the upstairs loft office that used to be Emily's small apartment. I made my way across the ranch. The loft was above the detached garage that sat next to the old Victorian home on the hill where Emily's grandmother Jean Parker still lived. I walked down the hilly slope and crossed the beautiful manicured green lawn headed toward the red barn.

We met clients here, because it was the easiest landmark on the ranch for guests to find. Just a short hike up from the parking lot areas at the entrance. It was also a great place for weddings now, and the place Emily and Stone would exchange their vows on December 31st at midnight. I wished I'd thought of it first.

A midnight wedding, they'd actually have two wedding dates. The 31st and the 1st. The barn, which normally sold art made by local artisans, had already been emptied in preparation. Rows of chairs were placed on either side of a makeshift altar Emily's father had constructed. Inside, the barn would be lit by soft candlelight as the two exchanged vows. Oh, sigh. So romantic.

"Welcome to Fortune Family Ranch!" I said to the couple who met me outside the red barn. Olivia and Jeff.

Introductions were made and I went into my prepared pitch. "As you know, Fortune Family Ranch just started having weddings and receptions, in addition to all of our other events. This is where we will have most weddings. You'll see that we've already started to set up for our December 31st wedding next month."

"Interesting." Olivia wrinkled her nose. "But I don't know if I see myself getting married in a barn."

"I don't know, I kind of think it's pretty cool," Jeff said. "Different."

I nodded. "I agree. But if you'd like to see our gazebo as another option, I can show you that, too."

Emily had taught me to never, *ever* take sides. Quite frankly, I couldn't get married in a barn, either. Because no matter how carefully their handyman tried, and he did, I'd guessed there was at least one spider in that barn. At *least*. Still, I reminded myself this wasn't my wedding. I only had to make two very different people happy. The couple followed me across the field to a gazebo in which Emily's younger sister, Molly, had been married a few years ago. It was lovely, and exactly where I had planned to marry Jimmy. Majestic El Toro Hill rose behind the gazebo and we were surrounded by a meadow. Not a clapboard church in the middle of the woods but close. In June the weather would have been perfect.

"Huh." Jeff scratched the side of his head as he stared at the gazebo. "Kind of small, isn't it?"

It had recently been re-painted white and the wood distressed for the shabby chic look so popular. I was still a bit in awe. I could picture standing next to Jimmy in his black tux, holding hands, surrounded by family and friends.

"To me, it's the height of romance. So much like the gazebo in The Sound of Music. What do you think?" I hoped I didn't sound too pushy. This would be my first choice for Olivia and Jeff.

"I love it!" Olivia said, bouncing up and down. "And since we're getting married in June it will be perfect."

"June?" I reviewed my notes. "I…I thought we were talking about August."

"No, it's June 21st." Olivia scowled. "Please tell me it's still available!"

"Calm down, honey," Jeff said. "If this doesn't work, we'll find something else."

"But I want this! It's just like the gazebo in The Sound of Music."

"We still have other places to see."

"For a June wedding, we're already pushing it for dates. Everything is going to be booked and nothing else is going to be this nice. Don't you want me to be happy?"

"Of course, but I don't know…isn't this kind of pretentious?"

Pretentious? I held back, refraining from telling Jeff to stick a sock in it.

"You want to know what's pretentious? That church my mother wants me to get married in! We went to church once a *year*, but now that I'm getting married she's the church lady. Well, no way. This is *my* day. I get to decide. I want to get married outside!"

Jeff, poor guy, despite his horrible taste and misuse of the word pretentious, seemed so miserable that I almost felt sorry for him.

"Is it available?" Olivia turned to me.

I paged through the clipboard till I got to the June calendar. And there on June 21st I saw that "Trish and Jimmy" had been erased. But Emily had scratched in a note to the side that said: keep open? Aw, sweet Emily. Ever the hopeful romantic and faithful friend. But it wasn't going to happen. I had to let it go.

"Oh, no, it's fine. Perfect. June is pretty full, and our most popular month as you know. We had a wedding scheduled for that date, but it's been cancelled."

Jeff quirked a brow. "Cancelled?"

"Things happen." I penciled in "Olivia and Jeff" on June 21st. Next to Emily's note I wrote: "No."

"Wow! This is our lucky day, baby!" Olivia jumped into her fiance's arms. "We got in."

Jeff smiled and spun her around, clearly a man in love. He had that gobsmacked, head-over-heels look in his eyes. No longer looking miserable, he simply appeared to be a man desperately in-love with his bride-to-be. Willing to do whatever it took to make her happy.

God bless him. I hoped Olivia appreciated what a rare find she had.

It wasn't until later, once Olivia and Jeff had paid their deposit and were gone, that I realized no one had thought to ask Jeff whether or not he'd changed his mind about the gazebo.

Chapter 4

Jimmy

On Thanksgiving Day morning, I woke with a boner. Hard as a rock. I'd dreamt of Trish, lying next to me on this very bed. In my dream, she wore her red boots and…nothing else. I'd decided to wake her up.

The fun way.

I blinked now, stared up at the ceiling, and ran a hand down my bristly beard. Yeah, I had a beard. Trish hated my prior attempts at a beard, saying it gave her a beard burn every time I went down on her. And since I loved nothing more than going down on her, the choice had been a no-brainer. Now, I had a beard simply because I could.

And, were I being honest, because Trish hated it.

I didn't know why I'd agreed to this sham today. The tears shouldn't have swayed me. It wasn't fair that I'd have to see her today and pretend everything was great. It wasn't fair that even though she'd been gone a month there were still touches of her everywhere.

The drapes she'd picked out, the lamps, our bed, all the furniture. Everything had her touch. I'd washed the sheets four times and still caught her sweet scent in my bed. And this…this charade today was not the way to get over someone. It was a way to prolong the agony. Not smart.

I should have said "hell, no."

But she'd proved that she still had me, didn't she? Truthfully, I also loved her grandparents and would suggest after today that maybe we should tell them together. Soften the blow, so to speak, if that could be done at all. They'd welcomed this southern boy when I'd settled out west. I'd become a part of their family the moment we met.

Reina and Jorge were salt of the earth people who'd been in Gilroy for decades. Consequently, they owned a couple of acres of land now worth well over a million dollars. On paper. They had no intention of selling their home, and lived modestly in the twelve hundred square foot, two bedroom single family home where they'd raised their only daughter, and then Trish. She was the center of their lives and a visit from her meant Reina would likely rise at sunrise and cook all day.

If nothing else, I'd get a good meal out of this. And Reina would send us home with plenty of leftovers. It would be interesting to see which one of us would wind up with them. I was to pick Trish up at her condo at one-thirty and make the fifteen minute drive to Gilroy. A holiday "dinner" was always served by two o'clock at the Garcia household. Pretty much smack dab in the middle of the day so that it was tough to fit in anything else.

That was because dinner was about far more than eating. There was also all the talking. There would be plenty of Garcias there, some coming from as far away as Stockton. Trish's mother's side of the family. Aunts, uncles, cousins. Their children. Most of these relatives we saw about once a year. Before our meal, of course, there would be the intense pressure to be thankful for something that could be announced in mixed company.

We'd eat ourselves into comas. We were usually home before eight o'clock and had the rest of the evening to do a lot of...whatever. There would be no "whatever" for me this year. But sure, I could do this. One more time. Of course, I'd likely come out of the day even more bitter and resentful than I already felt but hey. I was doing Trish a favor.

She, who was so fixated on a wedding day that she'd left me in the dust. What I thought, what I wanted, didn't matter because everything had to be "perfect." An illusion created by satin, lace and flowers. Doves. And perfect, in Trish's book, didn't involve eloping. Sue me if I thought the idea of running away to get married was romantic. Different. I was obviously a damn fool.

Because Trish wanted a wedding, not a marriage.

A marriage to her I could do. But this wedding business...no. So we were at an impasse. We might both be two tough and stubborn fools, but I'd reached the point where I had to believe that she'd stay with me no matter what. Even if we had to elope and live in a hut somewhere on a deserted island.

Okay, I was exaggerating. But once, that's exactly how it had been between us. We'd lived unglamorously for years in base housing before we both got out, had deployments that had separated us for months at a time, but still managed to stay together.

This wedding had been our only battleground. My personal nemesis. And I had won the battle, but lost the war.

When I pulled up to Trish's condo complex on time, she waited for me outside. She wasn't wearing the red boots today, but what I had to face was no better. Dark pants were tucked into long, black boots that went up to just below her thighs. Tight red sweater emphasizing her amazing rack. Happy Thanksgiving to me. I knew what I was thankful for, but again I could hardly say it in mixed company.

I opened the passenger door for her. "Ready for this?"

She brushed up against me as she got in, I was sure accidentally, but even so I got a good whiff of her flowery scent. Yep. Same smell I woke up to every morning. Seemed she was haunting my bedroom.

"Don't worry. I'll do all the talking when it comes to the wedding."

I slid back into the driver's side and buckled my seatbelt. "So…business as usual."

She gave me a quick glare. "That way we don't have to worry about keeping our stories straight."

"Right." I pulled out of the complex and headed toward Gilroy on 101.

"Let's not start off the day pissed off at each other."

I could feel the heat of her gaze on me.

"I'm not pissed." I gripped the wheel tighter.

Man, I was angry. She was torturing me.

"Okay, then." She spoke softly and when I turned to glance at her she had the whisper of a smile on her face. "I believe you."

Stop the presses. It was the kindest thing she'd said to me in months. Maybe I could be thankful for that today. When we pulled in front of the Garcia home on Old Fruitvale Lane, there were already several cars parked along the tree-lined street.

"The gang's all here." I parked and turned to Trish. "Showtime."

But Trish grabbed my arm before I opened my door. "Wait."

"Yeah?"

"Hold my hand? I just want us to look as convincing as possible."

"Of course."

When I came around to her side of the car and held out my hand, she took it. Her hand was cold as per the usual, but also so damn soft. For a second I remembered the first time I'd held her hand. The first time I'd believed "she's mine." We walked quietly toward the Garcia house, children already spilling out at the seams.

"Auntie Trish!" One of the little girls ran up to Trish and clinched her in a hug.

"Uncle Jimmy!" The other girl, one of cousin Lydia's kids if I recalled, grabbed on to my leg.

"Hi, girls," Trish said, laughing. "Easy on Uncle Jimmy, now."

"Sure!" The girl clutching my leg said. Yolanda? I was so bad with names.

She grabbed my free hand and started skipping down the sidewalk, tugging all of us along. "There's lots of food. I'm so *hungry*. Can we eat now?"

"You'll have to ask your Tia," Trish said, referring to Reina.

"I already did!" said the other girl. "She just said, 'Out of my kitchen, Mija.'"

"I hope you listened," Trish said.

I grinned. You did not want to ignore Reina, especially when it came to her kitchen.

There were more hugs once we were inside the full

house, with aunts and uncles shaking my hand and clapping me on the back. I got pulled away from Trish.

"A beard? Que eso?" Reina gave me a hug, then leaned back to study my chin.

I already knew that meant, "what's this?" but usually, "what the hell is *this*?"

"Do you like it?" I rubbed it.

"Whatever you want." She threw up her hands. "I don't understand you men. Why you want all that itchy hair on your face. Eh, to each his own." She went back into the kitchen.

Huh. Not the reaction I'd expected.

"Salud! You're going to be a married man like the rest of us." This was from her Uncle Tommy, who'd been married for approximately half of his life and still seemed normal.

"Thank God," said Aunt Rosario, his long-suffering wife. Eight kids. *Eight*. "I was praying hard. Praying and a-praying. And then when Reina called and said you two were getting married, I dropped the phone. 'Madre de Dios!' At last, I said! At last! That girl! So picky."

"Well, uh. Sure." I stuck my hands in my pockets and rocked back on my heels. "That's right."

I caught Trish's worried gaze, a few feet away from me. She too was surrounded by aunt, uncles and cousins probably all wanting the scoop on our non-wedding day.

"I'm sure you have no idea what's happening with your wedding." Uncle Tommy elbowed me. "But we've got you covered on the bachelor party. I'll need a list of your friends."

"My bachelor party?" Oh, hell. Knew this was a bad idea. I decided to improvise. "Well, I own a bar, so…"

"Exactly why you need to let me handle this for you. You don't want a bachelor party where you work. People talk." Uncle Tommy leaned in. "I've got a stripper lined up."

"What did you say, viejo?" Aunt Rosario smacked his shoulder. "No estripper!"

Sometimes Aunt Rosario automatically added an "eh" in front of words beginning with an "s." Especially when she was pissed off.

"No, no, mi amor." Uncle Tommy held up his hands. "No naked women."

I bit back a laugh as Tommy backed up, giving me a wink as he did.

Finally Trish rejoined me, grabbing my arm. "Everything go okay here?"

"Sure, except Uncle Tommy is giving me a bachelor party with an estripper."

"Oh, geez. I'll talk to Aunt Rosario and she'll get him in line."

Probably not.

"Would you have been okay with that?"

"With what?"

"My having a stripper at my bachelor party." I hadn't planned on one. Stone had been handling that and when he'd asked for my input on whether I wanted one, I'd passed.

"What happens at a bachelor party would have been your business. A bride has nothing to do with that." She glanced up at me. "But if I'm being honest here, I wouldn't have liked it very much. I always hated the idea of you looking at other naked, or nearly naked women."

Finally it was time to eat and Reina called everyone to the table. It was so crowded that as usual Trish was almost in my lap. Jorge said grace and everyone began the long process of finding something to be thankful for so that Reina would allow us to eat.

"I'm thankful for Netflix," said six-year-old Tony, the youngest cousin.

His mother tapped his hand lightly. "Try again."

"Okay," Tony stared at the ceiling. "I'm thankful for… um…uh…"

"Tony! We are all estarving here." Aunt Rosario held her clasped hands up, prayer-like.

His older brother nudged him and Tony spit out, "Good grades! I'm thankful for good grades."

"Much better," his mother said.

We went around the table, everyone saying something, anything, so we could dig in. Good health. Nice weather. Football. Trees. Mashed potatoes. Turkey. The more time passed, the more food seemed to be mentioned.

When we got to Trish she said, "I'm thankful for a kind wedding planner. She puts up with me and my demands."

Everyone laughed.

"Trish and her wedding day," a cousin said, "I've been hearing about it all my life."

"You're exaggerating," Trish said, biting her lower lip.

"Since she was a child," Lydia said.

It was my turn, and Trish glanced at me, a worried look crossing her eyes. *Seriously?* Did she think I was grateful for being single again? What did she think I was going to say to her family? I'd always restrained myself in the past from announcing the honest truth.

Stuff like "I'm thankful Trish gives great blow jobs," or "I'm thankful I fell in love with a woman with big breasts." I always wound up with a sanitized version and usually said something safe like, "I'm thankful I don't have to go shopping tomorrow morning at four AM. That's Trish's deal."

But everyone here thought I was still getting married. Trish had rather skillfully been thankful for something related to the wedding. I needed something like that. What would I be grateful for that I could say in front of children, if I was still engaged to Trish? Oh, the pressure!

I surprised even myself when I said, "I'm thankful for family."

And *that* got me a round of applause.

––––––––––––––––––

Chapter 5

––––––––––––––––––

Jimmy

A few hours, a food coma, and a college football game later, it was time to go home. We said our goodbyes to everyone (it took a half hour) and Trish carried out our usual plate of leftovers for the week.

"You can have some of this," she said to me once we were outside. "I'll divide it up and give you half."

"I'm good. Don't care if I see turkey again for another year." I opened the passenger door for her.

"You always say that."

We hadn't been on the road three minutes when Trish sighed loudly. "Thank you. That went well."

"No worries." I was still surprised we'd fooled everyone, but with the amount of people present today the attention wasn't exclusively on the two of us.

"I'll tell Nonna tomorrow."

"That's what I wanted to tell you…I'll help out. Soften the blow."

"You mean we tell her together?"

"Let me be the bad guy." I gripped the steering wheel tighter. "I have a wandering eye, or I…shit, I don't know. You think of something."

She turned to me. "Wandering eye? Why? You want them to hate you? They adore you!"

"I don't want them to hate *you*. Or blame you."

"Why not? It's my fault, isn't it?"

"Alright. Let's not get into this."

"We can argue now. Our show is over, and we don't have to pretend anymore."

I slid her a look. "I hate arguing."

"That's right. You just like to sulk and shut me out." She folded her arms in front of her chest.

"That won't work anymore. You're trying to bait me into a fight."

"Forget it. You're right. In order to fight you would have to *feel* something.

Damn it! It was working.

I spoke through gritted teeth. "We're not doing this. You had a choice and you made it."

"If you say so, but that was no real choice."

I pulled my truck curbside to her condo complex and shut it off. "You want a wedding. I want a *marriage*."

"Most people have both!"

"Well, I found out I'm not most people."

"Fine!" Trish made a jerky movement to get out the passenger door and then stopped her forward momentum.

She stared straight ahead, her hand poised on the handle.

"What's wrong?"

"There's a…huge problem with my condo. I-I might have to move."

"What kind of a problem?"

She had a landlord who was responsible for repairs.

Regardless, Trish was mechanically inclined and could fix a leaky sink herself. There wasn't much she couldn't fix, in fact, and I wondered how I could help her. Unless…

"I saw a spider." Her jaw quivered.

Bingo. Would have been my first guess. Trish had been through boot camp but a tiny spider still freaked her out. I hadn't fully understood in the beginning, but easily fallen into head spider killer without complaint.

"You want me to get it?"

She nodded several times. My heart dropped to my stomach at the misery I saw in the way she held herself, arms circled around her waist. Clearly, she didn't *want* to need me. But she also didn't need me beyond the spider killing.

And selfish though it was of me, I wanted her to need me for more than being the convenient groom and head spider killer. An exterminator could kill a spider. Of course, they weren't on call 24/7, or on Thanksgiving Day like a dutiful fiancé. Um, *ex*-fiancé.

" I don't know how you'll find it." She shuddered. "It's in there, somewhere. Hiding."

"Maybe because you're one hundred times bigger."

She shot me a pained look I read too well. And true, I above all people understood her phobia. I'd read up on it after her first incident in my presence and understood it didn't have to make sense. It *wasn't* logical. I wouldn't be able to talk her out of it. So I made sure to have our home sprayed regularly and was always on active spider duty.

"Sorry. Didn't mean that." I climbed out of my truck and led the way to her upper level condo unit.

She unlocked the door and damn if her hands weren't shaking. "I saw it just before it was time to leave today. Fat and furry. *Huge.* It ran across the floor that way."

I followed her finger pointing to the kitchen. And yes,

she'd barricaded the area with kitchen stools and upturned bowls. There would be yellow police tape, too, if she had any. Again, didn't make sense. Didn't have to.

"It's probably going to crawl out again while I'm sleeping." She threw a terrified look in the direction of the bedroom. "Do you think a rolled-up towel lined at the edge of the door jamb would keep it out?"

"Of course." Hell if I knew, but the answer was always yes to anything that might alleviate the fear. "But it would be better if I find and kill the sucker."

"That's what I was thinking."

I rolled up my sleeves and went to work, removing stools and Tupperware bowls from the floor. Kept one bowl, because it might come in handy to throw over the thing if it scurried past me too quickly. Although I'd probably have to throw away the bowl after that, or take it home with me.

The bowl would be dead to Trish. Anyway, this was all mostly for show and to comfort Trish. No idea how long this spider stand-off would last. I should probably get comfortable.

"Why don't you go in the bedroom and wait it out? It's safer in there."

"Thank you." She handed me the broom and opened the bedroom door shutting it behind her.

I supposed I was here for the duration. Then again, if I really wanted to get out of here I could just pretend I'd caught the thing, make a few loud sounds with the broom, and be done with it. I didn't want to ask myself why I had no intention of doing that. One possible answer might be that I was still madly in-love with the woman.

So clearly, I was an idiot.

My logical, non-phobic brain told me the spider was hiding. Terrified. It wasn't likely to crawl out now. Trish was right. It would come out at night and scurry round the kitchen. Make a web. Catch flies.

If only my life could be that simple.

"Jimmmmmy!"

The wild, guttural scream coming from the bedroom had me dropping everything and running. I threw open the bedroom door and found her standing on the bed, no longer wearing her boots. No longer wearing anything but her panties and red sweater. Pointing to the carpet below her.

"It's right there! *There!*"

It took two steps and the sole of my boot to end the evil thing. "Got it."

"Are you sure?"

"Yeah. I just need a tissue so I can give it a proper burial."

I did just that, removing my boot and walking towards her bathroom where I wiped the squished spider off my sole. Flushed it down the toilet. Put the boot back on. Now, time for a little reconnaissance. Sure enough, Trish was hiding under the blankets. Sobbing.

I'd expected this. The aftermath of a phobic incident usually involved a few tears and a lot of humiliation. In particular because Trish was a strong woman, former Army, a soldier who had traveled to parts of the world with real problems, she remained mortified by her fear.

"Boots," I said quietly. "It's okay."

"No, no, it's not." More sobbing and hiccuping.

I kicked off my boots and joined her on the bed. Then pulled her into my arms. "C'mere."

"Why…why do I do this?" She said between hiccups.

"It's been a while."

This was true. It had been months. Then again, I had

the exterminator spray frequently to keep it that way. Maybe I'd have to discuss this with Trish's new landlord.

"It's a phobia. Not your fault. Nothing to be ashamed of." I held her tight, rubbing her spine until after several minutes the sobs slowed and her breathing became regular.

She'd once fallen asleep in my arms, emotionally spent. The other times…neither one of us fell asleep. For hours.

"You can go now."

She tried to move, but my grip on her was too tight. "Not yet."

"I don't want you feeling sorry for me. I'm okay now."

"I'm not feeling sorry for you."

She was so soft in my arms. And for the first time in a while, vulnerable. The scared recruit I'd met in Virginia. When she let her guard down at moments like these, I saw *my* Trish. Those moments had come too few and far between lately. But right now I craved her. Her hands on me. All over me.

"I don't want to hold you up." She said this into my neck and sent a bolt of blazing heat racing through my bloodstream.

"Nothing left to do today except watch the games I recorded on the DVR."

"Hmmm."

She licked my neck once, then kissed it, and my day took a decidedly interesting turn.

Chapter 6

Trish

On the level of my humiliation at having Jimmy witness my complete meltdown over a spider? It would have to be getting turned on simply by him holding me, tucked against him, as he had so many times. He was right. It had been some time since I'd freaked over a spider. So long I couldn't even recall. Occasionally a tiny one would skitter down a wall but Jimmy was always there. Always.

Mostly he carried the little ones outside. He seemed like a tiny god to me when he did that. No fear. Just a gentle giant of a man. I'd believed my phobia under control, or maybe I'd fooled myself. Because it was Jimmy at the heart of my equation. Jimmy the one factor I couldn't do without. I wouldn't resist him. Never had.

He groaned when I licked and kissed his neck. When my hand drifted under his button-down shirt to curl my fingers through the light hairs on his chest down to his abs, his muscles tensed.

"God, Boots," he moaned and his hands tugged me closer still.

How I loved when he called me that. It was his pet name for me, and he always said it with such tenderness. Because it might as well have been "Babe" or "Sweetheart." But Boots had become a term of endearment that meant something only to the two of us. We'd been through so much together over the years, both as friends and then lovers. Two continents, three deployments for Jimmy, and too many duty stations for me. That had to be why it was so hard to let go.

But I didn't want to think about any of that right now.

I was suddenly touching him everywhere, under his shirt, squeezing his biceps, and caressing his beard. The beard didn't feel as prickly as I'd imagined. It was smooth and silky, and I pictured what it might feel like against my skin. Maybe it would tickle, or leave a burn. I didn't care about a burn anymore because I wanted to be branded by him. To feel him everywhere, both in pain and pleasure. Had I known our last time would be the *last* time, I wouldn't have taken it for granted. I would have memorized every part of him.

Jimmy's hands were busy too, skimming down the small of my back and lower to cup and squeeze my behind. He flipped me and was on top of me, his hands caressing my arms and raising them above my head. Then he slowly pulled my sweater up and off. I had the black push-up bra on because it worked so well with the sweater and not because I thought I'd be in this…position tonight.

But I wasn't about to complain.

Neither was Jimmy as dark eyes took me in and filled with heady lust. He kissed me then, a long and deep kiss, his tongue curling around mine, warm and insistent. The beard brushed against my skin, the scratchy and strange newness of it making me feel like another man had kissed me. But no, it was my Jimmy, or he used to be *my* Jimmy. Driving me crazy. I threaded my fingers through his hair, kissing him over and over again. We were both breathless when he broke the kiss.

"Maybe…maybe I should go."

"Don't you dare." I fisted his shirt, but then my palms went up against his chest. "Wait. Do you want to go?"

"What do you think?" When he pulled me to him so I could feel how hard he was, I saw how much he did *not* want to go.

"I missed you." I'd been afraid to say this out loud. Afraid it made me selfish to want so much. To want and need everything I had before.

"Right back at you." He lowered his head and teased my bra cup aside with his teeth.

Our problems and obstacles were forgotten for now. And it would be good because we *had* each other. He had me and I had him. We were practiced lovers with a powerful physical connection. I knew what he liked and wanted to give him…everything. His tongue and lips were busy doing their magic, pushing the bra cup aside and teasing my nipple, his tongue circling each nipple before he tugged gently. Then not so gently. I wrapped my legs around him and writhed, wanting more.

My hands skimmed up and down his spine and rested on the waistband of his jeans. "You have too many clothes on."

"You're right."

He remedied that by slowly unbuttoning his shirt without breaking my gaze. My mouth watered at his stunning hard body. I loved his pecs, his abs, his thighs. I didn't know which part of him I loved the most. He discarded his shirt to the side and went for his pants. Then he moved along faster, ending up naked and braced on top of me. I, however, still had my bra and panties on.

"Now *I* have too many clothes on." I wriggled under him.

"Or just the right amount." He grinned. "But let me take care of that."

Take care of it he did, removing my bra. His fingers tweaked a freed nipple. "Beautiful."

His tongue traced from my stomach down to my panty line. He pushed the gauzy material to the side as his wicked tongue probed and licked my core. His beard tickled in a way that I hadn't anticipated. An unexpectedly new sensation ground into my body and revved me into a frenzy.

Before long my hips were undulating and rocking with the sensation of his tongue and his lips and the soft bristle of his beard. Rocking my world. Within a few minutes I came hard against his lips, shuddering, nipples rock hard.

"Get in me." My nails dug into his biceps, because I wanted him inside me yesterday.

He obliged, bracing himself above me with his powerful arms. When he bent to kiss me, it was tender, soft, and lingering. Sweet. "So good."

"Hmmm." I tugged on his neck. "Now, please."

I was on The Pill and we'd had no other birth control for years. We slipped back into old habits, and he thrust into me, his long, hard length filling me completely. This was it for me, he was it for me…everything, and I didn't want this moment to end. Couldn't let it end. I had him back for now, as if nothing had ever been big enough to separate us. I held on for as long as I could, knowing that Jimmy wouldn't stop driving into me until I came first. Until I finally let go.

But if I could just hang on a little bit longer, and hold

back, I could make this last. He wouldn't leave me tonight. We wouldn't really be done. I clung to his shoulders, fingernails digging in, trying to push back the tide. But the tide came anyway, and it washed over me, pulsating in long waves and making me cry out. Minutes later, Jimmy didn't hold back either. With one last hard thrust he groaned and followed me over.

And it was done. I didn't want to talk about what this meant or didn't mean. I just wanted to keep going as if nothing had ever stopped between us. As if there had never been an ultimatum.

"Hey, Boots." He rolled me next to him and pressed a kiss to my forehead. "You wreck me every time."

"Ditto, Sarge."

This was so good. So right. But I didn't want to think about tomorrow or what I'd say to myself later. Could it mean something had changed between us? Did it have to mean anything at all?

I fell asleep in his arms, because that too was an old habit.

But when I woke the next morning at dawn, Jimmy was already gone.

Chapter 7

Trish

"Get it, mija! Get it for me! Quick! I can't reach."

When I grabbed the last fifty-two inch plasmas, I knew my tia had scored the deal of the year. It barely fit in the back-up shopping cart I pushed alongside Nonna's cart inside the absolutely annoying Jiffy Mart. Right on cue one day past Thanksgiving, Christmas music drifted through speakers, reminding everyone to be "jolly." But if one more person shoulder-checked me I was going to kick them in their jolly.

I was in a foul mood anyway, hardly fit for company, much less a bunch of unruly strangers. This was definitely not the way to start the holiday season.

"Where are you even going to fit this TV?" I couldn't imagine the plasma fitting anywhere inside their small and cluttered home.

"Don't matter. Maybe I'll give it to Jimmy for Christmas."

"He already—" I bit my lower lip. "I mean, we already have one."

The lying. It had become exhausting. Thank God it would end today.

"I know but could you use another one? Maybe a man cave for Jimmy. If not, I'll think of someone. Might even give it to your Poppi. *If* he's good."

"Right. No sense in missing out on the deal."

I understood the method to Nonna's Black Friday madness. First the gift, then the giftee. For all big ticket and unsentimental gifts, the first point was the price. There *was* no other point. It was six AM and we'd been at it for nearly two hours. There wasn't enough coffee in the free world for this madness. I'd left my warm, soft bed reluctantly and under duress at four AM. But it would have been all that much harder to get out of bed with Jimmy nestled in next to me. Instead, there had been a cold spot.

So, we were no longer getting married. I'd taken his ultimatum and he wasn't backing down as I thought he might. How was I supposed to explain this to Nonna, for whom life was so simple? Find a good man, marry him, have children, live your life.

Like my mother, Nonna hadn't had a big wedding. Not because she was pregnant, but because it would have been impractical and outrageous for her father to spend so much money on one day. Nonna didn't understand (or know about) all the elaborate plans that I'd made, but she'd been supportive every step of the way. She above all others understood how much this day meant to me.

When we were seated for brunch at the Brown Bear Diner in Gilroy, as was our Black Friday tradition, I waited until we'd both ordered to drop the bomb.

"I have some bad news." Keeping busy, I moved the

salt shaker closer to the pepper shaker. "Jimmy and I… we're…see, we're not…"

"Dios mio! Don't tell me you've decided not to have children. Please just don't tell me that. Look, I know Yolanda needs braces and Tony picks his nose, but mi amor, you and Jimmy will have beautiful and well behaved children."

"I-I want children." I moved the pepper shaker away from the salt.

"And what about Jimmy?"

"Yes. He wants two boys and a girl." I thought it so cute, too, the way he thought he might be able to order them like a pizza from Roundtable.

Nonna crossed herself. "Thank God."

Maybe not. I thought I might cry, so I moved the pepper shaker back to the salt shaker. He looked lonely. "W-we're not getting married."

Nonna's crinkly eyes narrowed. "What does that mean?"

"It means we broke up."

"Last night?"

"No, we broke up a month ago. Yesterday he did as a favor to me. I didn't want to ruin Thanksgiving for you and Poppi. So we pretended for a little while. I'm sorry."

The waitress arrived with our plates of eggs, bacon, and chorizo. Nonna glanced at her food with muted interest.

She patted my hand. "Why, mija? I thought it was going so well, with the wedding planning and the…doves, was it?"

Sort of the beginning of the end. I had battled it out with Emily. I wanted doves released after we exchanged our vows. But like so many of my dream wedding ideas, it got way too complicated. Emily claimed the poor doves would suffer, unable to defend themselves against predators after they flew away to certain death.

She'd suggested chickens because they wouldn't go far. I was sure the suggestion had to be a joke. Chickens? At *my* wedding? The idea of doves released was such a beautiful touch but I hadn't thought it all the way through. And I didn't want to be responsible for their untimely deaths.

"I decided against the doves."

"But what *happened*?"

"Jimmy got tired of it all, I guess." I poked at my scrambled eggs. "He gave me an ultimatum. No wedding unless we elope."

"*Elope*?"

"I know. That's the worst thing he could have ever said to me. I thought he'd change his mind when he realized I wouldn't do it. But he hasn't. I've waited so long for my wedding day. Remember how Mami and I used to plan and dream every Saturday?"

Nonna's hand went to her cheek. "Ay. Why did you just not elope?"

"Elope? Do you even know what that *means*?"

"Yes, it means you get married."

"Somewhere *else*. You and Poppi wouldn't be there. It would be me, Jimmy, and a stranger. No time for the perfect dress, or the perfect flowers, or the perfect string quartet playing a perfect hymn as I walk down the aisle."

"There *is* no perfect. There is only right or wrong."

"But all the photos Mami and I used to cut out of magazines. She'd be disappointed if I eloped. I'd be disappointed."

"Ah, your poor Mami. She wasn't grounded. Always with the dreams. And with the picking the wrong men. I was glad when you were sensible. Smart. You signed up for the Army. Jorge needed five new shirts he popped so many buttons, his chest sticking out with pride. When I met Jimmy for the first time, I said to your Poppi, 'This one picked the *right* man.' And I knew you would."

onIt seemed I was crying now, Nonna getting blurry. I reached for the paper napkin and dabbed at my eyes. "Oh, Nonna, I love him so much, but he's *not* the right man. If he were, wouldn't we still be together?"

"Let me think." Nonna made a big show of opening her yellow packet of cane sugar and stirring it into her cup of coffee.

Oh, boy. I recognized this as her "I'm getting ready to lecture you, so gird your loins" look. Her lips were pressed together. I knew I sounded unreasonable, but Jimmy had asked too much. Running away to get married felt cheap. Wrong.

"Is he the *right* man?" Nonna tilted her head heavenward, as if consulting with the Almighty. "What do we think of a man who put up with all the wedding cakes, the photographers, the ten dresses, the doves I'm now hearing about? You almost sound like one of those…bridezillas."

"Nonna!"

Excuse me, but I was *not* a bridezilla. Oh, I'd heard the horror stories. Brides who demanded their bridesmaids gain weight just to make them look thinner in comparison. Brides who yelled and screamed at their friends if they dared to question any of their choices.

Emily and I had been in a few heated arguments, but I would have never yelled at anyone, and certainly not Emily. Okay, sure, I had been opinionated, and I was quite used to having to defend my choices, to fight to be heard, but that was different.

"Well, what was wrong with the *first* wedding dress?"

"Nothing, but I changed my mind. I wanted a sweetheart collar instead."

Nonna quirked a brow. "And the second dress?"

I winced. "Jimmy saw a photo of it on my phone and that's bad luck."

Nonna stopped stirring her coffee. "You want to know bad luck? Changing your mind ten times and spending all your money and time on just one day. Do you think maybe Jimmy thought you were more interested in the wedding than in him?"

My heart squeezed. He'd said something very much like that.

You want a wedding. I want a marriage.

"Um, maybe. But how could he think that? He knows I'm crazy about him."

"Mija, as I've told you before, sometimes what's in your heart also has to be on your lips. Frequently. Especially with a man. They don't read minds like we women do."

"He knows how I feel about running away to get married. It's cheap. The easy way out. If he loved me, he would understand and care about how I feel. If he loved me enough."

"Or maybe if you loved *him* enough you'd give up on perfection and just take what's real and right in front of you. A man who would come with you to Thanksgiving with your crazy Latina family *after* you left him, just because you asked him to. A man who cherishes you and your family. And by the way, a man you love with all your heart. Don't be foolish. You already *have* the right man."

Chapter 8

Jimmy

I was an idiot. An idiot to the nth degree. I suspected there wasn't a level high enough to account for the kind of idiot *I'd* become. Because…sleeping with the ex-fiancée? Bad move. Idiotic. My only explanation was that I was in new territory and I didn't know how to behave like a complete jackass.

But I'd done a fairly good imitation of it Thursday night. Should have just left after killing her spider, and not been so affected by her tongue on my neck. But I'd never claimed to be a saint, and Trish clearly remained my greatest weakness.

I'd closed the bar Thursday and Friday for the holiday and by Saturday I arrived early to do some inventory. The pre-holiday rush was upon us, and if I didn't know that already, I surely did when I turned on my favorite country station and heard *Grandma Got Run Over by a Reindeer.* It wasn't even December!

Regardless, the holidays were a time when I wanted to be overstocked. Figured I might as well get a jump on it. This was actually the job of the assistant manager I'd recently hired to take Trish's place. I had waited her out almost a month, doing both jobs, expecting her to fold and come back to me.

Or at least back to her old job. But hell, if there was anyone on this planet more stubborn than me, it was Trish. So, she was seriously now working for Emily, helping to plan other couple's weddings. Because she hadn't had enough of that with ours.

"What are *you* doing here?" Pete, my new assistant manager, said when he saw me walk in.

"Inventory."

"I thought I was doing that."

"Yeah, but you could use some help."

"Sure." Pete went behind the bar. "Is it my job to clean up all the fall fest stuff and put out the Christmas fru-fru?"

"Nah, but Trish used to do all that. It wasn't in the job description but I guess we'll have to do something. No overkill."

"I hear you. Nothing worse than Christmas when it tries too hard." Pete put up half empty box of Bacardi Rum and made a few notes. "Heard Trish was in here on Ladies' Night. How'd that go?"

"She needed a favor. No worries."

"So she's really not coming back?"

"Wouldn't have offered you the job if she was."

"I know, and thanks, Jimmy." Pete rested his hip against the edge of the bar. "I'm grateful for the work."

"You got it. Glad to help."

Pete had been downsized from the tech industry so many times in the past few years that at sixty-two, he didn't want to go back. All he wanted was an easy job until it was time to retire in a few years.

"But Trish not working here…that still mean you two are done?"

"Looks like it."

In order to be with Trish, I'd almost have to give up a part of myself. Much as I loved her, and I did, I couldn't do that.

"That's such B.S."

I scowled. "How's that?"

"You love her, man. It's obvious. You walk around here looking like someone hit you over the head with a bat. You ever heard of a thing called compromise?"

"Yeah, and last I heard two people have to be willing."

"Women are good at compromise."

I scoffed. "You don't know *Trish*."

My feisty woman was, at least for me, the perfect storm. And hindsight twenty-twenty, I probably shouldn't have issued her an ultimatum. It had been storming since then and frankly, I was tired of being wet.

But I still felt like I had to defend her. "It's complicated. She lost her mother when she was very young, and Trish has always been, at least outwardly, tough as nails. I think she believes that means she can't compromise. To be fair, the Army did some of that to her. Toughened her up. Made her a fighter. Sometimes, she comes out swinging."

"She's still a woman, and believe me, I know women."

I nodded and cracked a smile. Considering Pete had been married five times, I guessed Pete did know women. However, I didn't exactly want to take relationship advice from the man. I had hoped I could do this marriage thing only once.

"I'm guessing your silence means you don't want advice from a man married so many times."

I snorted and helped Pete move the box back to its place. I didn't say a word, but Pete kept talking.

"That's good because I can't give you any advice on marriage. But I can give you advice on love. I'll tell you what, five marriages for me, but my only regret is the woman I *didn't* marry."

"You mean there's someone you didn't marry? I thought that was your thing."

"Hey, wise guy." Pete elbowed me. "I'm trying to give you a life lesson here. Or at least, make you think twice."

"Um, okay. Sure. Go ahead."

"Years ago, before I moved out here, I was about your age and crazy in-love with a woman. Met her back east, when I lived in Pennsylvania. I wanted her to move here with me to start a new life in Silicon Valley. I'd studied computer technology and I knew where I had to be. Asked her to marry me, and she said no. Not because she didn't love me, you know, or so she said, but because she didn't want to leave her home and family. California was too far, and hey, I guess she didn't love me enough. She married some other guy a year later. They're still in Pennsylvania. Three kids."

"I'm sorry, man."

I thought about Trish, a few years from now, married to some other dude. Having *his* children. The thought made me sick to my stomach, because I'd have to kill the guy.

"It was a long time ago. All I'm saying is the only regrets you'll have in life are the chances you didn't take. Do you have any idea how many times I ask myself if I could have done something differently with her? Like maybe some grand gesture to convince her to take a chance on me. On us. I've since learned women love the grand gestures, you know. I got pretty good at them, too." He winked.

"Five marriages."

"Exacta-mundo. It's not like I didn't think about buying her a one-way ticket to California. But in the end, it seemed like too big of a risk to take. I'd be out the cost of the airline ticket if she didn't show up."

I clapped his back. "Damn. You're almost a romantic."

"Who knew, right? But don't tell my wife. I like to keep the standards nice and low so I can still please her."

The man was brilliant, if a little jaded. "Hey, I'm going to the office to check on some payroll stuff. You've got this."

"Sure do, boss."

When I sat at my desk and powered up my laptop, it wasn't payroll records I reviewed. Instead, I searched "best resorts" in Maui. Because call me crazy but I wasn't done. It was possible I hadn't managed to show Trish that running away to get married wasn't about saving money. And I had said the words: I don't give a shit about our wedding. Yeah, wrong word choice. Best of intentions. Terrible delivery.

The problem was I cared *too much* about our wedding. Because I'd never meant Reno or Vegas and a drive-by chapel. It wasn't about being cheap. Granted, I wasn't the most romantic guy in the world, or maybe my idea of romance differed from hers. I liked to be spontaneous. Spur of the moment.

Trish knew this about me. But if I demonstrated exactly what I had in mind, she'd see for herself what I meant. She'd understand that what I wanted was privacy and peace to take my vows. Privacy, peace, and Trish.

After this, she'd understand I wasn't giving up on us. Never.

A couple of hours later, I walked out of my office and found Pete.

"Hey, I'm going to be taking some time off next week. You're promoted to temporary manager."

Chapter 9

Trish

By Monday, I was back to work. I had an initial planning meeting scheduled with Olivia, who had called three times since securing the June date. On one of the calls, she wanted to make sure that someone would spray the gazebo for bugs and spiders far enough in advance that the smell wouldn't be an issue. Olivia was one lucky bride, because I was way ahead of her.

"I meant to ask you," I said from my desk now, "Is your fiancé feeling better about the gazebo?"

"Oh, yeah. He's fine."

After my talk with Nonna on Friday, I had spent most of the weekend thinking about what she'd said. *Had* I been a mini-version of a Bridezilla? Joanne, owner of the only bridal shop in town, was strangely unavailable the last few times I called to talk possible alterations on my latest dress. I dealt only with her assistant. I'd assumed Joanne was busy, but every single time?

And for the life of me, I couldn't remember whether or

not Jimmy liked the idea of the gazebo or if he preferred the red barn. Or if I'd even asked him. It was hard to believe I could have been so caught up in the details that I'd missed big-picture stuff like making sure he was happy with our wedding, too. And obviously, I'd missed something big.

Or several somethings.

In typical Nonna fashion, she'd asked me not whether Jimmy might love me enough, but whether I loved *him* enough. So did I love him enough, or did I love him too much?

I was so confused.

"And also, I have a list." Olivia pulled out a yellow legal pad and pushed it over the desk to me. "Just a few things I had in mind to make my day extra special."

I glanced through approximately seven pages worth of handwritten notes. Everything I glimpsed seemed reasonable until I got to page four, line item twenty. "Beautiful June day with an ideal temperature in the range of about 70-72."

Apparently Olivia had just asked us to control the weather.

When I glanced up, she had a lovely smile on her face. Funny. She *looked* perfectly normal.

"Okay, well, this looks good," I lied and set the pad aside. "I'll just run it by Emily."

"Great. I'm going to go shopping for dresses this weekend."

"That's always such fun. Are you going to *Joanne's*?"

"Oh, no. I couldn't find anything in that little store. We're going up to San Francisco. I'll go all the way down to L.A., if I have to, just to find the right dress. "

"What's your budget?"

She giggled and tossed her dark hair. "I have no budget! Daddy said just get what I want."

Dear God, was that what I'd sounded like to other people? No, no. I'd had a budget. I would have *never* asked for Nonna and Poppi to help, and it was just me and Jimmy fronting the whole thing. Hence one of the reasons I'd been so picky.

"I'll bet you've dreamed about this day for a long time," I said, wanting to find some common ground.

"Not really. I never thought I'd get married or have a wedding. It's such an antiquated way of thinking. I take you, you take me. Really ancient ritual." She made a face.

"Really." I sucked in a breath. "But you fell in love."

"Guess I did, you know. Jeff is kinda old-fashioned. And as for me, I figure it's going to be one great big partay!"

Okay. Olivia was young, only twenty-three. So she could be excused for her vapid mind. What was that about the brain not being fully developed until twenty-five? "Your wedding should be a special day for the two of you. A day you can always remember."

"Yeah, as long as I get everything I want, I'm good." She threw a significant look in the direction of the yellow legal pad.

"How many bridesmaids will you have?" I asked, pushing the pad further away.

"Ten, but actually five. I'll have ten bridesmaids but only five are going to stand up with me."

"I see. Is there a reason why?"

"Jeff is new to California, and some of his good friends can't make the trip. So he doesn't have as many friends as I do. Only five, including his brothers. I'm only going to be able to have five bridesmaids up there to make it nice and even."

I made a note. Five bridesmaids who would be dressed in their expensive gowns, hair done up, make-up, and simply sit near the front. Only five would be standing up with Olivia. It just didn't make sense. Didn't Olivia realize the cost involved to her bridesmaids? Just a guess, but it seemed the cost would far outweigh the honor of being asked, if you happened to be one of the five to sit.

An hour or so later, I was ready to write letters of apology to Joanne's, A Piece of Cake, and of course, Emily. When she walked in the office near the end of the day wearing her Mcallister Charters black slacks and white button-up, I almost hugged her.

"Emily, I'm so, *so*, sorry."

"Why? What's wrong?"

"I was a complete idiot." I stood. "I don't deserve you as a friend after what I put you through with my wedding."

"Let me guess. Olivia put you through your paces today."

I held up the pad. "She's asked us to control the weather!"

Emily laughed. "That's a new one."

"Tell me, was I really that bad?"

"Hey, so did we get much mail today?" Emily picked up an envelope from the desk and inspected it with far too much interest.

"C'mon, Em. You can tell me. I already know. It's the reason I lost Jimmy."

"You didn't lose him!"

"Of course I didn't *lose* him. I know exactly where to find him. With all the rest of the single men."

Emily crossed her arms. "That was your decision. He loves you. And you love him. I'm sorry, but you're both being complete knuckleheads. Sometimes I just want to crack both of your heads together and knock some sense into you."

"Honestly, I didn't realize I was being unreasonable. I just got so caught up in everything. The dream. But no wedding day can be perfect, can it?"

"No, but we can aim for our best. I've been to a lot of weddings and something always goes wrong. The groom drops the ring because he's so nervous, or your flower girl trips and falls. That's when you look at each other and realize you already have the only thing that really matters."

And all Jimmy had wanted to do was bring our wedding day down to the two of us. Maybe not to punish me, but just to wake me up to the fact that I'd forgotten what this was all about.

Because, God help me, I had.

"Do you think I can get him back?"

"Are you kidding me? Of course! He's crazy about you. You know that."

"Okay. Then I need to make a plan. Yeah, it's crazy, and I'm going to have to insist on no Elvis impersonators, but unless he's changed his mind on us…I'm running away to get married."

Chapter 10

Jimmy

The rest of the weekend and many keyboard clicks later, I had planned my wedding to Trish. The resort in Maui was a top rated place for large party destination beach weddings for the most part, but they'd been more than willing to accommodate a party of two. Then I'd had to find an officiant. And apply for a marriage license. Within a few minutes I'd been in over my head.

Luckily the concierge had been extremely helpful. Trish was right. A wedding required…planning. It occurred to me that I hadn't appreciated all the work and time Trish had spent on our wedding day. No wonder she'd been so angry with me at the suggestion that none of that preparation mattered.

I intended to make it all up to her, if she'd let me.

I'd purchased two plane tickets, first-class. One of them I could only hope would be claimed. But unlike my new assistant manager, "fifth times the charm" Pete, I was willing to take a risk. One way or another, I was about to spend a week in Maui. I'd either come back a married man, or with a tan, having spent my days paddle boarding and surfing. I fervently hoped I'd come home tan-less, having spent my days in our extremely expensive honeymoon suite with the heart-shaped tub. Yes, *heart-shaped* tub.

But there were no guarantees. There had been no guarantees when I'd joined up with the United States Army that I'd come back alive and in one piece but I'd risked life and limb. No guarantee that Trish would say "yes" the first time I asked her out and taken our friendship to another level. But I'd risked all we already had for more.

I'd had no guarantee the Silver Saddle would become the moderate success it had, but I was happy to be able to make a living hanging out with friends and listening to country music. And there had been no guarantee that Trish would say "yes" to marriage, but she had, making me happier than I'd ever been. Some people were worth the risk and I'd count Trish Jackson as number one, two, and three of my reasons to risk everything.

Late in the afternoon, I turned my truck right on Coyote Road at the sign that read Fortune Family Ranch: Events/Weddings/Picnics. Emily had informed me that Trish would be working till six, and also that she looked super hot today, and was in a particularly good mood. It was dark when I rolled my truck down the dusty driveway and parked near Trish's truck in one of the designated parking lots.

I hiked up the small hill past the red barn and up to the Victorian house sitting on the hill. In a few minutes, Trish would walk down the steps from the loft above the detached garage next to the house. And I'd be ready with my speech. I hoped. As I waited, I paced in the shadows, hands stuck in my pockets, nearly as nervous as I'd been on the day I asked her to marry me.

"Watch out, buddy. I've got a knife and I know how to use it!"

I'd apparently startled her, and one other thing I loved about Trish? I never had to worry about her going anywhere alone. Spiders were her only fear.

I stepped out of the darkness into the moonlight. "Hiya, Boots."

"H-hi."

"Didn't mean to scare you, but this is important."

"Are you okay?" She took several steps forward, stopping just inches from me. Her eyes searched mine. Earnest. Eyebrows lowered in concern.

"I'm good." A lot better now that she was so close, and I'd noticed the way those luminous eyes had softened when she recognized me. I reached for her, pulling her up against the wall of the barn. "Listen, I'm really sorry. I messed everything up."

"No, I—"

I put a finger on her lips. "Just let me say this. I was wrong when I said I didn't care about our wedding. When I let you think the day wasn't a big deal to me. I get it. It's a big day for both of us. For anyone who chooses to take those vows. I love you, which is why I just wanted it to be the two of us. Maybe that was selfish. What am I saying? It probably is. No, it definitely is. But I know you've waited your whole life for this day and I want to give that to you. I want to give you a day you won't ever forget."

Trish sucked in a breath, but I was afraid her thoughts were going in a different direction. Thoughts that I'd given in to her demands and was going to let the huge and unwieldy wedding go forward. Before her mind got too far on that track, I had to stop the train.

"It's your decision. I know it's sudden and spontaneous and that's not the way you roll. I won't be angry if you don't show." With that, I pulled out a folded piece of paper with her airline ticket printed on it and stuck it into her coat pocket.

"What's this? Jimmy?"

But before she could take it out of her pocket and take a look at it, I tugged her in for a long, deep kiss. It was filled with everything I wanted her to remember. Everything I wanted her to feel before she saw that I'd just given her a copy of her e-ticket itinerary, along with my detailed plans to marry her on the beach in Maui. Just the two of us.

She was breathless when I broke the kiss.

"Think it over. I'll see you soon. I hope."

With that I turned and walked away.

Chapter 11

Trish

My hands shook as I watched Jimmy stride back to his truck, start it up and drive away. That was some bone-melting kiss, and a speech that had my heart racing. Hoping. This wasn't over between us. We weren't done yet. Something had changed.

In the safety of my truck, the paper crinkled as I unfolded it. It was the confirmation of my airline ticket and an itinerary that had me on a plane from San Francisco International Airport flying into Maui, Hawaii. He'd printed information on the resort where he'd booked the honeymoon suite. He'd also listed the name of the hotel concierge, and the name of the officiant.

He'd planned our wedding.

The man who hated to commit to plans for the weekend had *planned* our wedding. I burst into tears.

I'd wanted this so much, though I couldn't have put it into words. An acknowledgment from him that the day *mattered*. All of it. Planning went against the grain for

Jimmy. He liked to take off camping for the weekend without reservations for a campground and drive until we found a spot somewhere. It made me bat shit crazy. I understood how far out of his comfort zone he'd come and it made my heart swell and the tears flow. When I regained my composure, I dialed Emily from the cab of my truck.

Emily heard my sniffling. "What's wrong?"

"Nothing. I'm just going to need a week off and I hope you understand."

"You're getting married?" Emily squealed.

"Yes. Jimmy…he planned it all. You should see this. The resort is beautiful. We can probably get married right on the beach."

"*So* romantic. Take all the time you need. Jimmy gave me a heads-up yesterday."

"*Yesterday?* And you didn't say anything to me today?"

"You better believe I told him to hurry up and tell you so you'd have time to pack. *Men.* But I didn't want to ruin the surprise and he made me promise. Don't worry, I'll get Molly to fill in while you're gone."

"Oh, no. Molly?" Molly was Emily's younger sister, a wild redhead that had scared a few brides off with her talk of wedding day disasters.

"Admit it. Olivia probably deserves her." Emily laughed.

I wasn't going to dispute that. "I've got to go home and pack! And decide what dress to wear for my wedding."

"Wear the blue one that makes you look like Angelina Jolie."

"I'm getting *married* tomorrow, Emily! Married!"

"What are you going to tell your family?"

"That I finally came to my senses?"

"You couldn't have picked a better man."

"The right man."

I hung up with Emily and almost dialed Jimmy to tell him how much I loved him and that I'd be claiming that ticket. I wanted to tell him right now that I wanted this. Just to run away with him. My finger was poised above the "call" button when I changed my mind. Whoever said I couldn't be spontaneous? Well, Jimmy, actually.

He always said I had a plan for my plan. So I'd surprise him at the airport where I'd fall into his arms at our flight gate. People would wonder if we were one of those couples who had been reunited after a long break, and if they asked I'd laugh and say, "The longest month of my life."

I drove home to pack. Once home I called Nonna, who said "Gracias a Dios" a few times, then made me promise to take plenty of photos, even if they had to be "selfies with that phone you say is a camera too" and not to think about anyone but herself and Jimmy. She also noted, her voice filling with emotion, that my mother, now in heaven, would be watching over me.

I would have to agree.

The next morning when I woke, I rolled over in my bed and almost called Jimmy. *Almost.* I couldn't stand to wait another minute to let him know I was coming, but I talked myself out of it. I wanted that moment. The look of surprise in his beautiful mocha eyes as he saw my approach. Knowing me, I'd probably arrive first and ruin my grand entrance. Accounting for my checked luggage, I allowed myself enough time to arrive at the gate and surprise Jimmy.

"I'm getting married!" I told my Uber driver when he arrived. A young-looking kid wearing a Seattle Mariners shirt. "So I can't be late."

"No worries. We got plenty of time." The kid put my luggage in the trunk. "Getting married at the airport? What are you? A stewardess?"

Nice. He didn't think I could be a pilot or anything like that. But no one could ruin this day for me. No one. I jutted my chin out.

"I'm running away to get married."

"Cool."

It started to rain shortly after we started up Highway 101 but there was plenty of time to get to San Francisco Airport. It was south of the actual city, after all, and it wasn't like this was high time commuter traffic. But when the light California rain came down hard, I panicked at the amount of red tail lights I saw straight ahead. We were barely out of San Jose.

I swiveled my neck. "Oh, boy. What is it?"

"An accident. Seriously, nobody around here can drive in the rain. Don't worry, I'll get you there."

He would or I'd strangle him. I dug inside my bag for my phone. I'd need to call Jimmy now and ruin the surprise. I'd be a little late and mess up my grand entrance, but I didn't want him sitting at the gate alone sweating it out. Wondering if I'd show up or not. That was plain mean.

"Oh, God. No." I'd forgotten my phone when I switched purses to the bigger one I traveled with.

"What? What is it?" my driver said.

"My phone! I forgot my phone. We don't have time to turn around. Please, let me borrow your phone?"

"Sure. No worries." He handed over his phone.

"Thank you so much! You're a life saver."

I dialed Jimmy, and sighed when I got to hear his deep and beautiful voice as he answered, "Jimmy Hopkins here."

"Baby, it's me. I love you. I don't care about the wedding anymore. I just want you. I've got my ticket and

I'm on my way to meet you. You know how I like a big entrance. We're a little delayed but I'll get there."

Silence.

Dead silence.

I glanced at the phone. Uber Kid's phone had died so I handed it back to him. "Tell me you have the charger up there."

"Oh, dude. Sorry, no, that hasn't been working. I think I need a new battery. Maybe it's because I've been listening to a book on audio, and trying to learn Spanish."

"Let me help you out. Mierda!"

My phone, ironically, was fully charged because I did that every night. Fully charged and currently in my other purse at home. How was it possible that with all the technology in Silicon Valley I sat in a sedan with one missing phone and one dead as a doornail phone? Unable to tell the love of my life I was on my way.

Okay, no worries. When I got there I'd apologize profusely to Jimmy for leaving him hanging. I'd explain and he'd understand. When I told him about the missing phone and the dead phone, and the rain and the traffic, well, we'd have a good laugh. I, Trish Jackson, who planned everything, had almost failed to make the plane to my wedding. If this wasn't one for the books! A story for the grandchildren.

I clutched Uber-Kid's headrest. "I can't miss this plane! Please, please, get me there, Uber-kid."

"Dude, you can count on me!"

Apparently a little too much, as he weaved dangerously in and out of lanes, cutting drivers off and earning glares. "Woohoo! I'm from Seattle and I know how to drive in the rain, suckers."

After we passed the accident, the traffic picked up considerably, and Uber-Kid seemed well up to the task of making up the time with a pedal to the metal action that reminded me of the Nascar races Jimmy liked to watch. He'd be so proud of me now, sitting back here, not losing my breakfast. As we took the exit to the airport, I glanced at the car's digital clock and realized I'd be too late to check my luggage.

But I would still make this flight. I had to. I couldn't have Jimmy alone in the suite with the heart-shaped tub, thinking even for a few hours that I didn't care enough to show up. Maybe he'd hook up with a hot Hawaiian babe and have crazy hammock sex on the beach. No!

San Francisco Airport was its usual long line of cars trying to find purchase for drop-offs, and uptight security guards waving their arms to "move along." Uber-Kid had slowed to a crawl as he followed the line, looking for a space to pull in. The rain had started to come down harder.

"I'll just get out here and walk." I leaned forward and handed him a slip of paper with Nonna's address and some cash. "One last favor. Please take my luggage back to this address. And tell them not to look inside. Here's a tip for you."

"Dude! Are you some kind of a spy?"

No, I just didn't want Nonna or Poppi seeing the kind of risqué lingerie I'd bought to seduce my husband. I winked. "If I were a spy, I couldn't tell you."

My hair got wet in the rain but no biggie. Rolling my carry-on behind me, I half jogged, half ran the rest of the way. I saved time by checking in at a kiosk and was limping a little bit by the time I got to the TSA line. I probably shouldn't have worn my pumps even if they made my legs look like those of a sex goddess.

They were killing my feet and slowing me down. But at least TSA should be a breeze. I had traveled so extensively

I knew all the rules by heart. No reason in heaven or hell that I should get slowed down. I grabbed a plastic tub and hoisted my carry-on.

"Random security check!"

The TSA agent headed straight for me.

Oh, Jimmy.

Jimmy

She wasn't coming.

When the ticket agent announced over the loudspeaker that military personnel, past or present, could now board, I waited. I never took the opportunity anyway, but especially not now, when I told myself that Trish might just be running late. Trish, who was never late. Trish, who hadn't phoned me. Of course, I could call her but I had a little bit of pride left. I'd given her everything I had last night and if she still didn't want to join me, I had nothing.

First class passengers were called next, and I still didn't move. Mostly because I never flew first class. Just today. Once every single section of the plane had been called and there was no one left waiting at the gate, I made my way to the ticket counter and handed over my boarding pass.

"Have a nice trip!" The friendly agent said.

Yeah. Not so much.

I found my seat in first class, stored my carry-on, and

took the aisle simply because I liked to stretch my leg, and *not* because Trish loved the window seat.

"Excuse me," I said to the stewardess, "How soon can I get a drink?"

"It's a light flight today, hon. Let me get us situated and I'll take good care of you."

"Tequila, please, and keep 'em coming."

"Aw, sweetheart." She patted my shoulder and kept walking down the aisle.

So I must look as pathetic as I felt. I'd planned this whole wedding and for what? A few stragglers kept coming in, rushing to their empty seats. Still no Trish. I didn't know why I kept glancing to the front of the plane. Time to face facts. It was over. I'd tried to get her back with this one last grand gesture. But maybe I'd waited too long. I rubbed my jaw, still unaccustomed to the missing facial hair. Shaved it all off this morning. For her.

And a new beginning.

"I'm getting married!"

Great. Was I hallucinating now? That sounded like Trish's voice toward the front of the boarding area of the plane.

"Congratulations," someone said.

I stood up and Trish appeared at the front of the aisle, boarding pass in one hand, tugging her roll-on behind her. "Jimmy! I made it!"

She looked a sight, her hair frizzy and disheveled, dark smudges under her eyes like she'd been crying. In addition to that, she seemed to be limping.

"You okay?"

I met her in the aisle, grabbed her carry-on and put it in the overheard compartment next to my own.

"Excuse me," said a stewardess. "But we're going to be

doing a little thing called take-off soon? So you'll both need to sit down and buckle up. Now."

"We're getting married," Trish told her.

This was a new stewardess. One she hadn't told yet.

"Not here you're not." She waved a hand for us both to get in our seats.

I maneuvered Trish toward the window seat, then sat down next to her and squeezed her leg. "Didn't think you were coming."

Once she explained everything that had gone wrong I was amazed she had managed to arrive at all.

"I love you so much. I'm sorry about the wedding. Things got crazy and out of hand. You were right. I'd forgotten what really matters."

"Don't worry about any of that now."

Her hands framed my face. "What happened to your beard?"

"You don't like it? I shaved it off for you."

"Actually, it didn't bother me. Feels kind of nice against my skin." She whispered into my neck.

"Yeah? I can always grow it back." I chuckled.

"Ahem! Excuse me, you two lovebirds," The stewardess said. "The Captain has just turned on the seatbelts sign."

"Sorry!" Trish gushed.

I buckled my seat belt and took her hand in mine. "Buckle up, Boots. It's going to be an unpredictable but very fun ride."

<hr>

Epilogue

<hr>

Trish

For two people who almost didn't get married at all, two weddings might seem like overkill.

Not to me.

The first wedding was on the beach in Maui during a glorious sunset. Me, Jimmy, and the officiant. A beautiful red and orange skyline was our only decoration. Add to that a flock of seagulls nearby who chose the moment we were declared officially wed to take flight. You couldn't plan that kind of thing.

A good sign.

Plenty of pictures, too, and they turned out quite lovely even if the photographer was someone we'd run into at the hotel resort. Jimmy had forgotten about the photographer, but other than that he'd planned a perfect wedding. Simple. And he'd done all this for me. He didn't need the honeymoon suite with the heart shaped tub (though he enjoyed it—I made sure of that.)

Soon after we'd arrived, I'd gone shopping on the island for a wedding dress and chosen a royal blue and white floor length cotton floral. Jimmy wore his black slacks and a blue button-down. No tie. I had insisted. We were both barefoot on the beach as we exchanged our vows. Waves lapped in the background, natural music when Jimmy recited his vows.

"I love you, Boots. You're my best friend, my lover, and my everything. I'm never going to lose you. I promise you that no matter what happens I'll never give up on us."

And as Jimmy had predicted, I didn't need to buy much else to replace the missing luggage other than underwear. All she'd needed was the wedding dress, a swimsuit, and …nothing else.

I spent most of the week in "nothing else."

The second wedding actually came about quite unexpectedly. Not surprisingly, our friends and family wanted to have a small reception to celebrate. But one thing led to another, this time mostly due to Emily getting involved, and when the June twenty-first date became available again (shocker) the gazebo was again a possibility.

A small group of friends and family (and Jimmy's parents, who flew out from Alabama) gathered around the gazebo as Jimmy and I exchanged vows once again. By that time, we were old pros. I wore the first wedding dress I'd ever tried on at Joanne's (it was still available) and Jimmy insisted on a tux.

The bouquet was made out of Baby's breath and made Nonna sneeze. The string quartet played "Perfect Storm" and the violinist dropped his bow halfway through. Most people didn't even notice. Jimmy was so nervous he dropped the ring. He recovered well and slipped it on my left ring finger.

The reception, of course, was held at the Silver Saddle.

And that's how we wound up with two wedding dates, six months apart.

Try and forget that anniversary.

The Christmas Bet
BONUS SHORT STORY

Chapter 1

Christmas Eve

Lieutenant Ty Gillham of the Starlight Hill Fire Department held out his collection boot at the corner of Main Street.

"Ho, ho, ho! Merry Christmas!"

"I'll pay anything if it will get you to quit that potty mouth of yours." The soccer Mom threw in some bills and then nudged her chin toward the passenger back, and her three adorable children. "I heard all about the bet. You have an example to set, Mister."

She did everything but wave a finger at him.

"Right." Ty saluted and smiled, winking at the kids.

As she drove away, Ty cursed under his breath. It was the only way he got to curse these days. He missed his favorite F word. But if he was going to win this bet with Mandy, then he had to keep the cursing down through the end of the year. If he managed, he'd win the bet and Mandy would agree to do anything *he* said. And he had a few ideas of what he wanted to do with his girlfriend of two years, the gorgeous, leggy woman who drove him out of his mind with lust.

He'd met Mandy Mulvaney through her sister, Diana, during the firefighter calendar shoot they'd done a couple of years ago. Scott, now Diana's husband, had been Mr. September. Ty had been tasked with December, complete with a Santa hat. He'd been so irritated by the entire ordeal that he'd cursed a blue streak on the way to the shoot and during it.

But when he'd laid eyes on Mandy, it was impossible to look away. When she'd come closer to take the cigar he'd brought along to irritate the photographer, she had to pull it from between his teeth. Mandy had been the one bright light in that whole calendar fiasco.

Before he'd even realized it, within weeks he'd fallen in love with her. She made it easy. Mandy was funny and playful, equal parts sex kitten and Lucille Ball. A tough spitfire, Mandy gave him hell when he needed it. Called him out on his bullshit. He was a passionate guy, sometimes filled with righteous anger. But he'd had girlfriends in the past who he was afraid to be honest around or risk hurting their feelings.

From the beginning, Mandy had been clear with him: *I don't need to be protected. Or coddled. Tell it to me straight, or don't tell me at all.*

She was a magnificent woman, and he was crazy about her.

But if he lost this Christmas bet, he'd be at *her* mercy. She wouldn't cut him any slack. He foresaw lots of re-runs of The Bachelor and binging her current obsession all weekend. Also, finishing the remodel on her bathroom, which he'd promised to do for weeks, and hadn't gotten around to.

So, even if it killed him, and it just might, no cursing

until after New Year's Eve. He could do this. But it didn't help that Mandy had a spy around every corner.

The other day at the fire station, the vending machine had taken his money. All he'd wanted was a Mountain Dew, so he could get through the forty-eight-hour shift that would not end.

Ty shook the machine, which he'd just given his last coins. "Mother fu—"

"Excuse me?" Scott Turlock had appeared out of literally nowhere, a wry smirk on his lips. "I know you don't want to finish that sentence.

Ty had simply growled and gone back to work, without his drink. He would *not* lose this bet.

Now, finished with collection, Ty handed the boot off to the next firefighter, and found his parked truck. There was a ticket on it!

"What the fu— is this?" This time, he censored himself.

He waved the ticket at Bert, Chief of Police, handing out parking tickets like they were candy canes.

"Red zone," Bert said happily. Why not? He was retiring soon.

"There was nowhere else to park!" Ty shouted. "How about a little professional courtesy here?"

"Sorry, no can do," Bert said and kept walking down the line of cars and trucks. "Just think of it as your donation to the town's coffers. Merry Christmas!"

"Merry Christmas, you fu—"

"Hi, baby."

Ty whipped around to find the source of that breathy, sexy sound. *Mandy.* She looked smoking hot dressed in an…elf costume. Short green skirt and shoes, silly hat. Long, delicious legs covered in some kind of candy-striped pattern.

Only Mandy could pull this look off and still look like every single man's fantasy lover. If she was a candy cane, he'd lick her from head to toe.

"Hey," he said, probably sounding a little breathy himself.

"Are we still on for tonight? My place?" She strutted up to him, her fingers deftly sliding up and down his arm before she squeezed his bicep.

"You better believe it. I'm off rotation now." He shoved the ticket in his turn-out gear pocket.

"Is that a parking ticket?"

"Yeah, it is." He straightened. "Bert's Christmas gift to me."

"Aw," Mandy said. "It has to be hard not to let loose a blue streak with that bad luck. So unfair, and on Christmas Eve."

He grinned. She loved teasing him. "I'm going to win this bet."

"Hm, we'll see about that."

She stepped with away with a sly grin, making him wonder how she would toy with him. He looked forward to every second.

Because he had a surprise of his own tonight.

Chapter 2

Mandy rushed home, driving by the twenty-four-foot Starlight tree in the center of the square, past the twinkling fairy lights decorating every shrub and tree. The entire town was lit up for the holidays. She waved to friends and residents bustling about town doing last minute shopping.

There was Billy Turlock, holding his wife Brooke's hand as they walked. Mandy passed Genevieve Turlock's bakery, where she'd stopped by earlier. A few minutes later, Mandy pulled into her single-family home rental just down the street from her grandmother's.

Since she'd moved to town with her sister Diana and their mother, the beautiful and quaint Starlight Hill had become home. She'd have never imagined she could be happy in a small town, away from the pulse and energy of Los Angeles. But she fit here. Ty was a huge part of the equation.

True, he was every firefighter cliché: tall, built, chiseled jaw, sexy beard bristle, dark hair and eyes. The stuff of romance novels. But it wasn't just his looks that she loved. Ty was always the first one to volunteer for causes that involved children. An only child, he helped support his single mother, and visited his elderly grandmother regularly.

Ty didn't like anyone knowing that he was a regular boy scout behind the scenes. His only real flaw, if it could even be called one, was his cursing. Gran had already called him out on it once, even if he'd been too respectful to curse in front of her.

She'd simply *heard* about his rather legendary cursing and threatened him within an inch of his life if he dared curse at her table. So, this year, Mandy had issued the challenge just for fun. She loved watching Ty nearly trip over his own tongue trying to avoid dropping an F bomb.

She'd fallen hard for the big lug, and tonight, she would propose. There was no reason a modern woman couldn't be the one to do this. Ty already knew how she felt, and though they were both fully committed to each other, they'd only danced around the idea of marriage. They'd gone away for long, sexy weekends whenever possible, which wasn't often given her work in the bridal shop and his at the fire house.

She'd told him she loved him six months into their relationship when he'd taken her to visit his grandmother at Sunny Hills. A former bad boy, and former Marine, Ty turned into a sweet boy with his grandmother. He was sweeter than anyone in town would ever know, and he wanted it that way.

Tonight, before she proposed, she would have a little fun with him and their bet. Secretly, she was going to *let* him win. He'd learned his lesson over the last month. If he won, she'd have to do whatever he asked. She had a feeling this would involve two days of non-stop marathon sex which wouldn't exactly be a sacrifice for her.

If she lost, and he took another six months for her

bathroom remodel, those were the breaks. Ty worked hard as both a firefighter, and also taking the occasional construction jobs.

Wrapping her presents, she slid the pink box under the artificial tree. No way could she have a fresh tree with a firefighter for a boyfriend. Ty worried about her all the time, which was just one other lovable quality of many. The cookie was her biggest surprise. The giant sugar cookie Genevieve had baked especially for Mandy had bold and bright red icing that read:

Will you marry me?

Tonight was special, just the two of them for once. Tomorrow, they'd be going between her mother's house, Ty's mother's, and Sunny Hills. A full day. It was unusual for Ty to have the holiday off. This would be the first year they'd spend Christmas Eve and Day together since they'd started dating. It wouldn't happen every year and she wanted this Christmas to be memorable. Two hours later, Mandy had finished staging her special night, when Ty arrived. Early.

He had his tool belt and box along with his overnight bag. "Thought I'd do a little work on the bathroom before dinner."

"On Christmas Eve?" This was most unexpected.

"Look, babe, gotta do a little here and there. You're going to lose this bet." He grinned, set everything down, and pulled her into his arms.

He felt so good. So right. As always, he smelled delicious. Her palms immediately came up on his hard-muscled chest and she smiled. She gave him a slow, languid, and delicious kiss that had him pulling her tight against him, hip to hip.

"That's what you say."

She'd forgive him for this romantic faux paux. He

didn't know how to relax on Christmas Eve, since he usually worked a rotation. Either way, she would distract him enough that he'd forget all about the remodel. This was definitely not the time for practicality. Tonight, romance reigned.

As he set his toolbox down and went to work, Mandy took the moment to run in the bedroom and change. She rummaged in her drawer for the red and green bib apron she'd bought that said, "Merry Christmas, Baby." Then she removed every stitch of her clothing, panties and bra included, and tied the apron on.

She sashayed to the bathroom, where Ty stood, his back to her, holding the new trim for the base board.

"Hi, there."

Ty turned, hand on the wood slat. Jaw gaping, he dropped the panel and it fell against the wall. "Holy fu—"

She crooked her finger. "You're so close. Don't lose the bet tonight."

"Bet? What bet? I forgot my own name."

Not wasting any time, he rushed her, throwing her over his shoulder in a fireman's hold. She laughed as he carried her into the bedroom.

"Unwrap me."

He set her down, then slowly untied the apron, sending her a slow smile. "Are you my present?"

"One of them."

"Just the right size." He grazed his teeth over his lower lip.

He tipped her chin and bent to kiss her. Warm, wet and deep, there was nothing tender about Ty's kiss. Her mouth opened under his, fingers threading through his thick hair, then lowering to his shoulders, luxuriating in the feel of his muscles tensing under her fingertips. Her fingers trailed down the length of his back to his waist and back up again. They got a little wild as they moved toward the bed. She tore at his shirt, losing one of the buttons in the process. Pulling it off his broad shoulders, she branded each one with an open-mouthed kiss.

He tugged her on to the bed, covering her with his body. His hot branding kiss seared her skin as he kissed the column of her neck, arms, breasts, stomach, legs, thighs. When his tongue and lips licked and teased the most sensitive part of her mercilessly, she fisted the sheets. Ty always drove her right off a damn cliff. She came hard against his lips, bucking and moaning his name, clutching the hair on his beautiful head.

"You taste so good," he said, kissing her stomach as she slowly came back down to earth.

He removed a shiny package from his wallet then tugged off his pants and boxers and shucked them to the side. When he tore at the condom wrapper with his teeth, she almost climaxed just watching. He stroked himself once and did not break eye contact with her. She licked her lips, her body buzzing with heat. He was so gorgeous that for a moment she took him all in. His hard angles, sinewy arms and thighs. His flat abs and light smattering of dark chest hair.

Then he rolled her on top and in one long and powerful thrust was deep inside her, making her gasp. She followed his lead in a steady rhythm, him holding her hips and driving into her. She clung to him as his thrusts became harder. Faster. Pleasure rippled through her body, giving her pulses of ecstasy.

"Baby," he said and brought her face to his, hand at the nape of her neck. "Look at me. I need you."

It was as if he'd heard her thoughts. She opened her eyes and met his, her lashes damp and she was certain revealing far too much. This night mattered. She'd propose, and deep inside, she was terrified. And to think men did this all the time! What if Ty said no? She wrenched the thought from her mind. Too scary.

"Ty," she breathed, unable to hold the tide back any longer. "I'm—"

He rolled her underneath him and controlled his strokes. They were even and measured as he intentionally slowed them both down. Even though she knew that what waited for her was bigger and far more intense, in the moment she hated when he took the peak away. Hated when he took his time like he never wanted this to stop.

Her body slick with his sweat and hers mixed together, her face flushed, and hair plastered to her face, she must look a mess. Ty made her feel like the sexiest woman alive. He whispered dirty words in her ear. Words of what he was doing to her and finally, *finally* he lost his tight control. His eyes glazed over and he pumped faster. Harder. As if he couldn't help himself. Couldn't hold back any longer. In that reckless space she met him thrust for thrust, angling her hips so he'd go deeper.

Her entire body tightened, and she climaxed with a fierceness that took her breath. Ty came with her, growling her name and gripping her so tightly she might bruise later but hell, she didn't care. She didn't feel any pain, only the incredible sensations rippling through her seizing body one after another, like a powerful undertow pulling her under and bringing her back up again.

"I love you," she whispered, knowing this wasn't the only part of him that she loved.

She loved the way they were together. Playful, giving, funny, but serious when the need arose. They were the perfect match.

"Love you back." He kissed her temple.

They lay there for a few minutes in each other's

arms, breathing slowly, trying to catch their breaths. Ty always made her feel special and…new. This was the perfect time for her next gift, the cookie, even if she didn't want to move from nestling in his strong arms.

She nuzzled her face in his warm neck. "I have to get your next present. It's under the tree."

"First, I have one for you."

"Oh, goodie!" He'd given her absolutely no hint of her Christmas presents all month long.

Ty rolled out of bed and grabbed his pants from the floor. Out of his pocket, he pulled out a small black box and Mandy's heart stopped.

It couldn't be.

Really?

Calm down. It's probably just a necklace or a bracelet.

Naked as the day he was born, Ty dropped to one knee, holding the tiny black box in his hand. "Will you marry me?"

"Holy shit! Yes!" Mandy's hand flew up over her mouth.

Ty laughed. "I think I'm a bad influence on you. You're going to have to clean up your act if you want to marry me."

He slipped the ring on her finger, then re-joined her in bed, tucking her beside him. "Are you surprised?"

Mandy held up the ring and admired it glittering on her finger. "You have no idea."

"I love you. You've made me the luckiest guy in the world."

She kissed him. "Wait until you see my cookie."

HAPPY HOLIDAYS!

For those who are wondering, I see Mandy and Ty as having a long and happy life together.

Ty continues to advance in his career at the Starlight Hill Fire Department, winding up as Captain. Mandy quits her mother's bridal shop and goes back to school to become a nurse.

They have three children: two boys and one girl. Ty, naturally, dotes on his little girl, as you might imagine. He's a great father all around, and ironically, won't allow any of his kids to curse.

About the Author

Heatherly Bell is the author of over fifty-six published contemporary titles under two different pen names.

She lives for coffee, craves cupcakes, and occasionally wears real pants. She lives in Northern California with her family.

Also by Heatherly Bell

LUCKY COWBOY

NASHVILLE COWBOY

BUILT LIKE A COWBOY

COWBOY, IT'S CHRISTMAS

MR. COWBOY

SOLDIER COWBOY

UNEXPECTED COWBOY DAD

GRAND PRIZE COWBOY

WINNING MR. CHARMING

THE CHARMING CHECKLIST

A CHARMING CHRISTMAS ARRANGEMENT

A CHARMING SINGLE DAD

A CHARMING DOORSTEP BABY

ONCE UPON A CHARMING BOOKSHOP

HER FAKE BOYFRIEND

Coming on November 26th:
THE MAVERICKS CHRISTMAS COUNTDOWN

And don't miss:
THE EX-DOOR NEIGHBOR
Coming Summer of 2025

For a complete book catalog, please visit the author's website.

www.ingramcontent.com/pod-product-compliance
Lightning Source LLC
Chambersburg PA
CBHW061851310726
48972CB00004B/977